WATER DAMAGE

by Gregory Ward

WATER DAMAGE

by Gregory Ward

LITTLE, BROWN & COMPANY (CANADA) LIMITED

First published in Canada 1993 by Little, Brown (Canada).
This edition published 1994 by Little, Brown (Canada).

Canadian Cataloguing in Publication Data

Ward, Gregory
   Water damage

ISBN 0-316-92233-1 (bound) ISBN 0-316-92224-2 (pbk.)

I. Title.

PS8595.A74W3 1993   C813'.54   C93-093138-6
PR9199.3.W3W3 1993

Cover design: Tania Craan
Cover illustration: Andreas Zaretzki / Reactor
Interior design and typesetting: Pixel Graphics
Printed and bound in Canada by Best Gagné Printing Inc.

Little, Brown & Company (Canada) Limited
148 Yorkville Avenue, Toronto, Ontario, Canada

For my mother.
Your kindness, I hope, resides in me.

ACKNOWLEDGEMENTS

As always, I am indebted to my wife, Sally, for her support and critical encouragement. Thanks also to Judy Kendrick for our invaluable teatimes.

Thanks to the good doctors, Marlene Spruyt, Roy Butler, Ray Blanchard, and especially Ron Langevin. Many thanks to Sergeant Paul Wassill of the Durham Regional Police Tactical Support Unit for his generous and creative assistance.

I am also grateful, once again, to my editor Lynne Missen for her grace under pressure. Unquestionably an Ormiston girl!

P R O L O G U E

WHENEVER THE POOL is in use, Paul and Eva shift responsibility for the children one to another by a system of verbal transfer and acknowledgement. They have to actually say: "Transferring."

And respond: "Transferred."

They observe it unfailingly, knowing that the system avoids another brief exchange, the prologue to tragedy:

"He's not with you?"

"I thought he was with *you!*"

They never relax the system and teach it to their guests at the Huron Street house. In the confusion of feeding and entertaining multiple families, not one second elapses when there isn't adult supervision in the fenced pool area. They know the toll of North American children in backyard pools, that it takes a human brain three minutes to start dying underwater; they know that most pool accidents are related to diving boards so they have not installed one. Thomas and Clifford are never quite cured of running on the pool deck, but not for want of being told.

"Walk!"

"Jump well clear of the side!"

"Cliff stay by the steps or put your wings on!"

Since vigilance comes only with fear, Paul and Eva carry around a necessary, low-grade anxiety.

It is a hot Saturday. Eva has taken Thomas to an outdoor puppet show at Harbourfront, leaving Paul and Cliff together, the usual split.

They go out to the pool for a swim before lunch, at twelve-thirty. They check out the catch of the day in the skimmer basket, both relieved and disappointed to find only bugs, no mice, no frogs bloated up like little green balloons. They pad around the deck a long time, happy together with the hot concrete under their feet, Cliff spotting sweat-bees on the surface for Paul to fish out with the net. There is no sound from the neighbours, who both have summer cottages. The pump humming low in the cabana, the skimmer gurgling pleasantly, the jets puffing bubbles under the soft aquamarine, its surface rippling in a thousand smiles...times like this convince Paul that a swimming pool is worth all the trouble and expense.

At three and a half, Cliff can't swim, so they play submarine, Paul pulling him through his legs under the water; then seahorse, taking Cliff on his back, delighting in the slippery sensation of his son's sturdy body, the strength of his grip. After that, Paul swims lengths, hurrying to the deep end to turn and make sure Cliff is near the shallow end steps.

It would have been no good Clifford going to the puppet show; he would have missed most of it, kneeling on the seat, making faces to distract the people behind, because he is three and a half, because he is a natural clown. Both Paul and Eva have told Cliff about being too friendly with people he doesn't know, with strangers. It is never too early to say it.

Thomas needs no telling. He walks back from grade one now, with a buddy. He is naturally reserved, so quiet, Paul never knows where he is in the house, except that it will be near Eva.

Thomas and Eva.

Clifford and Paul.

The brothers seldom fight because they seldom invade each other's territory. The drawing pads and colouring books, the markers and crayons are for Thomas, who could read at four, and at six is writing stories with beginnings, middles and ends, the way Eva has taught him.

The Duplo, Lego, building bricks — anything tactile that can be assembled, stripped down and reassembled — belongs to Cliff. He is going to be an engineer like his father, the family observe. "He's been sent for you. A gift," Eva says. "Your soulmate. Your teacher."

They get out of the pool at one o'clock and dry off and leave the pool enclosure. The fence stands five feet, as required by the Metro bylaw, with a padlock on the gate. Paul fastens it, withdraws the key, then tests the gate, routine as breathing.

They eat leftover Cajun meatloaf and dill pickles, adding toothpick arms and legs to make pickle people, making them jump out of the jar and splash about in brine puddles on the kitchen table. Paul has a theory that bad table manners are necessary, occasionally, if children are to appreciate good ones. Cliff tells his father that the pickles like being eaten. Neither of them wants the last one but Cliff, earnestly kind, worries that it will be unhappy all alone in the jar, so they give it an anaesthetic and chop it in half. Afterwards, Paul leaves him in the sandbox on the narrow area of lawn between the backyard and pool enclosure, playing with a slow-running garden hose while he goes in to shower.

Family life unrolls like a bolt of cloth with a busy but repeating design; Paul knows that this situation is tried and tested safe. Cliff knows he can go around to the front of the house but not near the street; he knows about sharp scissors and steep stairs. The swimming pool is fenced and the gate is locked and the key is hanging from a red woolen loop high in the mudroom closet. Paul feels no compunction whatever as he climbs to the master bedroom and bath on the converted third floor. It's big for a downtown Toronto house, wide and tall on a convenient and fashionable Annex street. The Huron Street house is a testament to Paul's success as a consulting engineer, the transport ministry contracts that have tripled his firm in the last five years.

At one point, halfway through his shower, Paul wonders if he has heard the door bell. It is something they have overlooked in the conversion, wiring the bell up to the third floor — it is too hard to hear, singing "Moon River" under the drumming water. He shuts it off and waits about thirty seconds, soaping himself. When he hears nothing more, he continues with his shower.

Paul is fairly convinced that the second ring is also his imagination, but he gets out anyway and runs, dripping across the carpet, to the open bedroom window that overlooks the front drive. He puts his head out but there is no one at the front door. He goes to the back of the house, through the walk-in closet, to where a small closed window overlooks the back yard two floors below. He sees Cliff immersed in play, throwing his L.A. Lakers junior-size basketball against the fence. Satisfied, Paul returns to his shower.

While he is getting dressed, he turns on the portable colour TV at the end of the bed to catch the Mexican Grand Prix on TSN. He likes Nigel Mansell, the English driver, is anxious to see if Mansell can win again on the difficult Autodromo Rodriguez.

Paul's instinct now begins to tell him that Cliff has been alone long enough. He is drifting back to the closet to check him again when Mansell skids into the curb on the Esses and a damaged back tire threatens his four-second lead on Senna, his Brazilian arch-rival.

Paul squats, glued to the screen, absently lacing his running shoes while the two drivers go neck and neck, rooting aloud for Mansell until he is flagged out of the Peralta Curve and Senna takes the lead.

Paul feels clean and refreshed and only mildly disappointed in Mansell as he trots down the two flights of stairs, hoping that Cliff will be occupied long enough to let him glance at the weekend edition. Thinking of the newspaper puts him in mind of the doorbell again, the possibility of something having been left by a neighbour, a canvasser, the residents' association.

He looks down as he opens the front door, but there is nothing on the stoop. Looking up and out into the hot summer Saturday, he wonders whether he caught a fleeting movement at the end of the driveway, or whether it was merely the shimmer rising from the asphalt, a trick of heat and light.

He remembers that Cliff is in his bathing suit, exposed to the sun. In spite of all the warnings, Paul isn't so good at remembering sunscreen, still conditioned by his own carefree childhood.

On a childish, mischievous impulse he shuts the front door softly behind him and goes around the side of the house towards the backyard, along the cool, buggy passage between the sidewall and the high cedar hedge on the property line. The wooden gate halfway along is open but that is normal; the real obstacle between the boys and the outside world of strangers and speeding cars is an invisible but sacrosanct line across the driveway twenty feet from the street, between two columnar maples planted when the boys were born.

Paul is tiptoeing as he reaches the end of the passage, readying himself to set the game in motion. They have played this lots of times: Paul will almost let Cliff catch him in the passage, again at the front door before racing through the house and out the back and around again.

"Can't catch me
 Can't catch me
 Cliffy stinks like a chimpanzee."

What he sees does not instantly traumatize him because it is plainly impossible.

He had locked it.

He had snapped the padlock. His fingers can still feel its smooth action, the minute ticking of the key as he pulled it out.

There is no ladder by the gate, no chair from the kitchen. Clifford is spirited but he could never, never...

Paul has never climbed the five-foot fence but he is over it now with a single unconscious effort, determinedly angry by the time he reaches his son hanging in the deep end with his yellow and purple Lakers ball bobbing near his hand, can admit nothing but anger as he throws himself in and tears Clifford from the water.

"What did I tell you what did I tell you..."

For a few minutes he holds reality at bay with his anger and the brute physical work he has learned at a lifesaving course. The knowledge he has gained from it, telling him that he is too late, in no way curtails his ferocious efforts to revive his child.

The last barricade is hope, but it is in ruins by the time the paramedics arrive, pump and shock his son and pronounce him dead.

"What do you know?" he rages as he rides with his love in the hooting ambulance. "You're not doctors! You're paramedics, you're not DOCTORS!"

But it is empty anger now, empty hope, the hammer falling impotently on spent charges. And the enemy is upon him, twirling its terrible doubled-edged blade.

PART I

C H A P T E R 1

PAUL PREEDY'S INVITATION arrived at the rented Durham, North Carolina, bungalow on a Friday. Paul was late home from work as usual and didn't see the small, typed envelope until early Saturday morning on his way back to the plant.

The invitation came from a private boarding school in southern Ontario, a school that, for a hundred and five years, had patterned itself on the much older English model. The Reunion, informed the sensible, masculine typeface, would be held on Sunday, August 25, from noon till six, at the school. Paul was advised that his early reply would be appreciated in order to give the Old Boys' Association an accurate idea of numbers. It was signed by the secretary of the association, a Leslie Meas, his return address a post office box in Scarborough, Ontario.

The invitation paralyzed Paul at the hall table, his forehead and newly shaved upper lip beading in a perfectly cool house.

There was a time when he had seen Felton School in his future as well as his past. Continuity had meant something to

Paul then. So had status. A private school education for his boys would have been a status symbol as well as a good investment, like the Toronto Annex house, the new Acura in the driveway. The pool.

Paul made a drooping moustache with his index finger and wiped the sweat off his lip and went out of the house, locking the front door quietly so as not to disturb Eva and Thomas.

He took Ravine Drive to the bridge, over the creek swollen by record summer rains, heading east out of Durham to US 70 in his grey, midsize company car. At seven on a Saturday morning, the lack of traffic drew his attention to the poor state of the highway — the untended medians, the apocalyptic cracks with things reaching through. Out of his spruce suburban neighbourhood, he passed the shanties — black or white, there seemed to be that monochrome edge, frayed and soiled, to every comfortable stronghold. At one time it had offended his privileged native decency, but that was in another incarnation, as a Canadian tourist in the American South. Now he was glad of it all. Glad of anything that was different from his life before.

He turned off the highway onto Mesa Park Circle, the co-operatively maintained perimeter road that bounded the light industries of Mesa Park. He turned right down one spoke of the wagon wheel configuration of access roads, into the CPE forecourt and the spot reserved for him, parking between sharp yellow lines on pristine blacktop.

The Carolina Polystyrene Extrusions plant resembled a very clean tractor-trailer, the picture-windowed brick office hauling a long, windowless shop clad in spotless mushroom aluminum. The new office windows and the cladding, the landscaping around the plant, the lawns mowed short as a marine's haircut and greened daily by in-ground sprinklers, the bright new stars and stripes, at ease this morning — all of it Paul's doing. It had been hard to part CPE's head office from the necessary quarter-million, but he had been proved right in the end about pride of place: productivity had doubled by the end of his first year as plant manager, had reached an all-time peak by the end of year two.

It wasn't just cosmetics: while the Carolina people would never see Paul Preedy as one of their own, they performed well for a manager who worked a white-collar day, then came back after supper in overalls, to that long aluminum shop. Respected a paper guy who had bothered to study the nuts and bolts of blowing polystyrene film until he was qualified to explode almost any piece of machinery in the factory and fly it back together again. A man who spoke quietly and politely yet gave away almost nothing of himself that wasn't their common business. Canadian, they said, until they learned that Preedy was handling his grief.

He spent an hour and a half with the maintenance crew, until nine-thirty when he was paged to the phone in the shift supervisor's office. He felt a light grip of anxiety when he heard his mother's voice from Toronto.

"Is everything alright?"

"'The time has come, the Walrus said.' Your father and I are selling the house. It's only been on the market since Thursday but we just got an offer. You know what? I'd much rather you and Eva bought it. We'll give you a sweetheart deal."

"You got another place?"

"We're at that impulsive age. It's near Bancroft, a couple of hours northeast of Toronto. About a hundred acres on a lake."

"A hundred acres?"

"Guaranteed privacy. There's a farmhouse on it but it's a mess. We'll tear it down as soon as the cottage is built."

"You've closed?"

"Almost. Now stop interrogating me. All further questions answered in person."

There was a pause between them, a weather change.

"We need you to come up, Paul. There's a lot of good stuff here we won't have room for." Another pause. "You have to collect your things from the Annex."

"We don't want them."

"*You* don't want them. Eva feels differently."

"How do you know?"

"I just spoke to her. We both feel you should come up this time. It's been two years, Paul. It's time to make your peace."

Celia Preedy knew she had crossed the line, but she proceeded blithely. She had worked hard for her family; she knew what was owing her.

"If you came at the end of August you could go to the Felton reunion. Did you get the invitation? It came here first. I wouldn't have opened it, but I thought it might be a begging letter, the Gymnasium Fund or something."

"Yes, I got it," Paul said flatly. "Thank you. I won't be attending. How's dad?"

"I see. So is this going to be the rest of your life? A rented bungalow in some redneck paradise, burying your past in a job that's nothing but hard work for half your previous salary?"

"I'd better go. I'm tying up the supervisor's phone."

"You do Clifford no honour by this."

Paul's voice rose with the effort. "You don't think I can say it, do you? You want me to say it? Listen: I'm not going to discuss Cliff and I'm not going to come and get Cliff's stuff. Did you hear? I said his name twice. Now drop it please."

"Do you know where your wife and firstborn are?"

"You sound like a public service announcement."

"It was a good one."

"I can only say at home since you just talked to Eva. Why don't you tell me?"

"They've gone to the Liberty fair; someone from Eva's writing class is driving them. You should have gone — you used to love the fair when you were a boy, those old farm machines. I found your model steam engine in the attic the other day, and all your Meccano. I think Thomas should have it, don't you?"

"You can send it COD."

Silence, more indicting than anything she could say. Finally: "You know who I grieve for most? For Thomas. And I suppose I'll grieve for you if Eva takes him and leaves you, but it won't be of my free choice. I feel so utterly stupid, Paul."

"Why?" he said reluctantly.

"Because you fooled me for forty years. All that time, I never dreamed you were this selfish."

Paul called Eva but the phone just rang. For a loose moment he considered Liberty, but there would be five thousand at the fair.

He drove home at noon as a kind of penance and regretted it. He wandered about the rented bungalow looking for busywork with the intensity of a man tracking a gas leak, aware of a dangerous rising pressure, a building headache. But there was nothing left to do, not even kitchen chores. He'd cleaned the oven Thursday night and the chrome wells under the elements with NevR-Dull. There were bricks in the toilet tanks, good bulbs in every socket, plants watered and fish fed.

He opened Thomas's door flinching from the stored, silent heat, against hard splinters of sunlight. Everything neat, shoes lined up, books put away, his stuffed animals — too many for an eight-year-old boy — propped in a row against the headboard, staring at nothing. The orderliness was Thomas's doing, not his parents. Quiet and neat. Only the desktop untidy because there was work in progress. Forests of felt-tips in carousels and jam jars, log spills of crayons and pencils. Thomas illustrated his stories these days. This one seemed to be about his school. There was a crayon drawing of the school building flying the stars and stripes. A disproportionately big flag because Thomas had drawn in every star. Was it his flag now?

Paul stared until the stars clustered, then turned out of the room with spikes of yellow pain in his head. He closed the door and went through to the kitchen. He had stipulated a bungalow, insisted. All his life he had gone upstairs at night and down in the morning, half a hundred stairs in the gabled Toronto house.

He swallowed three Bufferin, filled a pail and sponge-mopped a clean floor while he waited for the pain to subside. When it didn't, he ran the water deep cold in the kitchen sink and immersed his face until his skull ached worse than the inside, a distraction at least. Not every day was this bad — his mother calling, the invitation…

He went to the hall table where he had seen the deckled card this morning, to dispose of it, but Eva had moved it.

He put on dark glasses and threw aside the sliding door out to the patio. The lawn was mowed, the beds weeded, the barbecue gleamed. There was nowhere to hide. He should have stayed at work: at CPE he never ran out of things to do.

He heard it now, from the Reinholts two houses away, two hundred feet on wide suburban lots. A searing afternoon and he had expected the sound, surrendered to it now that he had scratched his other options. At times like this his loss was like a terrible hangover that you pray a little time and distraction and a couple of painkillers will alleviate, and when they don't, when it roots behind the eyes and down into the bowels, the only thing you can do is take a drink.

Mercifully the sound of swimming came without the accompaniment of the Reinholt children's laughter, without the plonk and splash of water play.

Someone — an adult — swimming lengths, a slow untidy crawl, it sounded like the measured rustling of tissue paper.

No.

It was like nothing on earth but a swimming pool.

Eva and Thomas came back from the Liberty fair at seven o'clock. They were dropped off by a woman about forty, wearing a lot of mascara. There was light reflecting on the windshield of her car, but Paul could see the panda eyes, black hair kicked up at the shoulder and held back by a wide band, in a style of thirty years ago — the way people remember Jackie Kennedy. But this woman wasn't pretty like Jackie; she looked hard. For a second she reminded Paul of someone else.

"How was the fair?"

"Ninety in the shade, except there wasn't any. I need a beer." Eva turned and waved and let the screen door slap shut behind them.

"How was it, Thomas?"

"Fine."

Eva had sat for a pencil portrait, the likeness but no life. Thomas had his fortune told.

"What did it say?"

The boy shrugged, diffident, tired. Eva waggled her hands around his face, a congested vampire accent: "He will be going on a long journey. He will meet a dark stranger." She shrugged. "Five bucks, what the heck." Thomas squirmed away towards the kitchen and Eva went after him. "Wash your hands before you touch that refrigerator."

Paul glanced behind him through the fly screen. The woman's car was waiting at the end of the driveway although the street was clear of traffic. She was stopped the way people stop to adjust their seatbelt or tune the radio or consult a map, but he could tell by the angle of her head that she was merely looking in the rearview mirror, back at the house. When she twisted in the seat to look directly, Paul's impulse was to draw back from the screen, his upper lip beading.

He called through to the kitchen. "So that's your writing student. What's her name?"

"Arabella Bauer. I've changed my mind, I'm going to have tea, you want?"

"No thank you."

Tea was a ritual that meant she wanted to talk. Most of the time they drank coffee. He knew what she wanted to say.

"So you talked to my mother," he said pre-emptively, still in the hall. He watched Arabella Bauer drive onto the street and turn left and disappear.

"You want cornbread? We picked up fresh, it's still warm."

She'd had a word with Thomas because he didn't follow her into the living room. She put the tray on the table, stirred the small teapot, daubed white butter on the yellow bread, poured milk and then tea through a silver strainer. The ritual prologue.

"Do you know why you put the milk in first? Arabella told me this, she knows some interesting things. Before central heating, a cup might crack if you poured hot tea straight in. I've got some budding historical novelists in my class; I'll have to pass that on."

Paul's wife taught creative writing at the University of North Carolina at Durham — a teacher like his mother and a published writer. Her first book of Canadian stories had been shortlisted for the Stephen Leacock Medal. She hadn't written anything since they moved south.

He watched while she stirred her cup, the movement of long, delicate bones in her brown hands. She didn't look like a thirty-eight-year-old woman who has spent all day at the fair and needs her tea. Something had already rejuvenated her.

"Is Arabella Bauer a good writer?"

"Very. She ought to be published."

"What does she do for a living?"

"Travels for a pharmaceutical company. She doesn't make it to every class. I think some of the more committed members are uncomfortable with that."

"Why?"

"I don't know, I think they're just uncomfortable with Arabella."

"Why?"

She glanced up, surprised by his interest. "She's not Ca'lina for a start."

"Nor are you."

"She writes better than them. She's tougher."

"She looks tough."

Eva raised her eyebrows at him as she sipped. "I like her. I don't have many friends down here."

"I thought you didn't make friends with your students."

"I'm learning to be flexible." She looked away. "Apparently she goes to Toronto all the time on business, knows it well. Actually she was supposed to go in August for a sales convention which fell through. She has a plane ticket she can't use, for August 23." She watched him over the rim of her cup. "Half price if you want it."

"Tell her to get a refund."

"It's a charter flight. They don't refund."

"They don't transfer charter either."

Eva shrugged. "I don't know, maybe her travel agent owes her a favour. She seems to think you'll be able to use it."

"Why should I? It's not my problem."

"No Paul. It's ours."

He looked away. Then back at her, waiting.

Her cup rolled in the saucer as she put it down, spilling an inch of tea. "I talk to her because I can't talk to you." She looked at him while the uncharacteristic anger burned off. Then, with her head slightly to one side, she found her sad smile. "Your parents need to see you."

"They were here at Christmas."

"I want our stuff. I want Clifford's things."

"You go then."

"You could go to the Felton reunion."

"My mother said that. I still don't know why."

Eva stiffened. "Because it's affirmative. Because you had a life before Clifford, and so did we. Hopes! Dreams! Remember?"

Thomas's anxious voice from the kitchen. "Mum?"

"It's okay, Thomas. Daddy and I are talking. I'll be there in a minute." She sat forward on the edge of the sofa. "I want you to use Arabella's ticket and I want you to get another one for Tom. I want you to take him."

Paul stared at her in disbelief.

Eva closed her eyes for a moment, nodded, took a deep breath. "I know I've kept him from you, but only because you let me. Only because you let me, Paul."

He looked away.

"Thomas needs you. He lost his brother, but I want him to have his father."

Paul was silent for a long time before he looked back at

her with his tired red eyes. "You read about leukaemia, whatever, any kind of tragedy…" He stalled, struggling with it. "You know how I used to think of death? Like something floating overhead with a hawk's view, looking down on all the houses, all the families, all the children asleep down there. This night-floating thing dispensing cancer and car wrecks." She nodded encouragingly. "Who was the guy, Eva, the artist who painted those big-eyed floating people?"

She smiled gently. They used to talk like this, generous with their imaginations and their respective knowledge. They used to talk a lot. She said softly: "Chagall."

But he couldn't allow her any encouragement. He stood up and turned away. "There's nothing random here. Nothing fateful. I wasn't paying attention. Clifford drowned. Cause and effect."

He walked into the hall. He glanced left towards the kitchen, saw Thomas turn quickly away from the arch, out of view. He went out onto the front porch, letting the screen door shut on Eva behind him. He heard Thomas call her again and suddenly turned, came right up to the screen until he was wearing it like a dirty veil.

"Tom didn't lose his brother. I lost him. You're going to trust me with number two?"

"I must."

"I've got molten steel in my head some days, Eva. I've got steel spikes for hair and fucking scythes for arms."

"I know."

"No you don't know."

"I know you need help."

"Ah, but do I deserve it? Who shall I blame? You for being at a puppet show? My father for being too careful all my life, which made me careless? Hmmn? There's no one else to blame. I was there that afternoon, no one else. My negligence killed our son as surely as if I'd held his head under the water."

"Stop it. You're not this cruel."

"I can't stop it."

"What do *I* deserve, Paul? What does Thomas deserve?"

"More than me."

"No."

"How long's your bag been packed, Eva? A year?"

Her silence confirmed it.

"Have I just had your ultimatum?"

She waited no more than a second and then, almost imperceptibly, she nodded.

It isn't a dream. He doesn't need to dream it. In the night, his imagination alone can drench him with sweat, can conjure the smell of pool water in his sinuses, so strongly he has to lick his sweat to make sure it's salt.

The not-a-dream is always in two parts. Both take place at the Annex house, on Huron Street in Toronto. In the first part, he is walking back from the variety store on Bloor, with the Saturday *Globe and Mail*. The house is flawlessly clear in his mind. He can smell pancakes as he enters the hallway with his paper, can hear the voices of his children over *Air Farce* on the CBC, Eva's easy admonishments, none of the urgency of a schoolday morning. That Saturday feeling, the future bright with a fresh, shining light. Paul sees a small silhouette in the kitchen doorway, growing as it hurtles towards him, rising in the air as it flies into his arms.

And is gone.

And the scene changes.

Part two has him still in the hallway by the front door. Another Saturday. Still looking forward to the newspaper, though it is afternoon and his progress is reversed and he is opening the door and looking *out* of the house.

Stopping.

Looking down to the threshold with the tinnitus of a doorbell in his mind's ear. Down then out into the parched and white-hot zenith of the day, to the street where the Thomas tree and the Clifford tree are no longer fresh green but withered and twisted, desecrated with fetishes that clitter in the dying branches without air to move them — feathers, bladders, skulls and bones of birds.

Further away, on the far side of the street, something… someone?…shimmering. Sometimes, for a split-second, not long enough to identify it, he can even see a face.

This is the part he has invented to preserve his sanity, that has turned on him. It disgusts him, and he encourages his disgust, hoping it will build to the point where his body rejects his cowardly invention, vomits it up.

"Paul?"

And he is so frightened that for once it is he, not Eva, that crosses the no man's land of their kingsize bed, into her arms.

"Do you remember," he whispered, "the first time we came to this state?" It had been before Thomas, as Canadian tourists, as married lovers, to a house on stilts at Holden Beach. "Remember how we knew the hurricane was coming? How the beach got suddenly empty one afternoon, and the pampas grass keeled over when the wind came up? The blowing sand sounded like fine rain against the windows. Remember how the waves crashed the night before we left?"

Her arms tightened around him, as they had that night.

"We knew it was coming but it wasn't coming just yet," he said. "We knew we had time to drive inland, to be safe." He pressed his cheek against her head. "I've made us wait too long this time. I'm sorry, Eva."

Her fingers strayed to his mouth, touched it softly to quiet him.

C H A P T E R   2

FOR THE RIGHT people, the Valmy Lodge Resort offered Lake Simcoe for sailing and water-skiing, two eighteen-hole golf courses, horseback riding and skeet shooting, curling and billiards. As it had done since the early 1900s, the Valmy continued to make itself as exclusive as was economically viable, witnessed by the *prix fixe* in the Trellis Room — a hundred dollars a head before wine. A week of tennis lessons from resident pro Andrew Adams, on one of the Valmy's eight clay courts, could easily go into four figures for a True Believer.

The courts ran in pairs alongside the adult and childrens' pools and the sun terrace outside the Portage Bar. Andy usually coached on court one nearest the bar, where guests could see him at work and sign up.

This evening he was fielding serves from a middle-aged record producer from Toronto. Not a bad club player, B ladder, trying to hit the ball too hard for his skill level, making a banquet of his serve, readjusting his body with endless stutter steps, wiggling his rear end, bouncing the ball with his racquet.

Badonk. Badonkbadonk. Show business.

Annoying, but the producer's work on his inner game gave Andy the opportunity to eye the producer's daughter, playing her brother on court two. Eighteen or nineteen, edible, with golden down on her tanned legs, like cornsilk. Her underwear, glimpsed every time the little tennis skirt flipped up, was pale mauve to match her socks. Andy had spent most of his life playing tennis, twenty years as a teaching pro, but still that flash of clean cotton panties under a pleated skirt bent him out of shape. Of course he'd been pleased to observe this young person in swimwear for the last three days, supine on the sun terrace, but the swirling pleats and nodding bobbles on her socks suited her much better than languor.

An orange ball flew over his head and socked into the chainlink.

"Fuck!" said the producer, raising admonition from the family.

Andy summoned him to the net, adjusted his grip from an Eastern to the more useful Continental, and for the umpteenth time told him to ease up:

"So you can hit it. So you can get ten aces a set with it. Rest of the time you can't get it in." Subdued derision from the next court. "Get it in, then worry about direction, then depth, then spin and *then* speed. Which serve are we working on?"

The producer mumbled.

"Remember," Andy said, "you're only as good as your second serve."

He felt tired as he watched the man scuff back to the supermarket cart full of balls at his baseline. Not Big Rich like many of the guests here, but a heavy hitter at his own game, a bunch of platinum records, hating it right now because he wasn't in control.

Andy glanced at his Rolex — ten to seven, last lesson of the day, the late summer sun low in his eyes, punishing in spite of his RayBans, though at Valmy prices he could hardly expect his students to take the sunset end.

They quit at seven and the producer went off for dinner with his family. Andy caught the girl watching him as he collected up orange balls — swiping back her hair, showing him a little private smile through the chainlink, reacting to his face and his physique like most females over five. The fact that she was off-limits caused him only mild heartache; the Valmy was just half of Andy's life story. His winters down south brought him many young conquests: hardbody surfer girls with their spandex and jargon, co-eds on March break, models on rollerblades along south Miami Beach.

Andy had long ago learned the power of his looks, but also of kindness and laughter and, above all, of not fearing women — neither their defences nor the real prospect of winning them. Loving women of all ages, fearlessly, was Andy Adams's natural gift, like his athletic ability, his balance and timing and eye for a ball.

He strolled along the deck beside the senior and junior pools, tilting the shopping cart up the single step onto the sun terrace. An hour earlier he would have had to navigate sunbathers, torporous as seals, but at seven o'clock most of the guests were back in their rooms, taking long baths, choosing evening outfits, perusing tonight's menu, making love.

He unlocked the equipment shed and pushed the cart inside with the umbrellas and folded Triconfort chairs and the canisters of pool chemicals. Then he went to the Portage Bar, quiet after the happy hour crowd, for a Perrier and lime.

He sat on a barstool with his RayBans on a turquoise cord around his neck and an acid yellow cotton sweater draped over his square shoulders. He sipped his Perrier, watching the quaint diorama behind the bar, the tiny *voyageurs* bobbing along in their canoe between *papier mâché* rapids and HO gauge pines, round and round the mountain. He kept an eye on his Rolex, a present from the lady guest who would be buying his dinner in fifteen minutes, a reminder that Mrs. Merrill was punctual and expected punctuality.

Andy's status as resident pro placed him in an undefined bracket somewhere above regular employees. Management understood that his effectiveness depended on his being able to mix freely with the guests, and thus he was permitted free range of the hotel.

He adored hotel life, could imagine no other. Because he rowed and bench-pressed and bicycled to stay in shape, because he drank lightly and didn't smoke and hardly ever took drugs even down south, time was still on his side at forty-three, as a teaching professional if not as a player. Living in resorts and hotels for twenty years, he hadn't needed to buy a house or pay rent, didn't own a car or a boat, and so had managed to build a tidy savings. About his only big-ticket possession was the white BMW motorcycle parked in the staff lot, on which he rode south every winter. His getaway bike, a sleek, 150-mile-an-hour symbol of his freedom. He sometimes thought about settling down, buying his own place in the sun one day — he actually had his eye on a little property in the Yucatan, just outside Cancun, where the secretaries sunned topless on Playa del Carmen. But if someone else bought it, that was okay; he wasn't in any hurry to invest in the future. Maintain an open attitude and something wonderful would always turn up.

He finished his drink and strolled out through the wide glass doors, slowing just a little as he came within range of a dark-haired woman seated at an umbrella table on the patio. He had been aware of her even from the tennis court, closely watching the producer's lesson. He saw a room key on a plastic fob on the table, for cabin six, a highball glass, empty except for ice, the September Italian *Vogue*; he saw an expensive sun dress, Paloma Picasso sunglasses; he sampled Calvin Klein Obsession, which was too young for her but, as Andy well knew, that so often *was* the obsession. He put her at thirty-eight.

"Hello," she said.

Andy turned in modest surprise.

"I understand you give lessons." A husky, silky voice, the usual cocktail of cynical amusement and insecurity.

He smiled his best shy smile. "I try." He offered his hand. "Andy Adams, how are you?"

She gave a him cool hand — it felt larger than it looked — but not her name. She did not take the sunglasses off. "Are you very good?"

Innuendo, a variety he had heard many times and which he did not, at this stage, ever reciprocate. At least not in the tone of his voice. "It depends on your level," he said openly. "I'm not really for beginners."

Her finger so casually brushed the room key. "I'm advanced."

"Is that right? I wouldn't have pegged you for a tennis player."

She smiled and picked up her *Vogue* and Andy walked on, grinning to himself when he heard, quietly behind him:

"I'm not."

❖   ❖   ❖

Like the guest cabins, the Valmy Resort's main building was of logs, a honey-varnished palace. This was Andy's seventh season, but it thrilled him to cross the wide expanse of the main lobby, the heart of a grand resort hotel with its cosmopolitan ambience. His place here assured, Andy felt some pride of ownership in the costly furnishings, the subtle lighting, the acres of pure wool underfoot, in striking contrast to the log construction and the towering fieldstone chimney. An old world Canadian hotel where the moose head trophies and the grizzly skins by the fireplace were immune to the new decrees of political correctness.

He sampled mouthwatering aromas as he passed the open double doors to the dining room; he saw guests seated at white-clothed tables amidst the twinkle of polished crystal and silver, a string quartet obliging them, softly, with show tunes.

Hotel music, hotel food, everyone in a holiday mood…

A little early for Mrs. Merrill, he stopped at reception to

pick up mail and messages. Charles had seen him coming and was already floating back from Andy's pigeon hole with a single, small envelope.

"Charles..." But the receptionist saw a guest approaching the desk and floated away. Andy picked up the envelope. He didn't get much mail, was spared the plague of bills and begging letters that afflict homeowners and apartment dwellers. The occasional letter from a departed guest or a winter friend down south, though this small typewritten envelope had a Scarborough, Ontario, postmark.

Who? He caressed the divot above his lip with a corner of the envelope. He liked guessing games. He liked games. The envelope carried a faint hint of perfume. Mrs. D'Arcy (first two weeks in May) wrote him what she called "notelets," but always with a Dunhill in green ink, and she lived in Montreal. The scent...Obsession again? That was probably just the lingering imprint from the woman at the Portage.

"The guest in cabin six," he said quietly when Charles was free. "Is she staying next week?"

The senior receptionist smiled and picked invisible lint off the sleeve of his hunter-green uniform. "What'll you do for me?"

"The usual — anything above the waist and below the neck."

Charles glanced sideways, confirmed that his two colleagues were busy, then leaned across the pine counter. "Ever wondered why men have nipples?"

"Fuck off, Charles. Just look and tell me how long she's staying. Please? I'm in a hurry."

"I can see that." The receptionist looked pointedly past him. Mrs. Merrill had arrived, seated to the left of the fireplace by the dining room doors, where the restaurant manager and the head waiter performed backflips for her, ignoring a group of businessmen with convention nametags.

When Andy turned back, Charles was on his way to the phone. He wanted to wait but Mrs. Merrill had seen him now, waving baby fingers across the lobby.

"*Love* your sweater," Charles called meanly over his shoulder. "Hard to beat yellow with a tan."

❖   ❖   ❖

The Trellis Room manager would normally have looked with disapproval on tennis clothes at dinner, but Mrs. Merrill liked Andy dressed that way. A straight-backed and regal sixty-two (freely admitted) in a full length Bill Blass gown tonight, Margaret Merrill was a regular. She arrived at the Valmy in a chauffeured Rolls Royce for four weeks every year, just as she had done throughout her childhood, and took the same premium cabin. It went without saying that she was given the best table in the Trellis Room, by the window overlooking the lake, in a pool of late golden sunshine.

"So what's in the mystery envelope?"

Andy had already opened it, had slipped it under his bread plate in the hope that she would ask. He pulled out the note and held it for them both to read.

Dear Mr. Adams:

We have pleasure in confirming your attendance at the Felton Old Boys' Reunion on Sunday, August 25, at the school. Please find enclosed a receipt for your cheque in the amount of $45.00. To remind you of the agenda:

12:00 noon.	Reception at Ormiston House.
12:00–1:00 p.m.	Cocktails on the Circle.
1:00 p.m.	Luncheon in the Dining Hall.
2:30 p.m.	Meeting of the Association in the Memorial Hall. Speeches.
3:30–5:30 p.m.	Walkabout.
5:00 p.m.	Evensong in the School Chapel.

Like the invitation Andy had readily accepted back in June, the note was signed by Leslie Meas, secretary of the Association.

"I don't know how they traced me here. I haven't been in touch with the school for twenty-five years."

"You're not in the Old Boys' Club?" Mrs. Merrill smiled. "No, I shouldn't imagine you've ever needed the network, given your...unorthodox lifestyle." Her lacquered fingernail traced one of the veins, numerous and prominent, in his muscular hand. "But I expect you were happy at school, weren't you? I'll bet you were captain of absolutely everything."

Andy reclined, bathed by the low sun filtered through willows on the lakeshore. It was true: though never remotely academic, he had been a star at Felton. Captain of tennis and squash, naturally, but also of cricket and field hockey, popular as only an athletic hero can be, one of a rare handful of Felton boys known to both pupils and staff by their Christian name. Certainly he had struggled against the restraints of an old-fashioned boarding school, had been caned for his exploits on several occasions, but he had never for one minute regretted his days there. He had always been grateful to Felton. Its spartan regime had toughened him, taught him self-sufficiency, the ability to make do with essentials. The close quarters of dayroom and dormitory living had socialized him, made him a good mingler, essential to his present career.

"All four of my children went away to school," Mrs. Merrill said. "They complained at the time, but they thanked me later. The academic and social advantages go without saying, of course, but it breeds damn good manners and something...something else." She looked at him appreciatively. "Are the uninitiated even aware of it? I don't know. But we are, aren't we? I knew it the moment I laid eyes on you." She gave his hand a squeeze and let it go. "So what are we drinking?"

She always made Andy take the wine list. As usual, he showed good manners and selected a medium price — a relative term at the Valmy — and as usual, Mrs. Merrill told him not to be such a tightwad and indicated the Margaux '79.

When they had ordered food and the waiter had gone, she said: "Actually, I don't think you should go."

He looked surprised. "To the reunion? What makes you say that?"

"It wouldn't be fair."

He saw it now, the slight smile with its hint of carnality, and imitated it. Their signal. "Why wouldn't it be fair, Margaret?"

"Oh, I was just thinking of all your balding, potbellied contemporaries. How perfectly lousy you'll make them feel, not to mention their poor wives." She had slipped off her backless sandals, began feathering the hair on his left leg with the toes on her right foot. "Did they make you wear short trousers at Felton?"

"Only for games."

"Jolly hockey sticks. Or do you mean sticking your hands up each other's shorts in the cricket pavilion? Or was it in class under the desk? In the dining hall perhaps, right under the headmaster's nose?" Her foot travelled up, pressed him teasingly, then withdrew. She straightened and looked imperiously around the room, rising an inch or two off her seat as she hitched the Bill Blass gown above her knees. Andy knew this signal too, and crossed his right leg over his knee to unlace his Reebok. He removed the shoe, then the cotton sock, and was gently extending his foot as the prosciutto arrived.

"Delicious," sighed Mrs. Merrill. She stared at Andy, encouraging him as the waiter carved honeydew melon beside the table, letting him get so far then clamping his foot between her knees. Her laugh was almost girlish: "I can't think of a more mouthwatering appetizer, can you, Mr. Adams?"

Andy smiled his good white smile, in genuine admiration and affection for a generous, spirited sixty-two-year-old woman. But he was also pretending, that beneath the silver and crystal and white linen, below the table where she wasn't wearing underwear, Mrs. Merrill was eighteen, spreading tanned, cornsilk legs.

❖   ❖   ❖

For the sake of decorum, they never went back to her cabin together, which gave Andy time to try Charles again.

"Which cabin was it?"

"Six."

"Ah yes." Charles picked at his sleeves. "Nice work if you can get it: terrace on the lake, hot tub and sauna, big screen TV."

"Is she staying next week? Just bloody tell me, okay?"

"What about dear Mrs. Em? Are we moonlighting now?"

"She's flying to New York Monday night for an auction, won't be back till Wednesday."

"I see." Charles surrendered with a sigh. "You're lucky, six is booked all next week. Nice luggage — Vuitton, eight pieces. I didn't see the car, probably something racy like an xjs. You'll have to ask the parking valet."

"Thanks." Andy turned away.

"You don't want the name?"

"What for?" Andy winked. "I've got her number."

"You make me sick."

"Really? I thought you just got sticky."

"Andy?"

He stopped and turned again, impatiently, expecting another retort, but Charles was serious. "You talked to her?"

"Briefly. Why?"

"You didn't notice anything…different about her?"

"Such as?"

Charles looked searchingly at him for a moment, then shrugged. "Nothing, don't worry. Off you go, Mrs. Em hates waiting, doesn't she?"

"Come on, Charles. What?"

Charles busied himself with his paperwork. "Her name's different for a start."

Andy could tell that wasn't it, but he asked now anyway: "Alright, what *is* her name?"

Charles made big eyes. "Can you dig Arabella? Arabella Bauer."

C H A P T E R   3

THUNDER HAD ROLLED across the country town of Port
Hope all afternoon. It had been a dull and constipated exhibition that had released no rain to flush the humidity. David
King was unaware of weather conditions, having lain all day
on his bed, sealed up in the big house his parents had left
him, chainsmoking cigarettes and reading about Alzheimer's. Forty-three was young to be worrying, he knew that,
but he couldn't help it.

Worried, and thoroughly disappointed by the latest offering from the Port Hope Library's interloan system. While the
books offered caregivers reams of advice on the handling of
Alzheimer's patients (their behaviour becoming ever more
bizarre and unmanageable), they held out no hope to its victims. As far as treatment or cure was concerned, the esteemed
and much-lettered authors knew as much about the disease
as they did about time travel. They couldn't even diagnose it
properly!

Abandoned by medical science, David's imagination was
given free rein. Of course he already knew what the lead-up

would be like, the general forgetfulness, misplacing things, then forgetting what you were looking for — the very experiences that had prompted his research in the first place. (His wallet never seemed to be where he'd left it these days; he was always searching for his car keys or his music before church; he'd let a saucepan boil dry last week, something that had never happened before. The pan had become so hot that the plastic knob slipped down off the lid and melted like a black snowball on the stove top.)

But what about the deeper reaches, what about the lost time, the minutes, hours, days in limbo, the utter disconnection that made the prospect of Alzheimer's such a terrifying one?

Sometimes he imagined a snow scene, all the more insidious in its prettiness: he was standing in the middle of a bridge covered with virgin snow, soft, slow flakes falling all around from a low grey ceiling. There was no wind to disturb their graceful descent. Somehow he had got himself "turned around" in the middle of the bridge, but the snow had obliterated his footprints so that it was impossible to tell from which direction he had come, nor that in which he was supposed to be travelling. Behind him and in front, both ends of the bridge were blind, obscured by mist and the soft curtain of snow. Beneath the bridge, a wide grey river flowed with infinite patience from one lost horizon to the next. There was no sound, not even the kiss of snowflakes. There was no way of measuring time.

He imagined the first flicker of anxiety, becoming fear then panic then terror as the grey figures appeared at either end of the bridge, closing on him. Strangers, all the more menacing because they had learned his name, hiding their intentions behind masks of kindliness; the strangers children were warned about, closer, reaching for him...

David started, staring through his thick glasses, blinking his magnified eyes rapidly to focus on the open book in his lap. But what it offered was no less frightening: a map of the human brain labelled in outlandish Latin, names such as

Renaissance cartographers gave their own dark, unexplored regions: isthmus, hippocampus, septum pellucidum, corpus callosum...missing only the illustrations of sea monsters and savages. And on the facing page was the brain damage, the inexorable, terminal rot that was only measurable by autopsy, after the victim's head had been cleaved like rotten fruit: the terrible neurofibrillary tangles that characterized Alzheimer's. Enlarged 125,000 times in the electron micrographic sketch, they formed the very picture of dementia, a frantic scrabbling of claws.

Of course, forgetfulness wasn't necessarily a symptom of Alzheimer's. Sudden stress could cause it, what the psychologists called "fugue." Or depression, and of course he *had* been highly stressed and depressed lately. Fugue and variations! But spinocerebellar degeneration could also account for memory loss, and so could the unspeakable Creutzfeldt-Jakob disease that made Alzheimer's seem like a reprieve, the absentmindedness followed in a matter of weeks by blindness, insanity and agonizing death.

David felt a familiar thrill of dread as he lay on his bed, staring spellbound at the brain map, his hand straying occasionally to the brimming ashtray on his night table. He recoiled when the telephone bleated, irritated at first, until he recognized her voice.

"So glad I caught you."

"I wasn't expecting to hear from you." He heard his own voice, strained and nasal, and tried to relax it. "It's been a few weeks."

"I know, David. I couldn't help it. I've been filling in for one of the other salespeople, looking after his patch. I've been in Montreal since Monday but I'm on my way home. I'm calling from Cobourg."

Cobourg was five miles down the road. His heart began to speed up.

She said: "Are you going to practise tonight?"

"Yes. I'm leaving in a minute."

"Can I come and listen?"

He made her wait while he chain-lit a cigarette and crushed out the butt. If he gave away his excitement, if she knew how much he wanted to see her, she might not come. She was so unpredictable, so full of surprises. So exciting.

"I don't mind," he said.

"See you at the church then. By the way, did you have any more thoughts about that school thing?"

"I'm not going."

"Just wondered," she said brightly. "None of my business anyway, right?"

His silence agreed with her.

"Right. See you at the church then. You'll leave the vestry door open?"

"Yes."

He put the phone down and fell back against the pillows, his hand over his heart to see how fast it was beating.

He waited for it to slow, for the sudden turmoil of his thoughts to settle. When they didn't, he swung his heavy legs off the side of his custom bed and stood, slowly and carefully until he had attained his full height. He made his difficult way across the big bedroom to the ensuite bathroom, hauling his size-fourteen feet over piled newspapers and mounds of soiled laundry, ducking low to clear the bathroom door.

At seven feet one inch, David King was well outside the recognized normal range, and had done much of his growing before the age of sixteen. Such a spurt had prescribed a life of poor health and inactivity, which in turn had left him soft and ungainly, narrow-shouldered and wide in the hips. In the last decade he had developed a stoop, both to do with his height and his melancholy disposition. Though severely my-opic, he read a great deal, mostly on medical subjects, through which he had developed a morbid hypochondria over the years, especially virulent when he was depressed.

It depressed him just *thinking* about the Felton reunion — about *them*, all together on Sunday. It was unthinkable that he would actually *go* to it. What would happen? He would find that time and so-called maturity had changed nothing in

their behaviour; there would be the same smirking and cov-
ert glances, the same little muted eruptions of laughter from
his former tormentors. And then it would escalate just as it
had always done, until they had egged someone on to put
something in his cocktail or his lunch, to pick his pockets or
trip him up, just for old time's sake.

His hand trembled as he stood in front of the toilet trying
to unzip himself, as the thoughts, recurrent since the invitation arrived three months ago, came again. Thoughts in
which he had the five or six core offenders at his mercy, in
which he flayed them alive, then sawed off their flesh, then
ground their bones to powder and inhaled it through his
nostrils like cocaine.

Usually he could keep the memories and the urges under
control, dissipated, in weak solution. But then something
would happen and they would suddenly congeal, floating to
the surface like curdled milk in a cup of coffee.

He wished he'd never mentioned Felton to Arabella
Bauer.

David shook himself off and gazed down into the toilet
bowl, reassured by the chrome yellow puddle that meant he
had remembered his high-potency vitamin C. He zipped up,
then went to the encrusted sink and washed his hands with
obsessive thoroughness, under the nails and up his wrists,
rinsing, re-soaping, then rinsing again, then drying them on
a towel as grey with dirt as the fixtures.

He turned to the big medicine cabinet that was the main
reason he had moved from his boyhood bedroom into his
parents' room. He reached in amongst his standing army of
bottles and tubes, shook out two 400-milligram tablets of
Meprobamate, chewing the tranquilizer raw as he went down
the grand curving staircase to find his shoes and his music.

The handsome gothic house, like David's financial independence, had been made possible by a chain of successful
music stores (instruments and instruction, repairs and recorded music) that his father had founded in 1947. George
King — formerly Kronowski — had been a popular profes-

sional accordionist in Poland before the war, a brash, flamboyant man who knew how to work a room. Roundly rejected at first by his gentile Dorset Street neighbours, George King had embarked on a program of systematic bribery, offering complimentary LPs and cut-price pianos and lessons. And soon, together with his pretty wife who demonstrated electric organs at the Cobourg store, he was as popular with his neighbours as his son was despised by their children.

David King's size stigmatized him of course, and perhaps the neighbours' children blamed him for the hours they were now obliged to sit indoors on hard benches plonking "Fur Elise." Upon release from their new pianos, they reformed like hounds to pursue their quarry through every byway and thicket of Port Hope, until David was forced to restrict himself to indoor activities — chiefly reading and music.

But the whips and snares of the neighbours' children were nothing compared to David's enemy within. By age thirteen, having attained a height of six feet four inches, he knew that the enemy was a growth hormone called somatotropin that marched forth against him from his anterior pituitary gland. He knew that his childhood disease had a prosaic name compared to the legion of diseases in his already well-thumbed medical encyclopedia, but what could be more frightening or shameful to a child than something called "giantism"?

David suspected that he was going to be the biggest man in the world, but the phrase brought no comic book flash of towering strength. Instead he saw the grainy photograph in his *Guinness Book of Records*, where the giant was posed next to a dwarf against a clinic background of white tiles: a stooped, bespectacled freak in a costume suit and tie, looking ill and leaning heavily on a cane.

He drove to the church in his mother's pale pink Cadillac. Once pristine, it was now disintegrating from lack of use and care, just like the Dorset Street house. Ten years ago, when

Hannah King still drove it to and from her pleasant duties at
the store, Port Hope had been a quiet country town of Victorian real estate bargains. Now it attracted Toronto
commuters and tourists, which meant health food stores and
antique shops and all-natural ice cream parlours — and nowhere to park. As usual, David had to leave the car halfway
down the hill and walk two blocks up Walton Street to Saint
Matt's.

He plodded half the distance then stopped to get his
breath and reward himself with a fresh cigarette, cursing the
humidity, slipping his hand inside his shirt and pressing it flat
against his soft, slightly lapping breast to feel his heartbeat.
One: his father had died of coronary thrombosis. Two: David
was overweight. Three: he smoked heavily. Still, if he had to
choose, he could do worse. Cancer, for instance, with all that
radiation burning and cutting, those frightful "ectomies" to
stop you eating yourself. Or diabetes, which turned you into
a pincushion and could make you blind, for which there was
always good old Creutzfeldt-Jakob.

David knew perfectly well that he was a hypochondriac,
that the contemplation of disease was his addiction, a dirty
and delicious habit like the cigarette smoking he had taken
up in his early teens because he heard it stunted growth,
which it never did. He knew that worrying about illness made
him more ill, but just as with the smoking, recognizing the
problem didn't solve it.

He started off again, bracing himself as he passed the
Queen's Hotel. They could tart up the town but they couldn't
get rid of the element outside the Queen's, always changing
but always there. Todd Grady was with them tonight, far removed from the boy soprano who used to sing in the church
choir, his face scrubbed to a pale translucence, his hair the
colour of ripe wheat. Now he was cable-muscled and tattooed, his head shaved, his pit bull panting at his feet, its
blunt, vicious head pillowed on his boot. David heard Todd
hawk and a gobbet of phlegm smack the concrete, he heard
the dog growl and waited for the inevitable insults.

"Fe fi fo fum! Hey! King Kong! Gonna play with your organ?" General amusement. "Queer...fuckin' freak."

They burned his insides like ulcers, the taunts and his own clever responses that never occurred to him until too late, which he would never have dared utter anyway.

He reached the church at last and hurried out of their sight, using his own key to open the vestry door. He entered and shut the door behind him with a long sigh as cool, blessed relief rolled over him.

Sanctuary.

David loved the empty church, its silent, perfumed twilight. He loved to be alone under its soaring, vaulted ceiling where he didn't even feel tall. He loved the Anglican liturgy too, its familiar, comforting rituals and rhythms, its essential contrasting images of purple-gold and sackcloth, its susuration like the wind amongst autumn leaves, its deep hushes.

But above all he loved the music, playing the music on a twelve-hundred-pipe double-manual organ he had voiced himself. He handled the instrument the way a champion driver handles a powerful and finely tuned race car, by instinct, with a sixth sense that goes beyond anything that can be learned. His heavy shoes tapped the slender bass pedals with a tap dancer's agility; he pulled and pushed stops by the fistful, in myriad and inspired combinations, never breaking the sure movement of his fingers on the keys.

Though his position as organist was modestly salaried (his sole source of earned income), he never thought of it as a job. Nonetheless he was fully committed to it, even dedicated. Tonight, for instance; Thursday nights he always came to practise even though he had already done so yesterday with the choir.

David settled himself at the console and switched on the pump, thrilled by the roar in the wind chest, feeling the great pipes towering above him, each one an intimate personality thirsting for its transfusion of air.

He cleared his throat with a series of armour-plated diminished seventh chords, all the stops out, until the panes buzzed in the altar window. Then he pushed nearly all the stops in and played a verse of his favourite evening hymn, drawing out the sweetest, most poignant melody in the hymnal:

The day Thou gavest Lord is ended
The darkness falls at thy behest

He played another, wonderfully therapeutic verse, improvising the melody on both manuals, dispersing all recollection of Todd Grady like a harmless vapour. He played his other favourites, "Love Divine, All Loves Excelling" and "Lo, He Comes." And then, healed and restored to his element, he played a Bach four-part invention to loosen his fingers, followed by the Sunday hymns, all of them familiar chestnuts, which didn't deter him from experimenting with dynamics and trying new voicings.

No, you couldn't say it was work.

When he had arrived this evening, the church had been flooded with evening light from the west windows. Saint Matthew's had more than its share of fine glass, intricately puzzled, stained clear and deep as if by the juice of ripe berries. Blazing an hour ago, even the west windows had cooled now, smouldering as the sun departed and shadows retook the church. He had to switch on the brass lamp above the manuals to see his music, playing in a little tent of light as the comfortable darkness gathered around him.

It had been like this when he met her back in early April, on a Wednesday after choir practice. It was always open to the public, usually one or two old people with nothing else to do who always left with the choir. He hadn't noticed her until he had finished a solitary recital, alarmed at first by the shadow-figure in the near-darkness, thinking of Todd Grady and the silverplate in the rector's office.

She said his playing "turned her on." But she really did know about music — church music — astonishing him when she said she liked Healey Willan and Ralph Vaughan Williams, his own favourites exactly. And Tallis. And Monteverdi. And Byrd.

It was incredible, all the more so because there was a definite unrefinement about her, a hardness she was trying to
overcome. He got the feeling there were some things in her
life she was learning later than she would have liked. He suspected that she, too, had been hurt in her past, something
that went beyond the usual deprivation of a poor, blue-collar
upbringing, a specific hurt that meant they had something
else in common besides the music.

She seemed so natural with him. There were none of the
usual subtle signals of discomfort or revulsion or pity. From
the first moment of their first meeting she had been completely at ease, and very soon, so was he. That Wednesday in
April had been the beginning of an irregular rendezvous.
Her visits, usually after choir practice, were dictated by her
sales itinerary, which was dictated by the pharmaceutical
company that employed her. She had never been on a Thursday before, but she was here now.

Right now.

He had not heard her because of the organ, but he could
feel her presence. He therefore indulged himself in a difficult Bach toccata, a showcase for his virtuosity with a
cascading, all-stops-out climax. He indulged the last tumultu-
ous chord and then released it, up to the vaulting and away
into the ozone. Then he switched the instrument off so that
they could both marvel at the deep, almost human sigh as the
air bled from the pipes.

When the last whisper had escaped, there was applause
from a single pair of hands. He rose from the console, smiling, and reached for the gang of switches behind the lay
reader's pew and turned on the choir lights.

"No! Turn them off!" He did so. "Turn off your lamp as well
— there's enough light from the street. It's perfect in the dark."

"My eyes always take so long to adjust."

"You didn't eat your carrots today. You'll go blind."

"I am already." David smiled to himself as he felt his way to
the choir steps, down them and along the right aisle, his permanently damp hand squeaking on the guiding edges of the

pews. He could never have said that to anyone else, about being blind. He would never have had the confidence. She gave him that.

He could just see her now, ahead and to his left, halfway down in the centre section. When he reached the row, she patted the place beside her.

"Come and sit down. It's so great here, I'm paralyzed."

He settled a small distance from her. "It's like an oasis, isn't it?" he commented. "That's how I think of it: an oasis in the middle of the town."

"You see?" she said. "You always say everything just the right way. It makes what I said sound ugly."

"That's not true."

"Yes it is. Paralyzed's an ugly word. I said an ugly word and you said it perfectly."

"Well I'm paralyzed too, so there!" By angling himself, his knees did not press into the front of the pew. They sat in comfortable, companionable silence.

"You must be wanting a cigarette," she said.

"Now that you mention it."

"Me too."

He shifted in the creaking pew, about to stand up again when he felt her hand on his arm.

"Why don't we have it here? Well, why not? They smoke the place up with incense every Sunday, what's the difference?"

He smiled. "Actually, they don't. That's high Anglican."

"And you're low and I'm lower. I know." She laughed before he could protest it, in her startling way, like a little shout. "Fine, okay, we'll go outside. Come on!" She was up and along the aisle, unpredictable, impulsive, exciting as always. "One cigarette then you have to play some more. And I want you to tell me more *things*. I've remembered everything." She stopped at the choir steps, on stage for him. "Double-manual stop-knob console, Tracker action, which I don't really know what it is except it has a backfall passing through the wind chest. Sounds uncomfortable!" She pointed up into the shadows, at the organ case. "Red oak. Twelve hundred and sixty-eight pipes in twenty-five ranks. Lead flue pipes, great and pedal reeds in the German Baroque style, fifty percent tin." She went closer to the case, pointing out individual pipes: "Viole celeste, spillflote, tierce...pretty, pretty. No, not all of them. Rohrflote, that's *a heavy*. And that's the nacht-horn, right? Night horn. Ooooh...gotcha!"

David stood, speechless, in the aisle.

She laughed. "Come on, what are we waiting for?"

They stood outside the vestry door, in shadow, hidden from the street. Occasionally the lights of passing cars washed over them like searchlights, giving David an exciting, fugitive feeling. He could see her then, as he had not been able to inside the church. Not very much younger than him, but everything about her was so dynamic: her supple figure and her dramatically made-up features, especially her eyes, which surprised him — frightened him? — sometimes, like her laugh. Her black hair — jet black — was always held back from her forehead by an Alice band, like the one his mother used to wear when he was a boy.

They smoked for a while in silence, until she broke it.

"So you've set yourself against this reunion on Sunday."

He stared past her, towards the lights on Walton Street. They seemed suddenly dimmer. Everything did.

"Are you going to answer me?" she said.

"No."

"Well poo poo to you too."

"I don't want to talk about this."

"You're not being very polite, you know."

He inhaled with a hiss, dropped his half-smoked cigarette on the path and ground it with his foot.

"That's a waste," she said.

He turned away and pulled the vestry door open.

"Daviiiid?"

"What?"

"Is this fair?"

"Not to me it isn't."

"Wait a minute, buster!" She reached past him and shoved the door back in its frame. "I remember the things you tell me. Don't you ever listen back?"

He waited, frightened and excited by her, still turned away.

"What did I say, David? Last time."

"I don't remember."

"Yes you do. Come on."

"You read too much of that self-help stuff."

"Come on, what did I say?"

He mumbled something.

"What?"

"CLOSURE!"

"Don't raise your voice to me."

"Closure. You talked about closure."

"What about it? That it never does any good trying to run away from the past, right? Confront it, right? *Them*. The ghosts, not half as bad as you remember. What else?"

"I don't know. You're the expert."

"I said that closure also means confronting all the good things you've blocked out. What was *good* about Felton, Dave?"

No one else in his life had ever called him that.

"There was the chapel, wasn't there? The chapel where you played the organ for the school services. There was the south window in the chapel."

He turned finally, staring at her in astonishment. "I told you about that?"

She laughed suddenly. "You see? A few *weeks* and you've blocked it! Imagine how much you've lost in twenty-five years!"

He spoke quietly now, subordinate: "What did I say about the window?"

"That it was beautiful. That it kept you going in hell school — that chapel, plus your music. Have you lost all that? That would be seriously tragic, Dave."

He had not forgotten Felton. What he had done was train himself not to remember. How he had been a big, slow-moving target for even the smallest Felton boys. How they soon learned that the giant had outgrown his strength, that he winded easily and was helpless without his glasses, was everywhere soft to the touch of stick and stone, foot and fist. What he glimpsed now, in dreams and moments of uncontrollable private rage, was a violent uproar, an emotional explosion that blew memory to smithereens, blew him back into the present, wounded and trembling.

"You don't get it, do you Dave? You gonna have to go, you know. And you know what?" She smiled and caught hold of his hand, almost painfully. "I'm coming with you."

David stared at her in sheer bewilderment. She was turned away from the street yet he could see moving points of light in her eyes. They widened. "You don't believe me? Okay. Come on." She flipped away her cigarette, opened the door and pulled him back into the vestry. He let himself be pulled along, stumbling after her, not daring to believe what she had just told him. Three months and he hadn't dared. This…the church was the unspoken limit of their relationship. He knew it. She knew it. That's why he had never invited her out for a coffee, let alone to the house, and why she had never asked. Why should she? She was attractive, desirable. He was her secret amusement, the Hunchback of Saint Matthew's. A temporary diversion because she was between relationships — she never discussed it but he had guessed, had never for a moment doubted that one day she would meet somebody and then there would be no more visits, not even a phone call to say she had a new route.

She led him to the choir steps and let go of his hand. It was true, his weak eyes did take a long time to adjust to the darkness so that he heard her voice before he saw her standing at the lectern with her hand on the big leather bible.

"I swear that three days from now, on Sunday, August twenty-fifth, in the year of our Lord…"

She laughed, a jet of laughter, hot and bright as a flame in the empty darkness.

"I, Arabella Bauer, hereby swear…"

C H A P T E R 4

THE COMMUNITY OF Slagg's Hollow is sequestered deep in the York Mills Valley. In the mostly flat city of Toronto, it can look almost alpine.

Viewed from the descending road in late August, the houses below are partially hidden in the soft bulk of deciduous trees, a view that tantalizes day trippers and househunters: big roofs down there, cedar-shingled or clay-tiled, lots of chimneys; between maple billows and the skirts of hundred-year-old spruce, they glimpse tennis courts and the jewel-blue wink of pools.

The residents enjoy the incongruity of the name Slagg's Hollow, pleased that it evokes images of tarpaper shacks and white lightning for the uninitiated, though these are few in the 1990s. The Hollow has been trendy for at least ten years, a favourite location for movies and TV. It has a high residential turnover now, and the few remaining older families yearn for the days when they lived in Toronto's best-kept secret.

The Hungerfords were gone, Celia told Paul as they twisted down Highvale Road, past the familiar houses, the landmarks of Paul's childhood. The Shepherds and the Berzins had sold, the Ingersolls still owned their place but they were in France all the time now.

"Chad Ingersoll was at Felton, wasn't he?" Celia asked.

"He was older. We only overlapped for a year."

"Maybe you'll see him at the reunion."

"I don't think I'd recognize him."

"You never really kept up with any of your Felton friends. I suppose that's the trouble with country boarding schools — term ends and you all go your separate ways, then the last term comes and you're still in the habit."

"It'll be interesting on Sunday. I wonder if it's changed."

"Not much. I expect it's still run by a wrathful Anglican God, cane in one hand, Latin primer in the other!"

Paul smiled as they wound past the Hamilton's, and then the Fairclough's long colonial — still the Fairclough's house even though it had been repainted, a convertible Mercedes in the driveway, someone else's children playing in the yard. Paul turned to the backseat. "How're you doing there?"

"Fine."

Celia glanced in the rearview mirror. "Feeling woozy, Tom?"

"Bit."

"Couple more minutes and we're there. You know, your father used to scare me half to death riding his bike down this hill, Thomas. He was a proper tearaway."

"And we didn't have pull brakes either, just coasters." Paul looked sideways at his mother. "Remember Mary Jane Fare losing it at the bottom here? Wasn't she in traction?"

"Over at Sunnybrook. Your father attended. She'd broken her femur, and you kids thought he said female: 'Mary Jane Fare's broken her female!' God, you were tingling with curiosity after that. Maybe it was just the little girls — they go in for prurience earlier than boys."

"What's that?" Thomas asked.

Celia smiled into the mirror. "Curiosity, but you'll find out

— the little boys more than make up for it in the end!"

It wasn't the objectivity of absence. Paul had always been able to see why his mother had been a popular teacher, why students had camped on the floor for her English classes. There would be a void at the University of Toronto in September, when Professor Preedy didn't return.

"Are you going to find some teaching near the farm? There's Peterborough, there's Kingston."

"We'll see. I'm going to be too busy to think about anything until the cottage is finished."

Celia held up crossed fingers. Unforseen difficulties had arisen over the building permit, severance permission on land zoned for agriculture. Paul's father was still in Bancroft, deep in red tape, preparing their brief for the hearing on Monday. Friday now, but Paul wouldn't see Jack till they drove out Sunday night after the reunion. He was glad.

Highvale ran straight now, tunneling through the trees. Down here the setting sun was hidden by the rim of the valley, the evening filtered to a cool, early twilight by the green canopy. It had been winter when he last saw the Hollow, through a mist of laboured breath, unloading boxes from the Annex house — one of those freakish late winter days when the rain freezes like a spell and makes a world of sudden, brittle glass.

Celia turned left on Fallingbrook, past the Dampney's corner house. "Still there. Nothing short of a Scud missile is going to budge Dal and Sheila!" She turned left again into the next driveway where an orange realtor's sign with a SOLD sticker gave Paul a sudden pang of regret.

With five bedrooms and a two-car garage on one half-acre, the house where Paul grew up was modest compared to the Hollow's many mansions. It was a family house, low-lying, with a pinkish roughplaster finish that would have been called rendering in the thirties when the house was built.

The garden was immaculate as ever: the weeded beds showed late annuals, hedges trimmed, the wide lawns that circled the house looked like striped green velvet; his parents' stewardship was undiminished just because the house was sold.

They went in single file up the tidy stone path to the front door, carrying bags, a representative from each of the three generations that had known this house.

"Your family seat," Celia announced as she unlocked the door and went in. "Anyone hungry or did they feed you relentlessly on the plane? How about you, Tom? Why don't you and me go and gaze into the fridge, see what we can see?"

Paul stood immobilized in the hallway. It seemed vast without the umbrella stand and the ottoman full of jumbled hats and gloves. There was an imprint on the wood floor where the hall rug had been, like pale flesh where a bandage has been torn off. The walls, too, bereft of grandmother Preedy's watercolours, looked naked and sore; where each familiar picture had been, its place was kept by a pale ghost.

Paul realized he was still holding his bags. He slowly lowered them, closed the front door, then walked across the bare, hard floor to the dining room. He was astonished by it, a mere arrangement of walls and windows without the encoded furniture, the grandfather clock where Paul's boys had listened for the mouse running down just as he had done as a small child.

Every Sunday, Paul and Eva used to bring them over from the Annex, even as babies. Standing here, it felt like yesterday: setting up the Fisher Price highchair, a sturdy one, well designed and engineered, in perfect condition when Thomas was finished with it. Thomas had always sat quietly with his bottle and his pabulum. It wasn't Tom that put the mileage on it.

Paul's breathing quickened. He squeezed his eyes shut but it didn't stop the room reassembling itself in relentless detail: the little boy with shining eyes, riding his highchair like a bronco buster, rocking out the rivets, making it walk and talk, squealing with purely joyful laughter…*Look at me!*

He went out quickly and shut the door firmly behind him.

He found Celia alone in the kitchen, putting away the groceries they had picked up on the way back from the airport.

"Where's Tom?"

"He went to check out the garden before the light goes."

"The house looks weird, mum."

She turned from the cupboard, saw the tight line of his mouth and smiled apologetically. "Burgled, I know. And an inside job, to boot. I'm sorry it had to be like this for your last time here. If we weren't closing in two weeks…"

"It's okay, I understand."

"Whatever's in storage, not a stick gets sold until we've furnished the cottage. You and Eva can have your pick. Meanwhile, we have an atticful to sort out, including your things from the Annex. I thought we'd spend tomorrow showing Thomas the sights, maybe make a start with the attic tomorrow night."

"Sounds good."

"What would he like to see? What don't you have in suburban North Carolina besides everything?"

"Mum…," he said warningly.

She smiled and reached out and curled her long fingers against his cheek. "But you and Eva *are* still talking about coming back?"

He took the hand and kissed it and let it go. "Still talking. Let's go ask Tom what he wants to do tomorrow." He turned and opened the glass-panelled back door, stuck his head out and called. He waited a moment, then called again.

"Shut the door," Celia admonished, "you're letting all the bugs in."

Paul walked out into the purple twilight and called a third time, louder, sudden tension in his voice. Celia followed him out and shut the door behind her. "Relax, he knows his way around here. It was his second home."

"Tom!" A shout this time, which brought his son at a run, out of breath. "God…didn't you hear me? I had to call you four times! What were you doing?"

Celia moved between them. "He's here, isn't he? You

don't have to give him the third degree." She took Tom's hand. "Did you find anything interesting?"

"I was up in the tree house," he said breathlessly. "The one Grampa built for me and..." He stopped himself, an uncertain glance at his father.

Paul turned away to the spill of light from the kitchen. "Come on, Tom," he said quietly. "Let's go find the bunkroom."

The boy started after him, but Celia kept tight hold of his hand. "That's right, Thomas. Grampa built it for you and Cliff. It's good that you remember. Don't you think so, Paul?"

He stood for a moment with his hand on the doorknob, which had grown slippery in his grasp. He waited with his back to them, remembering everything he had promised Eva and himself.

"Yes, Tom," he said at last. He cleared his throat and looked round, wishing he could smile. "Yes, it's good."

❖   ❖   ❖

Celia had made up the green guest room for Paul, with fresh towels draped over the familiar Lloyd Loom chair and a thoughtful posy of freesias on the night table, scenting the otherwise slightly musty room.

Paul hauled his bag onto the bed while Celia went round opening windows. "Let me know if you want something to read in bed; we haven't shipped out all the books yet."

Paul unzipped his bag and threw back the lid. "Actually I've brought *you* some reading matter." He lifted out the topmost item, the typewritten manuscript Eva had put in at the last minute.

Celia looked pleased and surprised. "Eva's writing again?"

"It's by someone in her class, supposed to be pretty hot. She thought you'd be interested." He handed it to her.

Celia read aloud: "*Running Out* by Arabella Bauer. Arabella! My, my... surely do sound Southern, don't it?"

"We got here on the cheap thanks to Arabella Bauer."

"Hmmn?" His mother was already leafing through the manuscript.

"She had a ticket for Toronto she couldn't use, sold it to us half price."

"That was nice." Celia perched on the green Lloyd Loom, frowning. "Has this person ever been published?"

"Apparently not."

"It's funny."

"I don't hear you laughing."

"It's familiar somehow." Celia shut it and stood up, gave Tom a bright smile. "Look at this poor guy without a room and we're sitting reading! Come on, let's get you fixed up."

She led the way down the corridor, to the last door before the back stairs. "I thought it might be nice for you to have your father's old room." She flicked the wall switch and stood aside, watching Tom's face.

Almost every flat surface in the small room was covered by models, racing cars and planes and some working mechanisms, cranes and winches and hoists — the colourful, complicated dazzle of Meccano.

"Where did you find them?" said Paul wonderingly.

"In the attic."

"I'd forgotten…" He walked into the room, towards the centrepiece of the display, the traction engine that powered many of the Meccano models.

"I gave it a little spit and polish."

"You sure did. Look at this, Tom." The boy came obediently to his side. "This isn't a toy, you know. This is a real, working steam engine. That's a solid brass boiler. That's the firebox underneath. See that lamp? You put methylated spirits in there, work up a head of steam in the boiler so the pressure…" Paul caught himself and looked around at Celia in the doorway. "Why are you smiling like that?"

"I'm so happy you both came." She turned out of the room. "Come see me when you're in your jammies, Tom, and I'll fix you up with a facecloth and a towel."

Paul helped him unpack, bemused by his son's neatness,

his purposeful journeys between his suitcase and the chest of
drawers that had contained Paul's things all his childhood —
drawers lined with brittle yellowed paper and exuding the
faint, comforting smell of mothballs. He left Tom to finish
when his attention was caught by a black-and-white framed
photograph partially hidden behind the open bedroom
door. Celia must have found this in the attic, too, and rein-
stated it in honour of Sunday's reunion.

He swung the door aside and stepped up for a close inspection. There had been other Felton shots, team photos
and graduation pictures, but this was the only one ever to be
framed of the school *en masse*.

Summer term, 1966. Three hundred and fifty faces, in
four slightly undulating rows, radiating out from the headmaster, Mister Jock Beale.

Faces, most of them long buried in the dead files section
of Paul's memory, but now, amazingly, he had names on instant recall: crazy Blenkinsop and Howard Jane, The Human
Brain; wimpy Hollom and Dean Crutwell who wasn't supposed to play contact sports because he had a hole in his
heart but could fence like D'Artagnan. Ronson in the back
row, swaggering under his Beatle haircut — Ronson and
Keel, giving attitude they'd call it now. The school prefects in
the centre, head boy Flogger Harris with his nose in the air,
rubbing shoulders with Beale.

Suck Jock's bone, Flogger!

The freaks: Nickerson with his horizontally buck teeth; the
giant, King; Riddle, the African Elephant, cruelly fat at
fifteen, with ears like pizza dough. But Riddle had a sister
called Carol, didn't he, produced bianually for Open Day and
the Christmas service, the weight of her small-eared body differently distributed. The Carol service!

There was Everett who died rolling a tractor on his father's
farm, and McNaughton Minor who could never fight his way
out of his athletic older brother's shadow until he distinguished himself at last, one of a handful of Canadian

mercenaries, blown to bits by an American claymore mine in a place called Phuc something.

But McNaughton Minor was immortal here — all of them were, the eternal prisoners of that callow summer of '66.

Paul himself stood in the second row, two places from the left.

Preedy. A smiling, carefree boy with his whole life ahead of him: college, a brilliant career…

…plainly impossible.

He had locked it.

He had snapped the padlock.

Like an ambush, he never saw it coming. The familiar rising pressure, the first pulse of the yellow pain in his head. Paul wanted to look away from the photograph but it held him in a vise.

Preedy. In the second row. A clear quarter century to spare but already powerless, locked on track with the pattern of Clifford, complete and perfect, already written in his genes and his soul.

Soulmates.

Running together, whilst somewhere far up the track, the train had already begun its inexorable journey, slow enough to give them a little time, but eventually…

"I'm ready, dad."

Paul stood frozen, blinking. It was a long moment before he dared turn round.

When Tom was in bed he put two Bufferin in his shirt pocket and went downstairs. He heard Celia on the phone in her study, and went into the kitchen. There was a pale moon on the wall where the big clock used to hang, but his watch gave him eight-twenty. He'd wait fifteen minutes before he took the painkillers, see if the headache would recede on its own. Fresh air sometimes helped. A walk.

He went out of the back door, into deepening twilight that had nudged back the trees and hedges, making the garden seem bigger as he crossed Jack's perfect lawn.

Shipshape. Jack's garden was just like Jack's boat.

Chop chop, hop to it, listen up, here's the drill!

Everyone chopped and hopped for Jack, scraping and scrubbing and hauling and tying. It was the firing squad for a loose life jacket; it was harnesses and lifelines at the first sign of bad weather. Jack was a doctor; he knew about the fragility as well as the sanctity of life, knew what the smallest slip could mean.

He stopped and looked up at the dark shape of the tree house in the big oak: pressure-treated spruce, three-quarter-inch ply, twenty-year shingles and galvanized nails; no scrap up there, some real houses weren't built so well. No half measures, that was Jack. The tree house was built to last forever.

An indestructible, empty nest.

He heard the back door open, turned and waved to Celia to locate himself. While he waited, he heard an eruption of laughter and the maraca sound of a cocktail shaker beyond the hedge, from the Dampneys next door. Dal and Sheila having a shindig on their porch. A few years older than Paul's parents, but still all kinds of life in their cultured voices, ripe and irreverent and privileged. He heard another burst of laughter, then a moan of theatrical dismay as someone blew their bridge hand.

Uncle Dal (everyone called him that) and Sheila Dampney and cronies, slightly in their cups...a pure evocation of the fat fifties and sixties in the Hollow, as right as vintage Sinatra.

He turned, smiling, as Celia came up. "Did you and Jack find a bridge game out in Bancroft?"

"We will. But we'll never find anyone who can mix a vodka martini like Dal Dampney!"

"Shall we go say hi?"

She took his arm and squeezed against him. "No."

They walked on together, a comfortable fit. Celia Preedy was tall, almost shoulder to shoulder with her son, still slender rather than thin. All the time he was growing up, Paul held the belief, rare in children, that he had the kind of mother other children envied: educated and enterprising, funny and attractive and generous-natured. It made him wonder why she had married Jack. He had wondered aloud once, casually, trying to hide his bias, and he had never forgotten her reply; not so much what she said but the way she said it, absent for a moment, girlish and starry-eyed, no longer his mother but Jack's wife:

"He's ornery but I like him."

Paul did not appreciate his father any better after that, as jealousy spiced the old antipathy. Which Celia understood — she spent a good deal of her time moderating Jack's demands on his son.

They turned away from the Dampneys, still arm in arm, towards the house standing thirty yards away, its lights pooling yellow as butter in the twilight. "You'll miss it, I know you will," Paul said. "Was it Jack's idea to move?"

She ignored the question. "I miss it already. Don't you?"

It was a moment before Paul replied. "I miss the happiness we had here. I know they say a man's home is his castle, but this home really felt like one: those thick rough walls, lawns all around it like a moat, a magic circle of trees and hedges. I miss being in the valley, it felt…"

"Inviolable?"

He smiled gently. "I took it for granted that no bad spell could touch us here."

His mother turned and kissed his cheek. "Nothing can protect us against ourselves — except ourselves." She walked him slowly forward towards the house. "Things have been better the last couple of months, haven't they?"

"Eva and I have been talking more. I've been spending more time with her. And Thomas."

"It shows. You're still a bit formal with each other, a bit anxious, but it does show."

They had reached the back door. As he went to open it for her, Paul realized, suddenly, that his headache had completely lifted.

"I want to tell you about Arabella Bauer's story now," Celia said. "I found out why it was familiar."

Paul shut the door on a loitering mosquito and followed her into the kitchen. He saw Arabella Bauer's manuscript on the counter beside a thin blue paperback. Celia picked it up. "*Queen's Quarterly* is a literary magazine — interviews, some poetry, but mostly serious short fiction. What old bookworms like me refer to as a 'Little Magazine.' I subscribe to some of them — *The Capilano Review, Impulse, Descant*— have been for years. I have a lot of back issues, which is why I couldn't immediately place your friend's story."

"She's Eva's friend, not mine. I've never actually met her."

"She's an imposter."

"What?"

"A literary imposter anyway." She opened the magazine at her bookmark and handed it to him.

He read the title aloud: "*Running Out* by Robert Iaboni." He scanned the title page while his mother held up Arabella Bauer's manuscript for comparison.

"See?" she said. "It's word for word the same story."

Paul frowned between the matching texts. "Maybe Robert Iaboni is a pen name? But why would she tell Eva that she'd never been published?"

"Probably because she never has. I know Robert Iaboni isn't a *nom de plume* because I know Robert Iaboni, at least I've met him at the odd party. Is Arabella Bauer mostly bald with a full beard to compensate?"

"What?" He dropped the *Queen's Quarterly* back on the counter and looked at her. "It makes no sense."

"Why not? If Ms. Bauer's intention is to impress her teacher and get good marks then she couldn't have picked a finer story. The only other possibility was a misprint, so I called one of the magazine's editorial staff, an old friend of mine. She assured me that *Running Out* is quintessential Iaboni, required reading in fact. Who did you say Arabella Bauer was?"

Paul shrugged. "She's a student of Eva's. Around my age, sales rep for a drug company or something. They've become friends. Tom seems to like her a lot."

"Does Eva often make friends of her students?"

"No, for the same reason you don't."

She gave him a sharp look. "A *good* reason when you have to hand out an F for plagiarism."

"Why would she risk it? What's to stop Eva seeing the original? She reads widely."

"*Queen's Quarterly* is a university publication, fairly obscure even here, probably non-existent in North Carolina. I only get it because I'm a Queen's alumnus."

Paul shook his head helplessly. "What can I say?"

"If they're friends, how come you've never met her?"

"It just hasn't happened. I've been busy at work; she never comes to the house. They go off and do their thing." Paul squirmed slightly. "She came along at a time when Eva needed support, somebody to talk to; I certainly haven't been the most receptive person in the world. I think Arabella convinced Eva to work on me about coming here." He smiled at his mother. "That was a good idea." He picked up the manuscript, leafed through it for a moment then dropped it back on the table. "Somebody mistyped it. I don't know. There's bound to be some simple explanation."

Celia sniffed. "Okay. Let's have some herb tea. Just mention it to Eva when you call her."

Paul felt different that night as he waited for sleep, soothed by his mother's camomile tea, the sensation of the telephone still warm on his ear. He had mentioned the story to Eva, but neither of them wanted to pay it any mind. Although physically a thousand miles apart, they had felt closer than ever and told each other so. Paul said he felt on the edge of something, a new beginning. He told his wife she was the wisest, most wonderful woman in the world. Eva told him she already knew that.

Paul lay warm in bed, smiling. He felt at home, even in the guest room, too happy to countenance the shimmering Annex driveway tonight, or the place under the trees across the Annex street, less than half a city away. There could be no profane smudge of hope tonight, no basting of sweat in self-disgust.

He went to sleep contentedly and easily, long before the first distant murmur of thunder beyond the Hollow, before the first intimate sigh of wind in the eaves, before the padding of raindrops, like soft paws.

They visited the Science Centre on Saturday, then the museum. They added vertigo to museum fatigue, climbing a thousand feet above the city in the CN Tower's glass elevator.

Toy boats on one side, plying the bathtub curve of Ontario's shoreline. On the other side, a green carpet hiding all but the tallest building. Paul put a quarter in the emplaced binoculars and tried to count the Annex blocks — Bedford, St. George, Huron — but his old neighbourhood looked like another patch in the vast green quilt.

They picked up a pizza on the way back to the Hollow and ate it in front of the television, in aluminum garden chairs. Celia put her bare feet up and drank a beer from the bottle. "We've had our culture, now we can be slobs in good conscience!" But with the cable disconnected and nothing on network prime time to interest the adults, they left Tom to watch while they made their first sortie into the attic.

Access was by a pull-down ladder in the corridor outside Paul's old room. It was stifling at first, breathing the day's trapped air, but necessity drove them on: they were going to the farm the next day, as soon as Paul and Tom came back from the reunion, and Celia wanted to take up a load. Decisions had to be made, so they worked as quickly as they could in the light from two naked bulbs, careful of headroom and exposed nails and splinters from the tinder-dry, rough spruce members.

They organized three categories: keepers, Salvation Army and garbage. Paul was glad to find his undergraduate textbooks after twenty years, as well as a stack of old Felton magazines, which he set aside for bedtime reading, primers for the reunion tomorrow.

But there was a lot of junk: warped tennis racquets and dehydrated, rusty skates; a hundredweight of magazines with fused and rippled pages; LPs of subscription classics by undistinguished studio orchestras; a tarnished fondue set; French onion soup bowls in seventies earth tones. The things that appear with mysterious regularity at thrift shops and lawn sales.

All Jack's old toys were here, trampled low by the march of technology and his relentless quest for efficiency. The pre-central air conditioning unit, the pre-central vacuum canister like an Art Deco jet-pack, the pre-propane hibachi, the pre-video 8mm camera. In fairness, Paul reasoned that the same appliances must gather dust in upper- middle-class attics all over North America, chronicles of privilege and progress, the refining of the dream.

He found the original black-and-white RCA and its once proud successor, a twenty-inch Japanese colour set on tapering, Flintstones-modern legs. Strangely, it still seemed like "the new TV."

Like yesterday…the Leafs' last Stanley Cup, Neil Armstrong's giant step, Nixon's resignation speech. And always Jack, up and down, back and forth to the set, tuning it, adjusting contrast, brightness, volume — working, perfecting, improving.

Paul had had a careful five-minute telephone conversation with his father this morning. They'd kept it businesslike, the building permit, things to bring on Sunday. Jack gave him directions to the farm, a new route that would shave ten minutes, as though Celia hadn't made the trip a hundred times.

Paul was looking to escape the heat by the time they had worked through to the Annex boxes. He stood up.

"Pizza thirst! Want another beer, mum?"

"No thanks."

"You know, we could finish this in the morning." He was passing Celia on his way to the ladder when she gently caught his arm.

"A couple more boxes, then we'll call it quits for tonight."

"I'd better see how Tom's doing."

"He's fine, Paul. Just two more boxes. Just look at them."

"Tomorrow."

"You've got a reunion tomorrow."

Her arm around his shoulder now, Paul's whole body stiffening as she led him back, towards the two unacknowledged boxes that contained his former life.

There was little of monetary value from the Annex house — they had sold it furnished with the appliances. Eva had given him instructions not to relinquish anything without her approval, also a list of what to ship and what to store until the future was decided. All Clifford's belongings, his clothes and bedding and toys, were to go back with Paul.

He had come to understand her wisdom, the healing there might be in processing those things. They had agreed that the toys and clothes should go where they were most needed, to those shanties on the way to CPE, to give pleasure, to wear out usefully and naturally, play-dirty and pee-stained and sun-faded.

But his approval of that didn't seem to help Paul at this moment, steeling himself as he pulled at the interwoven flaps of Clifford's toybox.

But his anxiety was unnecessary. The moment he had dreaded for so long came with no shock of recollection. Cliff's playthings, so eloquent in memory and imagination, were mute.

Nothing.

Inarticulate plastic and die-cast metal. What had been shadow and chimera in Paul's fearful mind was now bright and loud and ordinary, disarmed by detail: the screws and the fake rivets and the decals, the earnest faces of the drivers and spacemen in their cabins, the sherbet discharge of leaking batteries. Cliff's favourite toys, the Duplo and Lego building bricks, were as numerous as pebbles on a beach — bright, resilient plastic that bore no imprints, no scars.

Some of the toys had belonged to Tom first. Some were still hot retail items, things Paul saw in stores at Christmas, products still pitched feverishly between Saturday morning cartoons.

Toys. Overhyped, overwound, missing wheels.

Just toys.

Paul felt his mother's tentative hand on his shoulder as he lifted a preening Ninja Turtle. "It's so strange," he said wonderingly. "I don't feel him here."

"Should you?"

"I don't know. Maybe I'm not dealing with it. I thought I was."

Both her hands, gently kneading his shoulder muscles with her long, strong thumbs. "You are. You're doing fine, just fine."

Paul crossed his left arm over his chest, reaching for her hand. He covered it for a moment, then unfolded himself and stood. "It's getting late. We'd better get Tom up to bed."

Paul drank his beer in front of the CBS news while Celia went up with Tom. He knew how much she cherished her occasional role, felt guilty for the distance he had placed between her and her only grandchild. She and Jack hadn't chosen to have only one offspring; they had bought a big house in the hope and expectation of a big family.

The news ended and the weather came on. Paul was about to turn it off and go upstairs when the announcer reported a hurricane advisory for the southeastern United States.

"When do you have to start worrying?"

He looked round at Celia in the doorway. "Shouldn't have to," he said. "It's way out in the North Atlantic, only just been upgraded from a tropical storm. It'll probably blow off. Tom ready?"

"I told him he could look in the attic till you came up. He's self-possessed, isn't he? I remember when you were his age, how that trapdoor used to frighten you at night. I had to reassure you that it was shut tight, that nothing was going to come down the ladder."

Paul smiled tightly at the TV, where CBS was enlivening the hurricane report with file footage of exploding waves and rivers in the streets, palm trees bending like limbo dancers, cars and boats jumbled like broken toys. They reported that the newborn hurricane was named Terry.

"Sounds more like a hairdresser," Celia said. "Is that Theresa or Terence, do you think? They can be either gender now, can't they?"

"An equal opportunity disaster."

"How long does it take them to go through the alphabet?"

"Couple of years. There's a whole bunch of hurricanes every season that never get going. They draw up the list of names in advance, and when they're through it they start back at A."

"A for Arabella."

Paul looked round from the TV. "Why did you say that?"

Celia looked at him wide-eyed, amused and surprised at herself. "I don't really know."

Paul hadn't expected to find Tom already tucked in with the light off.

"See anything neat in the attic?"

Tom shook his head against the pillow.

Paul hesitated, wondering how to say it. "Find any of the stuff from our old house?"

"No." A tiny voice muffled by the covers.

He sat on the edge of the bed. "Budge over, big guy." Tom wriggled over and Paul lay down beside him on the narrow bed with his feet sticking over the end. "This was my bed you know. I used to lie here just like this, looking at old Earnest."

"Who's Earnest?"

Paul slipped the crook of his arm under Tom's head. "See up there above the bed, those cracks in the ceiling? See the elephant?" He pointed. "He's got his trunk in the air like he's giving himself a showerbath. Earnest, meet my fine son Thomas."

Tom smiled faintly. "I thought you used to sleep at your school. At Felton."

"Yes, I did, but that was later. Even after I went away to school, this was always my home. You knew that." Tom had just turned six the last time he was here, asking fewer questions at that age. Taking everything for granted.

Everyone.

They lay still and silent for a while, Paul looking at the familiar shadowplay on the walls, the night world of long-ago.

"Granma was your mum, right?"

"That's right, Tom."

"And granpa was your dad."

"Yes." Paul could hear the drowsiness overtaking his son's voice.

"Did you ever used to wish you had a brother?"

Paul lay absolutely still. "Sometimes. I guess. Why do you ask?"

He stayed quiet for a long time, wanting to ask again but lacking the courage. He listened, waiting until the boy's breathing had stretched out and slowed down before he whispered at last "Do you?" knowing that Tom was gone.

Paul slowly withdrew his arm and got up. He stood by the bed, looking at his son asleep, seeing Eva in his face as never before. He leaned down and kissed them both goodnight, and it was only then that he noticed something in the small hand resting on the pillow beside Tom's face. Relaxed in sleep it had opened, revealing a square white object. Paul leaned closer and saw in the warm spill of light from the corridor that it was a piece of Lego.

PART II

C H A P T E R 5

PAUL AND TOM left Toronto at nine-thirty, driving west on the 401 in Celia's Subaru wagon, reaching the outskirts of Felton town at eleven.

Paul was shocked by the change. What had been farmers' fields were now subdivisions, stretching away in dreary, biscuit-coloured conformity. Once a characterful market town, Felton had become a bedroom for Cambridge and Kitchener: they had widened the main street and fenced it with parking meters. They had razed the Rialto Theatre, the Prince George Hotel was gone, the fine old red brick building replaced by an anaemic precinct dominated by a video superstore. The Chinese restaurant was still there, but it had pastel venetian blinds in the window and a sign offering "Sishwan Cuisine" on a blackboard in turquoise chalk.

In spite of the changes, the town centre looked rundown, and at Fiveways and School Road he saw why: the inevitable shopping mall, a rearing retail fortress where the county fairground used to be, surrounded by a glittering moat of cars, bleeding the old town centre even on a Sunday: Zellers, The

Bay, Canadian Tire, Miracle Food Mart, a six-screen cinema. They didn't need the Rialto anymore.

"Dad! Look! They've got the new *Star Trek*!"

"I thought those old guys promised not to do another one!" But Tom was glued to the billboard as they drove by. Paul looked at him in playful surprise: "You mean you'd rather go to a movie than the service at the school chapel?"

"Yeah right, dad."

He slowed the car. "When's the second show? Four-thirty? Okay, we'll see how we're fixed for time. As long as we're not too late getting to the farm."

"I could sleep in the car."

"Nice company!"

They drove along School Road and saw more development. But whatever had happened to Felton town, Paul knew that Celia would be proved right, that the school itself would have undergone minimal change. Other private schools might be going co-ed or dropping uniforms or mandatory religious instruction, but not Felton. A gym perhaps, a new chemistry lab, some computers; but there would have been no revolution here in the last quarter-century. Tradition, keeping things the same, was the whole point.

"Twenty-five years since I was along this road," he said quietly. "Time flies, buddy."

"Time flies when you're having fun!"

Paul smiled. It was what Eva said when there were dull chores to do. "Miss your mum?"

Tom shrugged with studied nonchalance. "I guess."

"Me too. And *are* we having fun?"

Tom gave him a look of mischief and mouthed something.

"What was that?"

"Star Trek!"

Paul hooked his right arm and caught Tom in a headlock. "I suppose you want popcorn too?"

"Yup."

"Jeeeez!"

He slowed for the school gates, making the turn with one

hand, reluctant to let go of his boy.

Fifty yards up the driveway, they saw a spire between the trees. The little Anglican church had been built in the 1860s, open to the local population when the school had been a private residence. But for a hundred years it had been exclusively the Felton chapel, to which the boys made a weekly pilgrimage, on foot down the half-mile driveway in all weathers.

As Paul drove past, he got his first real tug of memory, almost physical: the buoyant feeling that had carried him away from chapel after the Sunday morning service, relief that it was over for another week.

He slowed the car to walking pace, feeling himself within a moving grey column, the push and shove; hearing the cacophony of four hundred high spirits, the inexhaustible laughter and derision of schoolboys.

"Wow!"

"What, dad?"

"I dunno…it's like I'm fifteen again!"

The driveway had been resurfaced, but otherwise everything was exactly as he remembered. Cows still chewing their cud on rented school pasture beyond the fence. No one had cut down the blasted oak by the entrance to School Farm — it still looked like a sharp black beak open to the sky. Far to the north, beyond the screen of trees that hid the school buildings, Paul could see the distant Caledon hills, blue as smoke, calling as they had called to a more or less willing prisoner twenty-five years ago.

Paul gunned the Subaru over the creek bridge — he'd shot a water rat under there his first year with Chalmers' air pistol — and past the groundsman's cottage.

Crabby Alf, pop-eyed and hump-backed. Alfie with his black market beer, fifty cents a glass for grade twelves and up. But nobody was fooled; everyone knew Alfie Criddle and his light homebrew were a plant, Jock Beale's failed strategy for keeping the senior boys out of the Prince George in town. Alfie must have been sixty back then, no way he was still around. But a good memory, and there would be many more this afternoon, memories and stories ripe for extrapolation.

Would Johnny Innes be here? What about Pete Moreton and Keith Usher-Smith? Would *it* still be there, the *esprit de corps* that had kept them laughing and playing hard through five years of incarceration? Suddenly Paul could hear them, his own voice in there too, in the draft room at the George, or on the rugby team bus, bloodied and adrenalized:

> *Oh the mayor of Bayswater*
> *He had a lovely daughter*
> *And the hair on her dicky di do*
> *Hung down to her knees.*
>
> *One black one, one white one*
> *And one with a bit of shite on*
> *And the hair on her dicky di do*
> *Hung down to her knees!*

"Ha!" he cried aloud, then shocked Tom with a rebel yell out the open window as they rounded the last bend in the driveway, through the screen of maples and staghorn sumach bearing August flowers like strawberry ice cream cones, and onto Ormiston Circle.

Ormiston House was the original Felton building, the private house from which the school had grown a hundred years ago. Victorian tudor, with tracery windows and tall, clustered chimneys, its sand-struck brick warmed by time and weather. The impression of age was reinforced by a gleaming white BMW motorcycle parked beside the ivied porch as if for a brochure. It was the only vehicle in sight.

"Where is everyone?" Paul looked at the dash clock. They were only half an hour early. Ormiston was supposed to be hosting the reception. "Jeepers, I hope we haven't got the wrong day. Let's see if the Mem Hall's set up."

He drove around the Circle and stopped outside the Memorial Hall, where the Old Boys' Association meeting was to take place at two-thirty. Dour and institutional compared to Ormiston, the hall had been built in the twenties to honour Felton's Great War dead, the usual venue for morning assembly, for concerts, lectures or prize giving.

They climbed the wide stone steps and entered its cool, humid atmosphere, their small noise ringing off the tile floor and damp stone walls of the entrance.

Paul pointed out the summer term's notices still posted on the long cork board — team lists and a prefects' roster, examination timetables, the program for the end-of-term concert.

"We should have come in term time, with stuff going on."

They went through double doors into the hall itself. It was empty, clearly unprepared for any kind of event. Three hundred chairs were stacked neatly at the back of the room, the stage was bare except for a grand piano under a dustcover.

"I thought it sounded quiet. They must have changed the venue. They've probably got it set up in the gym, or the theatre. Either that or we've blown it, kiddo."

Paul went further into the empty hall, assaulted by a wave of memories. A small thrill of dread, a long-dormant response at the clear recollection of Jock Beale on the podium in his black master's gown, issuing dire pronouncements.

"It has come to my attention...The boys responsible will report..."

He could hear the school song booming across the years. Was it still sung in Latin?

He looked around at the honour rolls flanking the stage, gold-on-black tablets, "Those Who Fell," the names shockingly familiar.

"Those were boys from this school who were killed in wars, Tom. Eighteen, nineteen years old, most of them."

"Were they fighting Saddam Hussein?"

Paul smiled sadly. "Before him. This is a very old school."

Blenkinsop J. Of wounds. Passchendaele 1917.

Tremaine D. In action. Verdun 1916.

Thirty such entries, somewhat less for the second war.

Nothing vulnerable nor provoking in the names, nothing that marked them for death; names shouted across playing fields and whispered in dormitories like all the others. When everything else was fair game, there had never been any schoolboy jokes about Blenkinsop J. and his ilk. These rolls, a reliable distraction from governors' speeches and dull lectures, represented a glimpse, however fleeting for teenagers, of their own mortality.

The Ormiston clock was striking half past eleven as they returned to the car. Chameleon chimes, they'd brought sweet relief when they marked the end of a Latin class, hung from you like iron weights on sleepless nights before exams or an interview with Jock. Paul hesitated after Tom got in, his gaze sweeping around the Circle where the cocktail party should have been, at the fine, opposing buildings within a jealous stockade of trees. Still intact, the sense of history and tradition that was the special provision of institutions like this. Classes of eight instead of twenty-eight; team games and close community living; a meritocracy that rewarded the all-rounder rather than the specialist. There was good here. Maybe even for Tom one day.

They drove north from the Circle in search of the reunion. Past Cluffy, Paul's own boarding house — potent with inarticulate memories — past the shooting range and the squash courts and an impressive new classroom block. They stopped briefly at the dining hall where lunch was to be served, just long enough for Paul to discover it locked and empty.

"Where is everyone, Thomas?"

Where was the staff, many of whom surely lived here year round? They hadn't seen anyone yet, not even any cars.

He fished the invitation out of his jacket pocket and read it aloud: "'Sunday, August 25, noon till six.' Do you reckon they changed the date?"

"Probably."

"Boy…nice of them to tell us!"

Paul's window had been down but he rolled it up now, irritably, as the wind gusted around the deserted dining hall.

The air seemed to have cooled and thickened since their arrival, hinting at rain.

There was no sign of life until they reached Wyttes House at the far north end of the campus. A plump, pink-complexioned young woman with a baby in her arms was herding two toddlers into an old Volvo. She was so far from the expectation of men *en masse* that Paul couldn't help smiling as he got out of the car.

The woman smiled back and walked to meet him, still carrying her baby. "Can I help you?" A soft, educated voice.

"I'm not sure. We're supposed to be here for an Old Boys' reunion but we can't find it."

The woman settled her baby in the crook of her arm. "Reunion? First I've heard of it. You don't mean the staff do? That's on today. The annual booze up, it's in Toronto at the Arts and Letters Club." She hitched the baby. "I didn't need the calories this year!"

"That's not it. This was definitely an Old Boys' reunion. Here. Today. I've got the invitation."

She looked at the deckle-edged card. "I don't know what to say. I certainly would have heard — my husband is the Wyttes housemaster." She looked the part, a type he remembered well — educated domesticated.

One of the toddlers called impatiently from the Volvo.

"I'm coming, Christopher." She turned back. "Sorry, but I don't really know how to help you. You wouldn't think they'd have it the same day as the staff thing, would you? Have you come far?"

"Try North Carolina."

"My God! I'll certainly mention this to my husband. Do you want to come in and use the phone or anything?"

There was no need to call. Celia was out visiting friends, wasn't expecting them until supper time. She gave Paul her number and urged him to phone her husband later tonight. He thanked her and went back to the Subaru.

"By the way," she called, "I did actually see a motorbike driving around about half an hour ago looking lost. Another alumnus?"

"Was it a white one?"

"Yes I think it was."

"We saw it parked by Ormiston."

"Good luck!"

"There's a bright side," he told Tom. "It's going to rain anyway, right? Let's have a quick look see who that bike belongs to, go get some lunch, see the two o'clock show. Yeah?"

Tom's grin showed all his teeth.

"Right then. Beam us up, Scotty!"

Now that the initial frustration had worn off, Paul found himself unexpectedly relieved as they drove back to Ormiston House. At least now he would be spared the fumblings for names, the spectacle of his contemporaries aged an instant quarter-century. Better to remember Innes and Moreton and Keith Usher-Smith the way he always had, as boys. A man reached forty one day at a time, in the fullness of time and dignity, the grey hairs and the lines feathering in gently, the process largely unperceived in the bathroom mirror. He didn't need the shock of seeing himself in boys turned to middle-aged men in an instant of time.

Most of all, he was relieved to be spared the cocktail party gloss concealing the unrealized dreams and little infamies that mar even privileged lives. Which meant there would be no need, now, to tell his own lies of omission.

The wind gusted, nudging the light car as they came around the Circle and stopped in front of Ormiston. The white BMW was still there. Little chance that it belonged to an Old Boy, let alone a contemporary; not too many guys, forty plus, rode racing motorcycles.

The bike meant that Ormiston was probably open. Having driven sixty miles, it was worth looking in. They had plenty of time before the movie.

They got out. As they came up to the ivied stone porch, Paul felt another, stronger gust of wind. He looked up into gathering grey and felt the first pricking of rain against his face like cold, tiny stars.

C H A P T E R   6

ANDY ADAMS HAD arrived at eleven, exhilarated from his
ride. He didn't go into Ormiston right away; he wanted a few
minutes alone. He knew exactly where he would make his
solitary communion.

He walked around to the east side of his old boarding
house and down to the playing fields, his black leather jacket
slung over his shoulder, his right hand hooked in the pocket
of his jeans.

He found a warm spot on the Tennis Steps between a pair
of fine ball-crowned brick gateposts — a sweeping, semi-cir-
cular flight that led down to the terraced grass courts and the
playing field beyond, bordered a quarter-mile away by a crescent of dark woods.

The brick step was sun-warmed, radiating through the seat
of his jeans, encouraging a cheerful semi-erection. Nothing
libidinous about it, a pure expression of his happiness at this
moment.

At his feet, the grass court where he had risen to stardom
his first summer term, murdering the best staff player in

straight sets with a laminated Slazenger Demon. He still had it, in its old wooden press with his initials — A.A. — in time-faded ink.

Right here! Senior boys running to fetch the balls he smashed past his exhausted opponent. Masters and prefects here on the steps, middle schoolers dangling their legs from the low wall, mouths agape as they watched history in the making.

He got up, trotted down the steps and across the courts to the cricket pavilion at the edge of the first team boundary. The pavilion was open. No equipment of course, but it was redolent with the smell of linseed oil, the dusty spice of the practice nets and the pads, the perfume of hard leather balls.

He stood on the veranda, looking out to the pitch, a pampered green oasis in the otherwise parched field. From his vantage point he could make out the faint white boundary, watched the ghost of Alf Criddle trundling around with his squeaking marker. He could feel his hands hot in rubber-spiked gloves, itching for work as he waited to bat. He could hear the delayed smack of willow on leather, the splatter of applause all around him as he walked out to the crease, properly handicapped by his stiff white pads — first eleven captain at sixteen.

Andy stooped to rub white boundary marker into his fingers. When he reached the crease, he dipped them into the deep, dry stump holes. He took a run up to the wicket, the graceful, uncoiling menace of the opening fast bowler.

The wind was up by the time he got back to the Tennis Steps, tarnished silver clouds tumbling across the bright dome of the sky, darkening it. He went through the gates and followed the low wall above the courts, back the way he had come, trailing his hand along the coping, enjoying the stored warmth in the rough limestone.

He left the wall and cut across the croquet lawn towards

Ormiston's east front, feeling the soft, sensual springing of turf beneath his shoes. No hoops out, which meant croquet wasn't on the agenda this afternoon. Pity. He could clean up at croquet too.

Andy stopped as a familiar din erupted from the north end of the house, where a deep stand of maples rose above its tall chimneys. The copse had been named by the school's creators, homesick Englishmen or overzealous anglophiles, because the "Rookery" had never been home to anything but plain Canadian crows. He could see the current familiars floating above the trees like black ashes, the air suddenly filled with their raucous, intelligent din. He waited, expecting to see someone down there, whoever had disturbed them.

Ormiston boys had always vilified the crows, thrilled to follow Alfie Criddle into the wood for the "culling," to watch Alf pump and pump his twelve-gauge and make it rain flopping black around them.

When he saw no one, he continued towards the south end and the way back to the Circle, through the housemaster's garden. Only now did it occur to him how quiet the school seemed, how odd that he hadn't seen anyone yet.

Andy glanced back as he reached the garden gate, nervously, taking in the distant crescent of woods, the Rookery, Ormiston's blind, reflecting silver windows — a response to the sudden, unreasonable feeling that he was being watched. Probably the crows, getting on his nerves already.

Proximity to the Rookery was about the only disadvantage of being an Ormiston boy. Always the favoured house, Ormiston had location, style and prestige. Cutting through the housemaster's garden, unchanged from Andy's day, he remembered how ambitious Basil McCrimmon had been for his house; how Basil had scouted preparatory schools shamelessly for the best of the best junior leavers, for the balance of academic and athletic excellence that would keep Ormiston on top. A glance at the Felton Register for any year showed that its most distinguished alumni were Ormiston boys, be they doctors or lawyers, politicians, captains of industry...

Or sportsmen.

Andy stopped again at the gate to the driveway and took a
deep breath, fortifying himself with the memory of his part-
ing conversation with Mrs. Merrill, in which she had
confirmed his image of himself as an independent spirit in a
world of grey conformity. It was no accident, she said, that he
had chosen the hotel life, so much like his life at school — a
microcosmic world with a distinct hierarchy, but one from
which his special skills set him apart and above.

He could see that. Just as his athletic ability had given him
special status at Felton, outside the main streams of academic
success or failure, so it set him apart at the Valmy or Club
Med, from the defined, segregated roles of host and guest.

"You're a wild card," Mrs. Merrill had told him. "A rare
breed these days. You'll blow them out of the water on Sunday. They'll turn up with their nine-till-fives, their bald
patches and bad backs and high blood pressure. You'll bring
on one mass middle-age crisis!"

The Ormiston clock chimed a quarter to twelve as he reached
the west gate, confirmed on his Rolex, but the driveway was
still empty.

He pulled the invitation from his jeans pocket. Ormiston
House. "Sunday, August 25, noon till six." There in black and
white.

He walked past his BMW and into Ormiston's stone porch.
He almost expected the heavy oak door to be locked, but it
wasn't. He pulled it open and stepped into the house that
had been his happy home for five years.

Under any other circumstances his eyes would have
roamed freely in the panelled hallway, relishing each detail in
a feast of nostalgia. But this morning, only one detail claimed
his attention: a bright yellow ribbon tied to the carved newel
at the foot of the staircase.

Andy crossed the waxed oak floor, around a billiards table

to the bottom of the stairs, from where he could see a second ribbon at the half-landing, a third at the top.

The house was empty. He knew it even before he called out and received no answer. There was no reception here but there was something…

A trail of yellow ribbons. Inviting him to follow it.

A game.

He loved games. He was good at them.

Andy's handsome features sharpened in curiosity. Without hesitation, certainly without fear, he placed his boot on the first creaking stair.

C H A P T E R   7

DAVID KING ALMOST didn't get into Felton in the winter of
1961.

It wasn't because of his academic record, which was more
than adequate. It certainly wasn't because his father lacked
the necessary funds. It wasn't even that there were no places,
though the headmaster tried to give Mr. King that impression.

Jock Beale, wearing a tweed sportscoat with leather elbow
patches, had been encouraging on the telephone. But at the
interview, seeing David in the flesh, Beale admitted that there
were "difficulties." He'd had no idea they were seeking immediate placement. The Kings realized, of course, that there was
a five-year waiting list for places, that many current students
had been "down for Felton" since birth and in some cases
even before? He further confessed that while David's musical
ability was admirable, music was unfortunately not a subject
that Felton supported to any great extent. They were "very
big on games" he reminded them, marvelling through a pall
of blue pipesmoke at David's great, knock knees.

But George King was too good a businessman not to have

done his homework. He knew that Felton was in financial trouble, that the school's conservative policies were no longer quite as attractive in the mid-sixties as they had once been, that enrollment was down. He knew that money talked and bullshit walked even when it held a classics MA and wore tweeds and smoked a pipe.

While David waited outside the headmaster's study, reading the school notices on the corkboard, enduring the gawks and titters of grey-uniformed passersby, his father bribed Jock Beale with ten thousand dollars cash money, on top of the hefty annual fee paid in advance.

It is easier for a camel to go through the eye of a needle than for a rich man to enter into the kingdom of God.

It made David grind his teeth every time he heard that at Saint Matthew's, when he considered the King family version: that a rich man had resorted to bribery to pay his son's way into hell.

He swerved to avoid the left gatepost and brought his mother's Cadillac to a barely controlled stop fifty yards up the driveway. He stamped angrily on the parking brake and switched off the ignition with trembling fingers.

Adrenalin — he could feel it storming out of his adrenal medulla, his body wolfing the stuff. Bronchioles and blood vessels in his heart and muscle tissue all dilating, pressure rising as the blood coagulated. Incredible wear and tear. Pure stress.

He lit another cigarette. He had smoked a lot in the car on the way here, until the windows were filmed and his dark Sunday jacket and trousers were streaked with ashes.

A tumbril ride. A nightmare journey. Just as unbearable today as it had been a quarter-century ago when his mother used to drive him. It was only the thought of Arabella Bauer meeting him at Ormiston House that had kept him from turning back.

"It's your rite of passage, Dave. Nobody said it would be easy. But just think how much better you'll feel for the rest of your life, knowing you've looked those old ghosts in the face and stared them down."

She had called this morning, a moment of despair when he heard her voice, expecting an excuse; but she was only prevented from travelling down with him, would meet him between twelve and one at the school. He had given her detailed directions, surprised that she didn't seem to be writing them down.

So he had been alone for the journey, listening to the jeers of his former tormentors, hearing their laughter in the roar of wind and tires. Taunting, urgent, sibilant, repetitive — rising to fever pitch until not even the radio at full volume could drown it.

David had conscientiously avoided this part of the province for twenty-five years; its roads had never conveyed him anywhere but here. Every signpost, every familiar, hated landmark was a mocking souvenir of terror and despair. He was a terrified boy again, being delivered to the prison gates for another stretch. As the odometer rolled with the passing miles, something had rolled and sloshed in his stomach, something blunt and slippery, like a whale with its internal compass shot, sick and disoriented. The thing had displaced his breakfast half an hour ago, into a ditch beside the car, the bile still scalding his throat and nasal passages.

It had taken every ounce of willpower to keep going. He was sorely tempted even now, in the shadow of the chapel, to turn around and drive home.

He looked up through the dirty windshield at the spire, a black exclamation mark against the grey sky. He opened the door, flipped his cigarette butt and got out, following the narrow flagged path through the trees.

Unto thee, O Lord, do I lift up my soul;
O my God, I trust in thee.
Show me thy ways, O Lord; teach me thy paths.

The chapel was locked but he'd been expecting that.

Once upon a time he'd been the only boy in the school with his own key, which he used in every kind of weather, angled forward against rain or snowstorm down that long driveway, hugging his organ music under his coat. He didn't mind not being able to go inside. He'd get his fill at evensong tonight.

With Arabella.

He glimpsed it again, the excitement that had lain under the heavy, dark and smothering quilt of his thoughts all morning. He tried to put it away, something he hardly dared admit for fear of disappointment, but right now it wouldn't stay put. Being here, right now, it was getting harder not to hope!

He walked around to the side of the chapel and pressed his face to one of the side windows. With the noon sun high and clouded, little light penetrated the chapel, which made it easier to fill darkened pews with the uniformed ranks of boys, to imagine Jock Beale in the pulpit, righteous and wrathful in his lay reader's vestments. Easier to imagine himself at the organ bench, delivered at last from his tormentors in the pews, from the pinches and pin-jabs, from getting squashed at the end of the row, getting his feet stamped on and his books snatched.

At that small, single-manual organ, for one hour every week, David had discovered empowerment for the first time in his life. He was the one in control, he was the one pulling out the stops; they marched to his tempo, they obeyed his dynamics...not just his tormentors, but the staff too, that snob Basil McCrimmon, Beale the hypocrite.

David pressed his face closer in order to see the south window above the altar. A masterpiece of composition and craftsmanship, it was said to have been designed and executed by Tiffany himself. It illustrated Luke 2, the twelve-year-old Jesus with the elders in the temple. Tiffany had chosen to stress Jesus' humility rather than his precocious intellect, had him cross-legged, in rapt attention. Yet such was the artist's skill that all the latent power and promise was there in the lovely, Pre-Raphaelite face.

The effect of a stained glass window depends on an equal partnership between glass and transmitted light; from outside the chapel, with the sun high and clouded, he could see none of the detail nor colour that elevated this window to the level of exquisite art. But he had been looking at it in flawless detail, almost daily, for twenty-five years — the central image of his life, burned deeply and permanently, not just on his memory, but on his soul. Now as then, this beautiful boy Jesus was an object not of inspiration or spiritual reverence, but of a fervent romantic love.

Was it possible, after all these years, that there could be competition?

He drew back at last from the window. As he straightened his glasses and drew himself up to his full, great height, David sent a silent prayer of thanks for Arabella Bauer to the God he had always tried to believe in. For however many — or few — days of hope there might be.

He was ready now.

THEY SAW THE approaching car from Ormiston's porch. An older model pink Cadillac, the driver so tall he was craning forward to clear the roof. Paul felt Tom's hand seek his own as the man got out, towering above the big car. He trudged towards them through the light rain.

At first he was just the tallest man Paul had ever seen. Then he was familiar. By the time he was near enough for them to hear his laboured breathing, Paul had the name.

"David King, right? Paul Preedy, I think I was a couple of years behind you, in Cluffy. This is my son Tom." Paul smiled and offered his hand in welcome, but King ignored it. The porch was spacious, with a high vaulted ceiling, but King darkened it as he entered.

"I got an invitation to a reunion."

The high, strained voice carried unpleasant, though indefinite, associations for Paul that he tried to ignore.

"I got one too," he said brightly.

"So what's going on? Where is everyone?"

"Good question. I'm afraid someone messed up. Either

that or they're hiding in the shrubbery about to leap out and surprise us!"

King turned his back to them, peering out of the porch. "There's no one here?" he demanded. "No staff?"

Paul recounted his conversation at Wyttes House, about the staff party in Toronto. King lit a cigarette while he listened, filling the porch with smoke.

"What about that motorcycle?"

"We were just on our way in to find out." Paul turned and reached for the door, but it moved away from his hand as someone opened it from the inside. He felt Tom's hand tighten its grip as a man revealed himself on the threshold. He was tanned and good looking, wearing jeans and cowboy boots, the casual impression heightened by the billiards cue he was rolling expertly between his fingers.

"What do they say…two's company, three's a reunion?" He smiled charmingly at Tom. "I'm sorry — four!" He shifted the cue to his left hand and reached down to shake Tom's. "You must be a Preedy. I was at school here with your dad." Amused, sun-faded blue eyes looked up at the men. "Paul Preedy, right? And you're David King. You used to play the organ in chapel." A double-take on King. "You okay? You look like you've seen a ghost."

A performance: the welcoming host at his country residence — a rehearsed quality only possible if he had been expecting them. Paul couldn't help but voice his disapproval.

"My memory obviously isn't as good as yours."

Still smiling — perfect teeth — the man offered Paul a strong hand. "I'm sorry. Andy Adams. I was a couple of years ahead of you. You were in Cluffy, right? I was in here for my sins, with Basil McCrimmon."

It only took Paul a moment. "Yes, I remember. You were a sportsman."

Adams grinned and brandished the cue. "Still availing myself of the recreational facilities!" He turned back to the door. "Shall we, gentlemen?"

"What the hell is this?"

Paul turned to look at King, his surliness now open animosity.

"What are you playing at, Adams?"

Adams' blue eyes were shot with wry amusement. "I didn't invite you here if that's what you're thinking. I came for a reunion same as you, all dressed up and nowhere to go. My only advantage was getting here before you. Gave me time to look around."

"At what?" snapped King.

Paul said evenly: "I get the feeling you were expecting us. How come?"

"I'll show you." He glanced at King's cigarette. "Come on in before we all asphyxiate."

Paul followed Adams and Tom inside then held the door. He was more curious than annoyed at King, who kept him waiting while he took another anxious look outside the porch. He flicked away his cigarette and blundered past Paul without acknowledgement.

There had always been a battered, three-quarter-size billiards table in Ormiston's reception hall. There were three balls on the threadbare baize today, lined up for a cannon and a possible in-off: spot, white, red — three-ball English billiards, a gentleman's game fit for Ormiston boys. The old table, the cracked leather sofa in front of the baronial limestone fireplace, the moth-eaten Persian carpet by the grate, the wood panelling around the hall buffed glossy at shoulder height from generations of loiterers — the overall impression of Ormiston House was one of very shabby gentility. Except for the sepia team photographs and the potent smell of institutional cleanser, the reception hall might still have belonged to a private house. The original staircase angled handsomely up to a minstrels' gallery with a carved oak balustrade. Beyond the billiards table, under the gallery and to the right, the housemaster's apartments and the house library occupied what had once been reception rooms. To the left, a glass-panelled passage door removed the long corridor from which ran the junior and senior dayrooms and the prefects' studies. Paul remembered it all.

The three of them waited while Adams crossed to the cue rack where a black leather jacket hung from a peg. His limber walk and trim physique suggested that he was still athletic, but in spite of his good shape and his Hollywood features, there was something dissolute about him, a weakness that went deeper than his tan.

Instead of replacing his cue, Adams took out another, shorter one, which he offered to Tom. "Ever play?"

Tom looked uncertainly at his father.

"He's played a little pool," Paul said carefully. "Why?"

Adams smiled at Tom. "If you can play pool, this is a breeze. How's about I get you going, then you can practise for a minute or two while I take your dad and Mr. King upstairs. Sound good?"

Tom looked at his father again.

"What are you talking about?" demanded Paul.

"Something I want to show you guys. Nothing that'll interest your boy though." He held Paul's gaze for a second, serious for the first time.

"Enough of this horseshit!" King thundered past Paul, up to the table. "You tell us *right now* what's going on. Who invited us? How did you know we were coming?"

Adams smiled, caressing his cheek with the shorter cue. "You haven't made the connection yet? Really, I can understand Preedy being a tad slow on the uptake; he was younger than us." The cue brushed his lips. "Come on, King. Why us three, out of all those hundreds — thousands — of old boys who might have turned up today? Contemporaries, too, all three of us. How about that? By the way, did we all get an invitation from a Mister Leslie Meas, P.O. box in Scarborough?"

Paul's nod and King's glowering silence confirmed it.

"Figured. So indulge me for a little minute, okay?" He turned his attention back to Tom. "You won't be missing anything, just some boring old stuff I want to show your dad."

Adams passed him his cue. "Just remember to grip the butt
and keep the tip up, as the actress said to the bishop. Here's
a cannon. It's easy. Watch." He made an elegant bridge,
sighted for a second then pumped. The cueball blurred
across the table into Paul's cupped hand.

"Stop it," he said quietly. He walked around the table and
took Tom's cue. "I don't know what you're up to, but Tom's
not staying down here on his own playing billiards or anything else."

Adams eyed the short cue, Paul's knuckles showing white
around it. He straightened up slowly from the table. "Don't
worry, I've been over the whole house, there's no one here
but us. We're definitely it this afternoon."

Paul took the cue over to the rack, thrust it impatiently
into its slot. "You want to show us something?"

"Right."

"Like what?"

"Like I said, a child wouldn't be interested. It's going to
require some grownup discussion."

Paul glanced at King. Clearly something was adding up for
him, enough to take him off the boil — he looked more anxious than angry now.

"How long are we going to be?" Paul said.

"Ten minutes...it's up to you."

He came to a decision. "Come on, Tom." He put his arm
around his boy and led him towards the front door.

"Hey Preedy..."

"Don't get worked up. I'm coming back."

He glanced up at the house as they came out of the porch,
confirming that there was a clear view from the upstairs windows down to the Subaru.

"I'm going to be right up there looking down. You keep
the doors locked and listen to the radio and you'll be snug as
a bug, okay? You want to beam me down, all you have to do is
sound the horn. Okay, Scotty?"

"Are we still going to the movie?"

"Absolutely. Ten minutes tops, and I'll be back."

"Okay."

"Are you sure? If you don't like the idea…"

"What does he want to show you?"

"Beats me."

Paul left the ignition key in, tested the horn, watched Tom power down the locks, then headed back to the porch. He'd be fine, because Celia was right — "self-possessed" described Tom exactly. It was one of the many new realizations that was making Paul so proud.

The rain hadn't picked up but the wind was gusting harder, the sparse drops swerving silver, zinging Paul's face. He glanced back to wave, but Tom was earnestly tuning the radio.

He hesitated a moment in the porch, before opening the front door. No good trying to conclude anything now, but first impressions were inescapable: David King was a sad sack, unsocialized and unwholesome, negativity hanging off him like a bad odour.

Adams? A peacock. A games player. That much hadn't changed.

But what was the game?

They were waiting for him at the foot of the stairs, separated from Paul by the billiards table. He could see instantly that some intelligence had passed between them in his absence, something that had seriously disturbed, and subdued, David King. His already pallid complexion looked like cottage cheese, accentuating the shadows nesting behind his thick glasses.

Paul had to smile as the door closed behind him. He couldn't help it: the impossible combination of types, the outrageous feeling of suspense — the *heaviness* of the whole situation. Securely out of Tom's hearing, he said what had to be said, slowly and with undeniable enjoyment:

"I hope I'm not being too inquisitive, but would somebody mind telling me just what the benighted *fuck* is going on here?"

"Certainly." Adams smiled matter-of-factly and walked up

to his side of the table. He reached into his pants pocket, and with the casual finesse of a croupier, tossed a six by four-inch deckle-edged card onto the green cloth. " 'Yours sincerely, Leslie Meas.' That what you got?"

Paul looked at it and nodded. "You know something I don't?"

"I know he didn't sign it with his full name." Adams leaned across the table and pointed a brown finger at the handwritten signature, where Leslie Meas had been abbreviated to 'Les Meas.'

Paul looked up frowning. "So?"

"What do you call a puzzle when the letters are reversed? An anagram, right? But this is kindergarten, all you have to do is switch the words around."

Unconsciously, Paul mouthed a two-syllable word.

"There you go! Bells ringing now?"

"I don't hear bells or whistles or any damn thing." Paul smiled derisively. "Measles? What is this? You're trying to tell me I came all this way for some kind of parlour game?"

Adams hesitated, caressing the red ball. He rolled it away, making it bound off the cushions in a perfect diamond around the invitation. "Actually, it was German measles. Christmas term, 1965." He caught the ball and sent it off again. "The school had an epidemic, the sanitorium filled up so Basil McCrimmon turned the third floor here into a temporary one. The three of us had the pleasure of each other's company for a number of days, in our affliction. You must have been — what? — thirteen, fourteen? King and I were older, of course, starting our last year. Right King?"

Paul shook his head like a man clearing water from his ears. "What are you saying? I was upstairs with you two, with German measles?"

"November '65. You were quite a bit younger than us, you were…how would you put it, King? Preedy was on the sidelines? Peripheral to certain…events?"

"That's absolutely enough, Adams." King had found his anger again. He lumbered forward, away from the stairs, the colour storming into his neck and face. White flecks from the corners of his mouth sailed onto the green cloth. "There's nothing to remember!" He glared at Paul. "Take your kid and go home. There's nothing here that concerns you!"

"Wait just a minute here," Adams soothed. "You seem to be forgetting Paul Preedy's on the guest list whether we like it or not. I didn't include him in our little get-together, Measles did." His hand went to his jeans pocket, the conjurer, and produced a bright tangle which he shook out into three yellow ribbons.

"Welcome home boys! I wouldn't have thought these were Felton style, exactly — I tend to think of country music, Desert Storm, you know." He brushed past King to the foot of the stairs. "They were tied all the way up, and there's more on the second floor. In fact, they go all the way up to the top of the house. It's a trail. How about it?"

Adams went up first, then Paul and then, reluctantly, King, the old oak stairs protesting under his weight. The staircase ended at a square landing. To the right was the minstrels' gallery overlooking the hall. To the left, through an archway, Paul could see a yellow ribbon taped to a light switch.

There were ribbons every twenty feet or so along the main second-floor corridor, the only cheerful notes in a depressingly bleak environment. For all its outward appeal, the interior of the house seemed deliberately charmless. The corridor was appointed with dark cream paint and brown linoleum, lit by intermittent pools of daylight, grey as dishwater, where dormitory doors lay open on the east side.

Glancing in, Paul saw the same dull cream and lino, black cast-iron beds marching towards curtainless windows overlooking the playing field. As a Cluffy boy, it was hard for him to guess what had changed up here in twenty-five years, but he suspected little: compared to the newer and more relaxed houses, Ormiston had always been notoriously spartan, a kind of reverse snobbery, another badge of exclusivity that its inhabitants saw as privilege and endured with pride.

In the narrow space between each bed, he recognized the

metal-reinforced wooden chests known to generations of Felton boys as "tuck boxes," although they were permitted to contain only slippers or books or other such personal items — boys were never allowed to bring food into the dormitory. The boxes, at least, were common throughout the school; since they might not be locked and were subject to arbitrary inspection, unsanctioned articles were safe only in secret compartments or under floorboards, certainly anything of an edible, combustible or pornographic nature.

They followed the trail to the end of the corridor, where the servants' staircase lay opposite the boys' bathroom: showers without doors, a rank of sterile white sinks. The west-facing window was old-fashioned privacy glass, denying Paul the chance to check on Tom.

"Come on up," Adams told him. "You can see the driveway clearly from the third floor."

There was a ribbon at the bottom of the servants' stairs, another one at the top. Paul took up the rear this time as they climbed to a dingy landing with a closed door either side. Long before Paul's time, these had been the servants' quarters, storage rooms when the days of live-in domestic staff had passed. The door on the left had a yellow bow tied to the knob.

"The sanitorium," Adams announced. "Which of you first?"

Not quite memory, but definite stirrings. Paul had been experiencing them all the way up from the hall, weak impulses carried through corroded circuits from remote, long-disused banks.

"Wait," he told them, and turned away to a small window tucked under the roof beside the servants' door. It was flyspeckled and stippled with rain, but it afforded him a clear view of the driveway and the Subaru. It was half the length of the house away but he could see Tom inside, working the steering wheel, guiding the car through imaginary hairpins. He had found the intermittent setting for the wipers.

Paul turned as the sanitarium door opened. He saw King's enormous, stooped silhouette filling the doorway.

"Go on in," Adams said.

He stayed rooted to the spot.

"Go for it, King. You're blocking the view!"

Still no response.

Adams glanced wickedly at Paul. "Hey! King Kong!"

When King moved, it was faster than Paul would have thought possible, so fast that Adams was caught off balance as King rounded on him, seized him with both hands and slammed him back against the wall.

"God damn you, what are you *playing* at?"

Paul was on King in a second, trying to find purchase on his soft, heavy mass, but the giant was bearing down with his full weight in an appalling rage. The white scum flew on his breath, a noxious miasma of tobacco and bile.

"Why are you doing this?" he screamed. "*Why?*"

"It isn't me!" Adams gasped. "I told you!"

"You've told me NOTHING!"

"Let go!" Paul entreated. "That's enough! Let him go, King!"

King pinned Adams for a moment longer, rigid and trembling, then his strength and conviction ebbed all at once. Adams slipped from beneath him, pulling himself back together, smoothing his blond hair.

King remained facing the wall after Paul had released him and retreated, his narrow shoulders sloped and heaving, glasses misted and askew.

"Jesus Christ!" Paul uttered in a voice of disbelief. "I'm in a bloody mad house!" At a loss, shaking from the confrontation, he crossed to the sickroom door and looked inside.

He saw an almost empty room about twenty feet square with bare floorboards and dull cream walls. A garret room, the water-damaged ceiling offering less than five feet of headroom under the slope. Meagre light filtered in through a small, north-facing window, darkened by overreaching trees, its outlook ending twenty feet away at the Rookery's green mass. The window had not been washed for a long time, splashed all over with droppings, the sill thickly encrusted. As

Paul watched, a crow flew near the window, slow and black, croaking. He could hear the irascible chorus now, black noise that must have been there all the time.

The room was familiar, though he remembered it furnished with half a dozen steel cots. Sick beds. The room's focus was still the washbasin to the left of the window, an old fashioned pedestal style with dull brass taps, its white enamel chipped black as licorice where the iron showed through. Draped around the rim were three plain white facecloths.

"Take a closer look," Adams said from the doorway.

There was water in the basin. Submerged clusters of tiny silver bubbles, like spawn, clung to the enamel.

"I left everything just as I found it. Look at the facecloths, the one on the right. Open it up." Paul lifted it from the rim of the basin. It was slightly damp. He unfolded it.

"Welcome to the reunion, Preedy."

Stitched neatly into the corner was an embroidered red nametape, the kind that mothers of private school children sew in by the yard, that Celia Preedy had painstakingly added to every item of Paul's Felton uniform. It was accurate to the letter, the middle initial M for Maynard, one he never used:

PAUL M. PREEDY.

There was a facecloth marked ANDREW ADAMS.

There was one for DAVID KING.

"That's how come I was expecting you," Adams said, smiling. "I just followed the ribbons to the nametapes."

Paul stood with the damp cloths festooning his hands. "Okay Adams, you got me good. What do I say now? Uncle? Injun? No more games, okay? Just tell me."

Adams left the doorway and came into the room. "It wasn't only the three of us here. There were two others. Don't you remember?"

"What's the matter with you? I remember beds with bodies in them. It was twenty-eight years ago."

"There was a middle-schooler called Everett, decent hockey player — farmer's son, got killed in a tractor accident right after he left."

"I know that. Who was the fourth?"

Adams hesitated. "A junior boy, I'd say even more junior than you. Tell Preedy his name, King."

King had taken Adams' place in the doorway, his anger spent, his breathing steady. His head was bowed to clear the architrave, but it was also an attitude of submission.

"Go on, tell him," Adams insisted.

"Maybe he doesn't want to know."

"Sure I want to know."

King's words came thick and slurred, on a sigh of defeat. "Dempsey. His name was Victor Dempsey."

Adams turned back to Paul. "Something happened here during our quarantine. Something happened to Victor Dempsey. Maybe you don't remember because you weren't really part of it. Not actively."

"Part of what?" Paul narrowed his eyes but he had already read the innuendo. "What are you saying here — you abused him? Is that what I'm hearing?"

"Don't get on your high horse," Adams said. "It wasn't unusual. Locking guys up together at that age, that's the cruel and unusual part."

Paul turned. "You too?"

King looked down at his big shoes.

Paul stared helplessly at them. "What is this for chrissake? You trying to tell me this is why we're here today? Victor Dempsey is Measles, is that the idea?"

"I don't know," Adams said.

"Oh you don't! Well you've certainly shot *your* load in a hurry. Is it what you think?"

"I said I don't know."

"Why? Blackmail, revenge?"

"You're guess is as good as mine."

Paul shook his head. "I don't think so, Adams. I don't think so at all." Paul glanced towards the basin. "What about this, these facecloths? This is significant, right?" He saw Adams exchange a look with King. "Come on, Adams, I've got my son waiting in the car and half-dozen more questions after this one, including what in God's name I'm doing here with you people. Now what happened?"

Adams' bravado was fast disappearing. He went to the window, gazed out for a moment, then turned. "I don't remember all that well. Dempsey was...I dunno. Different."

"Different how?"

"He hadn't been to a preparatory school. He didn't know the ropes."

"*Ropes?*"

"You know what I mean! Kids that've been in boarding school since the age of seven or eight get used to a certain...level of intimacy. In the showers, playing doctor in the dorm, just horsing around, checking each other out, it's inevitable. I guess this kid was from a blue-collar family. He was a scholarship boy, really smart, really high strung."

"What you're saying is, he was an unwilling participant in your 'intimacy.'"

For a second Adam's glance flicked from the washbasin to King, then he turned again to the window.

"Listen to those goddam birds! Twenty-five years and they still haven't shut up!"

For Paul it had become background noise again, but now he heard them. While not heavy enough to drive the crows to shelter, the gusting rain had provoked them: the air outside was oppressive with their scolding.

Adams spoke to the window. "I think we told him it was initiation, something like that, that it happened to all new boys. Standard procedure."

"What procedure? Get specific here."

When Adams turned, he was back behind his casual mask. "Just how am I supposed to get specific? As you pointed out, we're talking a few years ago here. It hasn't exactly been on my mind all this time."

Paul's anger rose, his voice buzzing off the angled bare walls: "Listen to me, whoever you are: somebody got me here all the way from goddam North Carolina and I want to know why. You're having a hard time with specifics? Fine. We'll work on the big picture. You said I was peripheral. What does that mean? *What the hell am I doing here?*"

He turned to confront King as well, saw that he had retreated from the doorway onto the landing, a look of fearful, rapt attention on his face.

"What is it?" As Paul moved towards the door, King raised a hand to quiet him. The crow-noise was diminished out on the landing, so that Paul could hear the other sound under it — slow, shuffling footsteps along the second-floor corridor, getting closer. He was aware of Adams coming up behind him. He saw a shadow, then a dark silhouette in the opening at the foot of the stairs.

"Gotcha!"

A figure was coming up, gaining dimension and detail: an old man with a naked brown head, extended turtle-like from the hump of his back. In his hands, emitting its own purple light, was an over-under twelve-gauge shotgun.

The turtle head extended further, sheened yellow eyes rolling over them. "Three of yous, is it? Thought you'd have the run of the place I suppose. This is private property, in case you were wonderin'."

Alfie Criddle paused on the middle step, his breath a stertorous whistling, filling the stairwell with the rank sweetness of second-hand homebrew. The shotgun was lowered to the stairs but he jabbed a denouncing finger, like a knotted twig, at King.

"I remember *you!*"

His yellow eyes swivelled to Adams, then Paul. "Old Boys, is it? Think that gives you the right to trespass? Which o' yours is that bloody kid blowin the horn down there, waking the whole place?" He saw Paul's face and scowled. "Gonna let 'im drain yer goddam battery?"

But Paul was already on the stairs, rushing down through the mist of alcohol breath, feeling a dull pain as his right kneecap caught the barrel of the shotgun. He hit the corridor running, hobbling as the hot pain caught up, the old man's voice falling away behind him.

"Don't panic. I didn't shoot him! Don't bother runnin' off either, I've got your licence number! Police'll be here any minute!"

Paul barely registered it. He had already heard Tom's voice calling from the minstrels' gallery at the far end of the corridor, on the edge of tears.

"It's okay, Tom! It's alright, I'm coming!"

Paul ran, seeing yellow bows flash by in his peripheral vision, then Tom at the end of the corridor.

Thomas, eight years old, holding back his tears, squared up and ready with a junior pool cue in his hand.

Paul hugged him, panting. "Jesus, I'm sorry, Tom! I didn't hear you, I didn't…" He held the boy by his shoulders at arm's length. "You okay?" Tom nodded bravely. Paul looked down at the cue. "What's this? What were you going to do, take him on all by yourself?" He frowned in wonder. "You were chasing after him? For me?"

"He was looking for you, dad. He had a gun."

"It's okay. I know him. He thought we were burglars or something. He's okay now. But you…" The words caught, growing in his throat and tugging at the corners of his mouth, pushing sudden tears into his eyes as he gazed at his son. "You crazy old coot." He hugged Tom close again, said quietly over his shoulder: "I didn't know I had a hero."

He stood, caught Tom's hand and led him down the stairs. "What did he do when he saw you?"

"He was really grumpy, shouting at the car. I was scared 'cause of the gun. Then he went inside. I honked and honked and honked, dad!"

"I'm really sorry, Thomas. We were right up on the third floor, in the middle of a bloody crows' nest. I'm serious, they were making so much noise, that's why I couldn't hear you."

"What did that other guy want to show you?"

"Big anti-climax. Just a dumb old room where we all got stuck with the German measles years and years ago."

"What's German measles?"

Paul explained, glad to distract him from other questions.

He kept Tom's hand across the hall to the cue rack. He replaced Tom's cue then hesitated, eyeing Adams's leather
jacket.

"We don't want to hang around here any more, do we
buddy?"

"I want to go."

"Okay then."

Adams's wallet was in the zippered right pocket. His driving licence gave his address as the Valmy Lodge Resort at
Jackson's Point, Ontario. Paul knew of the town, near Barrie
on Lake Simcoe. In the main compartment, behind a sheaf of
twenty-dollar bills, he found a Visa receipt with a phone
number under the signature.

"What are you doing, dad?"

"I'm not usually this nosey, but it's been sort of a weird
day."

Paul remembered the number, wrote it down with a pen
from the Subaru's glovebox. Not enough answers, and there
certainly *would* be answers. But not today. It was Tom's day
from now on. To hell with everything else.

He shoved the car into gear and drove fast away from the
Circle. Better not to find out if Alfie really had called the police. But he'd always been a bullshit artist.

As they drove through the trees, Paul watched Ormiston
House slipping away in the rearview mirror. No one came
out.

"Feel like some music?"

Tom had the radio tuned to a strong rock station. Paul
cranked it up as they cleared the creek bridge towards the
school gates, to drown the sound of crows.

THE HOUSE WAS full of heat and the smell of neglect: rotting food, unemptied ashtrays, soiled laundry, expired medicines.

The Dorset Street house was also full of small sounds during the early evening of Sunday, August 25, even while David King played the organ at Saint Matthew's church. One could have heard the patter and scratch of mice feeding with careless enthusiasm in the kitchen, inured to the sight of their fellow in a trap beside the toaster, yellow teeth bared from his long dehydration, leaving their droppings like black rice around the stacks of unwashed plates.

There was the intermittent buzz of a wasp paddling to death in an open jam jar, still sounding as the mice vanished, as soft footsteps crossed to the stove.

To the sink, where water hissed into a kettle.

Back to the stove, although there was no logical huff of gas.

Not yet.

❖   ❖   ❖

Half an hour later, there was only the buzzing from the jam jar, still optimistic, plangent as an oboe in the again-empty kitchen.

The mice had not reappeared. Although there had never been a cat in the Dorset house, instinct had been enough to alert them to the almost perfectly silent presence in the gloomy scullery behind the kitchen. They felt its patience and its predatory intent.

CHAPTER 10

THE RECTOR OF St. Matthew's, an ex-prison chaplain, finished his sermon and announced the offertory hymn. Attendance and contributions were always down in the summer, the reason he had chosen "laying up treasure in heaven" as his theme. With that, and a stern delivery, he had every hope that the sidesmen moving into place at the back of the church would reap at least a modest harvest this evening.

He waited a moment longer for the opening few bars from the organ, and when they didn't come he announced hymn 489 again, taking advantage of the delay by reciting the first verse. He jingled his loose change as he read in a loud voice:

> *Behold, a stranger at the door!*
> *He gently knocks, has knocked before,*
> *Has waited long, is waiting still:*
> *You treat no other friend so ill.*

The rector waited.

Damn King! What was the matter with him? He'd already

fluffed the Magnificat and started 112 with Nevin knowing perfectly well they were singing Darwall tonight.

He heard a rustling of gowns behind him and turned in the pulpit to find the choir inclined towards the organ bench, two of the tenors out of their places, going to King's aid. The rector glimpsed the organist between the billowing choir gowns, swaying drunkenly on the bench, heard a shrill and discordant alarm as he sagged forward onto the manuals.

A murmur arose from the congregation, pews creaking as they strained to see David King escorted to the vestry with the rector in close attendance.

King denied he was ill and shook off the choresters. All he needed was air. His supper had disagreed with him — they could return to the service now. Mrs. Crowther could take over the organ for the last two hymns.

It would be no trouble to drive him home.

"Leave me be," he snapped. "I'm fine!"

And the rector, remembering his sidesmen waiting in the aisles with their empty collection bags, took him at his word.

David's immediate need was for a cigarette, which he smoked in the car as he drove woozily home in pouring rain, sustained only by the promise of 800 milligrams of Meprobamate.

Steering was tricky with only his left hand, especially in the rain, but he needed his right, damp and icy, under his Sunday jacket to monitor his heart. He knew the degrees of his heart-beat as intimately as those of a metronome, and it was beating a dangerous *prestissimo*.

He had to force himself to concentrate on the road, to blinker himself from the images of the sickroom that had overwhelmed him during the sermon: the washbasin, the white-splashed window, the crow noise that was going to ex-plode his head any minute.

He was too distressed to give any thought to his break-down at the organ, his dramatic exit. He had been part of a terrifying and elaborate game: the invitations, the ribbons, the facecloths...choosing a day when the school was almost deserted.

Terrifying.

And would the game go on now? When and how and where?

Did he need protection?

He needed a friend.

He needed Arabella Bauer.

Thank God she'd been late at the school, that they hadn't connected. He wouldn't have known where to begin. He still didn't know. He would have to get in touch with her, soon of course, to apologize, to explain somehow. Would she call him? When? He needed time to think of an explanation...

He needed his tranquilizers.

The light changed to red at Mill Street and David skated to a stop, twitching with nerves and frustration.

He needed air, rain or no rain. He wound down his window, found himself looking through dripping black iron railings into the Mill Street school playground. Someone had tossed a green plastic trashcan over the railings, and rubbish had exploded across the shining asphalt. He thought of Todd Grady with hair the colour of ripe wheat. He thought of Victor Dempsey...

Green light, and David spun his drivewheels, the back end of the Cadillac planing sideways as he veered right then right again onto Dorset and sped up the hill. He almost hit one of his stone gateposts as he lurched into his driveway, wallowing to a halt at the side of the house.

David's hand brushed the hall telephone as he passed on his way to the stairs, as if he could tell by touch, by its warmth or vibration, whether it had been ringing.

In the ensuite bathroom, he shook two 400 milligram tablets of Meprobamate — then a third — into his hand. Three was too many to chew raw, so he bent with difficulty to the hot tap and sucked noisily at its thin trickle. He stood and let the water run over his hands, shutting his eyes as he felt the slowly growing warmth, waiting for the Meprobamate to kick in, waiting for his rescue.

He was safe here, behind locked doors. Safe in his mind and body, ready to travel with his medication on its river journey through a crimson-dark subterranean kingdom, along warm, obedient tributaries, hurrying their payload of tranquilizer towards his central medulla, the teeming capital — fresh supplies to quell the unrest, restoring the kingdom to calm, order, contentment. A journey through an enchanted landscape tinged with Romantic melancholy, past landmarks with names he knew so well. One day he would write an organ fantasia, a Romantic epic to describe and celebrate his river journey, an anatomical version of Smetana's *Moldau*. He would give his composition a romantic, darkly yearning title, *The Islets of Langerhans*, after the little endocrine cells in his glandular tissue.

David soaped and rinsed his hands, did it again, then went to his bed.

But there was no river journey, no lovely languorous music. No rescue. With twelve hundred milligrams he had taken a modest overdose, and now found himself locked down in a kind of synthetic sleep, a grotesque virtual reality in which he saw again the Mill Street schoolyard, rain falling steadily from a low and leaden Sunday-grey sky. Once again a green garbage bin had exploded across the slick asphalt, but now it had attracted birds, crows that flapped and lunged amongst the offal, snatching at bones and squibbles of fat. One of the crows was examining David with its wicked eyes. A cripple, he realized, as it flopped towards him, hauling unfastened, ruined wings. He struggled in terror as the thing dragged itself nearer, but his head was stuck fast between the dripping iron railings while something unseen pinned his hands behind him. David knew he was dreaming and prayed that he would wake before the bird reached him.

It reached him.

He could see the raindrops rolling on its blue-black feathers, beading on its greasy beak. He prayed that his glasses would be sufficient protection until it became clear that the crow didn't want his eyes. Alarm bells started ringing ringing ringing in the school across the filthy playground as the crippled bird pecked at the side of his neck, tentatively at first, then drew back and stabbed.

David King awoke to the dull bump of entry followed by the thin, treble sting of a hypodermic. The first five seconds of his consciousness were clouded but busy with registration.

He was lying on a bed.

There was a face above him.

Because he was not, in reality, wearing his glasses, he couldn't identify the face, but after a lifetime of severe myopia, he accepted that.

He had taken an injection in his neck.

He had had some kind of accident.

But he was alive and, apart from the sting of the needle, in no immediate pain.

These initial moments provided nothing to alarm him, especially since the Meprobamate was active in his system. He felt the first threads of distress only when his glasses were slipped onto his face as gently and carefully as the optometrist always did it, and he looked up, not at a hospital nurse, but into Arabella Bauer's dramatically mascara'd eyes, golden and flickering with dark confetti.

David blinked up at her with a massive lack of comprehension. With one foot still in his dream, it took him several moments more to realize that the Mill Street School alarm was the kettle in the kitchen downstairs, at the boil and squealing for attention.

He was home.

David tried weakly to sit up, surrendered to the firm hand that pressed him down.

He lifted his own slow right hand, heavier than he had ever thought possible, and touched the sting on his neck. He made a small interrogative squeak.

Arabella Bauer spoke matter-of-factly and loudly, the way people often talk to the disabled, as though they are deaf: "I have just given you an injection. Pancuronium bromine." She smiled. "Of course you can't speak, but I know you can hear me. Pancuronium bromine," she said again, enunciating like a quiz show host. "Recognize it? You know so much about these things."

He was awake. He could not mistake the categorical disrespect in her voice. It made his scalp crawl.

"Unfair? Okay, we'll forget the clinical extraction. How about curare?"

He knew it by both names, though the last one was more evocative, of *National Geographic* footage, a monkey high in a treetop while below, on the rainforest floor, a small brown man with a black bowl-cut raises a long pipe to his lips and blows. It takes only seconds before the monkey with the dart in its side begins moving in slow motion, crashing drunkenly from branch to branch until it drops onto soft brown leaves.

David broke into a cold sweat.

He tried to sit up again, but this time there was no need for restraint. Injected directly into the jugular, the curare was already overrunning his motor centres. He felt a numbness, inexorable as lava, rolling over him, cooling, petrifying. He had missed his chance to talk.

"You are experiencing paralysis of the voluntary muscles. Interesting effect? Sort of artificial quadriplegia. You must find it fascinating, knowing your interest in things like this. Illness. Sickness."

In her eyes, glimmering black mica, kaleidoscopic sticks and triangles.

Sticks and stones

"Pancuronium is non-depolarizing — nice big medical term for you. You can hear and see fine, can't you? You can feel too. Point-two-five milligrams won't last very long, so I'll have to give you another needle quite soon. We'll have to be careful because I think you've already taken your Meprobamate and I don't want your heart to stop yet."

Her face came very near, her nostrils quivering. "You understand, King? I'm not going to *let* you die — I'm going to *make* you die. Believe me, you'll feel the difference. That's why we're here…to feel."

He could not move his eyes, but her arms were extended across his limited field of vision as she rolled up her sleeves, showing him the grid of terrible scars on the soft white inner skin of her wrists and forearms.

"Let me take these for a minute." She removed his glasses with the same smooth and gentle motion, then hit him hard with her fist to break his nose. A sunburst of light and searing pain, worse because he could not react. He could not look to see the blood but he could feel the warm wetness, a moustache then a flowing beard of it. He could taste copper in his slightly open mouth.

He wanted very badly to cry.

She had replaced his glasses but he had no range of vision, his eyes were locked front and centre. He could only hear her going downstairs.

He heard the swooping *diminuendo* of the kettle.

He heard her returning, with slower, careful steps.

"It's time, King," she called cheerfully from halfway up the staircase. "Time for your blanket bath."

There was still sufficient tranquilizer in David's system that he was able to leave the coming horror to spark and fizz at the edge of his mind, for a few seconds at least. Automatically, he tried to fix its core on the south window above the altar in the Felton Chapel, to tap into all its nascent power and promise of delivery. For a moment he got nothing, like blanking out on his own name, but then he saw it.

David King's imagination had always been as morbid as it was potent, so it betrayed him now only by its consistency. What he saw, while Arabella Bauer removed his clothing, was an abomination, a startled hole, a smashed-out jagged black star where the lovely head had been. A star-head, monstrous and alien, wearing a crown of black thorns.

C H A P T E R 1 1

THEY LEFT TORONTO after an early supper and made good time to Bancroft, passing Sunday evening traffic jammed in the citybound highway lanes as far east as Cobourg.

Celia drove while Paul rode in the back with Tom. They gave her a lengthy synopsis of the Star Trek movie, then the three of them played I Spy and Twenty Questions. Tom was tired, but he didn't fall asleep until they had turned off the main Bancroft road for the last three miles of dirt roads, where Paul got his first opportunity to finish the account he had begun at the Hollow.

Celia did her best to listen while she negotiated potholes and punishing washboards, blinded by dust every time they met an oncoming car. It had been pouring rain all the way east through Durham Region, especially heavy at Port Hope, but Bancroft had obviously missed it.

The twilight was deeper here than on the highway, the forest rising in sheer walls either side of the road, collapsed here and there in deadfalls of jumbled silver. Signposts bristled at every sideroad, reminding Paul that somewhere behind these dark tree-walls was a network of lakes with cottages and marinas.

Paul finished his strange school story as Celia pulled in for gas at a dusty filling station-cum-variety store. It reminded him of North Carolina in a way, hillbilly-looking with its faded tin cola signs and its lopsided stoop up to the flimsy screen door. He noticed an ancient blue truck parked behind the store, a three-ton Fargo with a canvas tarpaulin, a kind he hadn't seen for years.

Tom was horizontal by now with his head in Paul's lap, so Celia got out, calling "It's okay, Fred, I've got it," to a lanky, arthritic-looking old man peering out from the screen door. He waved and went back inside leaving Celia to pump while she talked to Paul through his open window, amidst the seductive haze of gasoline fumes.

"I don't really know what to say. I've never heard anything like it. I'd completely forgotten you'd had German measles."

"So had I."

"You don't even remember being there?"

"Sure. Sort of. But I don't remember Dempsey."

"I think you'd better call this Adams character as soon as you can. I don't like the sound it. Any of it."

He leaned close enough to the window that he could see her face. "Shall I tell Jack?"

Celia frowned. "Sure. Why wouldn't you?"

"You know what he'll be like. He'll own it in two seconds. He'll be like a dog at a bone."

"You want to know what's going on, don't you? He's got a fine mind. Use it."

The nozzle clashed against the pump as she hooked it up. She screwed the gas cap on hard and walked away to the shop. "We need bread and milk."

"Need some money?"

"No thank you."

Her conjugal loyalty stung him and she knew it; when she came back with the grocery sack, her smile was tender if not contrite.

"You know what Jack's going to do?" she said as she got

back in the car. "He's going to call his buddy Jock." She qui-etly shut the door and started the engine.

"Jock Beale?"

She watched Paul's surprise in her rearview mirror. "I sup-pose 'buddy' is overstating it, but they go back since before you were at Felton. You knew that. That's why we chose it in the first place."

"I'd forgotten. I didn't even know he was still alive."

"He's in a retirement home somewhere. You'll have to ask your father."

"He'd have to be nearly ninety. He's not going to know anything."

"Who says? It's worth a try."

The road deteriorated after the store. Paul kept his fingers laced through Tom's hair to steady his head. It was another mile before Celia braked for a sharp left turn, the Subaru skidding slightly on the loose gravel. There was a sign at the junction — PREEDY— freshly hand-painted white on green with a folksy stencilled border.

"How d'you like my sign?"

"Your sign's fine."

A single name because the road served the farm exclu-sively; with a hundred acres around one end of Blackstone Lake, Celia and Jack had no immediate neighbours.

The sky all but disappeared on the winding sidetrack, densely overhung with softwood trees. And then, with star-tling suddenness, they broke into the open.

The hundred cleared acres rose gently straight ahead to the south, the rutted track running up to a tractor shed, now the garage, becoming a pathway to a nondescript, brown bungalow. On the east side to their left, shimmering purple in the twilight, a hay meadow deep in timothy and alfalfa rolled softly away to the encircling woods. To the west, past a fine old timber barn that shamed the house, the hayfield vaulted up to a ridge with an undulating fenceline; beyond the fence, the empty, dark blue haze promised Blackstone Lake below.

Jack Preedy had seen them coming. Paul watched his compact, thrusting figure descending the path from the house. The Subaru bottomed out halfway along the track and Tom began to stir awake. Celia slowed almost to a stop and glanced round.

"Paul?" Expectation, apology, caution — a complex signal in a single word. "Don't tell him I mentioned Jock Beale, alright? Wait till he thinks of it. It'll give him pleasure to help you clear up this business. Let him help, okay? He hasn't got used to retirement yet. He needs to know he's still resourceful. Promise?"

Jack had the door open before Celia had killed the engine, a squeeze on Paul's arm just short of painful, play-punching Tom.

"Look at these two great louts! I don't think the fatted calf's gonna be enough for these big fellas, Cele, reckon we'll have to go for the cow. How'd you come out of Burleigh Falls, on nineteen or did you try the Hainesville detour like I said?"

If anything, Jack seemed younger and fitter than he had at Christmas in Carolina. He had always tanned easily, looked like a Roman with his prominent nose and tight grey curls and his small height. Jack Preedy was more than a head shorter than his son, even Celia had some inches on him, but he overcame the lack of them with his scrappy physique and his intellect and his professional stature. Paul couldn't remember his father ever using the shorter word, "doctor"; Jack was, had always been, a "physician."

"Saw you bottom out down there, Celia." He winked at Tom. "Wouldn't have happened in the Trooper."

Celia grunted. "Your father just went and bought himself a mean machine. We tend to disagree on its indispensability."

"I thought you didn't like Japanese cars," Paul said.

"Only Subarus. Anyway, this is not a car." He started towards the tractor shed. "She's in here, only took delivery last week."

"For heaven's sake," Celia said, "let them catch their breath first."

But Jack was already hauling on one of the wide double doors. "If we're going to winter here, we'll need something that can handle snow. They don't plough the sideroads." A brutish black truck loomed in the shed, raised on its oversize tires so that the cab almost grazed the ceiling.

"Four wheel drive, 190 horsepower. When the Preedys want to go to Bancroft, they go to Bancroft. Damn thing'll climb trees."

Paul smiled. "I guess you've already considered, you know, the white Caddy and the condo in sunny Sarasota."

"Snowbirds? So we can hang out at the drug store with a bunch of old skeletons wanting free advice on their cataracts and their diverticulitis and the warts on the end of their decrepit peckers?"

"What your father means," said Celia, "is that it's extraordinarily beautiful here in winter." She turned back to her Subaru. "Come on, Tom, let's you and me take a load up to the house."

There were other new toys: a lawn tractor and cart, a gas-powered trimmer, a big walk-behind rototiller for Celia's vegetable garden up behind the house. It was pleasantly warm in the shed, the smell of gas and oil coming from the machines and the packed earth floor. They did what estranged fathers and sons do well, encoding their difficult feelings with the language of machines, with bearings and limited-slip-differentials and foot-pounds of torque.

Paul was puzzled by the green and yellow John Deere tractor: powerful enough to make short work of a regular yard, but next to useless for a hundred acres of hay.

"I thought about getting a Bush Hog," Jack said, "towing it behind the Trooper, then I guess you'd say the solution found me."

"Goats?"

"Nope."

"You get a farmer to cut it."

His father grinned. "Not quite."

"What?"

"Wait and see. Needs a second cut right now, very late this season. I've arranged a little demonstration for tomorrow."

"Come on, Jack."

"You wait and see." He led Paul out of the shed. They both closed the double doors, then Jack jammed a two-by-four through the handles. "How was your reunion?"

"Interesting."

His father read the look on his face and waited. "You'll have to do better than that, buddy."

"Then you'll have to give me a beer."

Jack started up towards the house. "Tit for tat, is it?"

Paul grinned. "Like father, like son."

❖   ❖   ❖

The house was a shock despite forewarning from Celia: the cheap three-bedroom bungalow belonged on a neglected subdivision: undulating green asphalt on the roof, peeling Insulbrick siding with "decorative" vinyl shutters. The wrought-metal storm door featured a rust-dappled fawn with splayed legs and a bow on her head.

Celia laughed as she welcomed Paul inside: "I never thought a house would bring out the sadist in me: I'm going to see to it that this one is destroyed with exquisite slowness and damn the overtime! Ready for this?"

She took a kind of defensive glee in the place, because in spite of her liberal education and feminist sympathies, in spite of an academic career, Celia had enjoyed her other, patrician life: the Slagg's Hollow doctor's wife, Havergal and Queen's, able to hold a bridge hand or knock a tennis ball around or fix a dry martini with the best — or most banal — of her neighbours.

She played them Dixie on the door chimes; she modelled the kitchen like a game show floozie — more imitation brick for the linoleum, the formica worktops swirl-patterned like chocolate ripple ice cream, pressboard cabinets with baroque handles. In the living room, the familiar, good furniture from the Hollow looked homesick on the powder blue shag.

"Elvis sighted at Blackstone Lake!" she said. "We get Geraldo on satellite and they deliver *The National Enquirer*! Heaven or what, eh?"

The emptiest of jests, proof of which lay everywhere in precarious stacks; Celia and Jack's books, by the hundreds, with boxes more in the basement. Their umbilicus.

Jack opened beers and a ginger ale for Tom, and they went to see the site of the new house, stopping half way up the ridge to look in the barn, into a rich pinstriped gloom still warm from the day, full of the musty sweetness of old hay and long-departed animals. Paul saw four dayglo orange life jackets hanging from nails near the door, the smallest one new in a plastic bag.

"Still got the Albacore?"

"Going to get something bigger as soon as the house is built. Maybe a motorboat, there's a 1938 Chriscraft for sale at the marina — pure mahogany, tandem cabins. It's a work of art. I'll build a boathouse if we get it."

"Lot of work."

They climbed the ridge where the cottage was staked out. Celia described the rooms while Jack competed for Paul's attention to talk about grading and water supply and drainage, until she bid him quiet to watch the low fire in the western sky, the scrawl of salmon red on turquoise water, grey rocks and deep green woods fading to black. Below them, Jack's fifteen-foot centerboard bumped with blind insistence against the dock. Paul could see the long cigar-shape of the canoe drawn up on the beach.

"Time this guy learned his ropes." Jack turned to Tom. "We're going out tomorrow morning, right Thomas?"

"We've got a Committee of Adjustment meeting at nine," Celia reminded him.

"Damned yokels! Why don't these people get a life and let us get on with ours?"

"Is it going to be okay for the permit?" Paul asked.

"'Course it is! But we're city slickers, see? We thrive on running around in circles, so they're actually doing us a great big favour."

Celia laughed and took Tom's hand and led him off across the ridge. "Come on, I've got a peach tree up by my garden that's been waiting to meet you."

She had taken over the previous owner's vegetable garden, along with half a dozen fruit trees. Jack pointed them out, on the slope fifty yards behind the house.

"You've done a good thing here," Paul said. "I'm sure you won't regret it."

"I know we won't. How's Eva?"

"Fine. She's teaching, not writing."

Jack cleared his throat: "So how was Felton?"

"Right."

"Right is right. Quit stalling, you got your beer."

A dog at a bone. The man Celia loved hadn't changed at all.

"There wasn't much to see," Paul said. "It was locked up except for Ormiston. The whole place was deserted. Not even any staff — they had some kind of conference in Toronto."

"What are you saying? You had the wrong day?"

Paul could hear the familiar testy impatience. Jack the scientist, Jack the sailor, organized, methodical, vexed by anything that wasn't so. Paul could hear his own reply, defensive and retaliatory.

"I went on the day specified by the invitation. I didn't misread it, I didn't misunderstand it." He took a long breath, struggling to keep the sap from rising. "There were two other alumni there besides me."

"You just said the place was deserted."

Paul raised his beer and drank, wishing he could drown the abysmal, angry voice, the child that wanted, just once, not to be steamrollered by this little man.

Paul slapped his head as the first mosquito whined past his ear. "You remember Ormiston House, don't you?"

"Sure I do. The inner sanctum. Tried to get you in there but Basil McCrimmon didn't want solid all-rounders. Arrogant sonofabitch."

"Well, I got in alright yesterday." He tipped the bottle and swallowed the last flat mouthful of suds. He turned back to the house. "I think this is a two-beer story. I'll tell you as we go."

He was half through his account by the time they were settled in the living room, in the familiar, comfortable armchairs from the Hollow. Jack had declined a second beer, sat forward with a pad on his knees, making notes, asking questions. He was a relentless inquisitor, interrupting constantly, gathering every last scrap of data, reviving details already buried by the last eight hours.

Paul felt no squeamishness because he felt no culpability, because there was no memory of Victor Dempsey. Nor was it Jack's style to indulge the emotional side; he was interested only in accuracy.

"What about these guys, King and Adams? Are you prepared to rule out their involvement, either separately or together?"

"King was a genuine mess, angry then scared. No one could act that well. I'm not sure about Adams. He seemed to be enjoying himself. Smooth, for sure, but he's probably like that all the time."

"I guess you'll find out if it's blackmail."

"You're not serious."

"It's a possibility. Look at the newspapers, those Christian Brothers going to the wall, thirty years after the fact, some of them. Prosecuting child abusers is becoming a national obsession, and perhaps rightly so. Maybe this is a new twist on it, settling out of court so to speak."

"Even if you were right, there'd be nothing to blackmail *me* with. Adams himself admitted I wasn't part of it."

"He said you were peripheral." Paul looked sharply at his father. Jack didn't flinch: "Why do you think you were invited then?"

"Great! Thanks for the vote of confidence!"

"Don't be softheaded. I'm a physician, it wouldn't shock me if you *had* been indiscreet. You weren't priests, you were schoolboys. At boarding school."

"Adams and King were eighteen."

"So? At that age it's a matter of testosterone, not morals!"

"But I don't have even the vaguest recollection of Victor Dempsey."

"What about this other guy in quarantine with you, Everett. Remember him at all?"

"Vaguely. Probably because he got killed while I was still at school."

"How?"

"Rolled a tractor on a hillside."

Jack nodded. "Okay. What about Adams and King, do you remember them as boys?"

"Sure, but they were both fairly conspicuous in their different ways."

"Wasn't Dempsey conspicuous?" Jack glanced at his notes. "Scholarship boy, exceptionally smart...working class! Isn't that what Adams told you?"

"What are you trying to say?"

"That I'm not surprised you remembered them since you were all cooped up in a sickroom for days on end. You remember Everett and King and Adams, yet you have no recollection of Victor Dempsey; doesn't that sound a bit selective to you? People block things out, you know, easy enough to do: memory says 'It was like this' and pride says 'It couldn't have been' and memory sometimes gives in. Who said that, by the way? Somebody famous."

"You're not going to give me the benefit of the doubt, are you, dad?"

"Don't be touchy. I'm hypothesizing."

"Sure." Paul got up, slightly unbalanced on the springy shag as he crossed the room towards the kitchen. "You want a beer?"

"You said a two-beer story — that's your third." Jack got up and followed him. "Alright, we won't hypothesize. Call Adams."

"I called from the Hollow. I left a message with this number."

"Call him again."

He used the phone in the hall. The same male reception-ist answered. Paul recognized the efficient lisp. Again there was no reply on Andrew Adams' extension.

"He's employed by the hotel, isn't he? He's not a guest?"

The voice was coldly correct: "Mr. Adams is the resident tennis professional. Would you care to leave a message?"

Paul left the farm number again.

He went into the kitchen for his beer, stopping at the kitchen window, but the twilight had deepened almost to night, the window showed him nothing but his own reflection.

"Mum and Tom are taking their time."

Jack glanced at his watch. "It's too late now, but tomorrow morning *I'm* going to make a phone call, see if we can't put together a couple of missing pieces here."

Paul went to the fridge, pulled out a beer. He levered the cap onto the chocolate ripple counter, watched it spin as he played the game for Celia.

"Call who, dad?"

Jack smiled. "Your headmaster. Jock Beale."

"I didn't know you were still in touch."

"Of course you didn't. But you knew we were friends be-fore you went to Felton. Jock's the old school, literally: he's a letter-writer, little jokes in Latin, that sort of thing. I guess you'd say we're pen pals."

"Jack and Jock? Cute. When did you meet him?"

"Years ago, before you were born. I was interning; he was a hospital patient, can't remember what for now. Then I ad-vised his daughter when she was trying to choose a medical school — *choose*, mark you; bright kid. Became a shrink."

"Jock had a daughter?"

"Still does as far as I know."

"I didn't even know he was married."

"His wife died very young. Mary Beale, the daughter, was grown and gone by the time you started at Felton." Jack pretended to look contrite. "I've been slack in my correspondence lately, what with the move and the new cottage. I owe Jock a couple of letters. I meant to write him in the spring after your invitation came. He's got prostate cancer, not that it's going to kill him before something else gives out. He's eighty-five."

"Where does he live?"

"He's in a retirement home out in Hamilton. Pretty fancy by his account. I've never been there."

"He must have been retired for years."

"I know what you're thinking: how's an old duffer in Hamilton going to have a handle on any of this. Thing is, he never really did retire, at least *he* doesn't think so. He's still nominally on the Felton board of governors, still contributes to the school magazine, makes a nuisance of himself with the Old Boys' Association. Felton School will always be his whole existence."

"But the invitations didn't come from the Association. If a snoop like Alfie Criddle doesn't know anything, and he's right there, I don't see…"

"There's nothing wrong with Jock's long-term memory. If anything it's improving. You want to know about Victor Dempsey? Jock Beale's the obvious place to start. You sound like you don't want me to help you."

A bubble bulged from the neck of Paul's beer, straining up, not bursting. "Are you going to tell him why you want to know about Victor Dempsey?"

"I can't predict that. I'll play it by ear."

"Jesus, dad. How about asking *me* how I feel about it?"

Jack leaned back against the fridge. "How do you feel about it?"

Paul glared at his father, helpless to stem it, his knuckles white around his beer. Suddenly, without any conscious decision to do so, he was raising his voice:

"I don't know, do I, Jack? Isn't that the whole fucking point here?"

Jack stiffened. "I don't know, Paul. Is it?"

"What do you mean?"

"You want to know why I've never forgiven you for Clifford.

Isn't *that* the whole fucking point, as you so nicely put it?"

Both of them had known all along, at some level, that this was on the agenda. Ever since Paul's arrival they had been carrying it like some volatile explosive substance.

Paul looked unwaveringly at his father. "You never said anything, but I knew."

"You didn't know. You were wrong. You *are* wrong."

"Sure. You who always gave everything a hundred and twenty percent. Always in control. You who never made even little mistakes, let alone fatal ones. Why *don't* you blame me, Jack?"

"Maybe if you'd shut up for a second you'd find out!"

Paul took a big drink without tasting it, his teeth clamped on the hard brown neck of the bottle. He looked down at the swirling formica. It made him feel dizzy and sick.

"Alright. Maybe I did blame you, but not for long." He moved a step closer. "Look at me, Paul."

"What?!"

"How can I blame you when I don't understand how it happened? The fence was there, it conformed to the bylaw. You tell me it was locked and the key was up on its nail in the mudroom. That's all I need to know. I looked at that fence. I went back and looked at it. I went back a dozen times and looked at it. I went back last goddam *week* and looked at it and I still don't have one single idea how he got over."

Paul looked at his father a long time before he said, quietly and unemotionally: "Thank you."

"I'm only sorry, son."

For the second time today, Paul, whose heart had been arid for two years, felt the prick of tears. Neither of them were ready to draw any closer, but they were looking at each other, a silent agreement to test the deep force that pulled them together while it pushed them apart. They were like that when they heard Celia's voice outside the kitchen door and moved quickly, sweeping away the broken pieces of the spell.

Jack overdid his brightness. "Memory and pride fighting, memory gives in: who said that, Cele?"

She stopped in the doorway, blocking Tom who was holding his shirt as a bag, pregnant with peaches. Slightly out of breath, she looked searchingly between her husband and her son.

"Nietzsche." A beat. "Were they?"

C H A P T E R 1 2

PAUL WOKE, DISORIENTED, in his sunlit, eggshell blue room. He got out of bed and went to the open window, which showed the meadow behind the house, rising to the circle of fruit trees that contained Celia's vegetable garden; he had to ask himself if he had dreamed the distant whinny of a horse.

His watch said nine o'clock — late holiday sleep that had refreshed him superbly. He fished a clean white T-shirt and underwear from his suitcase, pulled on his jeans and padded through to the kitchen, his bare feet making small sticky noises on the already-warm linoleum.

There was coffee on the stove and breakfast for two laid on the kitchen table, cantaloup and Welsh cakes and thick-cut marmalade. There was a note on his plate, in Jack's handwriting, illegible to all but pharmacists and his own family: "Gone to assassinate the planning department. Canoe and Albacore all yours. Life jackets, paddles, gas for outboard in barn. Have fun. See you when."

Paul smiled, inhaling the smell of coffee in the sun-warmed kitchen. He poured a cup, was on his way to Tom's room when he heard it again through the open kitchen window — unmistakable this time: a horse's deep snort.

He opened the front door. The sun was up and bright, dazzling until he made a shade with his hand.

Paul counted five teams about two hundred yards away, working the east meadow. Horsedrawn sickle mowers, two big Belgians for each machine, pretty horses in spite of their size, pale caramel with white-blonde manes and forelocks — the breed of choice for Mennonites. The primitive wood and iron mowers had arrived on wagons, parked under the trees at the bottom of the farm track where it broke from the woods.

At this distance Paul couldn't see the drivers' features, but their dress was the standard Mennonite uniform: dark hats with rounded crowns and wide brims, white shirts with black suspenders holding up black trousers. Paul had taken his engineering degree at McMaster in Hamilton, not far from Waterloo County where most of Ontario's Mennonite communities are established. In his four years at Mac, Paul had come to take for granted the sight of Old Order Mennonite families in their horse-drawn buggies and severe black clothes — or at work on their farms, with equipment like this, unchanged for a century. The biggest surprise for Paul was seeing them so far from their traditional southwestern home.

So this was Jack's surprise.

Paul heard a noise behind him and turned, smiling. "Good morning."

Tom came to his side, sleepy and warm, still in his pyjamas. He blinked into the bright morning, his hand automatically straying to Paul's as he caught sight of the activity in the lower meadow, the cocoon of sleep instantly falling away.

"Wow!"

Paul chuckled. "They're called Mennonites."

"They've got horses."

"They're people who like to do things the old-fashioned way. See those iron wheels on the mowers and those wagons down there? They won't even put rubber tires on."

"Why?"

"Because rubber's too modern. They don't drive cars, they don't even have electricity in their homes. Imagine that, lighting with candles and pumping all your water by hand from a well."

"Can we go see?"

"Run and get dressed then."

They stood at the edge of the meadow, exchanging sober nods with the mowers, watching the expert way they controlled the big horses, the alfalfa and timothy toppling under their relentless advance. The machines were at some distance, largely hidden except for the tops of their iron wheels and the long wooden tongues running up between the horses. But Paul knew what they were: Number Nine high gear mowers with the sickle bar gnashing off the right side, its teeth driven by a Pitman geared from an oil-bathed differential inside the traction wheel, the softly rounded gearbox looking wonderfully like a seal pup with two big bolts for its eyes.

He had first seen such machines — loved them — as a little boy, long before Waterloo County, in the countryside north of Slagg's Hollow, which was still farmed during Paul's childhood. Land that now bore developers' crass euphemisms had nurtured real communities in the fifties and sixties, with old-fashioned country fairs in summer and fall: tractor-pulls, step-dancing, fiddle contests and animal shows — and, of course, the vintage agricultural machines.

Always the machines for Paul. Years before his mind had grasped the principles of internal combustion, he had loved those simple, hundred-year-old contrivances, the mowers and threshers and corn binders. You didn't need adults to confuse you, you could *see* how they worked — how this shuttled back and forth, which twisted this, which turned that. Even when he had graduated to the steam traction engines and the old clacking motor tractors, even as a teenager coaxing contraband horsepower from a Chrysler hemi, he could never dismiss the elegance of those first transparent mechanisms — no more than a symphonist could ever cease to respond to a simple, lovely melody.

He played a game with Tom over breakfast, thinking of things they would have to forego if they lived without hydro, Tom back and forth from the window as the formation of mowers cut nearer the house. After breakfast, because they both missed her, Paul called Eva collect.

"How was the reunion?"

"We went to the movies in Felton town, the new Star Trek. Awesome."

"What are you saying, the reunion was a bust?"

"I'll tell you when I see you. Don't worry, we're having a great time. We're going canoeing in a minute. How's Hurricane Terry? Still an advisory, right?"

"That's all. It's building, but it's way out. You know how often we go through this in a season. It's not as if we're near the coast. Tom there?"

He chatted happily to his mother while Paul drank a second cup of coffee. Then he took the phone again.

"Did you get any explanation for that Iaboni story? Mum was wondering."

"Arabella must be on the road, I haven't heard from her. There's bound to be a simple explanation. Listen, I've got one or two students I would happily credit with plagiarism, but not Arabella Bauer. No way."

"Why so sure?"

"She's not out to impress anyone. She listens, she learns, she hands in wonderful work."

"Do you have any of her other stories?"

"Nope. I mark them and I hand them back."

"But you would remember if you saw one of them again, right?"

"What are you getting at?"

"Just say *Queen's Quarterly* was her regular source, you

could check out some back issues, see if there are any other stories that look familiar."

"Where am I supposed to get *Queen's Quarterly* down here?"

"What about the university library? Chapel Hill maybe?"

"My God, Celia's really got you spooked on this!"

"Has she? I'm sorry, I thought I was just curious."

"She's my friend, Paul. I've needed someone to talk to this year."

"I know, sweetheart. You're quite right."

"Arabella's a good listener, a wise one. I wish I could take the credit for getting you there with Tom, but it was Arabella. The moment the subject of the Felton reunion came up, she knew you and Tom should go, the right thing for all of us."

"I know. You were both right. Tom and I are right here proving it, believe me."

He apologized again, not quite sure why he had been so ready to jump on Celia's bandwagon. As he looked at Tom waiting by the front door in his bathing suit with the sun-screen on a yellow rope around his neck, Paul felt ungrateful: Arabella Bauer had done them an inestimable service, a true fact that yesterday's events didn't alter in any way.

It was the same old fibreglass canoe that had hung in the ga-rage at the Hollow for thirty years, big bellied and disinclined to tip. Paul stowed the water bottle and sun hats and cinched Tom's life jacket, then sat him in the bow and stroked away from the dock, keeping to the shoreline in shallow water. Tom's paddle bumped and splashed, but Paul was thrifty with his advice: Tom had all week to get technique; Jack would see to that. Let him enjoy the ride. After ten minutes, Paul was content for him to lay his paddle aside, happy to have him sit in the bottom of the canoe and trail his fingers in the black water.

Paul stripped off his shirt and felt the early morning sun

benignly warm on his skin. There were no powerboats out. The rocks and deep cool forest slid by in a magical silence broken only by the trickle from his blade between J-strokes, the whisper of Tom's fingers veeing through the water, the rustle of small, unseen creatures in the woods.

"Boy oh boy," he said quietly, inspired by the *Buoy O Boy* label on the back of Tom's lifejacket, but more so by the picture — he would never forget it — of Tom at the end of the corridor at Ormiston House, worried for his dad, his small fist wrapped around a pool cue.

Paul tipped his head back and sent a wordless prayer of thanks to the high blue sky. To the Manitou. To the Bancroft planning department for taking Celia and Jack away this morning. To Eva and her friend Arabella Bauer for the wisdom that had brought Tom and himself to this moment.

Paul resumed his stroke, trying to relax back to his previous easy rhythm, but he was somehow out of synch. He was beginning to feel a pre-blister tenderness on his left index finger, switched the paddle to his fresh right side, but he was long out of practice and it felt awkward. Across the flashing water, the morning's first speedboat inched distant white against the dark background of low hills, its insect whine drilling through the quiet.

The question came unplanned and unformulated: "What's Arabella Bauer like? Is she nice?"

"Yeah, really nice."

"Do you remember any of the things she and mummy used to talk about? When you guys were out together?" A wasted question on most kids, but Tom was thoughtful, observant.

But he shrugged. "I dunno."

A thirsty deer fly landed on Paul's arm, ribbed dusty grey. He slapped it away and swung the bow further out from the shore. Forget it. It wasn't any of his business. It felt sleazy asking Tom.

They had long been out of his parent's bay, passing other cottages, the ones that belonged to those signs on the dirt road. A girl in a bikini threw a frisbee for a golden lab, a little boy chased around with a water pistol, a man cutting a wide sweep of lawn with a push-mower waved cheerily to the canoe.

"They had a big fight once."

"A fight? Really? When was that?"

"The time we went to the Liberty fair."

Paul had not forgotten that day. It had been the beginning of this.

"Arabella told mummy it was time for her ultimation."

"What?"

"Mummy showed her that card you got from your school, and she said mummy had to give you her ultimation."

Ultimatum.

"Mummy got mad with her."

"What happened?"

"Mummy cried and then Arabella hugged her. She said you had to go. She said it lots of times."

"Arabella did?"

"It was funny. But she's usually nice."

He watched Tom's hand leave the water, the small glistening fingers picking with sudden disconsolation at the gunwale. As he had done on the phone to Eva, Paul chastened himself for his selfishness. But this was worse — he had just spoiled something precious.

He lifted his dripping paddle and laid it across the canoe. It was quiet again, the powerboat had gone, the cottages had fallen behind them. He sat, restoring the morning by observing his son, fixing him in this moment, the silver down on his nape and arms, the thoughtful angle of his head, the small clean hand falling still now on the gunwale. In a sudden, unbearable rush of love, Paul saw not only the enormity of Tom's loss, and his bravery, but the way he internalized his grief. Like father, like son, they had been holding onto that hard piece of Lego for too long. Now, at last, the never-spoken words came easily.

"Do you think about Cliff a lot?"

Tom's frozen stiffness was answer enough.

"You know what, darlin'? I believe he's here with us."

Tom looked around immediately, his face bearing all the human contradictions that are transparent in children but are never resolved: gratitude and resentment at the opening of dark places, fierce hope and terrified doubt.

"That's what mummy says."

"I believe she's right, Tom. I do. I believe he can see this sky and these trees and rocks. I believe he's on this canoe trip right along with his big brother and his old dad." He smiled, reached forward for Tom's hand.

For a moment Tom withheld it. A shade of stubbornness, his own ability to hurt. "Is he in the water?"

But Paul's smile remained strong and steady.

"Sure he is, Tom. Clifford's wherever we are. He's looking after us. He's our guardian angel."

They got back at eleven-thirty, beached the canoe and walked up to the barn. The mowers were idle now, the pretty Belgians out of harness, grazing. Several black buggies had joined the wagons at the end of the lower meadow; a lunch party was in progress beneath the trees. They could see Mennonite women wearing summer bonnets and aprons over long cotton dresses, plain but altogether feminine women moving with graceful ease. They had brought their children, Tom's age and younger, dressed exactly like their parents, even to the bonnets and the round-brimmed hats. The women and children were serving the men seated on the sides of the big wagons, Paul knew it would be some kind of hearty casserole, pasta and meat with half an inch of cheese on top, and spelt bread.

Paul realized how hungry he was as they walked along the fenceline towards the new cottage site, where Celia and Jack were with a tall, straight-backed Mennonite man. The man was pacing — Paul thought he was measuring until he turned and Paul could see the forked wand in his hands, the stem of the Y ahead of him like an antenna.

Celia saw them, waved and came down the fenceline.

"What do you think of our Mennonites, Tom? Did you think you'd woken up in another century?"

"Where do they come from?" Paul said.

"There's a community about ten miles from here. We only found out when they approached us about the hay."

"Old Order, right?"

"Ancient. No musical instruments, newspapers, not even curtains. Amazing people though."

Paul looked past her up the slope. "Is he doing what I think he's doing?"

"The original well's running dry. Mr. Toews is supposed to be the best witch in the county. He doesn't just divine — he tells you how deep the well's going to be, one nod of the wand for every foot. Come and meet him." She caught Tom's hand. "Didn't know there were men witches, did you? It's okay, he's a nice one."

Toews was in his middle sixties, lean and strong, his complexion mapped with delicate lines. When he tipped his round black hat in greeting, Paul saw a high, startlingly white forehead.

"Is that a hazel wand?" Paul asked.

Celia chuckled. "My son's an engineer, Mr. Toews. He's interested in anything technical."

Toews looked directly at Paul, his hybrid German accent low and neutral. "I use chokecherry. Do you know how it works?"

"No idea."

"Mr. Toews helped his father build this barn when he was fifteen," Celia said. "They built a fire letter into the foundation, an exhortation to the elements. What did it say, Mr. Toews?"

"'No lightning will strike you, no witchcraft nor ghost can harm you.'" The merest hint of a smile. "Barn's still there, *nein*?"

"Do you believe in the supernatural?" Paul asked him.

"We believe in tradition, Mr. Preedy." Toews raised the chokecherry wand and resumed his measured pacing. Then he turned.

"People always ask why we're different. But we ask the same question: why is the world different? Why has the world abandoned itself to immorality and crime? Why do we resist even small changes? Because every one leads to another, and then another. Always. Before you know it you are at the brink, then you are over it and into the torrent." He turned his neutral blue eyes to Tom. "You are going to be here for a few days?"

Tom nodded shyly.

"So are we. You are seven years?"

"Eight."

"So is my grandson. His name is Peter. He's the one in the black hat."

Tom frowned. "You all have black hats."

Toews flicked a glance at the smiling adults. "Then you'll have to come and ask all our names. You like Mennonite macaroni cheese?"

Tom shrugged.

Toews started down the hill towards the wagons. "Come on, all of you. The water's been there a good long time; it will still be there after lunch."

"Will there be enough food?" Celia called after him. "I could bring…"

"We are expecting you. We have plates, cutlery, everything."

Jack was just getting off the phone when Paul and Tom went in to wash up. Jack drew him aside.

"I just spoke to Jock Beale. I had to give him the details. I assumed I had your permission to do so."

Paul nodded. "What did he say?"

"It was an odd conversation to say the least. He was keeping something from me and he wouldn't tell me what it was."

"Why not?"

"He said he would rather tell you."

"What?"

"He wants to see you. Tonight."

Paul stared at his father. "*What?*"

"He wouldn't tell me why. He said he needed the day to think, and he would see you tonight around seven."

"And you said fine."

"Of course I did. Hamilton's under three hours from here. You could stay at the Hollow if you don't feel like driving back tonight. You could be back here by ten tomorrow morning."

"What about Tom?"

"What about him? We'll take good care of him."

Paul shook his head. "Hamilton tonight? Christ…I don't know, dad."

❖   ❖   ❖

But he knew. At four o'clock, bouncing down the farm track in the Subaru, his curiosity was already at flashpoint.

Jack had seen him off at the house, dispensing advice and caution, and a bottle of August lily tonic for Jock Beale, a Mennonite recipe of flowers and herbs that had caught his interest. Now Paul stopped at the end of the property where Celia was minding Tom, one of a gaggle of children playing tag through the stubble, the boys holding onto their black hats, the little girls lifting their long cotton skirts as they ran.

Paul got out of the car, caught Tom as he flew past and hugged him goodbye.

"Look, dad." Tom took a stone from his pocket, deep translucent yellow, worn smooth from touching. "Mr. Toews gave it to me."

"It's amber," Celia said quietly over Paul's shoulder. "Mennonites put a lot of stock in it."

Paul turned the pocket-warm stone in his fingertips. "How come?"

"Its association with preserving? I'm not sure. Toews carries a string of it, sort of a worrypiece cum good luck charm."

"Like the fire letter?" He grunted and popped the stone back in Tom's hand, then kissed the top of his head. "Take good care of your granma. I'll see you in the morning."

Tom ran back to his new friends while Celia took Paul's

arm back to the idling Subaru. "Think you might stay at the Hollow?"

"I'd rather come back. I'll see how I feel. I'll call you whatever I decide." He smiled grimly. "It's been a good few years since I was summoned by the headmaster."

"Six of the best!"

"Don't worry, I'm taking a cushion to stuff in my trousers!"

His mother grew serious. "Extraordinary, isn't it? I wonder what he's got to tell you. I hope it isn't just a lonely old man taking the opportunity to indulge his favourite subject."

"Jack doesn't seem to think so."

"Curiouser and curiouser, the whole affair. You'll have to come and see us more often. We obviously don't get enough excitement!" She touched her warm hand to the side of his face. "Take great care, my darling. And don't worry about Tom. He'll be fine."

Paul grinned. "He's got his amber, right? It's a load off my mind, I can tell you. Reassures a man to know his son's protected from witches."

CHAPTER 13

JUST AS HE could summon the woman from the girl, it was Andy Adams's gift and pleasure to be able to coax the girl from a mature lady of sixty-two.

Seeing pouched eyes sparkle with tears, watching Mrs. Merrill's inelastic, diminished body abandon itself to pleasure, hearing her voice ascend, even briefly, to a girlish soprano — it gave him almost evangelical satisfaction.

While Mrs. Merrill was transformed by his ministrations, she was by no means the passive object of them. She was, after all, one who dared. And she was rich, used to a life of privilege that had accustomed her to getting what she wanted when she wanted it, from a dominant position.

"'Ride a cock horse to Banbury Cross
  To see a fine lady on a white horse.'"

She rested at the top of her stroke, inclining her head forward, heedless of the unbecoming tug of gravity on her face, peering down between her straddled thighs, pressing in her tummy for an unobstructed view.

"Will you just *look* at that…I'm absolutely *stuffed!* No thank you, Mr. Adams, I simply couldn't manage another millimetre!" She pumped again, panting and giggling: "'Mrs. Margaret Merrill of Toronto and Palm Beach, widow of the late financier George R. Merrill, pictured here enjoying the hospitality of Simcoe's most exclusive resort!' Don't you just *love* it?!"

Margaret Merrill was far too wise to search his face for the answer; instead she bit her lip and inclined forward and settled herself, forcing him so deep he could feel the nudge inside. She moved slowly up and down, deliberately shunting him against her cervix, her face floating inches above his, monitoring his discomfort. In the absence of love, Mrs. Merrill had discovered she liked both ends of a little pain.

Andy decided it was time to go on the offensive. He pushed up onto his elbows, forcing her upright, freeing one hand to gently lift each pancake breast in turn, kissing the pale, concave nipples. He sat up further, assertively, catching her in the crook of his arm as she toppled backwards. Both arms wrapped around her now, a tango embrace and soft, fiercely tender kisses on her eyes. In his own were the beginnings of tears.

"Funny girl," he whispered, the tears suggesting vulnerability, the power of his feelings and therefore her own power. Tears for the news that she was leaving for her New York auction two hours from now, and would not be returning after all, even though the rest of the week was booked and paid for. There were staff problems at the Palm Beach place that couldn't wait till October. Her Lear would be landing at Barrie airport any time now with her housekeeper, coming to pack her and accompany her to New York. The auction was of paperweights, another one of Mrs. Merrill's passions; she had people down there, of course, but it was the thrill of the chase, wasn't it?

"This is our last night of the season, darling."

"Will you write to me?" he whispered. He kissed her nose. "I don't think I can go a whole year without your laughter."

Mrs. Merrill sighed deeply and surrendered to the fiction.

She knew enough, at sixty-two, to make the most of it when the acting was this good. He knew what he was doing and he wouldn't let her down. He was reliable in every way, and genuinely kind within his limits. He may even have believed a little of his sweet nonsense. She hoped so.

Mrs. Merrill felt a sudden pang at the prospect of leaving the Valmy tomorrow, felt the spectre of weakness, an embarrassing scene in which she implored him to come to Palm Beach in the fall, at whatever rate of compensation he required.

But she was too practical and really too aroused to spoil their last half hour with histrionics. And when the half hour had passed and he was dressing, a reconstituted and grateful Mrs. George R. Merrill handed him his envelope.

"What's this for?" A puzzled frown, bless him, as he slit it open and pulled out the cheque.

"I wanted to treat you to a farewell dinner tonight, but I've got a lot of packing and you know how I hate goodbyes. You'll have to buy your own."

His surprise at the amount was quite genuine. He returned the check to its envelope, folded it, and placed it carefully in the seat pocket of his tennis shorts. "Sweet Margaret," he said quietly, with a catch in his voice. "I'll toast you with champagne."

"I should hope so." Mrs. Merrill was feeling much better, and the practical side was regaining ascendancy; for a moment she wondered if she hadn't gone slightly overboard this year. Seven thousand dollars would buy Mr. Adams a lot of champagne dinners.

Andy closed the door behind him and inhaled deeply of the fragrance that pervaded the premium enclave, of Oriental lilies, his breath escaping in a sigh: apart from a couple of swims in the premium pool, he had not been out of Mrs. Merrill's cabin — or her bed — since late yesterday afternoon.

It didn't surprise him that there was a message at the desk for him to call Paul Preedy, though he wasn't sure how Preedy had traced him here.

"He's called three times, quite frantic," Charles said archly when Andy went by reception for his messages. "And someone called Mary Swoffa called twice." The name meant nothing. "And Ms. Arabella Bauer from number six came by half an hour ago. She wants to arrange a lesson as soon as possible."

"Did you give her my extension?"

"I thought that was your job."

"Ha ha."

"Of course I gave it to her. To serve you is my sole waking thought."

Andy looked at him, waiting. "What is it, Charles?" It was the way he was picking at the sleeves of his perfect green blazer, it was the smoulder. Charles glanced furtively sideways to make sure that Caitlin, his assistant, was out of hearing.

"And here's silly me thinking you were a connoisseur of the ladies." Charles tutted at his own folly. "What a letdown."

Andy smiled brightly. "Oh…you know me, Charles, anything with a pulse. Even then. Anything except road kill." Regretful: "And you of course."

Charles sighed. "Here I am, always trying to give you a little friendly advice. Impossible when you're always just *so* ungrateful."

"For what?"

"Off you go. And er…*vive la difference*, hmmn?"

"What?"

But Charles was already floating away to the far end of the desk, waggling surreptitious bye-bye fingers under the counter.

Andy crossed the oil-stained employees' parking lot towards his quarters near the Valmy's service entrance, forced to stand aside as a fuel-oil truck lumbered past, holding his breath against the thick diesel fumes. The nights would start getting cool soon, and the Valmy would be ready.

He stood for a moment, looking longingly at the white BMW in his spot, poised and ready. Andy was ready, too; still only August, leaves still green on the trees, towels and paperbacks still smelling of suntan lotion, yet he could feel already the itch to be gone, back in the saddle for his annual southbound ride. He was waiting to hear back from a new resort just opened on Eleuthera that was hiring pros, ATP rankers above 300. Serious tennis, he'd heard — ball-throwing machines, serving and ground stroke aids, rebound nets and instructional films. Not to mention the best marlin and amberjack fishing in the Bahamas.

The employees' quarters were in one long single-story structure, like motel units but with a kitchenette and a small living room area. He shut the door behind him and went into the bedroom and undressed, sliding Mrs. Merrill's cheque under the glass ashtray of change on the credenza beside the TV and his rented VCR.

He opened the closet and undid the suitcase in which he kept his tapes, narrowing his selection down to two, both early Marilyn, both classics. In fact, all the films in the case were oldies, none of the modern shot-on-tape garbage, shrewd little scrubbers with coke-clogged sinuses faking the same tired stunts.

He loaded a cassette and lay naked on the bed to watch, fondling himself half-heartedly, his body not yet ready to respond in spite of its stored potency, its need for release. Andy never permitted himself an orgasm with the likes of Mrs. Merrill, and since he, if not they, always insisted on condoms, and since a large part of his success rested on his Zenlike control, it was simple to fake his orgasms. It was a kind of pact he had with himself, a way of withholding himself — of saving something — with the result that he often liked to watch a movie afterwards.

Andy had enjoyed too many different kinds of women to have any set definition of beauty, but if he had to describe his ideal, he might have said the young Marilyn Chambers. Nubile, at the feminine end of the tomboy scale, with her soft brown hair and her wide American mouth. The girl next door. But it wasn't just Marilyn that had led him to select this particular film: *Behind The Green Door* was a movie with a message, one he needed to hear this evening.

Green Door was about initiation into pleasure, the casting away of shame. About discovery. In the film, a fresh, innocent girl is spirited away to a private club where nothing is taboo, where a madcap audience, a heterogeneous menage of homosexuals and hippies, transvestites and even a circus fat lady witness her sexual awakening. It had been revolutionary in an era when they were still called stag films, in which the out-of-shape actors looked at the camera and the guys kept their socks on. Andy knew that *Green Door* was flawed, earnestly artsy, but it was trying the way a whole generation — Andy's generation — had tried: to fuck guilt but good. Fuck it up its tight ass, fuck it in its deaf ears and its hypocritical mouth.

Fuck Felton!

Andy masturbated with hard, joyless, ineffectual strokes, unable to connect with the tension inside him, a black energy from which he had had Mrs. Merrill to distract him since he came back from the reunion yesterday afternoon.

What...he was supposed to feel guilty now, twenty-five years later? Christ, he'd been through the late sixties and seventies since then, on the front lines of the sexual revolution. Not that he'd ever been a switch-hitter. No, he was a tried and true ladies' man. At eighteen, in boarding school, boys had been a necessity.

That boy...

Fuck it. He had not personally used anything but the gentlest persuasion. Was it his problem if that pervert King had overdone it? So Dempsey had protested at first. So was Marilyn protesting at the beginning of this film. When it came to sex, most people hadn't the slightest idea what they wanted. As soon as they dumped the guilt, as soon as they got into the swing of things...

But the dusty black box was open and the images were loose in his memory and they kept on coming, crowding out the comfortable scenes on the TV. Sounds washing over the comfortable cries of pleasure…cries of terror, cries of agony, a child weeping for mercy and getting none, beyond reason and its little comprehension, begging for forgiveness…*I'm sorry…I'm sorry…*

Andy tried for another minute to stimulate himself, then got up and stabbed the television and the VCR to silence. He took a shower and washed his hair with *Clairol For Blondes* and was blowing it dry when the phone rang.

"Hello?"

If she had purred, dropped innuendos, he would have said no. He was in no mood tonight to go the whole distance, to play the game of inches, to spend half the night at the Portage warming a terrified middle-aged woman's cold feet. But the voice on the phone was all business.

"We talked last week at the Portage, about lessons. I'd like some."

"When."

"Tonight at eight? I'm in cabin six. I expect you like to be paid in advance."

"Not necessarily."

"Have you eaten?"

"No."

"I'll call room service. Shall I choose?"

"Be my guest."

"No. You'll be mine."

CHAPTER 14

CHARLES ALLIN FREER wore his good humour into the staff
dining room at seven o'clock, smiled right through his dinner, was humming very quietly to himself when he arrived
back at the front desk at eight.

The badinage with Andy Adams was especially enjoyable
when Charles got the upper hand, and this time it wasn't
merely advantage Freer. This time it was going to be game, set
and match! The thought of Andy's face when he found out
about cabin six was enough to brighten the prospect of the
next five hours on the desk with Caitlin.

Charles had nothing against the Valmy hiring students in
the summer, but it did seem unfair for them to take a dancer
instead of a kid in hotel management. Just because Hedley
the assistant manager had the hots for Caitlin, she of the
French braid and the turned-out ballet-academy feet, bouncing around all the time like a rubber ball.

He checked the reservation book while Caitlin registered
an elderly couple from Syracuse, both of them, it seemed,
hard of hearing. He glanced sideways with crimped lips when

he heard the unprofessional note of exasperation in Caitlin's voice, monitoring the transaction, ready to intercede.

A bellboy escorted the New Yorkers away. Caitlin took a phone call. Caitlin made a phone call. Caitlin bounced over with the first of what would be an endless night of questions.

Charles sighed audibly. "Yes, what is it?"

"What do you do if someone calls for room service and…"

"I hope you didn't sound weary and tell them to dial direct."

Caitlin beamed resiliently. "'Course not. I took the order and tried room service but there's no reply."

"Which is probably why the guest called us in the first place." Lately, room service had needed a bomb under them. He would be speaking to Hedley about it. "You'll just have to keep trying," he told her. "I hope you wrote the order down carefully." Charles returned to the reservation book, tugging his shirt cuffs to show that the consultation was over.

"Didn't need to."

He looked up sharply.

"There wasn't anything to forget," she said. "Easiest one I ever got: eight-thirty, cabin six, a large thermos of boiling water."

Charles arched his eyebrows. "Six?"

"Yeah."

"That was all? No tea or coffee, just hot water?"

Caitlin's unprofessionalism sounded again in her rich-and-spoiled-guest imitation. "Goodness me no, plain hot water wouldn't do at all, she stipulated that, said she could get *hot* water from the tap. It had to be *just* boiled and in a thermos, the largest one we have. Scalding, she said."

PAUL CROSSED THE Burlington Skyway at a quarter to seven, keeping to the slow lane to prolong his view across Hamilton Harbour. He had always liked the way this steeltown wore its heart on its sleeve: a hard heart, Stelco, looking part technopolis, part medieval hell from the bridge, the still evening water reflecting its baleful fires, carrying the din of unceasing labour.

Halfway across the bridge, he lowered his window to sample the familiar, sulphurous air. Paul had worked there all of his university summers, because the money was good and because he was enthralled, not only by the clamorous, infernal drama of steelmaking, but by the powerful and complex administrative apparatus that kept hell burning.

He had to check his father's directions to find Trindall Street, in a part of town he'd had no cause to visit as a student. He found himself driving on a broad parade, past opulent houses with graciously treed gardens and expensive cars in the driveways.

He found the number Jack had given him, surprised that

the retirement home didn't look like one, little different from the prosperous three-story Edwardian residences either side of it. He had to stop briefly before turning into the drive-way, as well-nourished boys on rollerblades snatched up their hockey net and swooped politely aside to let him pass.

The building had been extended at the back, sensitively, with minimal interference to the original house. Even with the extension, he realized that the home's capacity had to be small, fifteen or twenty residents at most. He left his car in a spruce parking lot at the side of the house and obeyed a sign directing visitors to the front door.

The entrance hall, broadloomed and wallpapered and greened with potted plants, dispelled any sort of institutional feeling, giving the impression rather of an intimate country hotel. Through open double doors to the right of the hallway, he glimpsed a comfortably furnished lounge that reinforced the hotel atmosphere — soft cream walls and carpet, arm-chairs arranged around a fireplace, occasional tables with softly shaded reading lamps and fanned-out magazines, recessed shelves of books. The furniture was good reproduc-tion pine for an upscale country look. So far it was an adult house, fresh and tasteful, nothing at all to indicate the age of its inhabitants.

Paul could hear activity behind a closed door to the left before the stairs. He found a spacious dining room where a plump, fiftyish woman wearing an apron over a puff-sleeved cotton dress was laying places for breakfast.

She looked up with an easy smile. "Sorry, didn't hear you come in, rattling about in here!" Twelve places at a large ob-long table, good silver on white linen, willow-pattern cereal bowls and side plates. Through an open hatchway behind her, presumably to the kitchen, Paul heard the clattering of dishes.

"I'm here to visit Jock Beale. My name's Paul Preedy. I be-lieve he's expecting me."

The woman looked surprised. "Jock doesn't get many visi-tors. Are you local?"

Paul explained that he had driven from Bancroft, showed her the bottle of Mennonite tonic he had carried in from the car.

"How thoughtful of you." She placed two silver toast racks. "I'll get Dinah to page him." The puff-sleeved dress was ankle length, rustling as she went to the hatch; given a mobcap, she might have been keeping a heritage house for tourists. In fact, the whole setup here had that genteel, fresh-baked quality.

"Dinah?"

"What?" came a harried reply from the kitchen.

"Could you page Mr. Beale, please. Paul Preedy is here to see him." She turned back to the table with an armload of linen napkins rolled in colour-coded rings, and a moment later the harried voice sounded simultaneously from the kitchen and the hallway.

"We don't like to use the intercom but we're short staffed today."

"It seems very quiet."

"Movie night on Mondays. We just got one of those new big-screen TVs, and the residents love it. They all have television in their rooms, of course, but we like to do things together as much as possible."

The cheerfulness was professional, a touch of self-promotion, but Paul liked her. He fell in with her work, taking half the napkins and placing them where she indicated. "Seems very comfortable here, not what I was expecting."

"An old folks' home? Well, we just like to keep the emphasis on home, that's all."

And they're paying for it, thought Paul. Jock must have retired with a sizeable nest egg.

He helped her straighten chairs while they waited, six each side of the table. "We tried separate tables," chatted the woman, "but the residents like it better this way. We're a tight group; we'll miss Jock." She glanced at the hall door. "You know he's ill, of course."

"My father told me."

"Don't expect him to show it, but he'll be pleased to have a visitor. He doesn't get many."

"He has a daughter, doesn't he?"

She glanced at the door and lowered her voice. "Never so much as a Christmas card till Jock got bad news from the doctor. Won't be the first time I've seen it. They're around like vultures once they can smell an inheritance. She came when he was in hospital for his tests, if you please, poking around in his private papers! He was a teacher, you know, headmaster of a private school," she added with a touch of pride. She shunted the last chair into place. "People don't care these days. Double-income families, kids in daycare. Family life is breaking down. No place anymore for the older generation."

She went to the door and stuck her head into the hall. "I don't think he heard. He's probably in his room with the headphones on. He loves his music." She came back, untying her apron. "I'll take you up. It's on the first floor."

"Mrs. Colcomb?" came the frustrated voice from the kitchen, and now a face appeared at the hatch, a pretty teenage face, red from exertion. When the girl saw Paul she tried in vain to brush back the hair sticking to her forehead.

"What's the matter, Dinah?"

"The stupid dishwasher won't go on again. That dial thing won't move."

Mrs. Colcomb turned to Paul in mild exasperation. "This might take a minute. You said Jock's expecting you?"

"Dad talked to him this morning."

"Why don't you go on up then? It's room two, just to your right on the first landing. If he isn't there, try the TV room. Door at the back of the hall into the new wing, you'll hear it. We rented an Alfred Hitchcock tonight — I love him, don't you?"

The warm, tasteful decor continued up the stairs: more reproduction pine and some genuine antiques, an extensive set of botanical prints on the walls, a fortune in wallpaper. Of course there would be medical facilities here, but he had seen nothing sanitized or institutional so far. He remembered going to a retirement home with his mother one Christmas with a food basket, one of her numerous charity projects; Leisureville, it had been called, "Seizureville" to the Slagg's Hollow volunteers. He had little visual recollection of it, but the olfactory memory lingered, a complicated, layered odour of cheap spray freshener over disinfectant over the sweetish smell of old age.

There was none of that here, the only smell a peppery fragrance from a cut crystal bowl of potpourri on a pine dresser on the landing. He could see the doors to four rooms now, each bearing an oval ceramic plaque, hand-painted with a border of flowers around the occupant's name.

He didn't smell pipe tobacco until he was right up to the door of room two — "Jock's Room" — but it was instantly familiar: an aromatic Dutch blend, the scent that invariably announced the headmaster's approach on a blue-grey cloud.

He stood for a moment on the quiet landing, held in thrall by the tobacco evocation: Jock crossing the Circle to morning assembly, stout brogues creaking, back so straight his spine might have been fused, his master's gown flapping from his shoulders like black wings as the wind raised sparks from his pipe. A black dragon.

Paul knocked, fighting a ridiculous urge to flee down the stairs and out to his car — the feeling of being thirteen again, summoned to Jock's study on a federal charge.

He listened. No sound of music, the whole house quiet except for the distant, and comforting, rattle of dishes from the kitchen. He knocked again, curiosity piqued by the tobacco smell, then opened the door.

Through a stale blue haze, he saw what had once been a generous bedroom now converted to a modest bachelor apartment. The room had a high ceiling, French grey walls with elegant white mouldings; it should have had a spacious, airy feeling, yet compared to the rest of the house, Jock's quarters were stuffy and oppressive in a way that went beyond the fug.

The major pieces of furniture, obviously imported by Jock, were far too heavy for the room: a maple sleigh bed, two studded leather armchairs by the delicate marble fireplace, a massive rolltop desk against the wall beside the single window. Every remaining square inch of wall space was occupied by dark bookshelves, giving the impression, against the receding sky-grey walls, of a barricade round an encampment.

Along with the books, there were several hundred record albums on the shelves (Paul could see numerous boxed operas), also a monolithic McIntosh stereo system, state of the art in its day. Jock's pipes inhabited two wall-mounted racks, an impressive collection of traditional briars ranked with the odd exotic — an extravagantly carved meerschaum, even a long-stemmed clay pipe.

The fact that the room was fastidiously neat drew attention to the disorder of the open rolltop desk, from which screwed-up balls of paper spilled into a wicker basket. Amongst the litter was a lined, legal-size pad crammed with handwriting in red ink.

Poking around in his private papers

He was leaving the bottle of tonic, that was all. No point in carrying it all over the building.

At first Paul saw only the calligraphy, as instantly familiar as the pipesmoke — he had had Jock for Latin in grades eleven and twelve, Caesar's interminable Gallic wars.

Maintaining the habits of a lifetime of schoolmastering, Jock had made corrections in the margins, in his careful hand, though the whole page had ultimately been crossed out. But it was perfectly readable:

> I could see it the moment I laid eyes on him: he had the look of a victim.
>
> He was musical. I told his father we had no music program to speak of, which was a lie. Why did I put the father off? Because the boy was so big, a giant for every Jack in the school? Or because they were Jews? How selfish, how dreadfully selfish I have been.
>
> It seems to me now, waiting to die, as though I can already hear the overture to my eternal torment leaking into the foyer where I wait in my black evening clothes, late for the

performance. But soon there will be a break in the program, and the Usher will come for me and it will be time to face the music!

What will my torment be? An eternity of Wagner, anti-Semites together? Will it be my beloved Wagner, *ad nauseam*? And to what nausea? The Ring Cycle round and round for eternity? Or will they take the other approach, endless Italian operettas, an infinity of infantile plots? Imagine never being able to leave one's seat, even to go to the lavatory (though I am already more or less denied that luxury), waiting forever and ever for the fat lady to sing!

I am such a coward.

The familiar, mordant humour, very much like a suit of evening clothes, darkly elegant, worn over the fear. Paul was unaware that he had sunk into the desk chair, distracted by this sudden, unexpected reminder of Jock Beale's playfulness.

I was always mortally afraid of Basil McCrimmon. For many years I worried that he was after my job at Felton's helm. But I was forgetting that he already had everything he wanted in Ormiston House, which he saw not only as the jewel in Felton's crown, but as a separate, not to mention superior, institution.

And of course Basil always got what he wanted. I should have realized that after he singlehandedly revived the Loftus Scholarship. Remember the Loftus, Preedy?

Paul turned slowly in the chair, his face burning, cringing from the sight he fully anticipated: the headmaster standing in the doorway, caped in his black master's gown like a roused vampire, smiling his wrath.

He rose and tiptoed to the door and peered out onto the empty landing, his heart thumping, although he couldn't go down yet: he had seen a second closely written page under the first.

He listened for a moment to the continuing clatter of china

from the kitchen. The "dial thing" must have proved immovable
— Mrs. Colcomb and Dinah were doing them by hand.

He returned to the desk.

Remember the Loftus, Preedy?

He drew the top page aside, holding it by the edges as if
afraid to leave fingerprints. Page two had also been cor-
rected, line by line, but it had not been crossed out.

> Its namesake was an Edwardian headmaster and philan-
> thropist who personally underwrote the tuition of a local boy
> who, owing to his family's relative poverty, would otherwise
> have been denied the full flowering of his prodigious gifts.
>
> *Noblesse Oblige.* How McCrimmon relished the role! Not
> only that, he used his campaign to revive the Loftus Scholar-
> ship as an exercise in the application of his favourite axiom,
> one with which he guided his Ormiston Elite both on the
> playing field and in the examination room: Grace Under
> Pressure. Their privilege and responsibility.
>
> To clarify: Basil McCrimmon chose to invoke the
> openhandedness of the governing body at the same moment
> that Felton faced the most serious financial crisis in its history.
> It was brought on, in large part, by our valiant defence of
> tradition, or, as others chose to put it, our stubborn resistance
> to a changing world. You may recall the 1960s.
>
> How typical of McCrimmon, that indefatigable talent
> scout, that he should already have a recipient lined up for the
> Loftus, a boy in mind. An exceptionally gifted thirteen-year-
> old, already an instinctive linguist, an intuitive
> mathematician. If not a bona fide prodigy, certainly the near-
> est Felton, or should I say Ormiston, had ever come to one.
>
> Not a local family, but then Basil's range was wide. Cer-
> tainly not a "good" family — I believe Victor Dempsey's father
> laboured for wages in a plant that processed radium. Far from
> an all-rounder, the boy would have stood little chance on the
> sportsfield, given his delicate physique.

Yes Preedy, a beautiful boy.

And how are you holding up? Gracefully? But then you are not an Ormiston Boy, are you. Except for that one brief, though significant stay.

Paul's hand was trembling slightly as he lifted the second page to reveal a third, almost free of corrections. His eyes raced along, so absorbed now, he barely cared whether he was discovered or not.

However much I hated and still hate McCrimmon, I cannot in conscience pretend that there was anything untoward about his interest in Victor Dempsey. At worst, Basil might have seen in him some kind of romantic stereotype — I must say, the labourer's son looked every inch the Little Lord Fauntleroy.

Dempsey was a hothouse plant, overtended by a doting anddominating mother. It was the father that encouraged McCrimmon's advances, quite against the mother's wishes. I'm sure Mr. Dempsey was only too glad to see the boy delivered from her influence. Aside from the prestige, he must have thought boarding school would toughen Victor up, purge the decidedly feminine characteristics he had adopted from his mother.

Unfortunately for all of us, the opposite occurred. Instead of purging them, Felton School, as represented by messrs. Everett, Adams, King and Preedy, wasted no time in taking advantage of those very qualities.

The effect on Dempsey began to show as soon as he came down from the Ormiston sanitarium, out of quarantine. His straight A's became B's, then C's. He was clinically depressed. The parents naturally demanded an explanation and McCrimmon, seeing Dempsey's decline as a personal failure, resolved to give them one. Though Victor did not return to the school for the Easter Term — he never returned — McCrimmon arranged for the boy to see a psychiatrist in Toronto, at the school's expense.

Thanks to the analyst's skill, it all came out, every shameful detail of Dempsey's ordeal. No wonder his academic performance had faltered, no wonder his marks plummeted. No wonder he became — in one short term — so utterly withdrawn that he had to be removed from the school, his pride and identity stripped from him, a brilliant young life in shreds!

It all came out. How, night after night in that makeshift sanitarium at the top of Ormiston House

The paragraph was crossed out — the first excision of the page. A second attempt began at the bottom:

No details were spared. How he was

Again it was crossed out, so hard that the nib of Jock's fountain pen had cut the paper.

Paul snatched up the page, but the one below was mockingly blank.

He tore open the paper balls littering the desk, pulled others from the wastebasket, but they were all false starts, prototypes of page one.

Defeated, his glance fell upon the uncapped fountain pen lying above the pad: an old Parker, its lacquer worn dull, its nib bent back forty-five degrees. Paul could see the fresh scar on the desktop, a red-stained hole where the nib had bitten the wood.

The TV room lay at the end of a corridor through the new wing. He passed several doors adorned with ceramic cameos like those upstairs: Mildred, Hamish, Dorothea, Ian.

The door to the television room was slightly open, he heard coughing above the sound, male then female, call and response.

Paul was old enough to have enjoyed Hitchcock's later films at the cinema, had seen all of them on TV. This was deservedly one of the most famous — he recognized it from the soundtrack before he looked at the screen: the relentless crop-dusting aircraft, the sibilant, furtive rustle of the corn-field that offers Cary Grant no refuge in *North By Northwest.*

The audience was seated in comfortable padded chairs facing a ten-foot screen, the kind taverns use to show ballgames and boxing matches.

But this was anything but a sports bar crowd: they had dressed for dinner, elegantly casual, the men wearing light jackets, the women in summer dresses. With the action build-ing to a climax, only one person looked round as he came in, a woman in the back row with dangling earrings. She smiled in welcome, then turned back to the screen where Cary Grant had graduated to the highway, desperately trying to flag a rescue from the gasoline tanker.

Was Beale here? It was impossible to tell from behind the audience in the near-dark, but under any conditions, after twenty-five years...

The woman with the earrings turned again and whis-pered: "Can I help you?" Someone else, a man, shushed her. Paul went to her and squatted. Expensive perfume.

"I'm looking for Jock Beale."

"Ssshhhh!" carped the man.

"He's had a bad day," the friendly woman whispered in Paul's ear, vodka and lipstick. "He's sulking poor beast. Won't talk to anyone. Try the back garden."

"Pipe down!"

Paul whispered his thanks and backed up to the door. He waited long enough to watch the spectacular explosion as the plane crashed into the gasoline truck, then went out into the corridor and through a glass-panelled garden door to the right.

Paul saw him immediately, on a bench at the far side of the lawn. He sat stiffly with his pipe in his mouth, compact balls of smoke drifting away on the still evening air.

Jock Beale watched but did not stir as Paul crossed the lawn, though the puffs of smoke came somewhat quicker. He had grown thinner with age, the nose and ears more promi-nent, but his condition would have accounted for some weight loss. It was his fused-upright posture that made him recognizable, and his style of clothing that hadn't changed at all: a college tie, grey flannel trousers, an unseasonal school-master's tweed jacket — a pipe smoker's jacket with bagged-out side pockets full of paraphernalia.

"Good evening, sir." The form of address came out quite automatically. "I'm Paul Preedy. You spoke to my father on the phone this morning." He stopped before the bench and offered his hand.

Jock Beale looked up at Paul with moist amber eyes. "I know what I did this morning, Mr. Preedy."

"They paged you when I arrived."

"I heard it. You will forgive me for not running over. I imagined Mohammed would come to the mountain." Though the years were in his voice, the weakness was confined to the instrument itself — irony and intensity were both intact. "But Dinah paged fifteen minutes ago," he continued. "Whatever could you have been doing?"

Paul felt his face grow hot. He sidestepped. "I stopped by the TV room to look for you. It looks like a comfortable setup here."

The damp, tired eyes held him. Paul tried to remind himself that he was grownup, forty-two years old, but somehow he didn't quite believe it. He pocketed his hands. "Mrs. Colcomb told me to try your room. My father sent you a bottle of tonic. I left it on the desk."

"I see." The old man kissed smoke from his pipe, watching Paul's years drop away like a discarded costume until he was a boy again, playing at being grownup. Beale smiled, all-knowing. "At least now we can avoid covering the same ground. You must have so many questions."

"Yes, I do," Paul said weakly.

"I suppose you're wondering why I would bother with a letter when I knew you were coming."

"I think I understand. It's not the easiest subject to discuss with a practical stranger."

"Worse than that: it got the better of my Parker, did you see?"

Paul waited.

"I assume you read to the end. The letter lacks a conclusion, of course. The burning question having to do with *your* involvement in the whole affair. Your father tells me you are in the dark regarding Victor Dempsey. I take it no light has dawned since this morning?"

"That's right, sir."

With an effort, the old man edged sideways along the bench. "Sit down. Upwind, unless you've a taste for second-hand Cavendish."

"You have quite a pipe collection."

Beale stared ahead across the lawn as Paul took his place on the bench. "It's supposed to be the tongue with pipe smokers, isn't it?" Paul heard a far-off bubbling in his chest that might have been amusement. "Actually, prostate cancer is quite unspectacular until you have to go to the lavatory or it metastasizes. Your father told you, I expect."

"I was sorry to hear you were ill."

"So was I, Preedy. Apparently I don't qualify for this place any more." He gazed across the lawn where the fine house glowed warmly, gilded by the evening. "They can't accommodate large health problems here. Serves me right, though; I've been as smug as the others about our situation — retired gentlefolk still in our prime! None of your old fogies here, none of your nodders and wetters. There are people on the waiting list who've been dead for years!" The bubbling again from his chest. "But they don't have the pain control people, you see, so I've been given my walking papers."

Beale reached into his pocket for his pipe tool. His hands were old, skeletal beneath tight, papery skin, tremoring as he tamped the bowl. He had shaved carelessly. Paul could see the glimmer of errant whiskers, a speck of tissue bonded to a razor cut, a tiny white flower with a crimson centre.

Paul watched the swallows cutting through the nourishing

evening air, heard a sudden, full-bloodied whoop from the hockey game in the street.

Beale dropped the tool back in his pocket. "You must be wondering why action wasn't taken against you boys after we learned what happened."

Paul's expression hardened slightly. "Mr. Beale...I don't think you understand. *I* don't know what happened."

Beale went on as though he hadn't heard. "We did so much more than merely turn a blind eye, you see. We suppressed everything that was divulged to the analyst, so thoroughly that not even Dempsey's parents ever found out."

"To protect the school?"

"Of course. David King's father had made a fortune in the retail music business, did you know?" He said it with a delicate disdain. "Thanks to that, and his insatiable desire for respectability, Mr. King was at that time the school's wealthiest and most generous patron. Those were difficult days for Felton; if Dempsey's parents had found out about his ordeal, we would have had no choice but to expel David King along with you others, thus killing the goose that laid the golden eggs. The scandal alone, its effect on enrollment, might have been enough to sink the school. It was vital that we monitor and control the flow of information."

"Who is 'we'?"

"Basil McCrimmon and myself. But naturally we needed the analyst's cooperation."

"Sounds unethical. Who was this, an Old Boy?"

Beale's jaw muscles pulsed faintly under the thin, blotched skin as he worked on his pipe. "Close ties to Felton but not an Old Boy. Let's just say someone whose loyalty to the school was considerably strengthened by a generous cheque from Mr. King. He would have done anything to avert his son's expulsion in his last year. The analyst was new in practice, ambitious, short of cash..."

Beale returned his pipe to his mouth and stared out across the lawn, working the muscles in his cheeks as he smoked.

"Victor Dempsey remained in analysis for over a year,

though it would be nearer the truth to call it indoctrination. The analyst advised Dempsey that his best — his only — chance of recovering from his trauma was to observe complete and perpetual silence. In other words, to deny his experience in the sanitarium, even to himself. That was the 'therapy' prescribed by Mr. King, Basil McCrimmon, and myself, when what poor Victor needed, of course, was exactly the opposite advice. Who knows what damage was done. Who knows…" His voice trailed off for a moment. "We sold him down the river, Mr. Preedy. You see? We betrayed him." He removed his pipe, inspected the wet, greenish-stained bit, then faced Paul squarely. "Naturally we convinced ourselves that we were acting in the best interest of the school. We made excuses: unusual circumstances, Adams and King's last year, all that. But really, of course, it was a payoff that saved the lot of you."

"You're still including me. Why? What did I need saving from? I didn't *do* anything!" Neither good manners nor his natural deference to Jock Beale could hold down Paul's impatience now. "I don't even know what *they* did to him!"

A stray thread of Bernard Hermann's edgy score blew across the lawn from the TV room. Beale turned his head to the sound, wagged his pipe.

"*North By Northwest.* Seen it?"

Paul looked at him with a distaste he could no longer hide, aware for the first time that this wasn't mere eccentricity, that Beale was playing with him, a deliberate and tasteless game of withholding.

"Appropriate, hmmn? I expect you see yourself rather like poor old Cary Grant, the innocent victim, mistaken identity and all that. Poor hapless chappie up to his ears in someone else's mess. But it was yours, too, according to Victor Dempsey in the psychiatrist's office. It made little difference to him that you were not actively involved, that you made no…intimate contribution to his misery. Almost as junior as Dempsey, you were excluded from the menage, were given the job of standing guard at the top of the servants' staircase.

You were supposed to warn them of approaching authority, usually in the form of Miss Dimmock, the Ormiston matron." The damp eyes widened encouragingly. "Hmmmn?"

Paul very slowly shook his head.

"Of course, it was a common enough occupation for juniors, wasn't it? Necessary to have someone on sentry duty for pillow fights, midnight feasts, all kinds of harmless nocturnal fun. Except that on one occasion, outside the Ormiston sanitarium, you apparently — how should I put it? — exceeded your mandate. It was in the early stage of Dempsey's ordeal, before he became hobbled by fear or torpor; on this particular occasion he endeavoured to escape his tormentors, had Miss Dimmock's name on his lips as he fled across the landing to the stairs. Though the same age, you enjoyed a vastly more robust physique, easily overpowered him, held him with your hand over his mouth to quiet him until his pursuers arrived to reclaim him. I doubt that your services in that capacity were required again: Dempsey quickly learned the code of silence. Perhaps, for his own survival, he learned to extract pleasure from his humiliation. Which is why victims of sexual abuse seldom complain, or so we are told; they feel responsible. Guilty.

"Your role was that of watchman, although boys in traditional schools such as ours don't keep watch, do they? Like their English cousins at Eton and Winchester, Felton boys keep *cave*, *n'est ce pas*?"

Beale's pale lips closed on the pipe, made quick little kissing sounds but the tobacco was cold.

"Though you have no doubt long abandoned your schoolboy argot, you have surely retained sufficient Latin to remember what *cave* means, hmmn?" He gave the bowl of his pipe a close inspection.

"'Beware.'" Paul cleared his throat. "It means 'beware.'"

Beale turned away and knocked the pipe against the end of the bench. The dottle shot out onto the lawn, a black nut that bounced on the short grass. "Should you 'beware' now,

Mr. Preedy? What is your feeling, based on yesterday's strange events?"

Paul watched him narrowly. "What do you mean?"

"Perhaps I should include myself in your company, even though I was… snubbed yesterday. I am, after all, more responsible than you for Victor Dempsey's having drifted off into a no-doubt tormented obscurity. Who knows what psychological ravages that torment has exacted over the years."

Paul felt something grow cold inside. "You're saying you think it was Victor Dempsey yesterday? You think he's…"

"Forgive me!" For the first time Beale smiled broadly enough to show long brown teeth. "Such melodrama! Actually my guess is that your little charade was organized by David King by way of confession. King was himself a tormented creature, though I'm sure his persecution began long before he joined us at Felton — sadism isn't the exclusive preserve of the privileged. King was not only weak, he was an angry boy, and predators can smell anger like blood in the water; anger promises rage, which escalates to frenzy, which is exquisite entertainment for the bully. Of course, it's no mystery that David King acted as he did towards Victor Dempsey: he had merely learned the ways of his tormentors as victims so often do. The vicious cycle of abuse. It's all about power, isn't it?"

"Mr. Beale, there's no way King set us up. I saw his reaction, he was terrified yesterday."

"Well it certainly wouldn't have been Adams. Not stupid, but mentally lazy, not nearly complex enough for something like this. Popular boy, the antithesis of King. A genuine school hero. Adams no doubt thought he was God's gift to a junior like Dempsey, probably thought Dempsey would enjoy himself like the devil if he gave it half a chance. As I say, a lazy, sensual boy, but there was nothing cruel in Adams. A case of hormones and *laissez faire*, I would imagine."

Paul tried again: "Exactly what form did the abuse take?"

Beale pocketed his empty briar and got up. He began

walking towards the house, stiffly, but with the same floating, ramrod gait. "Les Meas…measles! Isn't that fun!"

Paul followed hard, trying to hold down his anger, to keep it from terminating the interview.

"Mr. Beale…please. I know that's where your letter ended. I appreciate…"

"You know what the popular options are, Preedy — fondling, frottage, buggery…? Use your imagination."

"Tell me!"

Beale jerked to a stop so abruptly that Paul almost ran into him from behind. He tottered. Paul reached to steady him but he shrank away. He fumbled his hands into his jacket pockets, seeking the comfort of his still-warm pipe, his soft tobacco pouch.

"Listen Beale: I drove a long way tonight, at your request. I had games and innuendos yesterday, all I can take. I want to know what happened to Victor Dempsey. Now! Was he penetrated?"

The headmaster turned very slowly. "Do you remember Miss Dimmock, the Ormiston matron? Did you know that she was dismissed after the Dempsey affair? She really should have noticed the blood, even after their attempts to remove it. Actually they made Dempsey do it, scrub and soak his pyjamas and bedding and then lie in them, damp."

Beale watched the shock on Paul's face, heightened by weak, intermittent, but undeniable undershocks of memory: a boy at the basin, the sound of running water, swathes of white sheeting…

Seeing this, the old man's mordant, Latinate eloquence was rekindled. "But that was later," he continued. "They had to break him first, subdue him. David King was grand inquisitor, his imagination particularly fertile given his own long history of abuse. King chose the washbasin as his instrument of torment, made Everett hold Dempsey's head under the water, titillated by his struggles, lashing his buttocks until the struggles weakened. Blanket baths after that, something you were all regularly submitted to, in a brisk and modest fashion, by Miss Dimmock. But the blanket baths devised by King were different altogether — prolonged and anything but modest. Ormiston House was equipped with large, coal-fired boilers, Preedy; the water ran absolutely scalding hot, even up to the third floor. Apparently King became quite expert in its...application."

"What...?" Paul's voice was no more than a whisper.

"It was King and Everett, mostly King. Adams would have no part of Dempsey's initial subjugation, but he did nothing whatsoever to stop it. Nor did he hesitate to avail himself of the fruits of their labours. Dempsey told the analyst that Adams called him 'Victoria,' by the way."

For the first time it was clear to Paul that he was interviewing a dying man. He no longer felt anger, only pity and revulsion, the urge to be out of range of Beale's pitiless wet eyes and charnel breath, to run from the garden. But for a moment he couldn't move, immobilized by the first twinges of a familiar yellow pain, his upper lip cold with moisture.

It was Jock Beale who turned away, crossing the remaining short distance to the glass door at the back of the house. A swell of movie music as the door opened and Beale looked back.

"Give my regards to your father, won't you? Remind him that he owes me a letter. Two, in fact!"

The door almost closed behind him.

"And Mister Preedy? *Cave*, hmmnn?"

CHAPTER 16

THE VALMY LODGE Resort kept half a dozen four-litre thermos flasks on hand, to accompany guests on the many junkets it organized, whether on horseback, by boat or in hot air balloons.

When filled, a single flask weighed ten pounds, uncomfortable to carry far since the handle was thin wire and dug into the hand. But while Charles Allin Freer disliked physical exertion of almost any kind, he had made up a story for the room service manager so that he could personally undertake this errand in place of a waiter.

Charles stopped halfway across the empty sun terrace and put the thermos down. Night was falling earlier now, and they were getting the odd cool one; it was pleasant to feel the day's warmth, stored in the flagstones, radiating against his face and hands, to see the three-quarter moon rocking gently in the children's pool.

He jumped when the overhead lights snapped on at exactly eight-thirty, flooding the tennis courts, which made him think about Andy Adams again. A possibility had occurred to him on his way to the kitchen, and it did so again now: that Andy already knew what Charles knew about the guest in cabin six, and knowing made not the slightest difference to him.

Charles could easily have believed it; the man had the morals of a cat. On the other hand, Andy would surely never have been able to resist saying something — some little dropped remark, some casual innuendo to show he was in the game. After years of enjoying their back-and-forth, Charles was certain he could have instantly spotted such knowledge in his opponent.

He resumed his journey, confident that he had the upper hand, not even bothered by the weight of the flask, though he couldn't help wondering why she would want so much plain water. Perhaps she didn't trust the tapwater, as if anyone ever got Montezuma's at the Valmy! But then a lot of them were obsessed with bodily functions, he'd learned that from his favourite breakfast television show last week.

Charles always watched Sally Jessy Raphael unless he was on the morning shift. She'd had one of those people on before, but this time there was a whole chorus of them. Lovely people really, perfectly well balanced, which made complete sense when you considered the rigorous psychological testing they had to go through in order to get their surgery. A highly educational show, he'd nearly lost his eggs benedict when they started in with the anatomical details. In spite of the gruesome miracles of reconstructive surgery, Charles had learned, whatever else they could nip and tuck and pump you full of these days, hands and feet remained unalterable — what you were born with, that's what you got.

It was A. Bauer's hands and feet that had given her away — especially her hands, signing her Visa deposit on the first day. Totally convincing otherwise, he wouldn't even have looked twice at the hands if Sally Jessy hadn't been fresh in his mind. But as it was, the big hands had drawn his attention to the big feet, which had made him re-evaluate the smooth contralto.

But maybe he would have noticed anyway; he was in a people job after all. He had always found people fascinating, which was why he was going to be a writer one day, which was why he could not, over his dead body, have let the room service waiter run this particular errand tonight; it offered an irresistible opportunity to glimpse inside cabin six, a quick peek just to see how this person —transsexual person — *had* things.

Charles waltzed around a Triconfort resin recliner, his polished black shoes pattering happily on the flags, down broad stone steps, falling silent now on the velvet lawn around the premium enclave. One of the groundspeople had just finished shocking the premium pool, but even the caustic bite of unstabilized chlorine couldn't overpower the yin of oriental lilies around the cabin group. Behind them, the moon had rolled out a silver runway on Lake Simcoe, even the lights of Barrie looked romantic tonight, twinkling across the water — a dreadful place really, but if he squinted, he could almost imagine a Saint-Tropez or a Monte Carlo.

Charles stopped at the door of cabin six and pressed the bell, listening to its muted chimes. He'd known long before the show that they weren't all vamps and street walkers, that they didn't all put she-male come-ons in the personal section. He'd even known that the real ones weren't gay, nothing at all to do with it. What he hadn't known, and had somehow never imagined, was that some of them — this one at least — were rich enough for the Valmy.

He pressed the bell again, a flutter beneath his crisp hunter-green when a voice responded from within.

"It's open!"

Charles Allin Freer let himself in with a cheery, "Room service, madam!"

The resort's top-level cabins consisted of a spacious living room with adjoining bedroom and bath complex — Jacuzzi and sauna, with a hot tub on the enclosed bedroom balcony for winter nights. As in the main lobby, the cabin's opulent appointments seemed even more luxurious in contrast with the honeyed log walls.

Through the slightly open double doors to the bedroom, a perfunctory voice called: "You can leave it on the table." Then the doors closed fully.

To complete the anticlimax, Charles couldn't see a single one of A. Bauer's belongings: no clothing, shoes, makeup, no snacks, not even a paperback or a pack of cigarettes. He'd imagined Virginia Slims.

Nothing. None of the little telling things that were going to be in his book one day, his Valmy exposé that would put *him* on Sally Jessy, like those authors with the goods on the Royals, *raking* it in.

Charles crossed the room and placed the thermos on the bar coaster he had carried in his jacket pocket for that purpose — not even his keen disappointment could undermine his sense of propriety.

He was turning to go when he noticed a pair of sunglasses lying with open arms on the love seat. Not A. Bauer's. It was a man's pair, on a sporty turquoise cord.

They were Andy Adams's RayBan Wayfarers.

Charles was barely breathing as he tiptoed to the double doors, his polished shoes soundless on the Wilton carpet. The Valmy was a long-established resort, built in the days when all doors — even interior doors — were supplied with lock and key, though most of the keys had long since gone missing. He dipped to one knee, sinking into the plush carpet as he sighted down a classic keyhole.

What Charles Allin Freer saw was itself so garishly classic, so typical of any routine sex-farce, that at first he was certain he had imagined it.

He had a clear and complete view of the bed on which Andy Adams lay naked, bound hand and foot with yellow nylon rope.

Farcical or not, the sight robbed Charles of his saliva and his immediate sense of urgency. For a few seconds he failed to ask himself why Adams should have his head raised towards the door, or where outside his narrow field of vision A. Bauer might be. For a moment he saw nothing but Andy's erection arching up and back like a glorious rainbow, practically to his sternum, until the keyhole went black and the left-hand door flew open.

Charles was very quick. In an instant he had twisted away and was dabbing at the carpet with his pocket handkerchief.

"Just a bit of water, madam." He pressed his hanky onto the wool with a convincing grunt of thoroughness. "There we are, all gone. Sorry about that, madam." He stood and turned to the door, avoiding A. Bauer's eyes even though she was, as always, wearing the Picasso sunglasses as well as all her clothes. The eyes knew, a certainty that prickled the back of his neck and made him want to run. He didn't know why. He didn't expect her to believe him but what could she possibly do or say?

"Wait!"

Charles forced himself to smile as he turned. She was also smiling, though very slightly.

Her right hand was behind her back. She used her left to remove the glasses.

The sight of her eyes milling shapes like a kaleidoscope

sticks and stones

raised the hair on Charles's scalp. He stood frozen with a terror quite beyond the range of rational scrutiny while she came over the thick, soundless carpet at dreamspeed, taking forever,

her right hand behind her back

until she was an arm's length away, where she at last brought her hand into view and let him see the crisp new twenty-dollar bill.

"You may go now."

He swallowed dry. "Thank you."

Charles's voice, when he replayed it outside the door, again and again on the return journey to the lobby, sounded a full octave above hers.

By the time he was safely back behind his reception desk, Charles had made a resolution: there would be no more friendly banter with Adams over the counter; he would no longer aid and abet Adams's extracurricular activities, didn't even want to know about them any more. This would be the end of all that.

Charles knew when he was out of his depth.

His decisiveness made him feel a little better, though he still had to try very hard, all night, not to think about her eyes.

ANDY ADAMS HAD been surprised at first to hear Charles's voice from the living room, but not for long. He understood now what Charles had meant about Arabella Bauer and how interesting he must be finding it.

She had told him five minutes before room service arrived, right after she asked him whether he had any problem with bondage. Of course he didn't. Did she want him to tie her up, or vice versa?

Vice versa, both of them smiling at its resonance when she added, casually, that she was a transsexual.

Andy's smile and his easy body language betrayed neither surprise nor discomfort. He didn't really feel any. He had entertained too many older women, had dispensed too much reassurance about the imperfections of the flesh — veins and wrinkles, saddlebags and time-flattened behinds — to find himself at a loss now.

And he had been happily deceived in this way before, as a teenager on the Toronto subway, coming home late and quite drunk from a party, alone for once. A tall, unusually elegant young woman on the far platform with a black male companion. When the man had beckoned, Andy had seen a pimp with his best working girl and had clowned for them, pulling out his empty pockets with a rueful grin. When the man beckoned again, and the woman too, he had crossed over. Later, the black man had watched and poured champagne (incongruous and touching in their cold-water apartment), while Andy discovered that the elegant woman was an elegant and biologically intact male. Hormones had supplied lovely breasts, but the debit side, he was told sadly, still awaited the necessary funding — such operations were not, at the time, covered by health insurance. In the heat of the moment, Andy had barely noticed the unattended business tucked between her slim legs and the very slight rasp of beard as he took her, anally, with unreserved pleasure.

He assumed that funds would not have been a problem for Arabella Bauer. He imagined an operation at some exclusive and luxurious clinic in Switzerland or Scandinavia, and it was the thought of what they must have done for her — a perfect little custom vagina (from a catalogue?) and flawless silicon breasts (he actually preferred small nipples) that had inspired the erection he had been unable to achieve watching Marilyn Chambers. He thought he would probably break his own rule and let himself come tonight with Arabella Bauer.

Andy automatically reached down to stimulate himself, reminded of his situation by the gentle bite of the rope securing his wrist to the bedhead. Frustration, mild pain, significant pleasure — bondage wasn't really Andy's thing, but he'd done this before too.

He raised his head from the pillow, listening to the expectant silence in the cabin. He hoped she would surprise him, something other than black patent leather and a dog collar and a cheap toy whip from a sex boutique. After twelve solid hours of Mrs. Merrill, Andy didn't want to have to act interested.

Interesting that she hadn't taken her sunglasses off yet. He hoped she wouldn't now; the masquerade, where you didn't know your partner's identity, was a timelessly erotic idea.

Andy lifted his head again, but could see nothing through the partially open bedroom doors. It was two or three minutes since Charles had left (nosey little bugger, there'd be some mileage in that when Andy got a chance to think about it), but he hadn't heard another sound.

For a moment an alarming thought crossed his mind — that he was the victim of a practical joke, even something of Charles's doing, in which he would have to stay here like this, helpless, for the chambermaid to find in the morning.

Then Arabella Bauer came back into the bedroom.

She did surprise him, but only by the fact that she hadn't undressed or changed at all: the only difference was the roll of two-inch-wide black electrical tape in her hand.

"Would you object to being gagged? You don't have a cold or anything?"

Andy smiled. "No."

"Is that your last word? How ironic, you especially."

A six-inch strip of tape fixed his mouth in a somewhat puzzled but accommodating smile. She had already proposed to give him two thousand dollars tomorrow morning — for that size of gift, he was prepared to reciprocate in any way he could.

Andy's first alarm didn't sound until she had unbuttoned and was rolling up the sleeves of her pale blue silk blouse, and he saw her arms.

Her inner wrists and forearms were cross-hatched with deep white scars. Left and right arms, too specific to be anything but self-inflicted. He gave a muffled upward grunt.

"I think it's only fair to tell you right here," she said quite cheerfully. "I've got a hygiene problem."

Andy could see himself in her sunglasses as she faced him — two spreadeagled Andys with black Raggedy Andy smiles.

"Can you guess what my problem is, Adams? You like games, don't you? How about a clue? Okay, it's a bad problem. I think it's incurable."

He could see his eyes, two pairs of eyes, wide with apprehension. He could see the whites.

"Can't you guess?"

Sweat broke out on his face, spreading down his body like a storm front. He could hear his heart. His erection had telescoped in, a terrified animal.

Like everyone else in the last ten years, Andy had heard all the true and apocryphal stories, about the misogynists and man-haters with AIDS, committing deliberate, post-dated murder. This person was clearly unbalanced, the scars alone...

"Give up, Adams?"

Andy strained against the ropes. He began to make bovine sounds behind the gag.

"You're thinking about AIDS, aren't you? And so you should be." She smiled silently for many seconds, while his terror built itself into a darkly glittering monument.

"Kidding. Not AIDS. But don't relax. I have what's called a recto-vaginal fistula. It means I have to wear a colostomy. You understand? A shit bag."

She came closer, within arm's reach. He could smell the Obsession.

"I shit in a bag between my legs because they botched my cunt. I shit out of my cunt, Adams." Her smile again, like a raw crescent scar. "I always hated toilet mess and now I have all this shit and smell to carry around and I've never even said thank you. So here we are. See?"

Andy's eyes bulged, his face sheened with sweat as he strained in vain against the ropes, his hands and feet puffing purple because she had fashioned the knots to tighten. But if he lay still for even a second he *would* comprehend, the last thing in the universe he wanted to happen.

"Now we've got another hygiene problem: yours. I don't think we're ever going to get you clean, but believe me we're going to try." She started towards the door, then turned back as if on an afterthought. "Oh yes, I'm going to do something bad between your legs after your bath. I thought I'd mention it because I expect you've been worrying about that as well.

Anyway, you're going to have your bath first. Get you prepped. Ever had a blanket bath, Adams?"

Andy thrashed in a blind frenzy, but the bed was of the same solid quality as everything else at the Valmy. By the time he finally gave up, she had gone and come back and was standing close beside him holding a large stainless steel container in both her hands.

"We'll go slowly, how's that? Lots of time for me to answer your questions. You won't have to ask them — I already know what they are." She smiled and licked her lips. "You're in hot water, Adams. How hot? Okay, I'll give you some idea."

She took her sunglasses off. She was tipping the flask to pour as his pleading eyes found hers, brief wonder before he pinched them shut and began to shred his vocal chords.

C H A P T E R   1 8

PAUL ENTERED SLAGG'S Hollow shortly after nine-thirty, descending with the barometric pressure. He'd had the air conditioner on most of the way back from Hamilton, to cut the stifling atmosphere in the Subaru.

He got out of the car and stood for a moment outside the front door, tasting the promise of rain in the flinty air, beguiled by a waft of Perry Como from the Dampneys, the music of their lost era. Martini music. Like so many of their friends, Dal and Sheila Dampney had been boozers but never drunks, never relaxed their manners or their hospitality. "Uncle Dal" to all the children. The kind of man that offered everyone over twelve a cigarette, then lit it for them. What they used to call a "good mixer," people and cocktails.

Paul fumbled his front door key as the phone rang, reverberating harshly inside the empty house. He hurried to the only phone remaining in the house, in Celia's study, and picked it up mid-ring.

"Paul Preedy. Hello?"

Silence, a second too long, then a click, ominously gentle, then the unrelenting tone.

Someone who knew the house was in transition and usually unoccupied, waiting for the right moment to back up a moving van? Perhaps it was a good thing he had decided to stop by tonight.

Paul wasn't sure yet whether he wanted to stay, only that he was too tired at this moment to drive the remaining two hours to Bancroft. Exhausted, in fact, in no proportion to the relatively early hour. An emotional fatigue, courtesy of Jock Beale.

He wandered into the living room, disoriented for a moment as he stared down at the bright rectangular print on the otherwise sun-faded broadloom where the sofa had always been.

He climbed the stairs heavily, turning on lights as he went, some long-inactive homing device guiding him not to the green guest room but to his old narrow bed. He let his head sink into the pillow and shut his eyes, but his mind refused to rest. Houses of cards, the same kind he had built and collapsed and rebuilt, profitlessly, all the way back from Hamilton, replaying fragments of his conversation with Jock, nagged by things he felt powerless to resolve.

Why did he have no memory of Victor Dempsey? Because Dempsey's stay at Felton had been so brief, because he was in another house, because Paul had had no understanding of what was going on during his hours of keeping watch by the servants' stairs at Ormiston?

Or was it the other way round? Was Jack correct with his Nietzsche, about memory and pride? Had Paul known so well what was taking place behind the sickroom door that pride — or shame — had driven memory to ground?

Before Clifford's death, Paul had seen memory as a tantalising mystery — something that came in a taste or a sound, or sometimes, stunningly, in a smell. But often there was no identifiable trigger, as though a tiny seizure, a random electrical storm in the brain (though it felt like the soul), was

flashing him vital epiphanies. The first twinge, perhaps, of
the momentary spasm death is supposed to bring, wherein
your whole life passes before you.

Then, suddenly, there had been no past, no memory beyond Clifford. Paul's grief had been a solid red door
slamming shut behind him.

Cliff with only three years of memories, such a little stock,
such a poor show for his final doomed seconds.

Paul took a long breath and opened his eyes, mastering
the wave of sentiment, rerouting the energy of the deeper pain.

He could do that. Thinking of Tom could do it for him now.

He lay with his feet over the end of his childhood bed,
looking up at the old elephant with its trunk in the air, feeling
Tom close beside him with the Lego in his hand.

With a pool cue, coming to Paul's aid.

Boy oh boy.

Paul wanted to sleep on that, but his eyes wouldn't close.
They moved down to where the open bedroom door hid all
but a few inches of the framed photograph behind it. He
didn't want to see it now. He wanted to think about the future, not the past. He'd had enough of the past for one day.

He got out of bed and turned on the light and pulled back
the door, but the school photograph offered nothing more
than it had yesterday evening after the reunion. Once again
he found King (hunched and glowering) and Adams (cock of
the roost), comically antithetical as he had observed at the
reunion, as Jock Beale had pointed out tonight. He found
Everett, somewhere between them in type, a plain middle-
schooler, as little marking him for early death as marked any
of them for dire cruelty. He studied Jock Beale, smug and
erect amongst the prefects in the centre, a false god surrounded by his acolytes; after tonight, Paul would always see
in this picture the forebear of a sick old man in a Hamilton
garden, reduced to a cynical, lickerish cruelty.

Paul tried, as he had tried on Sunday evening, to find Victor Dempsey, had worked his way through half the juniors in
the first two rows when he stopped.

He wasn't there.

Of course. Dempsey would have already left the school by the summer of 1966. He only had one term, the Christmas term of '65.

His straight A's became B's, then C's...

He never came back in the new calendar year.

Somehow the realization brought Paul a sudden emptiness, an anxious, undeniable need to see Victor Dempsey's face.

What about the Felton magazines, the first items he had unearthed in the attic on Saturday night with Celia? The first annual surely covered Christmas Term 1965. A small picture, the briefest mention...anything was better than the sudden nothing of this photograph.

Paul went out into the corridor and was looking for the pole with the hook on the end to pull down the trapdoor when he heard the phone ringing downstairs in his mother's study.

As he expected, rather guiltily, it was Celia.

"I was just going to call you," Paul told her. "I'm on my way home."

"Good. How was Jock Beale? Does he know who Les Meas is?"

"He didn't shed any light on the present, but he told me one incredibly depressing story from the past. I'll fill you in when I get there."

"Did you get a call in the last half hour, from someone at your plant in North Carolina?"

"No. Why?"

"That's odd. Someone phoned here for you, about half an hour ago. A woman. She said she was from your work, from CPE, needed to talk to you."

"Did you ask her why?"

"She said it was to do with the extruding machinery, something technical. Said it was urgent, she needed to talk to you right away. I told her to try the Hollow in case you were planning to stay there tonight."

"What was her name?"

"I didn't ask. She said she was calling from Jim Jessop, the maintenance supervisor."

Paul frowned. "That's weird. If it was so urgent, why haven't I heard? Why wouldn't Jim call me himself?"

"I didn't particularly like her voice."

"What do you mean?"

"It certainly wasn't any North Carolina accent I've ever heard."

"So what?" Paul listened to a strange, suggestive quiet on the line.

At last Celia said: "Do you want to know what your father told me today? He reminded me of the clinical name for German measles."

"Sorry?"

"It's called Rubella."

"I'm not with you." Paul frowned at the phone. Then, gradually, he began to chuckle. "Not this again. Come on, you can't be serious. German Measles Bauer? Give me a slight break!"

"Is it any more far-fetched than Les Meas?"

"Certainly. Anyway, why are you telling me this now?"

"Okay, forget it," she said, airily indignant. "Just hurry up and come home."

"I'm going to call the plant first. If Jim —"

"Call from here. I don't want you staying at the Hollow any longer tonight. I want you back at the farm."

He smiled. "Curfew?"

"Don't be smart."

"Mother's intuition?"

"Just come home please. We want to hear about Jock Beale."

Paul called the plant. Jim Jessop wasn't there, or even home in bed. He was in Baltimore, Maryland, on a course. The night-shift supervisor, an experienced man named Royal Mitchell, informed Paul that all the machinery, including the extrusion equipment, was running sweet as syrup. He checked if anyone had phoned Canada long distance. No one had.

Paul sat at Celia's desk for several minutes, thinking about the phone call when he had arrived here tonight, the too-many moments of silence before the caller hung up. It would have been about twenty-five minutes ago, right after Celia's call.

He sat in his mother's old study chair, looking at the walls that had been hidden all his life by books. Celia's had always been the most accessible kind of intellect, feminine if you could put a gender on it. Intuitive. It was what made her a good teacher and a great parent. Paul remembered all the hours he had visited in this study with her; whether she was writing poetry or reading, or swamped with term papers, there was never a second's hesitation nor a trace of resentment in her welcome. School problems or affairs of the heart, even health worries would bring him to Celia long before he would ever —*if* ever — have confided in Jack. And his mother's advice — read intuition — was always on the money. It was a matter of record.

Paul went back upstairs, not to the attic but to the green guest room, to the drawer in the night table where he had left the return portion of his airline ticket. He carried it down to the study where he used directory assistance to get the American Airlines number at Pearson International. Checking in at Durham airport last Friday, it had struck him that his own name printed on the charter ticket was inconsistent with Arabella Bauer's story of the cancelled sales convention. He had meant to confirm it with the ticket agent, but Tom had distracted him. He hadn't thought of it again until now.

But now, somehow, it was time to look again.

A recorded voice came on and instructed him to push one for tickets and reservations, where a real young woman asked how she might help him.

"I have a question, please," Paul said. "Would it be unusual for a business traveller, say someone going to a sales convention, to be taking a charter flight?"

The young woman took the question in professional stride: "That depends, sir. If the company was sending enough representatives, if they were guaranteed that the convention would be going ahead on a specified date, then yes...they might book a charter. You wouldn't have seen it much in the eighties, but in the present economy, everyone's saving where they can."

"The company would want the convention dates guaranteed because you can't exchange charter-class tickets, isn't that so?"

"That's correct, sir."

"In fact, you can't even have the name changed, can you?"

"That's correct. It's not like a regular Y-class ticket. A charter ticket is non-transferable."

"I'm sorry to keep you on the phone with this."

"That's quite alright, sir."

"So let me get this straight: if someone had a charter ticket with American Airlines that they couldn't use, and they promised to sell it to me for half-price..."

"Then I'm afraid you'd be disappointed, sir. Has somebody promised you that?"

"They already sold me the ticket. I *flew* here, to Toronto, on it. I'm flying back to Durham on the return portion at the end of the week."

A judicious note in her voice: "Then that person's name must still be on the ticket. You realize, sir, that it's illegal to fly under someone else's name. I'm very surprised you got through security; your identification is supposed to match the name on the ticket."

"But it does. My name *is* on the ticket."

"Then it must have been originally purchased in your name, sir. Would you like me to double-check that it's charter class?"

Paul gave her the flight numbers, his mind generating questions at computer speed as he listened to the clacking of her keyboard.

Arabella Bauer had lied? She had bought the ticket in his name and tried to hide the fact?

Why had she bought it?

Because she had wanted him to fly to Ontario on August 23 to spend time with Tom, benignly promoting Eva's ultimatum?

Or because she wanted him to attend a school reunion?

"Yes, sir, that is a charter flight, both ways. Do you wish to be confirmed on the return flight?"

"Yes. Thank you. Thanks for your help."

"Uh huh."

Paul sat absolutely still for several minutes. He heard a sigh as the wind tested the circle of trees around the property. He heard the first light ticking of rain against the study window. At last he reached for the phone.

He didn't need to consult his wallet for Andrew Adams' number — he had called it often enough in the last twenty-four hours. His meeting with Beale had hardly diminished his store of questions, and now he had a new one, a specific question that burned for an answer.

But it was the usual story at the Valmy Lodge Resort: the same rather fussy male receptionist asking Paul to wait while he phoned through, then Adams' phone ringing unanswered, then the receptionist again, would he care to leave a message?

With nothing to lose, Paul fired off a wild shot: "I'm an old school friend of Andy Adams; I'm sorry to bother you with this, but are you personally acquainted with him?"

The man's voice took on a wary formality: "I'm not quite sure what you mean, sir."

"You don't know him?"

"We are employed by the same hotel. I believe you have called before, isn't that so?"

"That's right."

"May I ask the reason for your enquiry?"

"Yes you may. I'm looking for a mutual friend of ours. I was hoping Andy would know where I could get in touch with her."

"I can only give him the message, sir. Would you like me to pass on the name of this mutual friend?"

"Sure. It's Arabella Bauer."

Paul hear a sharp intake of breath. "I see," said the voice, no longer coolly composed.

"Does the name mean anything to you?" Paul asked.

For a moment he thought they had been cut off. Then the receptionist spoke again, quietly now, sounding much nearer: "You must understand, it's not hotel policy to divulge information regarding our guests."

"Of course not."

"However, since you have called several times already, I'm prepared to make an exception."

"I appreciate this."

"There is a guest by the name of Arabella Bauer presently registered in the hotel."

The receiver felt slippery in Paul's grasp. It took him several seconds to find his voice, even then he was muddled with excitement: "I'm...how long? I mean when did she book in?"

"I hope I haven't created any difficulty, sir." A glimmer of satisfaction in the voice. "I can give you her cabin extension if you require it, but you won't reach her now, she left the hotel half an hour ago."

"You're sure about that?"

"Positive, sir. I summoned the parking valet for her personally."

"About how long would you say it takes to get from the Valmy Lodge to Toronto?"

"What part of Toronto?"

"Do you know where Slagg's Hollow is?"

"I believe so. I would say three-quarters of an hour. Much longer, of course, in weekend traffic."

"Thank you. Thank you very much."

"Will you be visiting the resort?"

"No. But I want Mr. Adams to call me as soon as possible. Please tell him it's urgent." Paul left the Bancroft number again and hung up.

His finger went to his upper lip and came away damp.

Why had he asked that last question? Why did he feel an

overpowering desire to do as his mother said, to be up and
out of this house?

He was curious, excited, but surely not afraid. Of what? He
was a practical man, an engineer. Danger was when maintenance failed to check the breakers on a polyfilm roller and a
long-haired worker forgot to wear a safety bonnet. Danger
smelled of steel and machine oil and acrid electrical smoke.

It smelled of chlorine.

Paul slammed the thought away and stood up. He wasn't
going anywhere right this minute because he had some un-
finished business to attend to upstairs in the attic. Because
there was another reason now to look in the Felton magazines: one of them, he knew, was supplemented by a school
register, listing the name and address of every alumnus of
Felton School, current at the time of printing. He didn't expect to find anything on Victor Dempsey, given that his stay
was less than one term (Beale and McCrimmon would never
have permitted his inclusion anyway), but somewhere up
there he was sure to find an address for David King. It might
well be out of date now but it was worth a try, even on the off-
chance of finding out whether King, too, had a friend named
Arabella Bauer.

Paul retrieved the pole to unhook the trapdoor, then pulled
down the ladder and climbed. He'd never liked this part as a
child, still didn't — the light switch was at the top of the ladder inside the attic, which meant you had to reach in through
the black trap to turn it on.

As he reached the top of the ladder he could hear the rain
coming harder — sparse but heavy drops, striking the roof
with gathering syncopation.

C H A P T E R   1 9

DAL DAMPNEY SAT on the dark porch of his handsome corner house in an old, paddle-armed Muskoka chair — unpatriotic as hell to call them Adirondacks — and drained the last drops of a vodka martini, with a twist. He lifted his other hand in order to ascertain the status of his Rothman's King Size, and took a long draw, taking comfort from the cigarette's glow.

Dal didn't like drinking alone, but he liked the ballet less. His wife was there tonight with Hope Taylor, for the buns and bulges. He'd made them both laugh like drains with that.

He missed Sheila. She was good company, fond of a sundowner herself and a full partner in Dal's other hopeless addiction to duplicate bridge.

He poured himself a third consoling cocktail from the shaker beside his chair. He didn't want to go and get another twist right now because he was watching something, so he fished for the cheerful scribble of lemon peel at the bottom of his glass, giving it an affectionate pinch to coax out its oils, sucking his fingers while he kept his eye on the creepy crawler on Highvale Road.

Dal's porch offered a perfect vantage point, right over his double-planted cedar hedge onto Highvale where twin points of red light moved slowly through the darkness — an all too familiar sight these days. Dal possessed a duplicate-player's eye for detail and a proprietary interest in the Hollow that over the years had fetched up a mortal loathing of the TV people and the rubber-necked Sunday drivers and the relentless bloody house hunters.

The creepy crawlers.

Dal remembered the days when the Hollow was the best-kept secret in Toronto, and its most desirable location — screw your Rosedale and Forest Hill. A sleepy village in the city, a lost world. But now they crawled all over the Valley all the time like vermin...like *this*, on a Monday night in the rain!

He watched the slow-moving car turn onto Fallingbrook, creeping past his driveway until it was opposite Jack and Cele's place where the brake lights bloomed.

House hunters. They didn't seem to care that there was a sold sticker on the realtor's sign — they stopped and gawked anyway. Christ, they'd march right up to your front door in the middle of supper, demand how much you wanted for it whether you had a sign on your front lawn or not!

Not that Jack and Celia would have to worry anymore. His friends of a lifetime, almost the last of the old gang, had finally succumbed. A few more weeks and they'd be gone, lock, stock and barrel. It wasn't in Dal's nature to be morbid about it, especially on his third martini, or to wish them anything but well.

He watched as a figure got out of the car and shut the door. He couldn't see a face from this distance, only that it was a woman, with black hair and wearing a light-coloured mackintosh.

Dal tapped a chrysalis of ash from his cigarette, levered himself out of the chair and went to the rail for a better look. In the dark, his cigarette point was the only visible thing about him, but he could see everything she was doing.

Not doing.

Just bloody standing there like a statue in the rain. Not moving at all — just standing by her small white car, staring across the road at Jack Preedy's place.

Dal turned and entered his house, easing the screen door open and shut, hurrying to the bookcase in the den where he kept his compact Bushnells. He took down the leather case, disappointed by its lightness, remembering now that Sheila had put them in her purse for the ballet. He might rib her about it again when she got back, the two girls fighting over the binocs to watch those big nancy boys leaping about: the battle of the bulge!

In the short time that he was inside, the rain had picked up, heavy drops patting the broad leaves of the hosta along his garden path. From the hallway, through the screen door, he saw the white car still there on Fallingbrook, but the woman was gone.

THE AIR IN the attic was thick and stifling; Paul felt as though he were trying to breathe with something wrapped around his head. The noise of rain on the roof had grown oppressive, dinning a few feet above his head, the water sheeting down, babbling in the gutters. In a momentary decay, he caught the sound of dripping from a distant, shadowed part of the attic.

With his eyes still adjusting to the dim light, he had to peer closely at the leatherette spines of the magazines, for the extra width that would indicate the presence of the register. But he felt it as he lifted the 1971 annual out of the cardboard box, an extra pound of weight.

It was one of those issues of *The Buckler* that had gone on arriving at the Hollow for years after he had left the school. He wondered if he had even riffled through it: by '71 his ties to Felton — even to his far-flung schoolboy friends — had begun to atrophy, the narrow world of boarding school gladly exchanged for the broad uplands of university life.

The register itself was at the end of the magazine, and went back to 1901, before which no accurate records had

existed. There were a great many names in very small print,
grouped in chronological order according to which term
boys entered the school, the names within the term-groups
arranged alphabetically. Next to each boy's name was his
birthdate, the name of his house, his leaving date, a tightly
abbreviated description of his athletic and academic achievements, if any, a note of his higher education, if any, and his
last known address. In most cases there was no recent history;
only those school leavers who joined the Old Boys' Association — often those who had enjoyed a distinguished school
career — had kept the editors posted as to their adult development.

Handling the magazines, Paul's hope of finding any mention of Victor Dempsey, let alone a picture, had dwindled to
nothing; he was certain that Jock Beale and Basil
McCrimmon would have seen fit to have all trace of him ex-
cised from the school's official memory. For that reason, to
postpone almost certain disappointment, Paul looked up
David King first.

King would have been about four years older than Paul;
assuming he was the usual new boy's age of thirteen, he
would have arrived at Felton either for the Christmas term of
1961, or the Easter or summer term the following calendar
year. Paul found him listed for the Easter term of 1962.

"KING, David Hubert. b 29.7.47. Cluffy. Left summer,
1966. 15 Dorset Street, Port Hope, Ont."

No scholastic or athletic achievements noted, nothing
about higher education as of 1971. The Port Hope address
was probably out of date — no doubt it had been his parents'
house, from which they might well have moved in their old
age. But Paul made a mental note of it.

He found Andrew Adams at the head of the next group,
summer '62. Plenty of athletic distinction here: "Tennis VI
(Capt.). Cricket XI (Capt.). Rugby XV. Swimming." But again
there was nothing current for the date of publication, not
even a home address, which was unusual in the Register.

Paul went forward to 1965, Christmas term.

Delves. Demooy. Dyson.

No Dempsey. Not a trace. Felton's dirty little secret.

Paul shut the magazine with a disgusted, dusty snap and dropped it on the floor. There was only one other possibility: the oldest magazine here covered Christmas term, 1965. He would be glad of even the slightest mention, one background picture, any connection at all...

He skimmed badminton and boxing notes, rugby matches won and lost, self-conscious teenage poetry, *Sturm und Drang*, some nice pencil drawings. The Motor Club had acquired a Citroën Deux Chevaux, a group photo including a very junior Paul Preedy, grease-monkeys frowning at the Citroën's transmission in pieces at their feet. The Drama Society had done Shakespeare, a photographic montage of the characters in dress rehearsal, with a quote under each one. The Cadets had been active that term, toy soldiers on manoeuvres in the snow...

Paul stopped and turned back to the drama page for a closer inspection. He realized he had become distracted, so daunted by the odds against finding Dempsey's name that he had been unwilling to examine any more text.

He found a cast list presented in an antique typeface, conforming to the outmoded (and chauvinistic) tradition whereby female characters are listed separately at the end.

It took a moment for the dark irony to strike Paul — the fact that Victor Dempsey had taken a female part, that he had played Maria in the Felton Christmas production of *Twelfth Night*.

Paul had to grip the magazine to hold it steady. Again the smothering feeling, the need for air, but he couldn't move.

Olivia, Viola and Maria: all three female parts had been played by junior boys. They appeared separately in the montage, an individual photograph of each player, in Elizabethan garb for the dress rehearsal, but without greasepaint. In spite of that, the only face Paul recognized belonged to a boy called Coatesworth who had been in Cluffy with him.

So which of the other two was Dempsey?

But he did know, with a certainty that went far beyond recognition.

A pale, lovely face above a lace ruff. A flop of soft blond hair between wide-set eyes, high, delicate bones in the cheeks, a full, dark mouth. Victor Dempsey had made a ravishing girl.

"I have dogged him like his murderer. He does obey every point of the letter I dropped to betray him…"

Paul's Shakespeare was rusty, but he was enough his mother's son to know that the Maria quote referred to Malvolio.

Kneeling under the rain-lashed roof, looking at the face, Paul felt something tighten his throat, making it even harder to breathe the suffocating air. Victor Dempsey had been beautiful — Jock Beale had certainly been right about that — but there was much more here than mere puerile beauty; there was a deep intelligence in the face and the slender, articulate hands. A sensitive, catholic intelligence that must have been equally at home in the classroom or the laboratory as on the stage, that bore out everything else Beale had said, that brought home to Paul for the first time the full outrage of the thing he was supposed to have abetted: the betrayal of such promise.

Held in thrall by the photograph, deafened by the hammering rain and situated nearly twenty feet from the trapdoor, Paul had to ask himself whether he had imagined the sound of the doorbell two floors below.

He stood and the sound came again, longer, unmistakable now that he was listening for it.

He closed the magazine and carried it towards the trap, using the length of his index finger to wipe sudden beads of sweat from the stubble on his upper lip.

He saw his own silhouette on the sloping attic roof as he descended the ladder, in the bright square of light projected like a movie screen from the corridor below, his image sharpening until it reached the focal point, then dissolving on the screen.

The doorbell sounded again, alarmingly loud, as he

reached the bottom of the main staircase. He crossed the hall, turned on the porch light, then opened the front door.

There was no one there.

Nothing but the rain, slanting grey rods that had already created a boiling river in the driveway, that threw a delicate mist against his face.

He shut the door and hurried through to the kitchen and switched on the light, squinting against the sudden glare from the hard bare walls, startled by the figure at the glass-panelled door until he realized it was his own gauche and vulnerable reflection.

He made a tunnel with his hands against the big pane before he unlocked and opened the door. Still no one. He called out, his voice self-conscious and impotent, drowned by the rain's thousand sibilant voices.

Then squishing footsteps.

And then a figure, stout and bumbling under an enormous green umbrella, emerging from the darkness across the back lawn.

"Didn't think anyone was home! Saw your mother's car, thought you'd left it for a decoy! Nice weather for ducks!"

"Uncle Dal! What the...come on in!"

"Can't. Sheila's home any minute. Why don't you lot come next door?"

"It's only me here. I was..."

"All the more reason. Weather like this you need a dry one."

Paul grinned. "With a twist?"

"You see? Where the hell were *you* when this house went on the market? I need neighbours who understand the ways of the Hollow. I need *Preedys* here goddammit! Listen, reason I'm here, I was sitting on my porch when I saw this character checking out your place from the road. Thought it looked a bit funny so I got the brolly and came over for a looksee. Found her round the other side of the house if you please, peering in the window!"

Paul's amusement had long dissolved. "A woman?"

"Thought maybe she'd seen the realtor's sign — getting so bloody cheeky these days."

"Did you talk to her?"

"Didn't get a chance to. That was the crazy part of it: soon as I called out — oh yes I did, I damn well told her she was trespassing on private property. They think they've got some God-given right. You'd think a bloody car in the driveway would tell them something, but oh no. Last week Sheila and I are having breakfast if you please... *breakfast...*" Dal caught the glint in Paul's eye and flapped his hand in hopeless dismissal. "Aaach! Who cares? Anyway, she took off."

"Maybe she was a friend of my parents."

"'Course she wasn't — they have the same friends I have! She was snooping's what she was doing."

"Did she say anything?"

"Hardly looked around. Just walked back to her car, calm as you please, drove away. Three minutes ago if that. Thought I'd better just ring the bell."

"I'm glad you did. Young? Old?"

"That's another thing, she looked frightful: no umbrella, nothing on her head — black hair all plastered down, mascara running all over the place — looked like the Fall of the House of Usher!" Dal flapped his hand again. "Anyway, you're home so we don't need to worry. You get yer galoshes on and come over!"

"I'd love to but they're expecting me in Bancroft. I only stopped by."

"How's everything? Tom having a good time at the farm? Listen...I never got a chance to say this the last few days, but Sheila and I, we were...what I mean is, we were very sad to hear what happened, Paul."

"We appreciated the card."

"Sheila was going to write again but...well..."

"I understand. Hey, I'll see you before we go, for sure."

"You better! And don't worry about the house, any more creepy crawlers, I'll send 'em packing."

Both men saluted, then Dal turned away. Paul watched, his

brow deeply furrowed, until his neighbour had disappeared into the darkness across the lawn, then he retreated back into the kitchen. He locked and bolted the back door, then turned off the lights on his way out into the hall.

He was hot with excitement now, his throat tight with it, his body very slightly trembling. The need to be gone, in the car and driving away, was so pressing he could actually taste it.

Five minutes and he would be. After one last call.

He went back into his mother's study and sat on the edge of the desk rather than in her swivel chair. He called directory assistance for Port Hope, Ontario, and asked the operator for a listing for King, initial D., 15 Dorset Street. He sustained a fresh spasm of excitement when the robot voice intoned a seven-digit number, then one of frustration when the number produced an answering machine. But it was unmistakably King's voice, high and nasal and pessimistic:

"I am unable to get to the phone right now..."

The universal message with its implied deterrent to would-be intruders: that the householder is at home but temporarily preoccupied — asleep or in the bathroom, or just at the tricky part of actually getting the ship into the bottle.

It would be worth a try anyway, no more than a two-mile diversion. Port Hope was on the way to Bancroft, its exit right there on the eastbound highway.

Two miles was nothing. He would drive all night if it helped him find out who was calling herself Arabella Bauer. Or did he already know?

CHAPTER 21

DAL LIKED SITTING on his porch in the rain, high and dry, but tonight's production had driven him indoors by ten-thirty.

The whole deck was taking water, his Muskoka was slick with mist, his Rothmans had fizzled out. Really something. It reminded him of the last Atlantic crossing they had made, on the Queen Mary with half a dozen of the gang just to be sure of a decent bridge game. Sheila talked about going again, but he hated to leave the house, justified after that creepy business just now, over at Jack's.

Dal stood in his hallway by the screen door and glanced nervously at his watch. The ballet would be letting out about now. Hope Taylor was driving. She'd had a cataract operation in the spring. Maybe they'd do the smart thing, go somewhere for a nightcap til the rain let up.

Dal jerked as he saw his garden in cold detail in a sudden stagger of blue-white light, jumped again three seconds later, at an ear-splitting crack of thunder.

He saw headlights in the driveway next door, Paul Preedy

poor sod, turning out onto Fallingbrook for his unenviable two-hour journey to Bancroft.

Another jagged flash, another terrific thunderclap, and another set of lights on Fallingbrook, coming from the east. For an optimistic moment he wondered if it might be the girls back early, but as the car came nearer, he saw that it wasn't Hope's.

It was the white car he had seen before, parked outside the Preedy's. That woman's car. Almost as if she had been waiting for Paul to leave!

Dal pushed the screen door open and went out onto the porch, heedless of the rain, watching to see if she turned into the Preedy's drive, perfectly ready to call the police if she did. But the car continued past. From his corner lot, Dal had a clear view of both roads; he could still see Paul's lights, climbing Highvale Road out of the Hollow to York Mills on the way to the highway east. He could see the woman's white car, creeping around the corner onto Highvale, accelerating now, but only enough to maintain her distance behind Paul.

Dal hung off the porch rail until both cars were out of sight, barely aware of the spume beading him from head to toe.

Something…the memory of the woman's face caught for a second in his flashlight in the garden; her lank hair, her eyes leaking black tears…

Something made Dal wonder if Jack Preedy had ever installed a car phone in the Subaru. It would be like Jack — another useful toy. Efficient. But then again, it was Celia's car, and Celia would hate the idea.

At least he had the number at the farm. He would call there.

CHAPTER 22

PAUL TRAVELLED EAST through the storm, his wipers flogging the driving rain. His jaw ached from clenching his teeth by the time he reached Port Hope at a quarter past midnight. He stopped at a self-serve gas station on the outskirts of town, where the cashier directed him to Dorset Street.

It ran steeply down the side of a hill overlooking Lake Ontario, the upper slope boasting a row of idiosyncratic mansions, everything from delicate clapboard to glowering Gothic stone. The houses on the lower slope were more secluded and had the best lake view, even bigger, judging by the sheaves of chimneys and high pointed gables thrusting up between massive trees.

Paul rolled slowly down Dorset, his side window open in order to see the numbers, his hair and collar soaked by the encroaching rain. He was already chilled from the air-conditioner that had been on since Toronto to stop the windshield fogging — he was asking to wake up with a sore throat tomorrow and for what? King probably wasn't at home, even if he was, he'd be in bed. He had been closed and uncommunicative yesterday at the school; he wasn't likely to open up after being dragged out of bed in the middle of the night.

Paul was on the point of deciding that his detour had been misguided after all when he saw the number fifteen engraved on the furthest of two stone gateposts on the south side. He had overshot the driveway slightly in order to read it, but he waited before reversing, so that the car coming down the hill behind him could pass. When it didn't, he looked again in the rearview mirror and realized that it must have turned off or parked because the lights were no longer visible. He backed up, then turned down a steep, overgrown drive, following it around an ill-defined turning circle. His lights had swung past two vehicles parked at the side of the house, King's pink Cadillac and another, smaller car. It looked like someone was home.

The house was of the Gothic stone variety, large and grimly handsome from a distance, but as his headlights crawled over it, he could see peeling paint on the front door and the window frames, a broken upstairs window boarded from the inside, missing shingles. It was still raining hard, the water sluicing from rotted eavestroughs, exploding onto the roof of the sagging porch below, about to punch through in one spot.

He left the lights and the engine on, and ran a gauntlet of weeds growing knee-high through the gravel, his trousers soaked and clinging to his legs by the time he reached the porch steps, hazardously soft and springy under his weight.

He pressed the doorbell button, but with water falling all around him, it was impossible to hear whether or not it had sounded; given the state of the place so far, it seemed doubtful enough.

He thumped with his fist and waited. Finally he tried the large hexagonal knob, more out of hopelessness than in any expectation of it opening.

But it did open, with a rising groan of protest from its stiff hinges. Embarrassed, he tried the bell again, listening through the open door to confirm that it was out of order.

He called self-consciously: "David? Is anyone home?" But even with the door open, the din of falling water would have drowned any reply from inside the house.

He stepped inside and pulled the door closed behind him, lifting his other hand in a swift involuntary motion to cup his nose and mouth.

The stench was palpable — of stale cigarette smoke and fried food and a general lack of sanitation. Worse somehow in the thick and stuffy darkness, without the car's lights shining through the open door. He removed his hand, tentatively, and called again, a sudden feeling of anxiety increasing at the sound of his own voice, unanswered in the dark.

Paul quickly opened the front door again and the Subaru's high beams thrust in, enough to show him a row of old-fashioned light buttons ganged in a brass plate just to the right of the door. The nearest one wouldn't depress, the next two were ineffectual, but the third produced a weak glow at the top of the stairs.

Paul went to the bottom step and strained to hear movement or snoring — he would have pegged King as a heavy snorer. Surely he was here, why else would the front door have been unlocked? And he had seen the cars...

"King?"

He called again — "David King?" — loudly, almost angrily from the stair's mid point, and again he heard nothing. There was only the smell, an unpleasant new one added to the farrago now, one that had grown stronger with every upward step. A diluted, rather bland meat smell that vaguely recalled boiled chicken.

He ought to go. He was in a ridiculous position. King — or perhaps his elderly parents — would be scared to death, maybe literally, if he woke up now. What if he had a gun? He was certainly the paranoid type.

Another step and he could see the dimly lit landing, closed doors and a single partially open one directly opposite the top of the stairs, darkness and deep quiet beyond the threshold.

Paul stood transfixed, in a sudden chilling sweat of indecision. His whole body tingled with the desire to turn and flee down the stairs and out to his car, a feeling so intense it was almost sexual.

He was looking at an ordinary panelled door, open a crack, and yet he felt a terror so childish, and for that reason so complete and with such potential to haunt him later, Paul had no choice but to exorcise it with a simple adult procedure, one he had performed for his own children on many occasions.

He was up the stairs before he could think any more, pushing first the door, then another light button on the wall beside it, turning to the bed to expose his fear as childish nonsense...

Paul staggered back as though he had been punched in the face, the point of his shoulderblade exactly striking the light button and plunging the room back into darkness.

He stood frozen, pressed against the wall, trying to pretend that the fleeting image of David King naked and rigid on the bed had been his imagination. But his eyes needed only a few seconds to adjust to the darkness, and then he could see the bulking shadow, the swell of the belly, the promontories of two big feet.

He reached, slowly, trembling, for the light.

He stared, with an undeniable curiosity now that the moment of his initial shock had passed, at the large, light brownish patches that appeared to cover King's giant body. They weren't blood. There was no blood anywhere except around his nose and open mouth.

Paul took a single, careful step forward. The blotches...what were they? Some kind of skin disease, something King had carried that was unconnected with his death? They almost looked attached to him, parasitical, repulsive.

As he took another, bolder step, his shoe caught something hollow and metallic, a gonging sound as a large steel kettle rolled ahead of him across the carpet, gleaming balefully in the weak light, lolling back and forth then lying still.

Paul stared at it for a long, frowning moment, long enough that when he looked back at the body, the physician's son — the boy who had pored over Jack's lurid medical texts — understood what the patches were.

They were blisters, monstrous blisters from which the fluid had evaporated so that the skin had gathered in loose bags. King's face was not directly affected, though the dried-flat, sunken eyes behind his thick glasses attested to the massive migration of body-fluid to the blistered areas.

Whether or not they had been the sole cause of his death, he had suffered massive third degree burns over most of his body.

Water burns.

David King had been horribly, deliberately scalded.

Paul's fear returned now, with the realization that the scalding could not possibly have been accidental, let alone self-inflicted: his posture was rigid, laid out; the bedding, still damp, was more or less undisturbed; his glasses rested properly across his nose. Not even someone with superhuman self-control could have sustained the mortal agony of such a burning and remained still.

He couldn't have been dead for long. Paul had seen him only yesterday. It was the manner of King's death, not his decay, that was the reason for the smell pervading the room, of boiled flesh.

Paul groped for the door, his gorge rising. He staggered out onto the landing, clutching the newel at the top of the stairs with both hands, anchoring himself as walls and doors waltzed sickeningly around him. Only the fact that he had not eaten since lunch, twelve hours ago, prevented him from vomiting, though it would have been less painful than the dry heaving that now racked and racked him until he was gasping for breath.

Until his spasms were cured, like childhood hiccups, by a shock.

"Paul?"

Shocked disbelief that he had heard his whispered name.

Damning his sick imagination and the irresistible impulse that forced his head around to look at the open door of King's bedroom.

He was dead.

The dead couldn't speak.

They couldn't walk.

Paul swooned, cold terror lancing down through his body, pinning him to the floor as he listened to the slow footsteps in King's room, saw the shadow on the carpet approaching the door.

"Paul Preedy?"

Paul groaned, the hairs all over his body dancing up from his skin as David King's tiny antithesis appeared in the doorway.

"Paul Preedy?"

A voice weak from its own trauma, and with the unnatural evenness of the traumatized.

"I was in his bathroom. You didn't see it. I heard you coming up. I didn't know who you were."

Paul's mouth hung in a stupid oval.

"I came here before you. A few minutes. I found him."

Paul didn't need to articulate it, his open mouth and a simple expulsion of breath produced the only word in his vocabulary:

"Who…?"

"Mary Swoffa. You saw my father tonight."

For a second the woman's eyes seemed to find focus. "Have you been contacted? Is that why you came?"

Registering nothing but his profound incomprehension, her tiny voice rose for a moment.

"My name was Mary Beale."

"Wha…?"

She gave up on him, turned back to the open door of King's room.

"I'm going to call the police now."

PART III

C H A P T E R 2 3

DETECTIVE SERGEANT SKOUFARIS weighed 250 pounds and wore a forty-two waist size. A fat man, but it didn't surprise anyone at Port Hope Police Headquarters — certainly not the female officers — that the framed photograph on his desk in the Criminal Investigation Branch showed the mother of his four children as a strikingly beautiful woman.

Skoufaris had sea-green eyes and a luxuriant Mediterranean moustache and a deep, resonant voice well-known to the residents of Northumberland and Durham regions: up until two years ago, when the demands of his young family precluded it, he had moonlighted as a disc jockey at CKFX out of Cobourg, an easy-listening station with low-key commercials — light classics and mellow jazz, no elevator stuff — taping his show if he was going to be on duty.

He had actually met David King once, back when the station had experimented with a serious classical program on Sunday nights, had taped an interview about organ music that had never gone to air; King's knowledge had been too esoteric, he had been too nervous and no amount of equalization could make his adenoidal voice fit for broadcast. It had been one of Skoufaris's rare failures. He was normally a sympathetic, skillful interviewer.

"Why were you surprised when your father called you last night?"

"We...haven't been close."

"Is there any particular reason for that?"

He saw the tightening. She had been in Interview Room One at the CIB for most of last night, couldn't have slept more than an hour or two. He decided to let the question lie.

"But your father called you shortly before nine last night to tell you that Paul Preedy had been to see him about the reunion, about Victor Dempsey."

"Yes."

"That he had explained Preedy's involvement to him, that he had revealed the details of the cover-up, how he and Basil McCrimmon and yourself alleviated the Dempsey problem."

"Not all the details."

"You mean he didn't tell Preedy that his daughter... that you were the psychiatrist who treated Dempsey."

"He did not tell him, no."

Skoufaris couldn't let it go now. "Why not? You said you weren't close. But close enough that he would want to protect you?"

"Himself. He feels guilty."

He noted the hardened tone. "For coercing you in the Dempsey affair?"

"Of course."

But there was more unsaid. Skoufaris wrote a note in the corner of Detective Wynnyates's original report and let it go at that. At nine o'clock this morning, even after a night of questioning, Mary Swoffa had impressed him: her silver hair cropped short to flatter her small, well-shaped head, an expensively plain grey linen dress with bravura touches of silver at her wrist and throat. At nine o'clock she had looked like what she was — a successful psychiatrist. Now, at nearly noon, she was reduced to a small, tired, middle-aged woman.

"Would you like another coffee?"

"Yes, please."

He got it himself, black without sugar, from the tiny coffee room at the back of the detectives' area. She held the china mug in both her thin hands, warming them in an already too-warm interview room, while Skoufaris flicked his green eyes around the confused, abominably written report. An offence to the eye, but for once he could forgive Wynnyates: it was surely the most baroque case he had seen in twenty-five years on the job, even more difficult now that the Barrie Police, the provincial and Metropolitan Toronto forces were all juggling pieces of it. Plus Detective Wynnyates had had to deal with last night's shock and tears.

"So your father called you to tell you that the Dempsey affair had resurrected itself with this reunion. I take it, then, that he was not aware of your current involvement with Victor Dempsey, in his present incarnation."

"That's correct. He did not…he doesn't know."

She drank half the coffee without enjoyment, in precise measures, like medicine. Skoufaris wished he didn't have to go over this difficult course a second time, but there was too much at stake to rely on her original statement in Wynnyates' report, to forego the extra dimension of a personal interview. Tired as she was, Dr. Mary Swoffa was being patient and cooperative because she, too, had logged enough hours of analysis to understand the importance of one on one. She must also have known that it was in everyone's best interest, including her own; they had a psychopath on the loose and two tortured and mutilated bodies; this interview was part of a process that would decide whether Mary Swoffa was charged with mischief or as an accessory to murder.

He pushed the report away. "Okay. Bring me up to date on Victor Dempsey. Or do we call him Arabella Bauer? Is it two people here?"

"You mean multiple personality?" She shook her head tiredly. "No. A complex pathology, but not that, at least not in the clinical sense. No more than you or I."

Mary Swoffa finished her coffee before she began to talk. She was repeating last night's statement, but not verbatim, and the coffee seemed to have enlivened her: her voice was modulated and actually pleasant to listen to considering the far from pleasant details it described. Her voice, if not her tired eyes, revealed a compassionate intelligence. She would, he thought in a moment of distraction, have sounded great on radio.

"After Felton, I didn't see Victor Dempsey again for over twenty years. By then I was working at the Clarke Institute of Psychiatry in Toronto. Do you know of it?"

Skoufaris nodded: he'd spent four years at 52 Division downtown, had escorted plenty of tormented and often malicious souls to and from the Clarke, an ominously sterile megalith at the outer edge of the U. of T. campus.

"What you may not know is that the Clarke Institute houses one of the most respected gender reassignment clinics on the continent." He knew that too but did not interrupt. "Gender reassignment," she went on, "is another term for sex-change, the procedure by which men, and occasionally women, take on the physical *appearance* of the opposite sex. I use that word advisedly: the Clarke is good because it recognizes the difference between appearance and a deeper sense of gender identity. For that reason, hormone treatment is liberally prescribed at the Institute, but applicants for surgery are rigorously screened: Wechsler Scale, MMPI, Brief Symptom Inventory, EEGs, criminal record — a fine net to catch anyone who is not a true, committed transsexual, anyone with any psychopathy that might be aggravated by irreversible surgery. In other words, to make sure the wrong people don't go under the knife."

For a moment she seemed to falter, like a runner off to too good a start who has forgotten to pace herself.

"Are you alright?"

She closed her eyes for a second, then nodded.

"In the summer of 1990 an applicant for reassignment surgery was turned down when his MMPI showed a 4-8 violent psychotic profile — highly unusual in transsexuals. I wasn't involved in the case, had no knowledge of it until a week after his rejection, at which time everyone at the Institute heard."

She paused, not for effect, but to gather nerve.

"Mid-morning on a late-summer Monday, the patient arrived at the clinic for his scheduled appointment with his councillor. He went to the women's washroom. A few minutes later he emerged naked into the main reception area, where he amputated his penis with a straight razor."

Skoufaris's breath was audible in his nose.

"The receptionist is still in therapy, but in the moment she acted with great presence of mind. Anywhere but a hospital, of course, and he would have died in minutes from loss of blood. It was only then, along with everyone else, that I learned the patient's name."

She looked at Skoufaris unwaveringly, encouraging the answer that he of course already knew, as though she needed relief from her own voice.

"Victor Dempsey."

Mary Swoffa reached for her empty mug and dialled it slowly on the desk. "I can't describe the shock. Something I had thought buried for so many years…for it to come back in this way. Reading his file was like a personal indictment: the suicide attempts, arrests for prostitution, drugs, assault, no record of any meaningful employment despite an IQ of 150." Her delicate hand blanched as it closed around the mug. "And I had helped create him, this psychiatric Frankenstein. I had taken his life from him. Everything. Even his ability to live with himself. For my thirty pieces of silver, I had betrayed Victor Dempsey, my profession, myself. All I could think about then was trying to give something back.

"The Clarke's gender reassignment program is exclusive: radical penectomy, self-inflicted or not, does not of itself qualify an applicant for admission. So then, right or wrong, notwithstanding his MMPI scores, I resolved to give Victor Dempsey the only thing he seemed to want: the surgical procedure he had already crudely initiated.

"I dropped almost my entire caseload for him. I had to — he was a walking bomb, enough concentrated rage to blow us both all over the walls."

"You told him who you were? He remembered you?"

"Yes, but not as his betrayer. The whole point was that he had trusted me, I had been his friend."

"Did you set him straight now?"

"I called in all my favours. I used every ounce of my influence at the Institute to adopt him as my patient. He had no money. I gave him money. I rented him an apartment, I helped him with…"

"Did you tell him?"

"I saw him through the bureaucratic nightmare of changing his legal identity after the operation, getting his name changed."

Skoufaris decided to let her off the hook. "He changed it to Arabella Bauer?"

"Yes." He saw a glimmer of gratitude in her eyes.

"How did the surgery go?"

"Not well. After the self-mutilation, there was no living penile tissue with which to…" She drew back slightly. "Do you wish me to be specific?"

"You're saying there were medical problems."

"Not immediately. They developed later. Detective Sergeant — does Paul Preedy know that Arabella Bauer is Victor Dempsey?"

"Only as of last night, on your information. He had begun to suspect that Arabella Bauer was the Les Meas of the invitation, but not that she was Dempsey, or a transsexual. Why do you ask, doctor?"

Mary Swoffa smiled for the first time this morning, her tired eyes suddenly glowing. "So his wife never told him. He might have put two and two together sooner if she had."

She saw Skoufaris frowning at the report and smiled again, tenderly. "Eva Preedy knew, you see. She saw it from the beginning but she was a loyal friend, as Paul Preedy well knows. She would have seen it as a betrayal of friendship, of sisterhood, to draw attention to such an insignificant detail about Arabella Bauer, even to her husband. She is a woman who believes in the power of transformation, of transcendence. Paul would testify to that."

She had drifted; now her tired eyes found him again. "But I'm ahead of myself." She sat up and took a breath.

"I had denied Victor Dempsey his truth and his anger and now I had to give them back, to Arabella Bauer. She had entirely blocked it, do you know that?" Mary Swoffa smiled bitterly. "I had been one hundred percent successful in my 'treatment' of the boy, so much so that the woman had no conscious recollection of the quarantine period, denied ever having had German measles. Do you know, she tried to prove it by having her GP mail me an old questionnaire she'd filled out, showed me her negative response to the rubella question! She had no explanation as to why she had chosen the name Arabella, insisted that it was a coincidence.

"We had daily, two-hour appointments. Weekends too, wherever he…" The remotest of smiles. "Wherever she felt most comfortable. As friends. It wasn't strictly psychoanalysis. I trained as a Freudian — interpretation, free-association, dream therapy — but this time I didn't need any techniques because I wasn't searching; I knew, of course, exactly what we were looking for and where to find it; we merely had to undertake the journey together. I knew only too well what trauma had led to my patient's present condition, knew that the outward symptoms — the early transvestism, the desire for an operation, the self-mutilation — that none of them sprang from a genuine desire to transform but to *escape…* from *all* sexual impulses, all of which carried a heavy freight of guilt and pain. It shouldn't take a psychiatrist to understand why."

She looked hard across the table at him. "He was deeply scarred, scars that had never healed. He was angry. Pathogenic anger in terrifying measure, his MMPI had showed it long before his spectacular performance with the razor. I had to give it its proper focus. I had to foment it." She looked closely at Skoufaris. "I had to teach Victor Dempsey — the boy — to feel his original pain again, directly, and then his anger. I had to teach him to hate again." Her voice dropped. "King and Adams and Everett and Preedy."

Skoufaris tilted his head. "And you?" It couldn't be avoided now.

She straightened defensively. "I had to gain my patient's confidence. That was my first priority now. It was not necessary to the therapy, at first, for Arabella or the deeper Victor to understand anything but the original trauma."

"I see." Skoufaris tried not to let his distaste show. "Go on."

"You must understand..."

"Please continue, Doctor Swoffa."

She took a deep breath, gathering strength and resolve. "Have you ever heard the term psychodrama? Encounter groups?"

He shrugged slightly.

"They are techniques for acting out emotional problems. Another contrasting form is Morita therapy, involvement in social activities where the patient is *discouraged* from baring his soul or analyzing his feelings, the rationale being that egocentricity makes neurosis worse."

He waited.

"I want you to understand that what we theorized was not so outrageous — really a kind of hybrid of some well-established therapies."

"But you did more than theorize, doctor."

Skoufaris hoped his voice did not betray a nudge of unproductive anger, but of course she was aware of it. She spread her delicate hands, palms down, on the desktop.

"The theory was to get the four of them to a reunion at Felton School. A sort of encounter group. The original idea was Arabella's. At first I thought it was misguided even in theory, harebrained, unwieldy, but I went along with it — *in theory* — helped her to develop it, encouraged her enthusiasm because it seemed to empower her, to give her life a focus. A healthy fantasy.

"I helped her research the four of them, nothing invasive, certainly nothing illegal — just enough at first to ascertain what they were doing and where they were living. We knew that Everett was dead, killed in a farm accident when he was nineteen, which left only three of them."

Her eyes opened wide. "You must believe that I never once imagined it coming to anything. Theoretically — professionally — the reunion idea had become intriguing. A role-reversal. Victor Dempsey now transformed, exercising *his* power over *them* to bring them back to the place from which a part of him had never really escaped. A confrontation, always the first step towards release. And closure. And forgiveness. Of them, then himself." Her eyes sparkled at Skoufaris. "In theory it was exquisite!"

He drew back from her appeal, into the report. "But Arabella Bauer *wasn't* at the reunion, doctor. There *wasn't* any confrontation at Felton."

She nodded vigorously. "We decided that the school was not the right context, that the encounters should be one on one, a short time later, that King and Adams and Preedy had enough to confront in one afternoon, enough to work on. And when that work was done, their memories fully restored, they would be contacted. We…"

She stopped suddenly as she realized what she was saying.

Skoufaris smiled gently, without satisfaction. "That doesn't sound much like theory. And David King and Andrew Adams most definitely *were* contacted. And we're sitting here, aren't we?"

Mary Swoffa blinked at him, as though she had just remembered where she was and why.

She turned inward again, a woman in grave distress. Her hands went back to the coffee mug, dialing it around and around while he waited.

It was many minutes before she said: "It happened gradually. I can't remember exactly when we crossed the line."

C H A P T E R   2 4

PAUL HADN'T BEEN able to get back to the farm until Tuesday midday, after a night and a morning of questions at Port Hope CIB. Now, at midnight, exhausted yet unable to sleep, he declined assistance from Jack's medical bag until he had called his wife. It was their fifth conversation in the last twelve hours. Eva wasn't sleeping either.

"I don't like the thought of you in the middle of nowhere. She knows where the farm is, Paul. I told her."

"We've got surveillance, two of Bancroft's finest, parked right in front of the house, armed to the teeth. Don't worry."

"Sure."

"Did the local cops talk to you yet?"

"For half an hour, some routine questions. I got the feeling they had other things on their mind."

"The hurricane maybe?"

"Not yet. It's still a routine coastal advisory. Apparently it's stalled in the Atlantic. We're far enough inland here anyway." She laughed dryly. "Now you're doing it. Relax, you've got enough to sweat about already."

"But you've got a designated shelter if it happens?"

"The gym at Tom's school. How is he?"

"Fine. He doesn't know anything yet. Skoufaris must want to talk to him. He's avoided the subject so far — this truly is a nice man, as well as smart. We're lucky in that."

"What could Tom possibly tell them? That she was nice? That she bought him ice cream cones? She was working on me, not Tom."

"I know, babe. But we have to be glad that Skoufaris is thorough. He wants me back at Port Hope tomorrow. They'll have finished with Mary Swoffa by then, and at least I'll be able to find out how they worked it."

"'Stranger than fiction.' I always told my students that, but I never believed it. Are they going to let you fly home on Monday?"

"I don't know. You'll have Tom anyway. You want to talk to him?"

"Yeah. And you be careful, hear me?"

"You too. Any inland movement on that hurricane, you get to the shelter. You don't have to be a hero, it's rented."

Eva chuckled. "Maybe it'll blow away."

"Maybe it will."

"Go get some shuteye."

He watched over the family, listening to Jack's shortwave radio at the kitchen table. He heard the full hurricane warning and called Eva again. The first damage reports came in from Wilmington and the storm began to move west across the state. Paul called again. He tried to feel relieved when there was no reply, which surely meant she had left for the shelter.

He made coffee for the surveillance team from Bancroft and took it to the cruiser parked outside the tractor shed, passing nearly an hour with them, grateful for the fellowship while their searchlight probed the woods around the clearing.

He tried to read, picking up and discarding half a dozen books, always returning to the shortwave on the kitchen table, trying in vain to get an accurate track of the hurricane. He was no better informed at seven-thirty when the surveillance relief arrived, a Constable Melanson in a marked Chevy Caprice. Melanson was just half an hour ahead of the Mennonites, on hay wagons today, to gather the windrows left drying since Monday.

Paul breakfasted with his family, avoiding open discussion of the hurricane so as not to upset Tom. Instead, Paul and his mother corroborated Jack's fiction of burglars in the area, boat thieves — pirates really — to account to Tom for the police presence.

Jack had impressed Paul in the last forty-eight hours, his willingness to stay in the background, to be a shield and a distraction for his grandson. They were planning an expedition to look for the pirates this morning, a scouting party in the Albacore while Paul was in Port Hope.

He stopped by the Caprice on his way. Melanson was a farmer's son — Paul was glad to see he had size, also a 12-gauge pump under the dash and a picture of Arabella Bauer on the passenger seat. It was a high resolution colour Xerox faxed up from Port Hope, just as he remembered her from that first glimpse at the Carolina house — black hair in an Alice band, the heavy mascara giving her panda eyes. Unsmiling. The furthest thing imaginable from a blithe boy in a school play.

"She knows where the farm is, Constable. You do understand that."

"I understand, sir."

"I'll be back by lunchtime. Okay?"

"I'm not going anywhere, don't you worry."

"I can't promise you that."

He took the Subaru and walked into Port Hope police headquarters on Walton Street slightly after ten. He was escorted up to Skoufaris's second-floor office by Detective Constable Wynnyates, who had conducted Paul's initial interview. Wynnyates was almost as young as Melanson, wearing cloying drugstore aftershave this morning. He had nothing to say on the subject of Mary Swoffa, was leaving it to Skoufaris to bring Paul up to date on the Port Hope enquiry. He had some questions relayed from the Barrie police investigating Andrew Adams's death, focusing mainly on Sunday at Felton, Paul's encounter with Adams, impressions of him, what he said, most of it covered by Paul's earlier interviews. Wynnyates had copies of photographs taken early Tuesday morning at the Valmy Lodge cabin where Barrie homicide had discovered Adams after their tipoff from Port Hope. Barrie wanted Paul to look at them, to confirm that it was the same man Paul had encountered on Sunday. Paul discerned a reticence in Wynnyates' request, a hesitation that prickled his skin. His upper lip was beading cold as he took the half-dozen police photographs.

It was not the same man.

Certainly the thing spreadeagled on the bed might once have been Andrew Adams — the grinning death mask bore every suggestion of that — but what had happened to the body removed it altogether from Paul's memory of the healthy, handsome athlete of Sunday afternoon.

The same scalding, the terrible grey blisters identical to David King's, but there was a further outrage here, one that King had not suffered, a mutilation that stopped Paul's heart and shrivelled his male flesh with primary fear.

Andy Adams had been radically castrated, the penis and testicles forming a single dollop of gore on the corpse's chest.

Paul waited alone in the upstairs office for Skoufaris, by the window. Glad to be alone.

He stared out along Walton Street, wondering if she knew he was here. Port Hope was big enough to hide her. She wouldn't think twice about the risk.

He could see morning shoppers giving a wide berth to a knot of adolescent males outside the hotel: local skinheads, Doc Martens and pimples, the oldest with a pit bull terrier on a chain. Normally the sight of them in this gracious town would have affronted, even alarmed him. This morning they seemed benignly obvious. None of those shoppers was about to step on the dog's tail or collectively insult them, and so remained predictably safe. Their black boots and their shaved heads were a uniform, their brutality, real or aspired to, nothing but a frustrated need to belong, a longing for order, maybe even for love. So much more terrible the chaotic threat, the danger you couldn't predict or prevent, or even explain afterwards in a way that made any real sense.

He thought anxiously about Eva. He'd seen a TV news report through a showroom window on the way in: Carolina Beach and Wilmington had been pretty hard hit, but TV always showed the worst. The chances of it tracking through Durham were minimal. She would have called the farm by the time he got back.

"How are you, Paul?"

He turned, surprised to see Skoufaris already in the room. "You're quiet for a big man."

"I've got small feet."

Paul smiled vaguely and nodded at the window. "Those guys give you much trouble?"

Skoufaris came up, looked out over Paul's shoulder. "Todd Grady's got problems, the one with the dog. The rest are babies — close haircut, thrash-metal, end of story for now. The trouble comes a year or two down the road when they hit biker age. Always been a problem in this town, except they recruit in suits now, with designer drugs. Never thought I'd miss the old days, chopped Harleys and pot. Grady's serving his apprenticeship, he's already done a year for dealing acid. Seems like only yesterday he was a boy soprano at David King's church."

"That right? How did he get to this?"

"We're starting to wonder, officially as a matter of fact. Seems some of the choir practices weren't altogether natural."

"Jesus." Paul shut his eyes and drew a deep breath. "Doesn't it ever end? I guess I shouldn't be surprised if King was involved. I imagine he was?"

"As far as we know, he was the only perpetrator. Remains to be seen if Todd Grady was the only victim. I just hope we can get him some help before he sets that Staffordshire terrier on someone."

"Or cuts off their dick."

Skoufaris went to the door and shut it. "I'm sorry you had to see that. Do you want to talk about it?" He sat down at his desk. None of his movements was heavy; there seemed to be none of the fat man's resentment or resignation about him, to failed diets or disparaging remarks or the spectre of heart disease.

"Probably. Not now." Paul stayed at the window. "Are you done with Mary Swoffa?"

"For the time being."

"What's the verdict? Did she know?"

"No. She made some professionally terrible judgments, got in way out of her depth, but there's no way she knew it would end like this."

"What are you going to charge her with?"

"It's academic. Her own people will skin her alive. Are you going to sit down?"

"I'm okay."

Skoufaris relaxed, put his hands behind his head. "Mary Swoffa got fooled, you know. They say it happens to every shrink once. They get a patient so insane they've come all the way around, started lapping normality." He cocked his head. "Did I just say that?"

"I understand. You're saying the craziest ones are sometimes the cleverest."

Skoufaris smiled. "Thank you."

"You're welcome."

They liked each other instinctively. Neither had said it, but both men wished they had met under happier circumstances.

"Of course, the hardball didn't start at any identifiable moment," Skoufaris went on. "As far as Swoffa was concerned, it was still theoretical when Arabella Bauer told her she'd sent invitations out. I guess Swoffa was hoping you'd all decline. It was only when one of you replied positively…"

"Adams."

"That's when Arabella Bauer started talking about going through with it, persuading you and King to attend."

Paul sat on the windowsill. "And Swoffa went for it?"

"She told me Arabella Bauer never suspected she'd sold her down the river twenty-five years ago. But I think the doc's kidding herself. Between you and me, I think Arabella Bauer knew very well, and used her. Used her guilt. Manipulated her into crossing over from theoretical into practical."

"But not murder?"

"No. When she didn't hear from Arabella on Sunday after the reunion, she really didn't know what was going on. I do believe Swoffa's clean on that. Last communication they had was on Saturday night, Arabella still working on King to get him to attend. I think saying yes to the reunion bought him one more day; I think she would have killed him Saturday if he'd gone on resisting the idea."

"He didn't want to go?"

"Absolutely not. He hated Felton, got torn to pieces there as a junior, you can imagine."

"So how did they work on him?"

Skoufaris smoothed down his heavy moustache and leaned back in his chair. "We're only an hour from Toronto, so the timing and the travelling was never a problem. But King was. He was in need of psychiatric help himself, that became clear to them as soon as they started researching his interests, largely church organs and the state of his health. A hypochondriac, a recluse…it wasn't easy. So they went through the only open channel — his music — and reached him through that. With a foot in that door and Swoffa as her silent partner, Arabella Bauer convinced him that returning to Felton would exorcise his demons…basically her own story. He'd been a victim like her, their situation wasn't much different because they were part of the same cycle." He glanced at the window. "And there's Todd Grady walking round with a pit bull seeing swastikas. Round and round it goes."

"How did she approach him, in what disguise?"

"Same as you — pharmaceutical rep. Actually she knows about drugs. Check this: she used pancuronium bromine — curare — to subdue King, forged one of Swoffa's prescriptions to get it." He looked candidly at Paul. "I wish I could pretend this 150 IQ doesn't worry me. I hate to say this to you of all people, but we could have an uphill climb ahead of us."

Paul wiped his upper lip. He'd forgotten to shave. "What about us? When did they figure out how to get to the Preedys, Detective Sergeant?"

"Larry. It's Lefterios really."

"Lefterios."

The sea green eyes smiled sadly. When Skoufaris spoke, a new softness enveloped his voice.

"You were the hardest. Your recent loss had made you unreachable. An island. Much more than King. They had to find another way to approach you. The logistics didn't bother them, Swoffa was bankrolling the whole thing, the flights back and forth to North Carolina, the writing classes, et cetera. She was committed to the reunion by now, to what Arabella Bauer had convinced her was a totally positive idea."

"And Eva," Paul said very quietly. "And me." His face darkened. The detective watched him, waiting to see if he was going to ride his anger or let it run, prepared for either.

"Go on," Paul said tightly.

"You want a coffee or anything? I didn't ask you."

"No."

Skoufaris went on carefully. "Logistically it worked fine: Arabella Bauer didn't have to be in constant contact with your wife to keep a light under the thing. Eva's writing class was bi-weekly and Arabella Bauer missed a number of classes. Her travelling job. Eva was naturally accommodating, especially when the student was handing in outstanding work. By the way, she *was* lifting the stories from that university magazine, we checked on that."

But Paul was only half listening. He got up and walked slowly to the door, then suddenly swung back, blinking his eyes. He took a gulp of air. "You're telling me this psycho, this...*freak* had the gumption to convince my wife...to use our grief..."

He did a theatrical double take, his eyes suddenly glittering with sarcasm. He laughed. "You know something? Maybe if I think about this long enough, you know...go a couple more days without sleep, find a couple more mutilated bodies...Hey! Maybe I could come up with some reason why this is happening to me. Think so?"

"Why don't I go get you a coffee?"

"Hey, how about hypnotism? You guys use that sometimes, don't you, so witnesses can recall events? But we could go right back, just like Shirley MacLaine." He grinned foolishly at Skoufaris, his voice ringing wild and giddy from lack of rest. "Hypnotic regression, right? 'Cause I'm beginning to think King and Adams and Mary Swoffa and Jock Fucking Beale maybe got it wrong, don't you? I mean, to go through this amount of *bullshit*, I reckon I must have done more than just keep watch up there, what do you say, Detective Sergeant?"

Skoufaris glanced at his phone. "I say maybe we should get you home, Paul."

"What's the matter? Don't you want to find out if maybe I packed a little fudge myself up there? Got into a little hot water? I mean, someone's trying to torture and kill me here, Skoufaris. Don't you think there's got to be some fucking REASON?"

Skoufaris reached for his phone. "Make a car available for Detective Wynnyates, please. Tell him he's driving Paul Preedy...it's okay, he's here." Skoufaris put down the phone and looked at the door where Wynnyates stood with a single sheet of paper.

"This just came in by fax. It's addressed to Paul Preedy. It was generated from a Sears agency and video store in Newcastle, west of here. I just called them, seems it was prepaid by a

tive flow, spoiling the creative mood: Celia's own voice, directed at the fifty warm bodies comprising English 300Y, absorbed by their luxurious manes and their black, unreflecting clothes.

But this wasn't Auden or Atwood — this was her own poem, a lame attempt thanks to that bullying, critical left brain, fattened by forty years of academia at the expense of its atrophied twin.

Celia moved the page, scanning it with a thin, intense shaft of morning light that pierced the barnboards at her back. Then she tore it out of the pad and stuffed it deep into her skirt pocket, out of sight. It didn't really matter — her bad poetry was only the by-product of something better. Inspiration, fruitful or not, was here for the taking: the sight of a hawk above the forest or of the trees themselves, fathomless striae of green and brown; the unseen yet constant presence of the wolf and the spectral muskie and the beaver pups in their lodges, on shelves in their dark, wet rooms — maybe she didn't need to put them into words to get in touch with them, to be empowered by her new life here.

Or was that the consolation of all bad poets?

She stood up, surrendering like a prisoner after an aborted escape, not just to the familiar failure, but to the worry and uncertainty of the day ahead, the helpless feeling that had made the last thirty-six hours some of the longest in her life.

She turned and put her eye to the widest gap between the barnboards, enough to give her a full view of the bay. No sign of the Albacore yet. That was something grandfathers did, atoned for their mistakes as fathers, with time to be kind.

An errant thought and she let it go. She loved Jack's energy. He'd been a pillar of strength these last few days.

She crossed the solid plank floor, her espadrilles crunching the dusty straw, sending dust motes teeming into the slanting pencil sunbeams until she reached the far east end of the hayloft. She stood in the open mow door overlooking the acreage and the ugly little house, further diminished by the big police car outside. She looked up the hill behind the house where the Mennonites were loading the hay, teenage Mennonite boys leading the great, docile Belgians in teams of four to pull the wagons. Behind, the men made fast work of the windrows, pitching tirelessly, building trembling mountains of dull gold.

Having arrived at eight this morning, they were almost at the high end of the property. Their last day, she would miss them. Mr. Toews had invited the Preedys to a barn-raising on Saturday, for one of the twenty families in his Ring; there would be a picnic, which the woman and children were already preparing — why only the men and older boys were here today. One of the women was coming by buggy with the usual carry-in meal, almost ten miles from their settlement. Toews must have read the unconscious disapproval on Celia's face, had smiled his enigmatic smile.

"She will use the time in many ways, Mrs. Preedy."

And eventually, thinking about it, Celia had found herself almost envying this anonymous woman in her grey bonnet and long grey dress, the rhythmic jostle of the buggy, the brown smell of the horse, the endless parade of small wonders slipping by at an appreciable speed.

She glanced at her watch: eleven-thirty — the men would be getting hungry given their early start, not that they showed any sign of slowing down. She could see Toews working with the dogged energy of a man half his age, the sun winking on the hornlike tines of his pitchfork as it rose and fell. Extraordinary people. It just didn't seem to be in them to lag or complain.

She went cautiously down the ladder, its treads hazardously smooth with wear. Once outside, squinting against the deluge of sunlight, she picked her way through the stubble towards the blue and white police car parked under the mountain ash in front of the tractor shed. She was halfway between the barn and the car when she stopped, shielding her eyes from the bright sun as she looked north to where the farm track disappeared into the forest below the house, her heart beating with unreasonable force. She glanced over at Melanson, but he was talking into his radio, writing something.

Damn this feeling! She had had it too often since Monday night. Weak and foolish. Old womanish, which was an unacceptable concept. Something had startled the crows, so what? Just the regular family that lived in the softwood trees down there, always in a flap about something. It was probably the Mennonite woman with the lunch, or Paul back already from Port Hope. There, they had stopped cawing, settling right down again.

Celia waited a few moments longer, her gaze fixed on the dark opening where the track ran into the forest, then walked on. She was about to stop and talk to Melanson when she heard the telephone ringing inside the house.

Four rings by the time she reached the kitchen, another while she tried to remember her instructions from the Bancroft police, what she should say if it was Arabella Bauer, how to keep her on the line while they traced the call.

But it was Paul.

"Are they done with you?"

"I'm on my way home. Did Eva call?"

"Yes, she did. Durham caught the tail end of it but everything's fine. She called from the shelter. She's helping straighten things up around the school before she goes home. There's been some flooding; she doesn't know exactly where. You want me to hold lunch? If you could pick up some olive oil and garlic…"

"Listen, mum: they can't keep up the surveillance. Skoufaris wants us off the farm, somewhere she doesn't know about. There's a safe house lined up, or we could go to friends. We'll have to talk about it."

Celia took a deep breath to steady herself. "I thought this would happen. When?"

"Today."

"How convenient." There was sudden, uncharacteristic anger in her voice. "They're going to get this bitch, aren't they?"

"Skoufaris is a good man. He's giving this a hundred percent." He must have realized how little he had reassured her, for he added softly: "I'm sorry. For all of this."

"You're *what*? Don't you *dare* let me hear you say that again, Paul Preedy."

"But it's me that's…"

"You are not going to start feeling sorry for yourself in *any* of its guises, and this is just about the dumbest. Do you hear me?"

"Yes ma'am."

"Good." She waited for calm to return, then forced a smile. "So they're going to run us off the farm, are they? Do I get to be Ma Joad? 'We could go all the way to California. There's work there and it never gets cold. Why, you can reach out anywhere and pick an orange.'"

"How's Tom doing?"

"Still out with his grampa. Jack's not going to like this, you know. He'd rather sit on the porch with a shotgun over his knees. What are we going to tell Tom? We can hardly pretend we're leaving the farm because of pirates."

Paul sighed. "I know. All I seem to come up with is the truth: Mister King and Mister Adams from Sunday just got horribly murdered by Tom's old friend Arabella Bauer who was really a man until he grew tits and cut his weewee off, and daddy might be next!"

"Paul…" Celia was appalled by the dizzy spiral of her son's voice, in which she heard all the shock and strain and sleeplessness of the last incredible two days. "Couldn't the police drive you home?"

"I'm okay. Olive oil and garlic?"

"Don't worry about it. Just get home safely."

"I'll see you in an hour."

Celia didn't want to think. She started packing, a mindless distraction, gathering momentum for the inevitable confrontation with Jack. But after half an hour, the walls of her hated little house began to close in, so she walked up the hill to harvest her garden.

She had always maintained a modest vegetable garden at the Hollow, and at first the temptation had been to upscale here, a short-lived fantasy featuring rustling acres of sweetcorn. But in the end her priorities had ordered themselves: there were too many books to read and forest paths to explore, too many bad poems lying undiscovered, within and without. There was a new cottage to build.

Celia plucked a small tomato and turned it in her hand, as much for the tactile pleasure as to inspect for caterpillar bores. She raised it to her lips and nipped its warm, silken skin with her front teeth, then bit hungrily, sucking out the sweet juice.

She filled a plastic shopping bag with ripe tomatoes then squatted, rooting for zucchinis, feeling her anger grow at the thought of the groundhogs getting all her lettuce, her zukes growing to baseball bats in her absence.

God damn Arabella Bauer, tormented or not! God *damn* a world so full of aberration. Maybe Toews was just dead right with his little sermon of the torrent. After all these years of liberal thinking, maybe it was just as pathetically simple as that.

She worked away her anger along the narrow strip of garden, weeding where the mulch had thinned, filling three bags with ripe produce to take with them, until she reached her pea plants, almost bare of pods.

Jack's work. He was a terror for fresh peas, "worse than the birds" she used to tell him. The boys had raided this morning and gone off with their pockets stuffed. She pictured the boat with a trail of bright green peapods widening behind it — Tom was probably getting a royal stomachache.

She picked the last pod of pickable size, slit it with her thumbnail and shook the jostling peas into her palm. The last pea, overeager, bounced out of her hand, and in jerking to catch it, she lost several more. She was frowning down, deciding whether or not to bother with them, when something else on the ground caught her eye.

Celia stooped and picked it up.

It was a round flat stone, deep yellow, translucent, worn smooth from touching.

It was the piece of amber Mr. Toews had given Tom on Monday afternoon, for luck. It must have slipped from his pocket this morning.

Celia straightened and took a deep breath, trying to relax the sudden grip of anxiety, her second attack of the morning.

She peered towards the lake, at first seeing nothing beyond the fenceline but the tops of the trees around the bay. Then she started, her fingers closing in relief around Tom's lucky stone as she saw the top of a mast above the ridge. Now she could hear it, the grumble of the Johnson outboard as the Albacore motored towards the dock.

Lunchtime. She stuffed the amber in her pocket, safe beneath her balled-up poem. She looked at her watch, then up the slope, where the Mennonites' uninterrupted work had taken them almost to the top of the property. What about *their* lunch? The woman with the buggy should have been here long ago, surely.

She counted them — a boy and two pitchers per wagon, four wagons. Twelve mouths, not counting her own family. Could she feed that many? Spaghetti maybe, or she or Jack could drive over to Frank's store and pick something up. Would Old Order Mennonites eat store-bought food?

Celia watched them, still pitching like automatons. It wasn't sensible for them to be working so long in the hot sun without rest or sustenance, especially the boys. What were they going to do if the woman didn't show? Would they keep on haying if the buggy had broken an axle or the horse had gone lame?

Celia set her bags aside and struck out up the slope towards the distant, toiling figures. Her thoughts in the vegetable garden had been fleeting, her sympathy tinged with irritation now, the natural set of a liberal mind distrustful of extreme zeal.

She was almost at the top of the hill, puffing slightly. She saw Toews laying aside his pitchfork, walking towards her, others behind him doing the same. Then she realized that she was not the focus of their attention, that it lay behind her, down the hill.

She turned, squinting against the sun until she made a visor with her hand. From her vegetable garden, her view of the farm track and the lower meadow had been blocked by the house and barn. Now, from this higher ground, she had a clear sightline to a black, covered buggy parked by the tractor shed, just beyond Melanson's patrol car.

The carry-in lunch had finally arrived. She watched distant, miniature figures, Constable Melanson helping the Mennonite woman unload a shallow steel container off the buggy, carrying it over to the old well beside the shed, setting it on the concrete wellhead. Now the woman was heading diagonally up the hill, through the gap between the house and the barn.

Celia turned to the men up the hill. "You guys don't know how lucky you are. You nearly got spaghetti."

Toews acknowledged her with a polite nudge of his round hat brim, and again she glimpsed the shocking whiteness of his forehead. Why doesn't he look hot, she wondered, why isn't he sweating?

"Thank you, Mrs. Preedy. And now you can eat with us."

"You can't keep feeding my family."

"We take your hay, *nicht wahr*?"

A number of the workers had started down the hill. She stared past them to where the woman was heading alongside the barn, up the ridge towards the fenceline, presumably for a view of the lake before serving lunch. Celia found herself inwardly applauding this small, uncharacteristic show of independence. It was hard to get more than an impression at this distance, of a young middle-aged Mennonite in the traditional bonnet and long grey dress, although there was something not altogether typical about her. The way she moved, Celia decided — a stiffness in her movements that had nothing of the natural grace of the Mennonite women she had observed all week — almost as though her clothes didn't quite fit.

Now Celia saw Tom scampering over the ridge on the path from the dock, still in his lifejacket, a brilliant pulse of orange against the blue sky. He stopped abruptly when he saw the woman. She beckoned to him. When he came, she put her hand on his shoulder, leaning intimately close.

Celia felt a sudden, inexplicable jolt of apprehension. She started forward, not taking her eyes off them even when her foot caught in the stubble and she momentarily lost her balance.

Then the anxiety dissolved as she saw her husband coming over the ridge, joining them on the path. Jack and the woman met, conversed for a moment, then the three of them started towards the tractor shed, back the way the woman had come, as though she had either forgotten about, or relinquished, her view of Blackstone Lake. Halfway to the shed, Tom left them, running happily ahead.

"Mrs. Preedy!" called Toews behind her. "Will you walk down with us?" He had been helping one of the teenagers unhitch his team, grazing now beside the wagon. For the first time she thought Toews looked something like his age, walking rather stiffly beside the loose-limbed blond boy. She waited, then the three of them joined the general migration down the hill.

"Will you come to the picnic on Saturday?"

She hesitated. "I'm not sure, Mr. Toews. We're going back to town for a few days. The police think it best under the circumstances." She had volunteered a sanitized and abridged explanation of Melanson's presence this morning, but Toews had asked no questions nor offered comment, probably for the same reason Mennonites declined to read newspapers or listen to the radio or watch TV — the world's business was none of theirs.

They were passing the vegetable garden now. Celia was retrieving her bags of produce when she saw Jack coming up around the house with Melanson. Seeing the look on her husband's face, she steeled herself and urged Toews and the boy to go on ahead.

"What the hell's going on, Celia? Melanson says they want us off the farm. What are we supposed to do, hide in a hotel somewhere, trembling?"

The constable gave her an apologetic shrug. "I'm only telling you what they tell me. We're low on personnel, see, being summer and all. We can't keep up the surveillance."

"No offence, Constable, but I can buy a twelve-gauge at Canadian Tire for little more than a hundred dollars. I can buy two for two hundred and so on. Unless she comes with a rocket launcher, I'd say my son and I have got this pretty well covered until you pick this freak up, which will be before sundown anyway, correct?"

Melanson looked appealingly at Celia. She couldn't help smiling.

"I'm not going to discuss this until Paul gets here, which should be any time now. What's Tom up to?"

"He's down there with God's people, checking out the horse and buggy."

Celia looked down the hill, but once again the house blocked her view of the tractor shed where the buggy was parked. She picked up her bags of produce and started down, Melanson and then Jack, reluctantly, falling into step beside her. Jack grunted when she gave him a bag and took his arm.

"Who's that Mennonite woman?"

"How would I know?" he grumbled. "Tom certainly seems to know her. She must have been around the last couple of days, at least. They were fairly in cahoots coming back from the dock." He glanced sideways, saw the sudden concern on his wife's face. "Why are you looking like that? It's a damn good thing they're not all as grim as old Toews."

"I like old Toews."

They came around the house. Ahead of them, the advance party of haymakers had reached the well. One of the boys was lifting the lid of the steel container, releasing the appetizing smell of onions, but few of the men were paying attention to the food; they stood, perplexed, watching the black buggy as it bounced away down the farm track, already a third of the way towards the mouth of the forest.

Celia called her grandson's name as she moved brusquely through the crowd. Maybe he was in the house. Probably. She saw Jan, the one with seven sisters. "Have you seen Tom, my grandson?"

"The boy with the orange?"

"Yes, a bright orange lifejacket. Did he go into the house?"

"He went in the buggy."

"He what?"

Toews came up, hat in hand, his high white brow compressed in a disapproving frown. "I did not see them go. She must be from one of the new families. Hardly appropriate behaviour when there are mouths to feed, *nein?*"

But Celia had already started down the track. The buggy was halfway to the woods by now but the horse was only walking. It was alright. She would soon catch up if she strode out.

The horse began to trot.

Celia's stride lengthened. She realized she was still carrying her produce bag and dropped it beside the path. Something was happening to her, a feeling of breathlessness, of lightness in her arms and legs, her heart beating out of proportion to her physical activity.

She must have been around the last couple of days.

But that wasn't true. Celia would surely have noticed her. Her body language…

They were fairly in cahoots coming back from the dock.

How could Tom know her?

How?

She began to jog, first in one of the wheel ruts, then on the median of scrubby grass between them.

"Tom?"

She stopped and cupped her hands and yelled: "Thomas!"

She saw a hand above the black canopy, too big to be Tom's, waving gaily. The buggy wriggled on its leaf springs, bouncing wildly as the chestnut horse broke into a canter.

Celia started to run.

Her left espadrille came loose, tumbling in her dust as her legs began to pump, as her whole body became injected with a high octane mixture of fear and adrenaline.

Long legs, still strong from tennis and daily walks and gardening, but hardly sprinter's legs anymore, too many years on the legs that had won leather-bound classics and silver cups at Havergal and Queen's, and only a sprinter could have caught the buggy now.

The horse pulled with effortless power, stretching the distance between them until its breaking point at the mouth of the tree-tunnel where the black vehicle tilted around the bend and out of sight.

Celia doubled, clutching her knees, gasping dust. She turned to wave her arms to the men and slipped off the median into the wheel rut, a bolt of white agony as her ankle buckled and sent her sprawling onto the verge. It was from here, on her hands and knees, that she heard the sound of a car engine starting up in the woods.

"Please oh please dear Jesus sweet Jesus don't take him..."

And the mocking response from the woods, the engine revving and pulling away.

She struggled to her feet, desperately waving, heedless of the pain, keening with anxiety as she witnessed the scene outside the tractor shed: her husband coming down the track with the Mennonites in an anxious knot, turning as one, like a shoal of fish, as Melanson's voice roared in frustration behind them:

"My keys! She took my goddam keys!"

Jack running.

A frantic conference.

The Mennonites pouring around the disabled Caprice, shouldering it out of the way as Jack ripped open the doors of the shed.

Melanson into the shed with the shotgun from his car.

How many seconds now? Celia counted ten in a dreamy way, suddenly quite objective, without pain in her ankle, unable to think beyond the instant as she heard the Trooper's engine.

Another four seconds before it emerged from the shed with Melanson at the wheel, applying the brakes once to lock the hubs into four-wheel-drive, a procedure in which Jack had recently instructed her.

The Trooper thrust forward, all four drive wheels spurting dust and stones, showering the Mennonites standing around the Caprice, unwilling and bewildered participants in a drama for which they could have no possible reference.

But Melanson had trained for this. He was in complete command of the powerful vehicle, controlling its torque on the loose surface so that he had already attained high speed by the time he passed Celia, when the homing chestnut horse cantered out of the forest with the empty buggy behind it.

Melanson kept his head, held the steering wheel in a vise-grip and stamped, letting the Trooper's anti-lock brakes do their work. But the horse panicked. It veered sideways off the track, stumbled, then collapsed onto its forelegs, jackknifing the buggy on its long traces, lifting it off the ground as it swung around like a gruesome old-time fairground ride, level with the Trooper's windshield at the moment of impact.

Melanson saw it coming and ducked the spoked iron wheel as it smashed through the windshield and severed his headrest, jamming against the roof.

Bleeding from windshield glass, trapped beneath the window line, Melanson could not see the horse, although he could hear its agonized frenzy, could feel the Trooper rocking as it struggled in its traces, tried to rise then collapsed on its injured forelegs, wallowing in pain and terror.

C H A P T E R 2 6

THE TRAFFIC WAS light heading into vacation country, mid-day, midweek in late summer. No one was following him.

Paul breathed deeply, holding it, tightening his abdomen to the count of eight, relaxing then repeating — Eva's yoga technique for staying awake at the wheel. He adjusted and readjusted the seat, each new position granting him a few alert minutes before the relentless fatigue claimed him again.

Coffee was no longer working, the last cup taken just twenty minutes ago at a restaurant and souvenir shop where he stopped for directions after missing a turn and getting briefly lost. He had fingered a pair of moccasins at the cash, thinking of Tom, until he saw they were made in Taiwan. So tired, he had driven into the place and almost out again without seeing "The World's Biggest Blackfly," a grotesque construct of fibreglass and re-bars, mounted on the roof. Distracted by it, he almost rammed a Winnebago with New York plates at the exit, a beefy, livid man wearing a yellow cap and aviator sunglasses, mouthing obscenities.

He checked the mirror again — just moving his eyes was

taxing — in preparation for the left turn onto Blackstone
Road. Still nothing behind, the road ahead trickling liquid
silver in the noonday heat. He signalled and made the turn,
the car chirruping complaint as pavement gave way to potholes and washboards.

This was the cottagers' common access road, the first mile
and a half cutting dead ahead through the forest, culminat-
ing at the hillbilly gas and grocery before it twisted and
branched to feed the network of lakes and bays.

He had forgotten about gas. With the gauge well into reserve, he pulled in beside the pumps and got out. He waited
in the sudden country quiet, hearing the Subaru's cooling
tick...tick. Now he could hear a car approaching on
Blackstone, heading out to the highway, at speed judging by
the insistent engine note and the wallop of its tires over the
pocked surface. Now he could see its dust above the trees,
thought himself lucky to be out of the road, too tired to pit
his nerves against some barely licensed headbanger hopping
potholes in his father's pickup.

Paul heard the screen door to the shop squeal open behind him, saw the proprietor look out of the shop with a
frosted carton in his hands and said "Hi there."

The tall old man nodded curtly as he squinted through
the sunlight at the passing car. Not a pickup but a midsize
green Chrysler, instantly hidden by a screen of swirling yellow
dust. "Need gas?"

"Fill up, please." Paul was still staring after the diminishing
funnel of dust as he said it, wondering how he could have
gotten such an unlikely impression of the driver: Old Order
Mennonites didn't drive cars, not at any speed, certainly not
like that. She must have been wearing some other kind of hat
that just *looked* like a grey cotton bonnet.

"You'll have to wait a minute," the old man told him.
"Freezer just went up the Khyber, got to get this stuff down to
the basement before it melts. Don't want to buy four dozen
Popsicles, do yer?"

"Might take one."

The shop was gloomy and overheated. As his eyes adjusted from the bright sunlight, he saw shelves crammed with every conceivable class of domestic item. There was a lovely nickle-plated cash register on the wooden counter, the disabled Coca Cola freezer chest looked old enough to be valuable.

"You want some help with that?"

Frank lifted out an armful of cartons and carried them towards a door behind the counter. "Nope. Won't take but a minute."

It took at least five, which Paul spent browsing the shelves. Having struck out with the Taiwanese moccasins, he was looking for a treat for Tom, a token apology for his absence the last few days, the way he must have appeared to his son — the way their holiday together was turning out.

Frank was carrying down the last load when the telephone rang behind the cash register. Frank called up the stairs: "Mind gettin' that?"

Paul reached over and lifted the greasy receiver from its battered dial base.

"Hello?"

"Frank?"

"I can get him."

"That d'Arcy?"

"No, I'm just…"

"Get Frank. Hurry, this is the police."

Paul felt a pang of anxiety. The voice sounded desperate, and vaguely familiar. "What's the…"

"Move it! This is an emergency!"

Frank was already halfway up the stairs when Paul summoned him, but took his time getting to the phone. He listened peevishly to it: "What did you say? You want me to *what*? You've got some nerve, sonny. I hope you know that."

A further ten seconds of testy impatience.

"Okay, okay, I heard you. Prob'ly missed the boat though…had a car come by a few minutes ago, goin' pretty fast. What? How the hell should I know?" He jerked his head at Paul. "What kind of car was that just went by?"

"Some kind of green Chrysler, I think. Midsize Plymouth, maybe a Dodge."

"Fella here reckons it was a midsize green Chrysler. Okay, I'll call you back."

"What was that?" Paul demanded.

Frank ignored him while he rummaged behind the counter. "God damn it, it's always when you need 'em in a hurry!" He spotted his keys, swiped them up and headed for the back door shouting "Customer, d'Arcy!" as he passed through.

Paul hung back for a few seconds, blinking against the hard light from the doorway. And against something else, as fleeting as the passing car, something he glimpsed there and in the officer's voice and tried to put away before it could properly register.

He looked out into a large yard cleared from the bush, littered with vehicles rusting into the stony ground between the shop and a cinderblock service bay. The Fargo three-ton was parked out in the sun, Frank climbing into the high cab, in hurried conversation with a middle-aged man in filthy overalls that emerged from the bay. The mechanic came towards the shop wiping his hands on an orange rag. He looked like the old man but without his stature — a son or a much younger brother. He stopped, turned back to watch Frank turn the diesel over and over.

"Christ almighty, get goin' if you're goin'!"

"Where *is* he going? What did the police say?"

"How the hell should I know? Some kind of bullshit over on Blackstone Lake."

Paul's stomach lifted. "What do you mean?"

The Fargo caught and fired, coughing smoke from the stack as it shuddered forward and around the end of the building. The mechanic shouldered past Paul into the shop, through it and out the front door to watch the truck's progress onto the road, where it turned left towards the highway.

Paul insisted. "Tell me what's happened."

"Who knows? Sounds to me like one o' them custody battles. Some crazy woman made off with someone's kid."

"What?"

The mechanic pointed after the truck. "There's a narrow bit just along the road there, they want dad to stall the Fargo and block it. He was the OPP Auxiliary round here for twenty-five years before they got a regional department in Bancroft. He didn't like that one little bit. Surprised he didn't tell that Melanson kid to go blow!" He nodded towards the pumps. "Want gas?"

But Paul didn't register the question. He stood in the doorway, staring at the road in front of the shop where the green midsize Plymouth or Dodge had flashed past. Seeing it again, the thing he had glimpsed before that could no longer be denied.

"Hey buddy, are you feeling alright?"

Paul was on his way to the Subaru when he stopped and swayed, the oil-mapped concrete tilting beneath his feet. He reached for the nearest pump to steady himself, in a sudden forgetful island of fumes, the faint, alluring sweetness of gasoline shimmering around him.

It had been here, last Sunday, early evening, while his mother filled the car and they sat in the back. Only Paul sitting. Tom had been lying down, at peace, in trust, reclaimed…his brave and handsome head warm in Paul's lap.

Paul pushed the pump away and ran for the car. He threw himself in, started it, savaged the transmission into drive, his tires singing blue smoke as they spun in place on the fore-court before they found purchase.

The Fargo must have been shy of the narrow section because Paul passed it thirty seconds along the road, blind in its dust, praying there was nothing in the oncoming lane. Another thirty seconds and he hit the highway junction, braking too late, skidding the last fifteen feet in a storm of dust.

God in heaven which way?

He leapt out and ran into the road, his head snapping right and left in a frantic burlesque of a man stranded in heavy traffic, although this road was gapingly empty.

She'd had almost ten minutes' start.

Paul drove south at the Subaru's limit, his face a staring crimson mask.

He was not afraid. The palsy in his arms and legs was something physical, to do with physical exhaustion, independent, in his ligaments. His mind was clear and fully competent, vigilant that the fear — grotesque and quite unfounded as yet — should gain not one millimetre of ground. He kept his mind's eye fixed on it, clear and bright and fearless, fixed on this insubstantial, darting thing, a cunning thing, at the outer edge of his reason.

Vigilant because the thing was diseased and ravished, hunting for a weak spot, for any opportunity as it waited for the clear bright fire of Paul's hope to die.

CHAPTER 27

THE AMERICAN IN the Winnebago wearing a yellow CAT DIESEL POWER cap and aviator sunglasses, the angry man Paul had so offended in the restaurant parking lot half an hour ago, was called Edward Walmsley.

While Eddie had never actually worked for the Caterpillar company, heavy diesels had been his life; starting as a mechanic with Army Transport Command in Korea, he had worn overalls at Kenworth, Peterbilt and Mack, right up to service manager at Central GMC Truck Sales in White Plains, New York. He had bought the full-dress Winnebago this summer as an early retirement present to himself. At least it had a General Motors engine so he didn't have to feel disloyal — a big block 454 with an enviable thirst. Eddie was only grateful it didn't run on beer.

"Beep beep!" he said to the slight Filipino beside him. Dolores was Eddie's wife of six months, his fourth wife, thirty-seven years his junior and with a less than rudimentary knowledge of English. But she was already well versed in the Walmsley Highway Code, and without hesitation retrieved

two Miller Genuine Draft from the optional console fridge
and zipped them snugly into the two fuzzy can-cozies (pink
for girls and blue for boys) that Eddie's last wife had gussied
up from washable polyester fleece.

Eddie didn't thank Dolores, although he expected her to
drink with him, beer for beer. He would have preferred to be
driving alone if he hadn't needed her for "beep beep" and
"honk honk," this last signal borrowed from the classic
bumper sticker and indicating, twice a day on average, his
readiness to pull over and service her on the optional
Simmons Beautyrest in the captain's cabin. The rest of the
time, as Eddie liked to boast while Dolores waited on his
Thursday poker game, silence was golden-skinned!

Eddie savoured his pun and considered a Beautyrest stop,
but decided to postpone it until his lunch had gone down.
Right now he was happy just driving and nursing his paunch,
the double cheeseburger and large fries he had eaten back at
the restaurant with the fly sculpture on the roof.

Eddie raised the cozy to his mouth, enjoying the contrast
of warm fleece with the cooly beading metal, but this time he
lowered the beer without drinking. He braked steadily but
hard, down to 20 mph, his eyes narrowing behind his aviators.

"Say what?"

A woman was running into the road, flagging him down.
She was dressed most oddly, in a long dress like out of a TV
western, "Little House on the Prairie," tight enough to show
her tall, strong figure. As she crossed to the Winnebago,
Eddie slowly unwrapped his aviators, powered down the window and smiled with helpful charm.

"Got some trouble here?"

"Know anything about engines?" No formalities, no introductions. She was in some kind of definite hurry.

"I guess I…sure…sure I could…" For some reason Eddie's
faculties of speech and thought were not cooperating.

He felt Dolores's hand on his arm and twitched it off.

"Sure I know about engines. That you over there?" He

noticed the car now, a green Plymouth Acclaim backed into some kind of farm track on the far side of the road.

"It's making this weird noise. If I start it up you'll hear what I mean."

Eddie looked closely at the woman's body as she crossed the road, then at the car. He didn't have much time for cars as a rule, particularly Chrysler products.

"Piece of garbage. No wonder we had to dig 'em out of their own shit back in '80." Dolores reacted nervously to Eddie's fist near her face. "See that scar? Got that pulling the transmission out of my brother's fuckin' K car. K for crap I told him." He peeled off his cap and sunglasses, carefully smoothed his hair in the visor mirror, then opened the door. "You stay here."

Eddie dropped heavily to the ground and crossed the road, massaging his tattooed forearms, hunching his beefy shoulders to loosen the driving knots. He came up behind the woman, aroused by the way the long dress flared out from her waist over her rump as she peered helplessly under the raised hood. He could see the muscles in her strong back visible under the tight material.

"What's the trouble, ma'am? What's this here noise?" He had injected what he considered to be an alluring quality into his voice, adding a southern twang to his native flat New York, the kind he admired in his country and western music. Eddie's bedside manner.

"Maybe you should have a look at this first," the woman urged him. "There's something dripping out of the back."

I'll just bet there is, Eddie thought, feeling a healthy pulse between his legs as he followed the woman around behind her car. He noticed, merely as a point of interest, that they were now out of sight of Dolores in the Winnebago, hidden behind the Plymouth's raised hood.

The woman pointed under the rear bumper. "Down there. What do you think that is?"

Eddie squatted, dipping his shoulder so that it brushed

the billow of her dress. He was leaning further, cocking his head down under the bumper when he raised it and sniffed. "What's that smell?"

"Gas?"

"Sure ain't gas."

It seemed to be strongest around the edge of the trunk. He sniffed again, closer to the seal. "Smells like…"

He didn't have time to say chloroform.

Eddie Walmsley had never turned away from a bar fight, and had he acted instantly on his instinct, he would have been a powerful adversary; but it was a woman, and he therefore failed to heed the full alert.

Massive, freezing shock before the pain, which allowed her to bury the knife twice to the hilt, down into the thickly muscled base of his neck. As he rolled to fight her, she struck a third time from a much lower angle, into his chest.

Eddie's arms made semaphore as the last agony cauterized him, and the woman stepped back, leaving the knife behind. The last thing he saw, before his vision milked over, was the wooden handle in scrupulous detail, moving as he moved, a brand new cheap kitchen knife with an orange price sticker on it for $5.95.

The Filipino woman in the Winnebago was used to being alone, abandoned, waiting for her husband. She sat unmoving, little worried about what was happening over at the car. She didn't like the woman who had stopped them, her first reaction had been caution, but shallow. All her feelings were like that now. She didn't really care what happened to Eddie or herself. After the last six months she was numb to everything except the dream of one day returning home to her family in Quezon City.

Then Dolores saw the child.

The woman in the long dress was running across the road with a child in her arms, and suddenly Dolores was scrambling to the big side door, struggling to open it for them, melting with concern when she saw how limp the boy was, how his head nodded as the woman ran, when she realized that he was not asleep.

"*Muchacho desmayado?*"

"Yes. Accident. We must go to hospital."

Surely the woman had trouble with her car, wasn't that why she had stopped them? Dolores didn't understand, but there was no time to think about it now. She helped the woman inside, threw open the main cabin, helped her lay the boy on the Simmons bed. "*Donde esta Eddie?* Where man?"

"Working on the car. He's going to follow." She pointed quickly. "*Camión. Comprende?*"

Dolores shrugged, totally confused but unconcerned now about anything but the boy. She leaned over him, stroking his warm forehead, making soothing noises while the woman hurried forward to the cab.

"I drive. You stay with him."

Dolores watched through the cabin's open door. She saw the woman glancing at the controls, fundamentally like those of any van, before starting up and pulling off the shoulder, northbound. Dolores arranged a pillow under the child's head then looked towards the cab again, further surprised to see the woman wearing Eddie's aviator sunglasses and stuffing her black hair under his yellow cap.

C H A P T E R 2 8

PAUL PASSED THE Winnebago approximately two minutes after turning south out of Blackstone Road. He registered the blue and orange New York plates, sunglasses and a yellow cap, and placed it immediately at the restaurant.

He drove on at 145 kilometres an hour, near the Subaru's limit, but not too fast to notice the green Plymouth up the farm track.

He could see immediately that it was empty. He found the man lying on his back behind the car, half underneath as though working on it, except that the dark pool around him was blood rather than oil. Paul didn't recognize him. Without sunglasses and a yellow cap, the staring face had no connection to the Winnebago travelling in the opposite direction a few minutes away.

The key was in the ignition. Paul opened the trunk. He vaguely noticed the smell of chloroform, although he was unable to focus on anything but the object inside, its orange colour in contrast to the dull grey carpeting.

He read the label.

Buoy O Boy
Over and over.

He was halfway back to Blackstone Road, on his way to the store to advise the police that she was no longer driving a green Plymouth, when he ran out of gas.

C H A P T E R 2 9

THE LAST AUGUST hurricane had been born as a tropical storm in the North Atlantic's eastern sector near the Cape Verde Islands. A massive, self-sustaining heat engine, it rose 25,000 feet above the deep, warm ocean on which it fed, its vortex deepening hourly as it walked with deceptive ease towards the east coast of the United States.

At latitude 25 degrees north, it stalled, prevaricating for twenty-four hours, taunting the monitors at the National Hurricane Center at Miami from the screens of their McIDAS supercomputers. In that one day of its hiatus, the computers disclosed that the hurricane had generated sixteen trillion kilowatt hours of electricity, more than enough to power the country for ten years.

At six o'clock on the night of Tuesday, August 27, it began to move again. While Paul Preedy had kept vigil in Bancroft, Ontario, the six-hour advisory was upgraded to a hurricane watch along the North Carolina coast from Cape Fear to Cape Hatteras, although the coastal dwellers didn't need TV or radio to alert them: they remembered Hazel in '54, they remembered Diane that had killed two hundred of their neighbours the following year, they remembered Hugo as yesterday. They had already seen the long, unnaturally slow waves running onto the beach, had felt the sultry air fret itself to a snapping wind by supper time, watched the high feathered cirrus above the sunset, red as blood and very beautiful.

As they knew it would, the watch now became a full warning, and just before one in the morning on Wednesday, Hurricane Terry devastated the coast along Onslow Bay. One hundred and fifteen miles per hour winds claimed twenty lives at Southport and Carolina Beach amidst imploding structures and scything debris, another thirty as it rocked Wilmington, killing and bereaving in an insane, upside-down world of floating cars and landborne yachts, prone trees and towers of water.

Only partially satisfied by its feast of human life and property, Terry was still a category 3 hurricane when it tracked west over the broad coastal plain, cutting a swath of destruction through the Piedmont Plateau, still at marginal hurricane force when it turned north and grazed the old university towns of Chapel Hill and Durham in the early hours of that Wednesday morning. From her designated shelter in a school gymnasium in a Durham suburb, the wind and deluging rain sounded to Eva Preedy like the roar of a gargantuan excavator about to claw the gym from the ground, or like some endless, hell-bound express train, its tracks spiked to the rooftree.

She had talked to Paul twice in the past eight hours, but still she joined the long lineup for one of the shelter's two payphones: she knew he would still be awake, worrying, glued to Jack's shortwave radio. Perhaps it was a diversion from the incredible events surrounding him there, the worry and uncertainty of something far more insidious than this hurricane.

When she was three callers away from the phones and the

aerial line went down, Eva felt such an overwhelming and surprising sense of isolation that she knew she had to get a grip on herself.

Since she did not have her own people to attend to, she made herself available to the officials at the shelter. She helped dish out two hundred hot breakfasts from the Southern Baptist portable kitchen, read to overexcited children, poured cocoa for the evacuated residents of two nursing homes and held their papery hands, held up blanket screens while nurses changed adult diapers or injected the day's first insulin.

The morning brought a long, collective sigh of relief, as the doors were unbattened and the sheltering throng realized that the world outside had not come to an end. They learned that the relatively unbroken state of the school was a good measure of conditions in the region: while Terry had whipped the stars and stripes to rags, had beaten down four large trees around the playground and gnawed the leaves from most of the others, while it had rolled two portables and blown the shingles from the roof of the main building, there had been no loss of life and the damage was all repairable.

Eva was among the last to leave the shelter late Wednesday afternoon, by which time the hurricane had been downgraded to storm status while it blew itself out, south and west through the Great Smoky Mountains into Tennessee. Helping coordinate the exodus from the shelter, she learned that only one local area had sustained severe storm damage, due to heavy rain rather than high wind, when an overloaded storm sewer let go along Battleford Ravine.

Eva said nothing to her co-workers about living on Ravine Drive. She didn't need sympathy, nor was she in any hurry to go and assess damage to the rented house in which they had suffered for two years. Her anxiety for her neighbours was no more than neighbourly, since she had made no real friends here. And when she did finally drive home, exhausted and exhilarated, making careful detours around storm debris and severed tree limbs, when she at last turned into Ravine Drive and saw the worst, a small, guilty light glowed bright and defiant under a bushel of sympathy.

The road had been badly hit, a fifty-foot section of it washed away less than a quarter-mile in, where Eva abandoned the car beside twenty others in a makeshift parking lot. She walked the remaining half-mile home, past variations of the same sad domestic scene, although the worst could have been much worse: the sewer had already been mended and the water pumped away. Sheltered from the hurricane wind, the houses along the ravine had suffered mostly internal damage from the brief though dramatic half-story rise in the water level. She saw people shovelling two feet of silt out of their front doors, cursing God and the weather bureau and the department of public works for the failure of their cheapjack-shit storm sewer. She listened to neighbours bickering across listing fences: "Boil it!" "Boiling don't do it, you treat it with chlorine." "I want to drink it, not swim in it!" "Fine, go ahead and get goddam hepatitis!"

She stopped and chatted briefly with acquaintances, and heard the horror stories that were already part of the apocrypha of Terry: someone was sandblasted on Carolina Beach, sixty seconds and nothing left but teeth and a belt buckle; someone else had their leg carried off at the hip by a coconut.

But she saw others just working, strong and silent for whatever private reasons, optimism or fatalism, old-time religion or perhaps they were merely keeping an ear cocked for a dry phone, for the insurance adjustor. She saw those of plain good character pitching in to help neighbours haul out their ruined rugs and sofas, peoples' lives displayed on their damp, shifted porches as though for a neighbourhood-wide yard sale. She saw a boy scout troop mucking in and was impressed and touched. She decided that as soon as they were settled back in Toronto — or maybe some picture-perfect village within easy commuting distance where her first novel would catch and burn and take off like a rocket — wherever it was they ended up living, Tom really ought to give the scouts a shot.

The house looked largely as she had left it late yesterday afternoon, except that the front door was wide open and the barbeque, which Eva knew for a fact she had left tied down on the back patio, was now in the front yard.

She wasn't worried about the open door — she had been able to fit everything valuable or important into two suitcases now locked in the trunk of the car, and looting was not a real danger in this dull suburb. In any event, it was rented, just like Paul said, furniture and appliances along with the house.

Eva was fascinated rather than distressed by the condition of the interior, its surreal possibilities: the wall to wall carpet of mud left by the receding water, smooth as chocolate pudding, decorated with a strange assortment of debris, some of it imported in exchange for whatever of the Preedys had floated away. There was a ruler-straight waterline a third of the way up the wall around every room including the kitchen, bisecting the hole in the sliding glass doors where the barbeque, buoyed up by its propane tank, had torpedoed the house at shoulder level. There was a swimming pool gently lapping the basement steps, or was it a subterranean grotto?

With her deeper responses already overburdened by the events of the last few days, with her thoughts trained towards Ontario, Eva Preedy felt none of the sense of loss that her neighbours must have been suffering at this moment. No sense of violation during her initial inspection, not until she pushed open her son's door.

Tom, whose neatness had almost worried her sometimes. Tom's stuffed animals littering his small, perfect room, crushed beneath his upended bed, flung across his broken desk, their saturated limbs twisted into all-too-human postures of flood victims.

Tom's stories, his careful illustrations, things she had intended to keep forever, reduced to pulp.

Eva was standing in the doorway, experiencing a reprise of her earlier anxiety in the shelter, the distance from her family catching up at last, catching in her throat and her tired, stinging eyes, when the telephone rang.

She turned to the sound and sniffed away her trouble, brightening at the likelihood of it being Paul, smiling now at the absolute perfection of his timing.

Into the kitchen, leaving resolute footprints in the chocolate pudding, towards the wall phone fastened a lucky few inches above the waterline. Unlike the school, Ravine Drive enjoyed cable telephone service, unaffected by wind or water.

Eva felt actual laughter bubbling up as she reached for the receiver, the product of an exhausted mind and body and an almost unbearable relief at the prospect of hearing their voices. As she snatched it up, as she heard her caller, as she listened to what Arabella Bauer was telling her, the giddiness did not decrease, although its spiral had reversed and she was spinning down now…ensnared by a violent and inescapable vortex. Now Eva Preedy knew she had made the classic mistake, believing herself to be in windless sunlight when all the time it had been the fatally deceptive centre of the hurricane.

The eye.

Where a person stands naked to their soul amidst the plummeting pressure, with bulging eardrums and blood in their mouth as the greater fury draws on.

C H A P T E R 3 0

DETECTIVE SERGEANT SKOUFARIS picked Wynnyates up at ten o'clock on Saturday morning. He lived in a shabby bachelor apartment on Wellington Street, on the high ground near Trinity College School, Port Hope's own, progressive version of Felton. He answered the door with a beard of shaving cream.

"You're early."

"We'll need the time. Last weekend of the Exhibition. It's going to be a slow drag into the city."

"I haven't been to the Ex since I was a kid."

"Don't let me spoil your plans. Far as I'm concerned you're off duty."

"Are you kidding? I wouldn't miss this." Wynnyates saw the distaste on the older detective's face, and rearranged his own expression. "How's Preedy? Poor bastard, I'll be surprised if he's still sane after today, however it comes out."

"Okay, let's go, let's go." Skoufaris turned back to the car idling at the end of the walkway, mildly regretting having asked Wynnyates along. But he'd been handling the dog work capably and without complaint since Monday — it was his case as much as anyone's. As long as he stayed in the background, Metro Homicide would hardly notice him.

Skoufaris drove to the end of Wellington where he surprised Wynnyates by turning away from the highway and onto Deblaquire, past the boarding school.

"I thought we were in a hurry."

Skoufaris stopped the car, sat staring at the big limestone gates. "My dad used to teach phys. ed. at Trinity you know. Great boxer he was. They cleaned up in intramural boxing when he was there."

"I didn't know that."

"Amazing he ever got the job, a Greek guy. The other teachers were all called Angus and Gordon. He always knew he wasn't on par with them, but mom didn't; she was a Master's Wife, made sure they got invited to all the teas, you know?"

"Yeah?" Wynnyates sounded lost.

"She was so proud of it, filled our little house up with school stuff, team photographs, all these things that didn't hardly have anything to do with us. It was the disappointment of her life when they couldn't afford to send me."

He drove on around the block. "She had me thinking like her, looking at those Trinity boys and wishing I had a blue blazer like them, their way of walking and talking like the rest of the world owed them something." He glanced sideways at Wynnyates. "Know something? Nearly forty years I carried that chip on my shoulder, and it's taken just five days to blow it off."

Skoufaris swung the unmarked car into Ontario Street towards the highway. Wynnyates waited until they were off the ramp and merged with the westbound traffic before he asked: "Who's in charge in Toronto?"

"A homicide staff inspector called Jellun." Skoufaris was silent for a moment. "I knew him at 52 Division. Jellun's a cool customer, but I guess that makes him good."

"What about SWAT?"

"Say 'Emergency Task Force.' Metro SWAT hate being called that except by each other. Apparently they've got a command post set up on the corner of Huron and Bloor, just down from the house. They've got an explosives demolition unit, snipers, the whole shebang." He slowed to eighty kilometres an hour behind the first traffic buildup. "Lookit, not even in Oshawa and it's started." He glanced right, at the empty, beckoning shoulder lane. "May have to pull rank if this keeps up."

"So no one's heard a word from her since Wednesday?"

"Nope. There's been no communication since the call to Eva Preedy. She wants Paul at the house, one in the afternoon Saturday with a portable phone, so that's what she's got."

"Did you talk to him this morning?"

Skoufaris nodded almost imperceptibly.

"Bad shape, eh?"

"What do you think?"

"Imagine. Guy's lost one kid already, and now the other one like…"

"Can it!" Skoufaris's resonant voice exploded with shocking suddenness in the car. "Don't talk like that again. You understand? This isn't a fucking joyride. We're going to get this child *back* for them, you hear me?"

Wynnyates coloured.

"Damn!" Skoufaris hauled down his window, grabbed the beacon and swung it up onto the roof. He flicked on the power, shunted sideways onto the soft shoulder and accelerated hard, loose gravel pinging inside the fenders.

In the two years of their acquaintance, Wynnyates had never heard the sergeant of detectives raise his voice or use profanity. He stared at the road ahead in shocked and embarrassed silence, but he understood: while he had kept marathon hours himself since Wednesday, Skoufaris had literally slept in the office. That too was unusual; two years of departmental ball games and barbeques had revealed Skoufaris as a dedicated family man — maybe that was why he was taking the Preedy case so much to heart, why he had in-

sisted on escorting Paul today, instead of delivering him to
the impersonal machine that was Metro homicide.

They picked Paul up at a quarter to twelve from the nondescript house in Scarborough where the Preedys had been
installed for the last three days, under plainclothes guard.
The safe house had phone relays from both Ontario numbers
known to Arabella Bauer, also from the Carolina house in the
hope that she would call, but there had been no word since
Wednesday afternoon.

Wynnyates settled Paul in the car for the ride downtown.
Eva Preedy watched him go, standing absolutely still in the
doorway, chalk-white, wearing dark glasses and saying nothing during Skoufaris's gentle monologue. He knew she had
heard it all before from Jellun, but he couldn't just walk away,
see you later, don't wait up. Not today. So he explained again,
in his deep, soft voice, why Metro felt Eva should not accompany her husband this afternoon: emotions always ran high
in situations like this, her presence would represent added
danger not only for Paul and the highly trained personnel at
the scene, but also for Tom. Discipline, precision routine and
the best available technology — that alone would restore
their boy to them.

Eva nodded slightly, her only other movement a slight dis-
tension of her nostrils. When Skoufaris looked back on his
way to the car, he saw Celia Preedy draw her gently and firmly
back from the doorway, like an invalid. Eva's husband, alone
in the rear seat of the police car, did not once look back at the
house as they pulled away.

CHAPTER 31

IT WASN'T DRUGS. He had refused sedation from Jack and from the police doctor. He didn't need it. He had his special suit, unworn since the spring, dusted off for this occasion. And now, at last, Eva had one just like it.

Like armour, like a spacesuit from which he watched an alien, barren moonscape drift by, featureless grey dust. Skoufaris was driving him west along Bloor Street, carrying him into his old neighbourhood for the first time in two years, but no spark of recognition or interest could penetrate his carapace.

The air conditioning must have been on too high, he felt a deep, cellar chill, but could say nothing to them. The discomfort was all he deserved, and for some reason, in a way that was vaguely repugnant to him but that he had no power to censure, he did not want the two police officers in the front seat, especially Skoufaris, to think him weak or distracted; whenever Skoufaris turned to him with reassurance, which was often on the spasmodic downtown journey, he tried his best to respond in appropriate ways.

"It's all about power, don't forget that, Paul."

"I won't." Someone else had said that to him recently. He remembered it phonetically — the words were without meaning or significance.

"Tom is the main source of her power. Without him she loses it. She's not going to hand him back, I'd be crazy to try and sell you that, but she's not going to hurt him because she needs him. You understand…we have time to do our job, which is to get your boy back for you."

Paul nodded, but he had heard only the cadences.

"It's a power game for her. The whole reunion thing, and now she's dragging you back here, to the one place on earth she knows you never wanted to see again. A game, and without Tom she doesn't have one. In a sick way she needs him almost as much as you do."

Paul nodded again while he slipped backwards in time, his only escape route since he could no longer look forward.

Back three days and listening to the sound of a car at high speed, watching it pass on a country back road while he stands stupid on the forecourt of a gas-and-grocery. Watching it go by. Watching Tom go.

Listening to the roar of a Winnebago with New York plates heading towards him on the Bancroft highway, a fleeting glimpse of sunglasses and a yellow cap.

Wondering, now, why intuition had deserted him. Had there ever been a better time for paternal instinct?

But instinct and intuition hadn't worked last time either, watching a motor race while a much more exciting event took place in the yard.

It was a lie. There was no such thing as intuition. To hell with it.

And his thoughts raced forward again with the deafening thunder of rushing water behind them, locking him fast in the present as the torrent engulfed him. Hell was nowhere but here, where a man's children died in pain and terror. Hell was here and now and forever.

Skoufaris signalled and turned north onto Huron. They passed the task force command post, but saw nothing but a store with a FOR LEASE sign, newspapers masking the window. He knew that Metro had a mobile post, a white motorhome emblazoned with police ID, but no one wanted to disrupt the normal life of the street this afternoon; it could still be monitored and controlled without a high-profile police presence.

They were flagged down a hundred yards up the street by what appeared to be a regular Metro patrol officer, but he knew who they were before Skoufaris could find a badge.

"You're expected at the house, sir. I understand Detective Wynnyates is remaining at the command post?"

Skoufaris looked at the officer's uniform. "That's a cover, you're task force, right?"

"We're playing it close to the chest right now, sir. Don't want anyone getting hinky."

There was a SWAT word. Skoufaris looked around at what appeared to be a normal Saturday in a smart Toronto neighbourhood. "How did you manage to sweep the street?"

"Some of the residents had to be advised. Mobile Support's been here twenty-four hours a day since Thursday." He added with a touch of pride: "There are four marksmen with spotters covering you right now."

Skoufaris smiled tightly as Wynnyates got out. "Glad I wore a clean shirt. Take it easy, Winnie."

As they slowed for the house thirty yards up the street, he could see a Toronto Hydro truck preventing access from the north end of the block, two ETF officers in hard hats and Hydro coveralls doing makework in a cherry picker, as if attending to the overhead lines. Skoufaris pulled into the empty driveway, switched off the engine and turned to the back seat, his voice very low and even. "They've got a medic down at the command post. He'll come up if you need something."

Paul shook his head as he opened the door.

"Paul?"

Skoufaris reached back and let something trickle into his hand. "They're called *komboloi*. They were my father's. I'd like you to have them."

Paul looked down at a small heap of black beads on a silver chain. "Worry beads?"

"You'll still have them when you're not worried anymore." His soft gaze intensified. "When you're celebrating."

"Mennonites use amber."

"Yeah?"

Paul's voice came from some distant, hollow place. "They believe certain things ward off evil. None of them work." He reached to hand the beads back but Skoufaris turned and got out of the car.

There had been no connection with the street, and there was none with the house at first. Had Paul been open to such sentiment, he might have construed disloyalty from the way it smelled and looked, how easily it had switched allegiance to the new owners and made him a stranger. But today he noticed nothing like that. He was a stranger everywhere.

Homicide Staff Inspector Jellun came down to meet them in the hallway. He was nearly fifty, trim and handsome, with close-cropped grey hair and a heavy moustache, a combination that sometimes, wrongly, identified him as gay. He had personally questioned the Preedys yesterday at the safe house, and now, as then, there was nothing deferential or unduly sympathetic in his manner towards Paul, nothing to undermine his cool professionalism.

"We've got half an hour before she's supposed to call. I want to use that time to brief you on our operation and your part in it." His voice dropped. "Excuse me, but are you sedated?"

Skoufaris answered: "No."

"You're feeling like shit, right, but you can handle this?"

Paul answered for himself: "Yes."

Jellun's cool blue eyes appraised him a moment longer, then he nodded: "That's all I want to hear." He turned to the stairs. "We've got the operations centre set up on the top floor for the vantage point. Got one or two gadgets I'd like you to be familiar with."

"Who's in charge down at the command post?" Skoufaris asked, panting slightly as they climbed.

"I am. All Task Force personnel and equipment are under my direct command. If we're going to make a premeditated decision to use gas or live ammunition, I'm accountable to the incident commander at Metro CIB. We've got an inspector on a dedicated line all afternoon, but I'm the man at the scene."

Paul listened, unaware of how much Jellun's confidence was disarming him until they were past the second floor, creaking up to the attic.

I should have rebuilt the stairs when we remodelled, carpeting over was a mistake, both boys sleep light…

Climbing in single file, they didn't see his face, the brief rictus of agony before the fissure closed, sealing the carapace, shutting out all the other deadly stinging thoughts that swarmed around him, seeking entrance.

There were two task force officers on the third floor, in SWAT uniform this time, dark blue fatigues and baseball caps. One cradled a scoped, bolt action rifle while his partner trained binoculars through the high gable window.

Jellun made terse introductions, the marksman and spotter, and a technician behind a table cluttered with equipment. Jellun let the narrow-shouldered young man identify his gear: a passive telephone receiver wired through a voiceprint spectrograph into an amplifier and a state-of-the-art DAT tape recorder, incoming calls monitorable by headsets from the last two components. There was also a standard Toshiba answering machine.

"The system's been well tested," the young man told them. "We've had four calls for the McGlades this morning, including, ironically, the Police Benevolent Fund looking for a handout." A sharp look from Jellun vaporized his complacent smile.

"Is that the family? McGlade?" Paul asked quietly.

"The house has been through two owners since you sold it," Skoufaris said. "The McGlades bought it last December."

"Where are they?"

"They went to the Exhibition."

Paul's gaze drifted to a bureau pushed back against the wall opposite the bed, a photo-cube balanced on a pile of cleared-away magazines. He could see two of its faces: smiling, fair-haired children.

Jellun cleared his throat, directing Paul's attention back to the table. "Apart from the passive monitor, we've got three active phones here: a dedicated line to Metro Criminal Investigation Branch and the hotline to the command post at the corner store. Also, as stipulated by Arabella Bauer in her Wednesday call to your wife, there is a portable phone for you. We can only speculate on that, but since it implies freedom of movement, you'll be wearing a ballistic vest when the call comes. A precaution, don't read much into it; the street sweep is ongoing — my guys will spot a squirrel if it has even a partial sightline to the house. And they're backing that up with Remington 700-40XBs, the most accurate field weapon in the world. I'm guaranteeing you can range freely in the house and yard if that's what she wants."

Jellun sat on the edge of the table, looking at Paul, his arms folded across his hard chest. "As I've already told you and your wife, we've got one real hope here today, and that's a phone trace. Getting to her when she's not expecting it. It's the old thing, attack is the best defence."

Paul nodded.

"Now you have to understand that tracing procedure has changed. These days, anyone can walk into a Bell showroom and buy a Maestro phone that flashes your caller's number. In other words, no kidnapper — especially someone this smart — is going to call on a regular land line. Unless she wants us to find her, or unless she wants to play it risky moving from phone to phone, she's going to call you on a cellular."

"You can trace that?" Paul was trying his best to concentrate, to remind himself that he was comfortable with technology.

"Yes, we can. Most people don't know it, maybe she doesn't. You'll need to keep her on the line no more than a few seconds for us to tell which network she's on, after that it's the reverse of old style tracing, and this is key: you'll have to *terminate* the call before the call record shows up at the main exchange and the trace can begin."

"You mean hang up on her?"

"Immediately. I know, it's a bastard when you need to hear what she's got to say, but she'll call back. She'll think it was a technical glitch, that's all."

Skoufaris was frowning. "So he hangs up. How long does this trace take?"

Jellun looked at the technician.

"Land line from the house, then back through the main switching station. Then through the assigned voice channel to the cell site, finally down to the cell sector. That's a block, more or less. We can pinpoint it down to a city block."

"How long?" Skoufaris repeated with a touch of impatience.

"It's Saturday so there's less network traffic, which is good." The technician shrugged his narrow shoulders. "Say five minutes."

"We've got Bell and Cantel ready to scramble," Jellun said, "and we have the trace warrant. No one's going to be dragging their heels today."

Skoufaris continued to frown. "You're saying we terminate the call immediately and in five minutes we've narrowed her position down to a city block? Sounds like a big area to me."

"This is a well-policed city. I need about twenty minutes to stake out one block. If she's in transit, obviously we're going to lose her. Our best hope is that she's calling from a base, which makes sense: she knows the kind of heat on her right now. I can't see her wandering around, especially if she has Tom with her. If I've got a specific block and twenty minutes, I can get a small army of undercover on the surrounding streets. Eventually she'll come out for air, we spot her, take her out if she has Tom and it's safe to do so, tail her if she doesn't, let her lead us to him."

"What do you mean by 'in transit'?" Paul asked. "You mean if she's calling from a car?"

"A car phone or a hand-held. But I don't think she'll be in a car. She could steal one with a phone, but it's a big risk plus any half-decent car phone has a lock code. She could rent a car with a phone, but again there's too much heat: she's got to know the rental agencies have all been alerted, why chance it when you can buy a hand-held unit on special for a hundred and ninety-nine anywhere down Yonge Street? Bell and Cantel will usually put you on the air before they do a credit check — she'll have a clear two days before they discover false ID, which is all she needs for this." Jellun looked at his watch. "It's twelve-forty. My guess is, if she calls in twenty minutes like she said she would, she'll do it on a hand-held C phone."

"What if she calls from out of town?" Skoufaris asked.

"That's good and bad. There aren't as many cell sites, which means a broader map reference. Plus we won't be able to respond quickly. But if she's not in transit, if she's calling from some place she has Tom, they'll be easier to find even with a bigger net. And she'll be less anxious in the sticks, maybe less careful. We could get witnesses."

"I may be able to pick up some background noise," the technician added cheerfully. "Something that would help us identify the location — a train whistle, a clock chime, something like that. After you've terminated the first call and she calls back, the longer you can keep her on the line, the better."

"I don't think we have to worry," Jellun said. "She's a games player, she's going to do the talking, and she won't be watching the clock on a cellular."

His gaze narrowed on Paul and hardened. "I know we've already discussed this, but I want to make the point again: if she tries to arrange some kind of exchange, offering Tom for you…"

"Wait a second," Skoufaris interrupted. "How's she going to do that? This woman is bound to know we're monitoring the call."

"Of course. So we can't expect a time or a place, nothing we can take advantage of. But she may try and encode it in some way that is meaningful only to Paul. He and I have been over this: he knows it's ultimately his decision, but he has given me his assurance he won't play into her hands. Correct?"

Paul looked away from the cool, penetrating gaze.

"Trust us," Jellun said with the first trace of conciliation. "Play along, accept her arrangements — that's important — but keep us in the game."

CHAPTER 32

THE TELEPHONE RANG at 12:53.

The technician activated the spectrograph and the tape recorder. Jellun and Skoufaris put on headsets. Jellun signalled Paul.

For five seconds he stared at the bleating portable, frozen with terror and longing.

To hear his voice. Only that.

"Pick it up!" Jellun insisted.

It felt so insubstantial, he might have been closing his hand around a hologram, the receiver seemed to float up to his ear. For a moment there was silence. Paul forced his mouth open, then remembered not to speak first.

"Trick?" asked the woman's voice.

Except for the technician minutely adjusting his levels, everyone in the room was rigid, even the marksman and the spotter at the window, who had not heard the woman speak.

"Trick?" Confused and insistent now. "Patrick?"

A rush of air at the anticlimax, a collective sigh.

"Hello? Who is that?" The voice had grown irritated. "Is

that one of the children?" Softening: "It's nana, dear, please go and get your father."

Jellun signalled the technician who stabbed the answering machine, rigged to override Paul's portable. Patrick McGlade's voice said: *"I'm sorry, we are unable to take your call right now…"* Quicker than trying to explain their presence in the house, especially to family members and close friends. Grandmother McGlade left a message for Patrick to call back, and the line was clear again.

"Sorry about that," Jellun said. "How're you doing? Little warm?"

Paul shook his head. He had already put on the Kevlar vest, but he was far from overheating in the close body armour: the chill he had felt on the journey here had never left him.

"Earphone working?"

He nodded. Another of Jellun's gadgets, a wireless receiver snugged in Paul's left ear, which would allow him to leave the third-floor operations centre and still receive prompts and assistance.

At 12:59 the telephone rang again.

Spectrograph. Tape recorder. The technician signalled. Paul picked it up.

For five seemingly endless seconds there was nothing, but he knew.

Skoufaris and Jellun knew, by the quality of the silence — knew instinctively, with a synchronized bloom of sweat. Jellun knew with almost enough certainty to instruct Paul to hang up now — five seconds was enough to give them the network and allow the trace to begin — but they had to be sure.

After five seconds, Arabella Bauer uttered her first words.

"Welcome home, Paul."

"Hang up." Jellun's quiet command in his earphone couldn't have been closer or clearer, but Paul failed utterly to hear it.

"I want to speak to my son."

"Do you? Well…let's see."

"Hang up now!" ordered Jellun, but he knew Paul could not and had made provision for that, had seated himself directly beside the walljack for the portable's base. He reached for it, unaware of Skoufaris until a huge hand closed like a vise over his wrist. Skoufaris held up a single steady finger, his green eyes unequivocal in their message until Tom Preedy's anxious — though untraumatized — voice sparkled through the ether.

"Daddy? Where are you?"

"Tom? Oh my…" Paul's voice billowed like a sail blown full of sweet fresh air. "Are you alright?"

"When can I come home, dad? Where are you?"

"I'm right here. I'm right here, darling, I'm…"

Skoufaris tugged Jellun's wrist and the jack snapped out. Jellun's quick, hard eyes flicked between Skoufaris and Paul, staring in frozen disbelief at the dead receiver in his hand, then back to the Port Hope detective. His voice was balanced on a knife edge: "You're not here at my request, Skoufaris. Anything remotely like that again and I will take extreme disciplinary action. Do you absolutely understand?"

"Yes." Skoufaris threw off his headset and crossed to where Paul had sunk onto the edge of the bed, sitting motionless, still holding the receiver. He did not make a sound as Skoufaris gently removed it from his hand and switched it to STANDBY. Not until the detective's arm encircled his shoulder did it burst from him, unravelling, rioting in the air like streamers in the primary colours of joy and hope.

Only Jellun saw the red pulse of the hotline from Metro CIB, on mute in case Paul's line was open. He snatched it up while Paul wept, listened for a moment then hung up.

"Okay, she's in the Bell network, on a cellular. They've started the trace. Paul?" He raised his voice: "Preedy!"

Paul took a great, shuddering breath, let it out and took another, steadier, while Skoufaris unscrewed the cap from a leather hip flask.

"Metaxa. Go on, it'll help."

"Listen while you do it," Jellun snapped. "She's going to

think you lost the connection, she's going to call back now.
How long you keep her won't affect the trace, so just do your
thing. Ask for Tom, whatever you like. But if she wants to talk,
let her talk, she may give something away. We've still got to
find out what the hell we're doing here."

The portable telephone rang for the third time at 1:02.

"What happened?"

"I don't know."

"Maybe your friends know."

Paul looked across the room for Jellun, but the voice continued: "Who cares? Let them play games, we've got our own,
don't we, Preedy? You're going to do what I say now, aren't
you?"

"Yes."

"Good. Where are you all situated in the house?"

Paul hesitated again, but Jellun was nodding and mouthing, "Okay."

"Where?" The voice was suddenly, shockingly harsh.

"On the third floor."

"Good. Then you've saved yourself a climb. Go to the
shower. Turn it on full and let me hear it. Do it now."

Skoufaris watched as Paul crossed to the bathroom, saw
Jellun frowning because he was out of control now, because
the logic had already drawn ahead of them. Why the shower?
To try and make monitoring difficult?

Then you've saved yourself a climb.

What was that? How did she know about the shower? The
house had been crawling with police since Wednesday, there
was no way...

Skoufaris silenced his thoughts and concentrated on the
faint snow in his headphones, wondering if the technician's
amplifier was giving the tape deck something he was missing.
He couldn't hear her, but he could feel her presence in the
silence, more intensely than when she was speaking. As

though *he* were being monitored. He felt vulnerable, as if the phones were a conduit through which she could reach his mind. Vulnerable to her power, her ruined though still profound intelligence.

A separate shower enclosure. A Speakman shower head, with a top-range Moen control on the tiled wall near the enclosure door. Paul had built it himself. The McGlades were careless housekeepers, his white grout was speckled grey with mildew. As the water blurted out, Paul automatically — absurdly — found himself adjusting the familiar control for optimum temperature.

"Good," said the voice on the telephone. "You don't have to get in but you do have to sing. Do you know "Moon River"? I know you do. Sing it please."

Paul opened his mouth.

"'Moon River.' Come on. Sing it!"

But there was no hope of a sound. He could not hear the melody. A great weight seemed to be pressing on his chest, allowing him no air, his throat constricted by a cruel iron collar.

"*Moon River...wider than a mile.* You know it. Come on. SING!"

Flat and tuneless, he delivered a sort of metered moaning, although the lyrics came easily from his subconscious because she was right, he did know it, at least the first verse.

"I didn't say stop."

By sheer will, he sang it again.

"That's enough. You used to do better than that. In the shower. On Saturday afternoons? Alright, now you're to go downstairs. You'll leave the shower running and the bathroom door open and you'll go down to the front door. Wait in the hall until I call back, understand? You've been you, now you're going to be me. I hope you're going to play ball, Preedy."

And the line was dead, a howling void in which his son had ceased to exist.

Paul was not thinking as he walked out, careless of Skoufaris waiting attentively in the doorway. Out into the main room where Jellun watched him minutely.

"What is it, Paul?" Live and in his earphone, but Paul didn't hear. "She's making sense to you, isn't she? Tell me for chrissake!"

Paul started down the stairs, leaving behind Skoufaris's offer to accompany him and Jellun's harsh veto, and the snicker of the Remington's bolt action as the sniper came to full alert. The weeping had sprung from hope, but he was back inside the carapace now, with little awareness of the world around him. All effect of the strong brandy had evaporated, the chill seated deeply and completely now, because in her last words he had entered a cold room filling up with darkness, in which shadows leapt from their daylight hiding places to caper obscenely, heralds of something larger and darker and immeasurably more terrifying. Something that would at last reveal the true depth of her insanity, past, present and future. The truth that there was no hope after all: having entered her room, he would never see Tom again.

He didn't feel the stairs. He reached the front door like a dreamer, for whom there is no transition, no sense of time passing. He heard Jellun's voice, reached up distractedly and removed the earphone receiver, a mere annoyance that he dropped on the hall carpet.

Now the bleating phone, distant and dreamlike, his hand disembodied, a remotely controlled finger nudging the switch from STANDBY to TALK.

Arabella Bauer made the silence last for fifteen seconds, then asked: "Have you thought about it, Preedy? Are you ready to be me?"

"Yes."

"Then open the front door and leave it open while you ring the bell so I can hear it."

Paul opened the door, automatically squeezing his eyes

shut against the shock of sunlight. When he opened them again, he could see the heat twisting the air above the driveway.

"What are you waiting for? Ring it."

The same disembodied finger reached for the button on the door frame and pressed. Not chimes but an old-style bell and striker, strident in the hallway.

"Good. Now go outside and shut the front door. Shut it firmly so I can hear it."

Paul did so and waited on the step. He could feel the sun on his skin but there was no warming penetration, it seemed only to scorch him.

"I have never been here before. Say it."

"I have never been here before."

"I'm impressed. Say it!"

"I'm impressed."

"The house is impressive to me because I have nothing. Say that: 'I have nothing.'"

"I have nothing."

"I rent a dirty room with plywood walls, where cockroaches mate in the margarine. But this is a butter house, and inside lives a golden butter family. The head of this family has never had to steal or sell drugs or rent his handsome cock. He is healthy, wealthy and wise, that's the impression from the magazine pages in my pocket, so I have come to see for myself." Silence. "Say that."

"I have come to see for myself."

"I recognized him right away in the magazine, after so many years. Because I have never forgotten him. Not the way I told the doctors later. I haven't forgotten any of them. Say that."

"I haven't forgotten any of them."

"A magazine about smart houses, the kind where they take pains not to give away the location. Although the magazine has told me everything else: Paul Preedy with his good degree, Paul Preedy so young to be at the top of his profession, Paul Preedy's lovely wife, Paul Preedy's perfect children. Paul

Preedy's number is unlisted as befits his station, and I've worn out my cheap shoes looking for the house, but now I've found it. To see for myself. Please?"

"To see for myself."

"But now that I'm here I don't know what to say. Say that please."

"I don't know what to say."

"But I ring the doorbell anyway. Do so. Put the phone to the letter slot and ring."

Paul did it.

"I know it will come to me, whatever I have to say, and I know Paul Preedy is home because I can hear him through the open window on the third floor of his so fine house. He is taking a shower and singing "Moon River." Why not? It's Saturday afternoon and he has everything in the world he could wish for, why shouldn't he sing? But when I ring the bell, the singing stops and I hold my breath wondering if they'll come to me, the words I need to say. But maybe there is *nothing* to say. Maybe it will be enough for now, for this first visit, just to stand there on the threshold and say nothing. My appearance alone will be enough for now: my skin, my hair, my clothes. My eyes. Say that."

"My eyes."

"All of it!"

"My skin, my…"

"My hair!"

"My clothes, my eyes."

"Maybe that will frighten Paul Preedy enough for now, wondering who I am, because he surely will not recognize me." The phone crackled with sudden anger: "Why should he? His life has long ago moved onward and upward. He'll never recognize me in a cheap fucking *dress*!"

Arabella Bauer ordained another long pause. By the time she spoke again, the anger had drifted somewhere else. "Be me again, Paul Preedy. At the door. Tired and sick. Say that."

"Sick and tired."

"Sick and tired, tired and sick. Alright. So I am losing my

nerve. Oh yes. So that when I ring the doorbell a second time and the singing stops again, I am suddenly afraid. I'm not ready, far from it. I am two years away from ready.

"But where am I to run? There isn't time to make it to the road because Paul Preedy will see me and I realise now that I need to make future plans. So I run to the side of the house, to the alley. Do that, Preedy, go there now, go right through to the back."

The portable phone hissed as he moved into the building's dank shadow, as reception deteriorated. Putting one leg in front of the other, Paul reached the open wooden gate halfway to the back yard. By now the receiver was roaring like a waterfall. If Arabella Bauer was talking again, he could no longer hear her. He didn't need to. He knew what she would be telling him, had known the moment he approached the bathroom upstairs and turned on the shower.

Earlier.

Of course. He had known three days ago, after the call to North Carolina.

Earlier.

And for a moment, isolated from Arabella Bauer, Paul was himself again, making this same journey on a long ago afternoon, looking over his shoulder as he passed through the gate, back towards the molten heat of the summer afternoon, the white hot zenith of the day...

...*to the street where the Thomas tree and the Clifford tree are no longer fresh green but withered and twisted, desecrated with fetishes that clitter in the dying branches without air to move them — feathers, bladders, skulls and bones of birds.*

And...

Further away, on the far side of the street, something... someone?...shimmering. Sometimes, for a split-second, not long enough to identify it, he can even see a face.

Paul reached the end of the passage and the roar of the telephone diminished, and she was flowing into him again, more of her than his body could sustain. His cheeks bulged, burying his eyes before the surfeit broke, spewing across the dry lawn so that he could hear her voice clearly again, decompressed, from inside him where it had sounded for two years of waking nightmares:

"I can see a child in the back yard," Arabella Bauer was saying. "I can see a child at play."

CHAPTER 33

AT 1:03, WHILE Paul Preedy had tried to sing "Moon River," the Bloor Street command post received a report from a mobile support officer on Huron.

Constable Givney had stopped a cab heading north on the street. When asked his destination, the driver had given the address of the tactical operations centre. He had a delivery for a Paul Preedy, a package given to him by a woman three hours ago at Dufferin and King. She had paid him in advance, the modest fare plus thirty dollars to make certain the package arrived between 1:00 and 1:15 pm. Givney described it as a gift-wrapped box, approximately fifteen inches cubed. He had prevented the cabby from touching it again, but the man had handled it earlier and believed the package to be cardboard, described the contents as "something round, something bumping around inside."

Detective Wynnyates had seen a tactical unit at work before, as a weekend guest of the Army's hostage rescue team at Camp Borden, but he had never seen anything like the purpose and precision of the next ten minutes, as Metro's

Emergency Task Force scrambled.

Public safety now outweighed any question of subterfuge. Huron was cordoned off at Bloor, and the twelve houses immediately adjacent to the red and yellow taxi were evacuated. As soon as the area was clear, including officers, a small, unmanned electric vehicle quested up the street towards the taxi, its umbilical cable paying out behind it like a leash.

Wynnyates watched its progress through binoculars as a demolition unit officer explained its purpose. The EOD robot (for Explosive Ordnance Demolition) was one of two maintained by the Metro task force. The video camera and floodlight were standard equipment, so that its activities could be monitored from a safe distance. Options included a grab hook, X-ray equipment or, as in this case, mounting brackets for a disruptor — a water cannon loaded with a 12-gauge charge, capable of enough muzzle velocity to tear through a leather briefcase, to instantly drench, and thus short-circuit, any electrical device that might be inside.

Wynnyates watched the robot slow as it reached the open rear door of the taxi, saw it shuttle back and forth, side to side, while the controller at the video monitor aimed it, then fired. At eighty yards, Wynnyates saw the big car rock on its springs and the air around the robot storming with fragments of wet cardboard before he heard the crack of the cartridge. To his disappointment, there was no larger explosion. Instead, as an almost comic anticlimax, a round object rolled out of the taxi's open door, bounced off the robot and bumped in a leisurely fashion down the street towards the command post.

"What's happening? What the hell is that thing?"

The officer beside him sounded puzzled but calm: "If it's ordnance, it's been disarmed, but I don't think so. Reckon it's what it looks like."

What it looked like to Wynnyates was a somewhat deflated ball, its progress erratic, finally wobbling to a halt about fifteen yards from the taxi. Now that he could fix it in his binoculars, he could see the sectional markings of purple and yellow. Celebrated colours, enough that a lesser sports fan than Wynnyates would have recognized them instantly.

What it looked like, exactly, was a punctured junior-size L.A. Lakers basketball.

CHAPTER 34

THE SAME PATIO furniture beyond the fence. The same fence. The same cracks in the concrete pool surround that had frozen out Paul's filler every winter. The same delicate stream of bubbles from the returns that meant there was still an air leak somewhere in the pumping system.

"Tell me what they brought you, Preedy."

He saw Skoufaris watching him from the back door. He could not monitor from down here, there was no body armour big enough to fit him — he had breasted Jellun's displeasure to watch over Paul. Unlike Jellun, Skoufaris understood what the SWAT had brought.

"A ball." Paul's voice, like his movements, had the dynamic range of an automaton — cold, controlled, compliant.

"Which team?"

"Lakers."

"So you know *what*, but you don't know *how*, which is why we have the ball, to illustrate. Are you ready to be me again?"

"Yes."

"Don't fuck with me, Preedy! Are you *ready*?"

"Please…" A tiny human voice from somewhere inside the tin man, but she heard it.

"Aaaah…I suppose you want to speak to your son again."

"Please."

"Please? I remember 'please.' It was 'please Preedy' that time, wasn't it? 'Please Preedy, please let me go, pleeeeeease…' But you didn't. Thank you so much. So just throw the fucking ball into the pool. NOW!"

Did he throw it? Light as a balloon, it seemed to float over the fence, through the cloudless sky, to settle like gossamer on the still water. By now it had deflated to a bowl shape, remained on the surface near the skimmer, slowly spinning in the gentle swirl of a return jet.

"He kicked it. He didn't throw it, he kicked it right over into the pool. It happened while I was watching him. He called you, then he started running to the house and I said 'Your dad's in the shower' and he turned and saw me. Smiled at me. And I asked him would he like me to help him get it back. I expected him to run for the back door but he smiled just like his picture in the magazine.

"I didn't know what I was going to do till I started doing it, like when I rang the doorbell. I saw the gate was locked so I picked him up and lifted him onto the fence so he could scramble down the other side. I said 'Go on, Clifford.' I knew his name from the magazine. I said 'Go get it, Clifford,' but he didn't want to. He wasn't allowed."

A low, rising sound escaped from Paul's throat as he sagged forward against the fence, barely aware of Skoufaris's supporting arms.

"Whiiiyyyy?"

"Why? You have to ask me?" Her voice mocked the inanity of the question. "Because I hated you. Because I hated you like family, so much that I didn't dare see it. But I saw it now. I saw Paul Preedy's perfect child halfway to his luxurious swimming pool, looking back at me to make sure it was okay. I told him 'go on, it's fine, I'm watching, your dad said for me to watch you.' So he knelt down at the edge of the pool and reached for the ball. He was careless. He knocked it further away and when he reached again, he went too far. I guess he was in the deep end because he just sank. I hardly saw him, just an arm, then his foot. It didn't look like you'd think, there wasn't any splashing, he didn't scream or anything."

The voice took on a taunting petulance.

"What was I supposed to do? Climb over the fence and tear my dress? I can't even swim. No one ever taught me to swim."

Paul listened, speechless, to the silence. He thought she was gone.

"Preedy?"

"Yes."

"Say goodbye. We're going now. Say goodbye to Tom."

CHAPTER 35

SKOUFARIS TOOK PAUL in through the back door, into a blur of activity.

A Task Force officer by the open front door. Boots down the stairs, first the sniper with his black rifle case, then the spotter, then Jellun. A double take on Paul and Skoufaris. He'd forgotten them. He talked rapidly, impatient to be gone.

"We got the trace five minutes ago. Canadian National fucking Exhibition. Twenty-five thousand people, 'cept we can play games too."

"You're going down?"

"We've already mobilized the Public Order Unit down there, that's one hundred fifty officers. All the exits tight. No one's leaving the ground without my say so. We'll show her fun and games." He went to the front door. "You people drive on up to the safe house, you'll hear soon as we've got something."

Skoufaris watched his car accelerate out of the driveway and surge down Huron with its light-bar flashing. He tried not to let his anger show.

"He knows what he's doing, Paul. Be encouraged. The guy's a natural hunter. He'll get Tom for you."

Paul continued to stare in silence out through the front door.

"They're trained to find needles in haystacks. She'll be off her guard. She won't know they've traced her. Do you want to call the family?"

Paul knit his brows as though the decision was far beyond him.

Skoufaris walked around him and shut the door softly. "It's okay, buddy. I understand." He glanced through an archway off the hall, saw a living room with a comfortable leather sofa and led Paul through. "Come on, sit tight for a minute. I'll call. I'll make it quick so I'm not tying up the line when the good news comes through." He put his brandy flask on the coffee table where Paul could see it, then gently pried the portable phone from a too-cold hand that resisted only for a moment.

He began the breathless climb upstairs for the command post hotline; the most urgent call first, for a medic. They were losing Paul: the vague expression, the careless compliance — all the signs of progressive shock, a typical response to overwhelming stress.

There was extra equipment on the technician's table now, some kind of equalizer with rows of faders hooked into a Macintosh Power Book. The young man was sitting back listening to headphones with his eyes shut. Skoufaris had to nudge his arm to bring him back.

"We still got a line to the command post?"

"They scrambled as soon as the trace came in. There's no one there."

Skoufaris heard the doorbell, faintly, from two floors below. He went to the gable window and saw Wynnyates looking orphaned at the front door. He'd forgotten all about him.

"That's for me. Go let him in, would you? Tell him he's to stay with Paul Preedy until I come down."

The technician had been cuing up the DAT recorder. He pushed a set of headphones across the table, proud and excited. "Listen to this, okay? The trace said Exhibition, but this put her right at the midway. That's the beauty of digital, you can work with it real fast."

"Go on now, the guy's waiting."

The technician boasted all the way down the attic stairs: "You can hear the midway rides. I'm pretty sure it's the roller coaster. You can hear the wheels on the steel rails, the brake hiss, kids screaming their heads off, everything!"

Skoufaris used the portable to call 52, his old division, to request medical assistance. He was prepared to use Jellun's authority, but the desk sergeant at 52 knew him, promised immediate assistance.

He switched the phone to STANDBY. Then TALK, for the Preedys.

Back to STANDBY.

He needed a minute to work on it. He picked up the headphones. The technician was typical of his breed, emotionally stunted, annoying as hell, but no doubt able to work modern miracles with his technology.

He touched the DAT's PLAY button and found himself listening to the last sequence he had monitored before he went down — Arabella Bauer directing Paul to the back yard — just before the basketball arrived. A relatively long period of silence that was far from silent now.

Filtering, isolating, amplifying — the technician had conjured a familiar world of sound out of thin air: the clamour of the midway, the swish and rumble of cars along the rails, the cries of excited children. All the fun of the fair.

It wasn't hi-fi, the sounds would need a lab to scrub them clean, but it was a remarkable piece of audio detection: of the original listening, Skoufaris could remember nothing but silence under snow.

He rewound to the beginning of the half-minute sequence (it seemed to be the only one the technician had worked on), to listen for any trace of Arabella Bauer or Tom Preedy. He heard steps behind him as he cued the sequence, turned to see Paul with Wynnyates, the technician out of breath behind them.

"Did you call?" Paul asked, his voice small but steady.

"Not yet."

Paul reached his hand out for the phone. "I will."

Something had happened to him. Still pale and in shock, but he was seeing and hearing again, as though he had tapped some final, forgotten reserve of strength. Or hope.

Skoufaris held out the phone but the technician reached between them, thrust Jellun's headset into Paul's hand.

"Just check this out before I pack up. She was calling from right inside the midway."

Skoufaris felt his anger rising, was about to protest when Paul put on the headset. Maybe he, too, was grateful for a postponement, maybe he was hoping for a snatch of Tom.

The technician played the sequence, then stopped the tape. "See what I mean? I thought it was the roller coaster but it might be that other thing, the Wild Mouse? You know that thing on rails that makes like it's going to pitch off around the corners?"

"It isn't the midway."

Paul's voice was so quiet, Skoufaris wasn't sure what he had said.

"She wasn't in the midway. She was at the loop."

The technician stiffened. Skoufaris said gently: "What makes you say that, Paul?"

"That isn't a fairground ride. It's a Toronto streetcar. A CLRV."

The technician was bristling. "How do you know?"

"I'm a mechanical engineer. We did sub-systems work for Hawker Siddeley who built them. Brake components. That hiss is a Knorr pneumatic disc brake."

Skoufaris was standing now. "You're saying she called from the streetcar loop?"

"We did field testing down there."

"What about the kids?" challenged the technician. "I can hear music and kids yelling."

Wynnyates spoke for the first time: "I remember they always had Kiddieland out there by the loop, the little roundabouts for the youngsters."

"Yes," said Paul.

Skoufaris was smoothing down his moustache. He turned to the technician. "You were here when the trace came through, how did Jellun brief the Public Order Unit? What did he tell them?"

He shrugged his narrow shoulders. "To seal the exits. Princess Gate, Dufferin, Ontario Place…"

"What about the streetcars? The turnstiles by the loop?"

"I don't think so. I don't think he said streetcars."

"What time did you get the trace?"

"Between five and ten past one, when she had Mr. Preedy outside. The same time as the sequence we just listened to."

"So she was still there at ten past." Skoufaris glanced at his watch. "That was nearly twenty-five minutes ago." He snatched up the portable phone and stabbed zero, shaking his head in amazement as he waited for the Bell operator.

"I think she knew! God damn! I think she knew we were tracing her, maybe even how long it would take. She was on the edge of the Exhibition ground the whole time, ready to go!"

The operator came on.

"Connect me with the Toronto Transit Commission. Hurry please, this is a police emergency." Skoufaris was tugging at his moustache now. "If we've got this right…can you believe the balls? She knows we're going to pinpoint her at the Exhibition, makes her calls with one goddam foot on an outbound car. Needs a diversion? She tosses Jellun in amongst the pigeons — twenty-five thousand of them!"

The TTC switchboard came on the line.

"This is Detective Sergeant Skoufaris, Port Hope Police. Which of your Divisions handles the Exhibition route?"

"Roncesvalles."

"Get me whoever's in charge there. Very quickly please, this is a matter of life and death."

Acting Superintendent Poulton came on almost immediately.

"Listen very carefully," Skoufaris told him. "We have an abduction from the Exhibition. We have reason to believe a woman and child left by streetcar some time immediately following ten past one this afternoon. They left from the loop at the northeast corner of the Exhibition ground. You have two-way communication with your drivers?"

"Yes sir, we do."

"How many streetcars could have left the loop since 1:10?"

"No more than three. The traffic is all inbound right now."

"Call up those drivers. We are looking for a tall, slender woman around forty accompanied by an eight-year-old boy. She may be carrying a hand-held cellular phone. The boy may not appear to be in distress because he knows her. Should a driver report any persons fitting that description, it is vital that they be prevented from leaving the streetcar. Is it possible to do that mechanically, without arousing suspicion?"

"Yes sir, it is. The exit doors may be disabled by switching off the treadle set. As long as there's power to the car, the doors cannot be forced from inside."

Skoufaris mentally beatified Acting Superintendent Poulton. "Your drivers should know that this person is extremely dangerous and is not to be aroused in any way, definitely not confronted. If containing her seems likely to endanger other passengers, let her go."

"I understand."

"Go call. The second you hear back, you're to call me at this number."

C H A P T E R 3 6

MARTA PIIRONEN LISTENED to the rising hum of electric power as she propelled Canadian Light Rail Vehicle number 4004 up to where the governor kicked in at 50 miles per hour, which was always too soon.

It was almost exhilarating to have an open stretch of track at last. She didn't mind the regular stops, you got used to that, but she'd spent the last twenty minutes moving slower than an ice breaker out of the Ex, up against a solid wall of inbound cars and dazed pedestrians — wannabe amputees the way they wandered across the rails. Marta's hand was tired from sounding the gong.

At least she had the outbound day run, a nearly empty car and clear sailing now, north towards Bathurst subway station and her lunch hour. Pity the operators making the same run late tonight, with a crushload of kids in black baseball caps, crazed from weird gravity and heavy metal, barfing chilidogs into their hightops.

The fifty-foot, fifty-thousand-pound, red-and-white trolly glided north on Bathurst. Toronto has always enjoyed a love-hate relationship with its streetcars; the predecessor to Marta's CLRV, the "red rocket," is still used by Canadian artists as a symbol of what the city used to be — dowdy and reliable and endearing.

Car 4004 took on five passengers at Queen. No one wanted Robinson or Lennox. Two off at Alexander Park. Marta was moving away from the Dundas Street lights, pulling down the roll blind behind her seat to cut the glare on the control panel, when her LCD display registered an incoming call.

That was unusual. Normally messages were brief or routine enough to print out on the display — short turns, rerouting, a broken overhead. Marta unhooked the handset left of the panel, identified herself and listened for twenty seconds, unaware that she had let the car slow down to half speed, unaware of anything except what the Roncesvalles Division Inspector was telling her.

Marta recovered quickly, brought her vehicle back up to speed. "I'm pretty sure I've got them."

"Don't look now if it'll raise suspicion."

"It's okay, I've got the blind down. She can't see me except in the mirror and they're way at the back of the car."

"You can identify them from there?"

She hardly needed to look. She had a good memory for faces, would have remembered them if the car had been standing room. She had thought the woman looked jittery when she got on at the Ex, put it down to a morning on the midway. The boy had looked red-eyed as though he'd been crying, too much candy and excitement. He'd been holding a stuffed dinosaur in its plastic bag. He had it out of the bag now, hugging it tight in the second row from the back.

"Yes," she said quietly. "I've got them. Sitting at the back. She's got a shoulder bag — could be a portable phone in it."

"Where are you?"

"Just north of Dundas."

"Did they take transfers?"

Marta remembered that too — the hand that took the paper slip, how big it had looked on a woman. She wasn't a regular rider either: regulars just said "Transfer." This person had very politely asked for "A transfer for the subway please."

The Inspector sounded glad to hear it. "Keep your speed right down. Delay your arrival at Bathurst station any way you can without arousing suspicion. The police are already on their way. Until you receive further instructions, this is what you will do, either at Bathurst or earlier if the woman tries to leave the car."

Marta listened and understood: switch off the treadle set, make a routine call for emergency assistance and wait. Clear enough. She had replaced the handset by the time she reached College Street. The lights turned green as the doors closed behind the last passenger, but she managed to spin out the process of handing out transfers and helping an elderly Italian lady make exact change, long enough for the lights to change red again.

She looked in the observation mirror above the fare box. The woman was looking at her watch. It was hard to tell her expression at this distance. The little boy was staring out of the window, hugging his green dinosaur.

Marta announced the stops in her usual voice. She wasn't overly excited or alarmed by the call. Her instructions had been clear enough and she'd been trained for a proactive role. And she'd paid her dues, more than her share because she was a woman, young, blonde like most Finns. She had seen plenty of night service as a junior operator, countless graveyard runs along Queen west; she'd taken fares from enough drunks and druggies, transported enough extraterrestrials to and from the Queen Street mental health centre to be able to handle almost any situation. Admittedly none of them had ever warranted a call from her Division Inspector describing them as "extremely dangerous," but he'd also used the word "unpredictable," and for TTC operators, unpredictable was a pretty fair job description.

She got lucky at Harbord: a trucker making a botch of his left turn, underestimating his artic's turning circle which meant she had to back up. It took three minutes for the half-dozen drivers jammed up behind the streetcar to coordinate their retreat, amidst the usual hooting and gesticulating and insults to the Toronto Transit Commission.

She bought another minute at Lennox by getting out with her switch iron to pry an imaginary obstruction from the track. As she hefted the heavy steel lever, Marta found herself half-hoping that the woman would lose patience and try to leave the car here and now. After some careful thought, Marta was a reluctant believer in the death penalty for what she considered two unacceptable classes of criminals — cop killers and kidnappers.

But the woman and the boy were still in their seats as she climbed back on board and replaced the switch iron in its bracket in the front stairwell. Still seated as she rolled slowly up to the Bathurst lights. No one was getting on or off here. They were immediately below the station, the end of the line where the streetcar looped south again. Marta was meeting her mother for shopping, a special on upholstery fabric at Honest Ed's. There'd be quite a story to tell her.

She slowed to the prescribed three miles per hour as she followed the wide curve into the station, reached to the control panel and pressed a square yellow button, shutting off the treadle set as she had been instructed.

She looked at the LCD clock and realized that by good fortune and nifty improvisation she had managed to eat up nearly fifteen minutes since Roncesvalles called.

An unusually large crowd was gathered on the far side of the loop for the car's return trip to the Ex, but Marta's offload ramp was deserted.

Where were these police?

She braked to a halt, the hiss of the pneumatic discs amplified by the hard surfaces of the station building. She tried to add an extra touch of normalcy, even a hint of boredom, to her intercom announcement:

"Bathurst station. Connect with Bathurst bus and Bloor subway."

She watched in the mirror as the passengers left their seats and herded to the rear doors. Only three riders, two teenage girls and a great-looking guy in a loud Hawaiian shirt, came to the front exit. Normally she would have opened the front doors with a manual remote, enabling the rear set to open automatically as soon as a passenger stepped down onto the treadle. But with the treadle switch in the off position, neither set of doors responded.

The guy in the shirt was the first to react, raising titters from the teenage girls as he gave Marta sleepy eyes over the fare box and crooned: "Pleeeease release me let me gooo..."

"One in every car, pal, don't call us." Smiling as she got out of her seat and turned to the back. "Yours not working either?"

An animated chorus from the passengers around the rear door. The woman and the boy had risen with the others, but they were sitting down again now, inconspicuous, in the same seat near the back window.

Marta didn't look at them as she walked purposefully down the aisle.

"Why won't it open?" someone asked.

"We're trapped," someone else announced cheerfully.

Marta moved through the small crowd. "Clear the doors please." She trod on the upper step, then the lower step, to the right and then to the left of the steel handrail.

"Are we stuck?"

"Come on, I got a bus to catch!"

She repeated the sequence, stamping this time, with her heel, as if this had happened before and there was a knack to it. She put the heel of her hand against the rubber seals between the doors and shoved in a systematic sort of way, a useless procedure since none of the doors could be forced with the treadle switch off, as long as the pole was up on the line sending power to the car. Only once — only now — did Marta forget to ignore the woman sitting at the back of the streetcar.

She instantly regretted it.

The woman was looking back, with eyes Marta had not been able to see a car's length away. Intense. Unbearably intelligent.

Suspicious.

Marta felt her confidence and courage being swallowed like something sucked into a Garburator.

She turned quickly, walking back towards the front, praying that her sudden fear did not carry in her voice.

"Sorry for the inconvenience, folks. We seem to have gotten the doors out of sequence. I'm calling for assistance. We'll have an emergency crew here very shortly. Please return to your seats. Thank you for your patience."

She found the guy in the Hawaiian shirt squatting to inspect a metal cover inside the front stairwell.

"This the fuse box?"

"Please leave that alone, sir, and take your seat." All she needed was this comedian pulling the propulsion reset fuse and they'd lose power and both sets of doors would fly wide open.

"Don't sweat it." He started to unlatch the fuse box cover. "I'm a licensed electrician."

"Yeah? I thought you were a lounge act. Get back to your seat. NOW!"

Not bad. She was decent on her feet, something you learned in this job, grace under pressure.

The woman was still watching her. Closely, in the observation mirror. Marta didn't need to look, she could feel her whole body prickling, every blonde hair stirring, tiny antennas to a new and terrifying signal from the back of the streetcar. Movement in the mirror...

The woman was getting out of her seat.

As Marta reached for the handset to call the emergency crew, she glanced across at the switch iron by the door.

Where were the fucking police?

C H A P T E R   3 7

Skoufaris kicked the unmarked car back and forth across the centre line, on a slalom course along Bloor Street. The horn was largely inaudible under the wailing siren — he leaned on it only to relieve frustration.

Wynnyates sat up front beside him, Paul in the back seat — the same arrangement as the numb journey from the safehouse an eternity ago, but this time Paul saw every careless pedestrian and reluctant car that delayed their progress, saw the whole street in agonizing detail, pulsing red as it reflected their beacon.

Skoufaris braked hard, hurling Paul and Wynnyates forward, then sideways as he wheeled right into the last street north before the Bathurst lights. As arranged, the three-ton yellow TTC emergency truck was waiting for them a hundred yards from the corner.

"Thank God."

Two crew members stood by the open rear doors, one man in TTC regulation bib overalls and yellow hardhat, a younger one in jeans and a tee, carrying his work clothes and boots.

"He looks about your size, Winnie." Skoufaris braked close behind the van. "Go for it."

Wynnyates left his shoes in the footwell and his jacket and tie in a heap on the front seat. He ran towards the truck in sock feet, a set of handcuffs jingling in his right hand, his holster harness showing darkly against his white shirt. He took the blue overalls and stepped into them, then sat on the tail of the truck to pull on the heavy boots — a size too large — while the crewman fished the straps over his shoulders and snapped them.

"Nice going, guys," Skoufaris made monosyllabic introductions then addressed the older, work-dressed crewman. "Your people brief you?"

"Some."

"Okay, this is the drill: your partner stays behind. You and Detective Wynnyates ride in the front where she can see you. The boy's father and I stay out of sight in the back — she would certainly recognize him, maybe me. Make sure you drive the truck right up beside the streetcar. Have your beacon on, be conspicuous, impressive. What do you have to do to get the doors open?"

"Nothing. The driver just has to switch on the treadle set."

"She knows that?"

"Yep."

"But you're going to do some mechanical business, right? About a minute's worth before the doors open, just enough to make it look like the call was worth your while."

The man nodded.

"While you're doing that, Wynnyates will position himself by the doors. As the passengers come out, he will restrain the woman while you shield the child." Skoufaris hesitated. "Can I ask you to do that?"

The crewman was well into his fifties, but tall and heavily built, a lot bigger than Wynnyates. He glanced at Paul, licked his top lip with the point of his tongue.

"Don't worry, buddy. I've got kids of my own."

Wynnyates had the boots laced. "I need a jacket. The holster straps show around the bib."

"I don't have a jacket," the crewman said. "It's August."

"What about your lunchbox?" the older crewman said.

"Improvise," Skoufaris said. "We're going."

Paul got in first and gave Skoufaris a hand up. Wynnyates and the older crewman went to the front of the van while the other man swung the rear doors shut. "Good luck." He said it to Skoufaris, unable to meet Paul's eyes.

The box was lit by two slit windows at the front. They rode in semi-darkness, seated opposite each other on narrow steel benches, hemmed in by rattling tools and equipment.

"What time is it?"

Skoufaris brought his watch close to his face. "Two o'clock. Nearly forty-five minutes since Jellun lit out."

"Think he'll show up?"

"Nah. We're the Lean Team!" Smiling tightly, still trying to sound reassuring, but Paul knew what he must be thinking: if Jellun appeared now, even if he'd been issuing countervailing orders to the TTC, the crucial next five minutes would be seriously jeopardized.

"No one's called him, right?"

"He's not stupid. They'll have covered the streetcar exit almost right away. But I don't think he's figured her on an outbound car in time to slip out. My guess is he's still got her at the midway when the trace came through, too far from the loop to make it before they sealed it. I would've called him if we hadn't gotten lucky, but we threw Bathurst station, right round the corner, and a service truck close enough to respond." He reached across and gripped Paul's arm. "This is about as close to a grand slam as I've ever seen in twenty years of police work. You could even call it a miracle."

"How's Wynnyates?"

"Solid. He'll have her back to front and cuffed before she knows what's hit her. And Tom Preedy will be all yours." Skoufaris's lowered his eyes and smiled. "You want to watch that habit, you'll get hair on your palms and go blind doing that."

For a moment Paul didn't understand, then he realized that Skoufaris meant the black beads on a silver chain pouring back and forth between his shaking hands.

CHAPTER 38

"THIS IS VEHICLE 4004. I have a treadle system down, both doors inoperable, automatically or manually. Approximately thirty passengers on board. Requesting immediate assistance."

"You're doing just great, Marta." The Roncesvalles Inspector's voice sounded low and intimate on the handset. "Is everything under control?"

"Sort of."

"Can you talk?"

"No. Too close."

The woman was half a car's length away, casually inspecting the TTC system map above the rear steps. Listening.

"You're hanging in?"

"I guess."

"It won't be long. The police will be there in two minutes or less. They are using the emergency crew as their cover. There will be one actual crewman. He will appear to be working on the door mechanism. You are to stay in your seat while he does that. The crewman standing by the rear doors will be an armed police officer. You will wait until you get the go

ahead from the working crewman, then hit the button to ac-
tivate the treadle set. At that point, you are to issue a loud and
clear request for all passengers to use only the rear doors. Is
that clear?"

He waited.

"Marta?"

The inspector's voice was spiked with sudden urgency.
"Piironen? Do you read me?"

Marta spoke quickly in a dry whisper. "She's coming down
the aisle. What the fuck do I do?"

"Don't lose your head. Explain that the service crew will
be there any minute. They will be. Get out your waybill, be
filling it in so you don't have to give her your full attention.
Hit the emergency button and I'll be able to monitor."

Marta replaced the handset, punched the red emergency
button, then reached down beside the seat for her clipboard.
She didn't dare look in the mirror. She could feel cold fear
growing as the woman's steps approached, as though a freezing draft was surging down the car.

She started filling in the waybill with meaningless transfer
numbers and trip times.

The woman had almost reached her.

Marta tried to drop her climbing shoulders, flicked a
glance at the switch-iron in the stairwell, measuring the distance.

"Excuse me?"

"Just a minute please." She spent another five seconds
with nonsensical entries then cocked her head sideways, preoccupied, reluctant. "Can I help you?"

The woman outmanoeuvered her by the simple act of saying nothing, forcing her to look round.

"How many streetcars are there in service in the city?"

Marta frowned deeply but not at the question.

The woman's eyes, her irises like two slow kaleidoscopes
full of movement…sharp, tiny, rotating shapes moving to
some distant music from Marta's own memory.

Playground music.

Sticks and stones.

She had to make a concerted effort to retrieve the question. "I'm sorry, ma'am. I don't know. If you would take your seat please, I'm a little busy here. The emergency crew will be along any minute."

Marta turned back to her clipboard, saw it double and out of focus.

"Would you say there are two hundred?"

"Really ma'am, I wouldn't know that."

"But you must find it hard to believe that the design would permit a situation like this to occur. Are you sure there isn't some way to make the doors open?"

Marta's skin crawled as she listened to the insinuating, relentless voice. The fear was overcoming her, she felt herself slipping and made a desperate call on borrowed anger, trying to own the authority of her uniform, to act the part of herself. She turned again for a clear confrontation.

"I'm sure the emergency crew will be able to answer that question. Take your seat, please."

But she had overdone it, her voice far louder than the situation warranted. The falsehood — her fear — showed naked and ashamed.

The eyes held her like barbed hooks, the milling shapes turning everything around.

"I understand. What if everyone bothered you?" The woman used a softer voice, soft and rotten, its angry purpose seething below a transparent skin of control. "I'm sorry. I didn't mean to be a nuisance." The eyes dropped for a second before she turned, a glimmer of a smile at the dark, wet half-moons spreading under each short sleeve of Marta's regulation summer shirt.

Marta watched in the mirror as the woman returned to the boy at the back. Sweating all over, barely able to control her trembling fingers, she picked up the handset and entered the Roncesvalles division code on the CIS keypad. The inspector picked up instantly.

Marta whispered: "I think she suspects."

"Do you know that? I heard the conversation."

"Not for sure. I feel it."

"It's your call, Piironen. Do I contact the emergency truck? It may change the situation. They may reconsider the safety of the other passengers."

Marta hesitated, in an agony of indecision.

"Tell me very quickly, please. They're going to arrive any second."

But even as he said it, Marta caught a flash of yellow in the corner of her eye, turned to look through the side window at a midweight yellow truck with a pulsing amber beacon, its tires squelching over the incurving track from Bathurst Street. Coming in fast and braking hard twenty feet from the car, the driver and his passenger already out, acknowledging her with a wave.

"Forget it," she told the Roncesvalles inspector with a mixture of relief and terrible apprehension. "They're already here."

THE TTC EMERGENCY crewman had parked the truck with the rear doors facing away from the streetcar. He did not look at, or speak to, either occupant as he swung them open. He indicated that Paul should lift his feet, pulled out a tool-drawer under the bench and removed a four-foot-long wrench.

The crewman was perfectly credible in his work. None of the passengers peering down from the streetcar saw anything but heroic expertise as he laboured to free them, straining to loosen a bolt on the primary suspension assembly that had nothing at all to do with the doors.

Seeing Wynnyates waiting by the rear doors, the passengers may have wondered why he failed to assist the big man with the wrench, but every work crew was like that — road gangs or construction guys — one always working, one always standing watching.

Marta Piironen was watching Arabella Bauer and Tom Preedy. Like Marta, they remained seated. Tom was closest to the window, looking at the workman. Arabella Bauer was looking everywhere, with slow and inconspicuous movements of her head.

When his minute was up, the crewman stood back from the side of the car and made a cranking gesture in the air.

"Okay, try it."

Marta pushed the treadle set button and the rear doors folded smoothly open.

Arabella Bauer got up from her seat and drew Tom into the aisle, keeping tight hold of his hand as they came up behind the crush of passengers at the rear doors. She paused only a moment, then pulled Tom further along the car, far enough past the screen of people that Wynnyates had an unobstructed view of her. As soon as eye contact was established, she made her first abrupt and conspicuous movement, towards the front doors.

Marta saw her in the mirror, climbed out of her seat and came down the aisle to block the way. "Rear doors please."

Arabella Bauer registered her but she was watching Wynnyates.

Solid, as Skoufaris had pointed out, but Detective Constable Wynnyates was not a quick enough thinker. By acting instinctively, by matching her sudden movement towards the front doors — by noticing her at all — he had given her exactly what she needed to know.

Marta realized it before Wynnyates but she stood her ground in the aisle, between the driver's seat and the rear exit through which half the passengers had disembarked.

Arabella Bauer kept coming, ahead of Tom until, with a sudden whiplash motion, she flung him ahead, her left arm locked round his neck, her right middle and index fingers vee'd inches from his terrified eyes.

"Sit down or I'll blind him. I'll push them into his fucking BRAIN!"

Marta sat.

Arabella Bauer was carrying Tom by the neck as she reached the open front door and literally threw him down the steps at Wynnyates. Again he acted on instinct, under-

standably this time, opening his arms to catch the child so
that his .38 revolver pointed wide for a fatal moment, towards
a high distant part of the station. He didn't see Arabella
Bauer reach for the bracket on the right of the stairwell.

She literally flew out of the doorway, her right arm blurring back then down to smash the top of Wynnytes's skull
with the heavy switch-iron, dropping it and flying over him,
her arm sweeping again, sideways like a dark wing as she gathered the child and passed towards the subway escalator with
a shriek of triumph.

C H A P T E R 4 0

THE CREWMAN WITH the wrench was halfway down the first long, broad flight of steps when Paul outstripped him. Two, then three at a time, shouting to clear his headlong descent, his hand burning on the rail, his shoes blurring over the rough tile facing.

TO TRAINS

Running, a howling projectile behind the raked cage of his forearms, dodging bodies, weaving, slamming away the challenge of a man in a bright Hawaiian shirt.

EASTBOUND TRAINS WESTBOUND TRAINS

Screaming for direction at the huddled, terrified people, those first off the streetcar who had stood and watched the woman from their car handle her struggling boy, who had not interfered.

"That way!"

"Down there!"

"West!"

Their guilty consensus powering him across the wide, pillared hall. A large coffee splashed over at the sandwich bar.

A busker in dreadlocks snapped his guitar neck as he spun to watch the madman go.

WESTBOUND TRAINS

And Paul could hear the train now, could feel it in the thick air of the second stairwell, the vibration greater than the sound, growing out of the ground like the penultimate moment of an earthquake.

Paul flew down into the epicentre, challenging this moment to destroy him if it dared, to destroy them both if he failed, his commitment so complete it filled him with a savage joy as the sound grew to a deafening thunder, as he reached the final stair and saw the eastbound not the westbound train entering the station on the far track.

Midday Saturday, with most of the traffic heading south by streetcar to the Exhibition. The westbound platform was empty except for a half-circle of terrified bystanders, surging like kelp on a violent tide as Arabella Bauer accused one, then another, with the black barrel of Wynnyates' .38 pistol.

Her back to Paul as he stumbled onto the platform and saw.

Jumped.

Down onto the trackbed, his brain seared by the image of his boy fastened by the hair, forced to his knees at Arabella Bauer's side.

Low under the platform's overhang, duckwalking, using the greasy purple rail as a bannister, knees and ankles screaming from the drop, the departing train covering the hiss of his breath.

Paul heard a shot and a woman's scream, then the voice that had bent and broken his mind today, bellowing in anger although only the peaks reached him above the clamour of the eastbound train moving out, ten feet to his left.

But it was enough to locate her, about twenty feet ahead and he had to get it right — if he came up short or long he would never reach them; she would turn and see him and shoot him like a dog.

Another train, the westbound for sure, a backward glance

giving him its headlights growing in the black tunnel behind him.

Ten more feet. The eastbound train clear now, revealing its passengers on the far platform, already staring across the track, pointing, running now as the public address system crackled an evacuation order.

Paul faced the wall, crouched and sprang, caught the overhang and hauled himself up.

And over.

Almost on his feet, seeing the elderly passenger's face the moment she betrayed him, seeing Arabella Bauer release Tom's hair and turn with the pistol, watching her aim, now the white muzzle flash as she shot him in the chest at point-blank range.

Protected by Jellun's Kevlar vest, the blow of the .38 round might still have killed Paul, a direct heart-shot would at least have bucked him off the platform, allowing her to fire again. But the bullet struck inches wide, over the lung, and now at last Paul Preedy's insanity was greater than hers.

He came in low, under and up like a diver streaking to the surface, driving her back against the platform wall. His arms were around her, pinning her gun hand, when she drove the blunt hammer of her head full into his face. Twice. Three times.

She followed with her whole body, thrusting away from the wall, his back to the rails, five feet from the edge of the platform. She struggled to raise the gun, then clubbed him again.

Paul's lips had burst, his nose was gushing, both eyes already closing, but he hung on. She would bite now if he didn't time it right. He let the bloody head slug once more then lunged as she drew back, catching her on recoil, getting a full, deep bite on the meat of her jaw.

Arabella Bauer roared with pain and rage. His mouth was full of their mingled blood, hot blood pouring between his teeth and down his throat, forcing him to swallow, to drink her as she writhed and bucked in his arms, desperate to tear her flesh and muscle loose.

Paul was blind with blood, deaf to everything but her raging until the inrushing westbound train blasted its warning horn and he realized they were teetering at the very edge of the platform, that the train was ahead and to his left…that Arabella Bauer's back was to the rails.

And suddenly she was no longer struggling. Suddenly she was quite still in his arms, not even panting. She dropped the gun.

"Please Preedy…let me go."

Distorted, whispered words, but he heard them, not so much with his deafened ears as in his all but broken heart.

"Please Preedy… pleeeeease…"

And he did let go, first with his arms, then his teeth.

The eyes did not leave Paul's for one second as she floated effortlessly out into the air above the rails in a graceful backwards dive that seemed to require no momentum. Clear and grateful eyes, not a flicker of movement as Victor Dempsey surrendered to the total thunder.

Bathurst had directed the westbound train to continue through the station without stopping, but it did stop. The driver had never had a jumper before and his reaction was an instinctive lunge for the brake handle.

The train screamed to a halt and the doors swished open, revealing to the Exhibition-bound passengers in one packed carriage a sight that shocked them back from the exit, crushing those at the rear.

Shock and fear, which did not find a common voice until the blood-masked man waiting for the train turned slowly away from them, opening his arms as he tottered towards a dazed and shrinking child.

THE COTTAGE IS a log A-frame, and it won't be finished by Christmas whatever Jack may say. But the roof is on and the fieldstone chimney is built down the middle of the big A window-wall, and it draws perfectly. It's quite something, looking at the flames with Blackstone Lake, snow-covered, on either side.

Finished or not, they will have the housewarming over the holiday season. They've already invited Dal and Sheila, and Lefterios Skoufaris and his family. Wynnyates, too, who ought to be on his feet by then. Skoufaris says he'd be a lot smarter if his head wasn't so thick. That or dead.

Tom is down to once a week with his therapist. They had a psychiatrist in Cobourg but Paul and Eva let her go. The new one is a psychologist, ego is not a problem, he has a sense of humour. It's worth the extra drive into Toronto. They like his sunny building on Davenport Road. They like the sweet, clean smells from the massage therapist across the way, who plays Vivaldi instead of New Age or ragas.

Both doctors agree that Tom will be back at school in

January. The new one says it will be good for him to have a permanent home instead of staying at the farm, and they're working on that.

Thomas will be fine. The only real trauma occurred on the last day. Not to say she wouldn't have hurt him, but she did no gratuitous harm to the Mennonite woman when she hijacked the horse and buggy, nor to Dolores Walmsley, abandoned with the Winnebago. Physically, they had suffered nothing more than the temporary side effects of chloroform.

Tom remembers her apologizing for the way she took him. In a vague and haphazard way, he remembers her explaining many things to him, but if she mentioned what she had done to three men in the past week, he is still blocking it. He remembers being shown her private parts and is able to talk reasonably freely about it, which, according to the psychologist, speaks well of Paul and Eva. She did not indulge in sexual abuse of any further kind. Both doctors are almost a hundred percent on that. Above all, it seems she needed him to understand.

She told him on several occasions that she loved him. Once, he heard her call him Victor.

There was no prolonged distress. He was adequately comfortable in the tiny borrowed apartment in Riverdale. Other than the last few minutes at Bathurst station, Tom remembers no time when she led him to believe that his life was in danger, or that he would never see his family again. He remembers no graphic threats against Paul. During the phone call from the Exhibition, apart from those few words with his father, he rode the roundabout at Kiddieland.

The green dinosaur has not been out of his hand for three months. The doctor says it isn't a problem. That is the level of his fear. It'll take a while to get down to it but the ground's soft.

Paul has decided not to give Tom the model steam traction engine as part of his Christmas present. He liked the idea when he had the machine in pieces, cleaning and oiling it. But when it was assembled, when the lamp was burning

meths and the water began its muted groaning in the boiler,
when the flywheel started to gather revolutions and the pis-
tons finally blurred and spat tiny scalding needles at his hand
— then he blew out the lamp, let the engine cool, emptied it
and put it away in a box on a high shelf. Children preferred
brand new anyway.

Such incidents do not occur for days at a time. When the
cottage is finished, when they have found a house of their
own, when Paul has begun the process of resurrecting his
business, maybe then he'll talk to someone about those odd
days. And the nights.

In the meantime, he has the therapy of hard and satisfying
physical work by the lake. He has his family.

THE END